THE *HOLT FAMILY* SERIES

T.M. CROMER

ISBN 978-0-9965720-6-4 (EPUB)

ISBN 978-1-7338198-8-6 (Paperback)

Cover Design: Deranged Doctor Designs

Edits: Sarah Hegger & Trusted Accomplice

DEDICATIONS

To Mark:
You are my true soulmate.
Thank you for your endless support.
I love you.

To my high school bestie, Kemo:
You'll see I kept the truth of our first meeting.

To Sabrina York:
Thank you for showing me the *error* of my ways.

To Sarah Hegger,
Once more, you've stepped in to save the day!

PROLOGUE

*L*ightning, like long skeletal fingers, streaked down from the heavens. Thunder boomed so close and loud, the panels of the window rattled, and an involuntary shudder found its way down Samantha Holt's spine. Was it an omen? Perhaps. At one time, she would have believed so. At one time, she'd believed a lot of things —but not anymore. That was the past.

The sliding doors of the clinic mocked her unwillingness to leave. Once she walked out those doors, she would have to put the past behind her and start all over. She wasn't so sure she wanted to do that. How was she supposed to forget and go on as if nothing had ever happened? As if there had never been a Michael in her life? The sting of ever-present tears pricked her lids, and she blinked them away.

"Just a few short steps and you're free. Free to be whoever you choose to be from this moment forward."

Although Dr. Stephen Montgomery stood a few feet away, his words still startled her. His deep voice, always welcoming and kind, drew her close. He'd been with her from the beginning when she was admitted to the hospital eight months before. Had it really been that long since Michael's accident? *Eight months?*

"I can't do it, Stephen. I can't walk out that door today."

"Why?" he asked, though she suspected he might already know the answer.

Indignation surged through her. The feeling of being misunderstood, mocked, and helpless all rolled about in her chest, nearly suffocating her. He only meant to help. She was intelligent enough to realize his aim. Still, it didn't make her any less angry.

"Don't pull that doctor BS on me. You damned well know why!" Anxiety began to build in her, making her edgy and raw. "I'm expected to go out into a world of people who saw—and will still see me—as a lunatic. They'll watch me and wait for me to do something stupid again. How am I supposed to live under that kind of pressure? People judging me all the time?"

She gulped in a breath. "Also, I hate storms. I fucking hate lightning and thunder and the fear of being struck down." Raging was her release when she was frightened, as Stephen was well aware. There wasn't much he didn't know about her. Sometimes, it frustrated the hell out of them both.

He gripped her arms, giving her a gentle shake. "Stop it, Samantha. You've come too far. Do you remember what it was like when you first arrived here? What *you* were like? You were practically catatonic. You had no will to live. Now that's changed. You're a living, feeling human being again. You're experiencing fears and misgivings. That's normal. That's progress. You aren't the empty shell you were."

Her voice was a mere whisper as she said, "I'm scared."

"I wish you could see yourself the way I see you. I've seen your passion for living spark back to life. You're intelligent. Funny. I've caught glimpses of the person you want to become. The person we both know you can become. You only have to learn to believe in yourself again. No one can force you to do that in here. You have to pull that from deep within yourself." Something flashed in his eyes, but it flitted away before she could interpret it. Something fierce. Intense. An emotion uncomfortable to witness. He dropped his arms and shifted his gaze to the window, watching nature's light show. His voice was much softer when he said, "I believe in you, Samantha. Believe in yourself."

"What if I can't?" As she glanced around her, she saw none of the bustle of the hospital or the staff. She remembered another time, another place, another *life*...

PART I

CHAPTER 1

NINE YEARS EARLIER...

*S*aturdays were always crowded in Flagler Beach. Finding a parking spot close to the pier was next to impossible, and Sammy had to walk quite a few blocks to where her friends converged. When she saw the group, she groaned aloud.

Rob Marks. Who the hell had invited him?

Sammy couldn't catch a break. Rob was always hanging around, trying to get her to go out on a date. Whenever he was within ten feet of her, her skin would crawl and warning signals would light up her brain. The guy was bad news. Now, she would spend the day fighting the urge to wear a head-to-toe cover-up. Why he couldn't accept no for an answer was beyond her. She wanted to wear a PSA sign stating, "No Means No!"

Sammy stopped on the boardwalk and scanned the group in hopes she'd find a friend to run interference for her. Someone jostled her on the steps.

"Stop hogging the stairs, Lil' Bit."

The rough voice elicited her scream, and she spun around. Without meaning to, she nailed her brother in the stomach with her oversized green-and-white-striped beach bag. If the "umph" she heard was any indication, she'd gotten him good.

"Jamie!" Unable to contain her bubbling joy, she flung her arms around him and hugged him tight.

As James spun her around, she caught her first glimpse of the man leaning against the railing. His casual stance, legs crossed at the ankles with hands resting behind him against the weathered wood, drew her full attention. Sammy might have warned the stranger to be careful of splinters if she could form a coherent sentence. As it was, she was gobsmacked.

"Damn! He's hot!"

Both James and his friend burst out laughing at her blunder. She'd forgotten her filter and blurted it aloud. A warm flush started at her feet and moved to her face in point-six seconds. Sammy happened to be an all-over body blusher. It made for awkward moments such as these. One day, she would learn to think first and speak second, or at least she hoped she would.

"I mean it's hot. Today. The sun." It earned her another laugh from James at her expense. In an attempt to cover her slip, she turned back to her brother. "I thought you weren't expected until later today?"

"We decided to take turns driving and pushed through the night."

"Driving? Not flying?"

"No, we were hauling our bikes." James bent to remove new-looking motorcycle boots. "Mom said we'd just missed you. We got to the house about five minutes after you left. I wanted to show you my new Harley, so Michael and I unloaded then came straight here. We figured we could sleep on the beach. What took you so long? Looks like we all arrived at the same time."

"I didn't realize yours were the bikes I heard when I pulled in." The only thing that rivaled the sound of the waves crashing to the shore were the motorcyclists zooming up and down the coastal highway on their throaty Harleys.

Sammy laughed and held up the bundle dangling from her fingers. "Anyway, you know I can't come to the beach without snacks and sunscreen. I had to pop in to the store. But now you're here, I have a favor. I need your friend to be my boyfriend."

At the choking sound, she glanced at Michael, who went pale

before turning a brilliant shade of red. At this rate, neither of them would need the sun, because they were getting enough color with her stupid mouth embarrassing them both.

"Yeah, no," James stressed, pausing in stripping off his bike gear. "You're jailbait."

"Okay, A—you know I am perfectly legal. Only four years younger than you, I might add. B—it's not like I want him forever." *Liar!* She'd taken one look and was smitten, but they didn't need to know that. "I just want him to pretend to be my boyfriend for today. It's to keep one of the guys down there from bothering me."

As if to emphasize her desperate need, Rob jogged up to where they gathered, and started his harassment of her. Okay, maybe he only intended to say hi, but she really didn't like the guy. His creep factor was high and left her feeling as if a good skin scrubbing was in order. Rob breathing the same air as her felt like harassment.

Michael stepped forward and dropped his arm across her shoulders. The cold stare he focused on Rob was enough to give even the dullest-witted person a clue.

Sammy's sigh was impossible to contain, and she beamed up at Michael. In that instant, she lost her heart completely. A jolt of recognition cemented her initial impression of when he'd first touched her. Nothing could explain the sense of familiarity he had created by putting his arm around her shoulders. A crystal-clear vision of the future formed in her mind. She was almost breathless with the knowledge that this man would be very important to her world. The butterflies in her belly seconded the impression.

Michael chose that moment to glance down and grin.

Her heart stuttered. The lethal combination of shaggy dark blond hair, warm-honey eyes, and dimples almost did her in. Those looks, along with his hard jawline and the two-day growth, turned Sammy's knees to jello. The dude was seriously gorgeous.

"Who the hell are you?" Rob demanded.

Unfortunately, she'd given him more credit than was his due. Instead of respecting Sammy's boundaries, Rob became belligerent.

His attitude proved once and for all that he was dumber than a box of rocks.

The air became charged, and the change to Michael's and James's stances was downright aggressive. All that was left was for one of them to beat on his chest, neanderthal style.

She was a bit disappointed when it didn't happen.

"Sammy's boyfriend. Is there a problem?" Michael's voice could only be described as Southern drawl laced with a hint of steel. Shivers skated along her spine when he spoke.

"I… she… we… no, no problem," Rob stammered in his anger. The resentful glare he shot her way chilled her, and she almost felt sick to her stomach. A sharp pain caused her lower abdominal muscles to clench. *Again with the premonitions.* He intended to stir up mischief, and not the fun kind. Sooner rather than later, unless she missed her guess.

"Sammy, you watch yourself around him. I get the impression he's the spiteful kind, out to cause trouble," James warned when Rob took the hint and left. "I mean it. Be careful to never be alone with him."

"You don't have to tell me twice. He makes my skin crawl." She snuggled closer into her new bodyguard because he hadn't dropped his arm yet.

"For show." She grinned up at him.

His answering grin and "uh huh" made her laugh.

"Don't get too comfy, sis. We have to head back to school in a week, and you're still jailbait."

"I'm nineteen, you tool!"

Both men chuckled.

Once again, her body flushed in reaction.

Dammit!

MICHAEL HADN'T GIVEN MUCH THOUGHT TO MEETING SAMMY. SHE WAS, after all, his best friend's kid sister. Bro code meant hands-off. What he hadn't expected—and what alarmed him—was the instant attraction he felt for her.

Normally, Michael was quiet by nature, so he suspected James hadn't noticed when he was struck mute by Sammy's natural beauty. It was as if her ice-blue eyes could see through him. See directly into his soul. He gave an internal shudder.

But with her hair so dark as to almost be black, lips made for nibbling kisses... No, it was better not to let his mind think about the pleasure to be found in those full pink lips of hers.

His immediate angry reaction to the guy who'd approached their group was disturbing. The urge to stake a claim and physically hurt the kid had been overpowering. Acting on instinct, Michael had thrown his arm around Sammy before her brother could take charge of the situation and send the little pissant packing. Michael hadn't waited. He doubted he'd have been able to.

But he'd done it now. By declaring himself Sammy's boyfriend, he had set himself up for a week of torture. Her curvy little body had him sweating faster than the Florida sun. There was little doubt he'd be in close proximity to her throughout the next ten days. James wouldn't forego spending time with his beloved sister.

His friend's "jailbait" comments were a definitive reminder for Michael to keep his hands to himself. The fierce stare James directed at him now required fast thinking. He was tired from the long drive and had nothing, so he simply shrugged. The dry look his friend shot him concurred with Michael's inner voice that he was an idiot for getting involved. Also, he should've received a medal for the willpower it took not to watch Sammy's pert little ass walk away.

"Come on, let's strip down to our suits and enjoy the beach."

Michael was never more glad to have James change the subject. He suspected the blonde hottie talking to Sammy provided the real reason. Unable to resist getting some of his own back, Michael said, "Now that sweet little thing talking to your sister? Son, *she* is jailbait."

The fist to his arm wasn't unexpected and would surely leave a bruise, but he couldn't help his laughter.

A short time later, as he came out of the water, Michael noticed Sammy as she rested on her stomach and chatted with the young blonde. Feeling a bit mischievous, he stood over Sammy and shook like a dog, effectively soaking her. Her struggle to rise while maintaining control of the tiny bikini top—which she'd untied after lying down—gave him the much-needed time to escape.

Michael jogged backwards into the water up to his knees, just out of her reach. "Sammy Darlin', don't be mad. I was only having a bit of fun. You looked like you needed cooling off." Laughing, he dodged this way and that with his body and words as she swung at him.

Sammy stopped her actions and nodded politely to someone behind him. Curious, he glanced over his right shoulder.

The running attack caught him off-guard, and the impact propelled him much farther back into the water. She accompanied her prize-winning tackle with a vicious pinch to his ass cheek. His yelp brought with it a mouthful of water.

When Michael surfaced, Sammy was floating on her back, kicking away from him. Wicked delight was written all over her face.

"Michael Darlin', don't be mad," she mocked before she jackknifed and dove under as another wave crested.

He had to admire her. He truly did. She reminded him of a mermaid. Soft and sleek. Tempting and taunting… shit! He'd lost track of her while wrapped in his sexual fantasy.

A second hard pinch caught him on his other cheek. "Ouch! What the hell?"

She popped up about twenty feet away. "I have this thing about equality. If I pinch one side of your ass, I have to do the same for the other." Her laughter followed her as she used the flow of the ocean to body surf into shore.

"Potty mouth," he yelled after her.

As Sammy trudged her way back to her towel, her thoughts lingered on Michael and their instant attraction. How, at nineteen, was her heart in jeopardy from a guy she'd just met?

She had no real experience to go by. Sure, she'd dated. Who hadn't? But having never fallen victim to love, there was no way of telling what might be real or not. She had enough empathic ability to question whether her feelings were her own or whether they belonged to whomever was interested in her at the moment. Although, in Michael's case, it felt damned real. Curbing the desire to rub against him like a cat in heat—in addition to keeping her hands to herself all morning—had been a serious chore.

The wind picked up, and a whisper of warning floated to her on the airstream. The hair on the back of her neck lifted, and a quick glance around showed why. Rob sat and stared at her. His expression was so malicious, Sammy was forced to look away.

Another chill took her. *Rob was going to be a problem.* Her instinct never failed her.

A hand snaked around her waist and startled a squeak from her.

"You all right, darlin'?"

And suddenly, she was. With Michael next to her, solid and strong, she gained what she needed to shake off the cold invading her body. "Yes, thank you. Are you hungry? There's an awesome Italian place across from the pier."

Michael dried off and grabbed a shirt. He patiently waited for her to throw on her beach cover-up, grab her bag, and nudge her groggy brother to see if he wished to join them. All she received from that end was a grunt. She shot a look of inquiry at her friend, Renee.

"Kemo? You want to go?"

Sammy hadn't really expected her to say yes No, her bestie didn't care to be that far from James. Renee would have tethered herself to him if she could have. Her friend had pictured herself in love with James for the better part of the last four years. Her faith that one day they would be a couple never faltered. It didn't matter if James thought of Renee as another kid sister. She'd arrived determined to change his mind today with her skimpy bathing suit and over-glossed lips. "Just in case he shows up," Renee had told her. Sammy admired the hell out of her for going after what she wanted. Unlike her bestie, she wasn't sure she possessed the confidence.

"If it's an open invitation, I'll go."

Michael and Sammy turned as one to view a belligerent Rob.

"It isn't. Get lost," barked Michael as he rested his hand on Sammy's waist to guide her forward.

Raw hatred flared to life on Rob's face. Her companion didn't seem to care, and at the moment, neither did she. Rob—that pain in the ass —needed to get it through his head to leave her alone.

With the warm hand upon her hip came the impression that Michael didn't like conflict as a rule. Yet, he'd immediately stepped up to the challenge twice to protect her from the likes of Rob. Sammy was left to wonder why he'd trouble himself to do so. She shrugged it off and allowed Michael to guide her toward the center of town.

"The food joint is this way, right?"

"Yep."

The long line at the self-pickup encouraged them to choose an outside table. While the two of them alone felt very first-date-like to Sammy, she was almost positive he didn't view their meal together in the same light. James had probably stressed in no uncertain terms that Michael would be beaten bloody if he entertained any notion of hooking up with *any* of the Holt sisters. Her brother could be annoyingly overprotective.

With a mental shrug, Sammy made up her mind to take a page from Renee's book. All she could do was indicate her interest. The rest was up to her companion. Their time away from the others would allow her to get to know him better.

MICHAEL'S THOUGHTS WERE CONSUMED WITH THE ISSUE OF ROB. THE asshole was out to cause trouble, not caring who he hurt in the process. It only took a single look at Sammy, and he could understand the guy's obsession. She was stunning in a girl-next-door way.

Because Michael's brain was occupied with thoughts of the confrontation on the beach, he missed her next words. "I'm sorry? What were you asking?"

With a grin, she repeated her question. "Are you single?"

"Yes," he answered warily.

A small, smug smile played about her lips. He should have prevaricated or outright lied because now she might get the wrong idea. Oddly enough, he found himself continuing with the truth. "I just broke up with someone."

"What happened?"

"I thought I loved her. Thought she loved me, too. Apparently, she loved drugs and screwing other guys more."

"Oh, God! Michael, I'm so sorry."

Silence reigned as they dealt with the uncomfortableness of his confession. A perky waitress appeared and killed the awkwardness. As if by some silent, mutual agreement, Michael and Sammy tabled the "ex" discussion and changed the subject.

After their pizza slices arrived, Sammy took a deep, appreciative sniff. The first bite brought with it her groan of pleasure. Michael grinned. Who knew she would turn out to be such a foodie? Not surprisingly, her second sexy moan hit him low in the gut.

"What is your major?" Her abrupt question caught him off guard.

He shook his head with a laugh. "Would you believe I've changed it more than a few times already? I think I may have settled on mechanical engineering. I took a little time off before starting, but all my pre-reqs are now out of the way. From here on out, I need to get busy earning the remainder of my degree. What about you?"

"Business Management. It's the old standby because I don't know what I want to do with my life."

He paused for a bite before asking about her blonde friend. "So what is with your friend's name? Did her parents actually name her Kemo?"

Sammy broke into laughter and explained. "No. Kemo stands for Kemosabe. As in *The Lone Ranger*."

His lifted brow encouraged her to continue.

"One day, a few years back, a group of us were horseback riding. Renee happened to be on a nasty beast that couldn't stand being around other horses—there's one in every barn. Anyway, she was far, far ahead of the rest of us. At one point, she called back, 'I feel like The Lone Ranger.'" Sammy smiled at the memory. "I didn't really know her well at the time, but being the sarcastic one of the group, I hollered 'How, Kemosabe!' Right then and there, her horse made a break for it. She cried, 'Tonto, save me!' I almost fell out of the saddle because I was laughing so hard. Despite my lack of heroics, we became best friends, and the names stuck throughout high school."

"So the moral of this story is you are not the best one to have around in a crisis situation. You find everything funny."

"Pretty much," she agreed with a broad grin.

After that, their lunch discussion remained light and fun. They took their time eating and hadn't quite finished before a heavily accented voice bellowed Sammy's name from the doorway.

Her face lit up, and she jumped up to run into the arms of a burly Italian. "Vinnie!"

"I never see you. Why you no come more?" he asked.

Not waiting for a reply, the restaurant owner offered up his hand to Michael.

"Ah, I now know. Love, eh?" Vinnie was a bear of a man who was exceedingly jovial but was prone to speaking his mind apparently.

A blush dusted Sammy's cheeks.

"Um, no. This is my brother's friend, Michael. We were just—"

The brisk Italian waved off her excuse.

"I know love when I see it, and you no fool old Vinnie. I have my eye on you since you come."

He laughed, pounded Michael on the back, and walked away, but not before insisting they not be strangers.

"I'm sorry about that… he… you… Yeah, well it's why I never bring male friends here," she finished, embarrassment obvious.

Sammy's distress was adorable, and Michael could no more prevent his grin than he could stop the waves from crashing against the shoreline across the street.

"You're cute when you're flustered," he said.

Another rush of color flooded her face.

"Mud pie," she blurted.

He lifted his brows in question, fighting back a laugh.

"You have to try their mud pie."

And so he did.

After the first bite, he was sure he had died and gone to heaven. Only sex was better. He glanced up to see Sammy savoring her own bite. Eyes closed. Complete bliss written all over her face. Desire struck, and Michael went rock hard. The way she consumed her pie was the most erotic thing he'd ever witnessed. She withdrew the spoon from her mouth in slow increments, and the little mew of pleasure which escaped her lips mesmerized him.

Shit!

James would kill him if he even *suspected* Michael's x-rated thoughts.

As he was contemplating doing something totally moronic, like sweeping Sammy up and stealing her away on his motorcycle, a rowdy group of customers walked up.

"Well, look who's here," sneered the guy who was fast becoming his nemesis.

"It shouldn't be a surprise since you tried to invite yourself along earlier," Michael responded dryly. "But here, have our table. Sammy and I were just leaving. Weren't we, darlin'?"

He handed the waitress more than enough cash to cover the check plus a generous tip, then ushered Sammy out the patio gate. He heard someone behind him try to encourage Rob to let it go and move on.

"It's never going to happen, dude."

"Fuck off!" the little shit snapped back.

A brief moment of unease struck. Sammy would have a difficult time after he and James went back to college. The situation with that kid was deteriorating rapidly.

CHAPTER 2

Sammy's mother had declared James's homecoming dinner a private affair for immediate family and Michael only. No one refused Violet Holt when she demanded all her children be in attendance. Their mother was a force to be reckoned with. None of them would dare even dream of being late. And although Sammy desperately wanted to go to a bonfire on the beach that night, she made sure not to commit when her friends had asked.

Most of the meal was spent listening to James regale them with stories of college and the various scrapes he managed to get himself into. Michael would interject here or there to clarify parts of the story —the way only a good friend could do.

"Sounds like Michael's the voice of reason in this duo." Her father, Martin, smothered an indulgent smile. "He's a good friend to have around."

James was a fan of exaggeration. Michael, on the other hand, downplayed things upon witnessing Violet's horrified reaction to some of the shadier situations. Consideration was a good quality to have. A trait Sammy's older sister Margie currently held in short supply.

"Margie, cut them a break already," Sammy said, effectively halting another lecture from her older sister on how James had been stupid to do this stunt or the other.

Sammy and Margie failed to see eye to eye on a great many subjects, and as a result, they didn't rub well together. Perhaps the age divide could be blamed. With Margie seven years her senior and having married right out of high school, the two of them had little to nothing in common. Lately, Margie always seemed depressed and bitter. Tonight, she bitched non-stop and was a complete buzzkill.

It wasn't that the siblings didn't all love one another. They absolutely did. However, the general consensus from the youngest generation of Holts was that Margie was best avoided if possible. *At least, until the woman got laid.* The last little bit was Sammy's personal opinion, but James and Annie hadn't disagreed when she mentioned it. Apparently, Margie's husband, Scott, was falling asleep and not getting the job done.

Sammy glanced at Annie to judge her reaction. Her sister fell between James and Sammy in age but in temperament was probably the most mild-mannered of the entire clan. Annie refused to be around Margie unless, like tonight, she had no choice. "Too painful," she would say.

Interrupted from her musings by Margie's grating tone, Sammy pasted on a look of rapt attention. Mentally, she calculated the number of drinks her sister had consumed tonight before and during dinner. A drunk Margie equaled a snarky Margie. All throughout what should have been a joyful reunion, her older sister felt the need to monopolize the conversation, complain about her husband, demand perfection from her three beautiful children, as well as insert a few digs on how Annie and Sammy lived their lives.

The victims of her tirade decided to leave the others to their own devices. Sammy came up with the first excuse to pop into her head. "I'll clear and make room for dessert," she stated and grabbed a few plates.

"I'll help," Annie and James piped up at the same time.

Three of the four Holt siblings gathered in the kitchen to get a respite from the fourth's barrage of insults.

"God, does she ever *stop?*" The frustration James felt was echoed in all their expressions.

"No," Annie and Sammy groaned in unison.

James paused in scrapping off his dish. "When did she become so bitter?"

Sammy didn't have an answer since she rarely saw Margie outside family dinners.

"She's hurting." Annie's empathic gift was strong and not something she could easily turn off. It required practice, diligence, and avoiding negative people for the most part.

James stared at Annie for a long moment, nodded, and continued his task.

Tired of the drama, Sammy hatched her escape plan. Michael sailed through the kitchen door, plates in hand, as she became enthusiastic about making a run for it.

"You can't just walk out on a family dinner," James warned. "Mom will have your ass."

"Sorry, bro. You know I love you, but not enough to listen to Margie another second. I promised Renee and Skye I would meet them at the bonfire tonight."

"Liar!" James charged. "You never said a word about it earlier."

MICHAEL NOTED THE SPARKLE OF AMUSEMENT IN SAMMY'S EYE. NOT having siblings of his own, he wasn't used to the constant heated discussions that seemed to go down in the Holt home. An only child couldn't fathom conversations like these were the norm.

Doing what he could to defuse the situation, he spoke up in Sammy's favor. Why? He had no idea. "Actually, she did. I heard her promise the two of us would catch up with them there. You were too busy snoring to hear it," he lied.

Catching sight of Sammy's laughing expression, he raised a brow in challenge. She wouldn't contradict him. At least, not if she planned to get away.

"A party sounds like a great idea right about now. I could use a drink after five minutes of Margie," James said as he loaded their plates in the dishwasher. "Why does she have to be so damned negative, or has she always been that way and I don't remember?"

"It started when she and Scott broke up," Annie offered by way of explanation.

"They broke up?" Sammy paused as she dished up the pie for the others.

"Keep up, Lil' Bit. Weren't you paying attention at all tonight?" James hunched over the counter to wolf down the slice Sammy had shoved his way.

A bit sheepishly, she confessed, "I tune Margie out more often than not."

Michael found himself mesmerized by her animated face. The fascination he felt was liable to create friction between him and James, but he was damned if he could ignore it. Being in her orbit was like having the sun shine continually on his face. She was bright, bold, and beautiful. The perfect trifecta.

"If I listened to a word she said, I would be forced to end it all. In her eyes, I am the worst human being to walk the Earth." Sammy worked herself up into a rant. "Did you hear her trying to encourage a date with Rob? *Rob!* Of all the losers to try to set me up with, she wants me to date *him?*" Though it looked like it, her shudder wasn't exaggerated. Michael had witnessed how much the guy disturbed her.

"How does she even know about him, besides his constant phone calls here?" Sammy asked.

"I'm sure Mom probably said he's been calling here twenty-four-seven," Annie answered with a shrug.

"Why does she want you to date that little waste of space?" Michael felt compelled to ask, outraged on her behalf. If indignation at the idea of her with another man was making his words a little extra harsh, he ignored it.

"Margie probably doesn't know he's such a dick. We aren't sure what her reasoning is," supplied Annie.

"Hatred from a past life?" joked Sammy. "Regardless, I can't take any more tonight. Anyone who wants to hitch a ride with me better be out front in five minutes." With that said, she jogged up the back stairs, presumably to grab her keys.

The remaining two siblings played rock paper scissors to determine who had the job of informing their parents they were heading out. James lost. Annie put a finger to her lips and dragged Michael out the kitchen door, hightailing it to Sammy's car with a laugh.

"What's with you and Sammy?" Annie asked after a few minutes of waiting for the others.

"Nothing!" Michael nearly shouted in protest. Sweat pooled on his lower back. In his mind's eye, he could clearly see himself getting busy with Sammy, but involvement with someone just this side of legal wasn't smart. "Jesus, she's practically a baby and my best friend's kid sister. I don't need, nor want, that kind of complication."

If Annie intended to respond, it was cut off by the commotion James made as he barreled into Sammy. "Damn, Sammy. A warning would be nice if you are going to stop."

Christ! She'd heard him. Feeling like an ass and wishing he could recall the words, Michael surged forward. He'd been watching for her. How could he not when she had him tangled up inside? It seemed the second he'd been diverted by Annie's question, Sammy arrived to hear his stupid little speech. The shock on her face was absolute. She wasn't savvy enough to hide her secondary reaction of hurt.

Fucking great. Now he had wounded her pride *and* her feelings. He was as bad as her oldest sister. If he could've cut out his tongue right then, he would've.

Sammy sidestepped and shoved James in front of her. "I dropped my keys. You look here, and I'll retrace my steps."

"I'll help her look," Michael muttered, latching on to her fake excuse to follow her. He raced after her to do damage control.

He didn't miss the smile on Annie's face and the frown forming on James's.

"What the hell..." James trailed off as Michael darted around the corner of the house.

. . .

WHEN JAMES'S VOICE CARRIED TO MICHAEL AND ANNIE, SAMMY HAD wished the ground would open and swallow her whole. Did anyone actually die of humiliation? *Not with her luck.* Seeing Michael had followed her, she bent over and pretended to be looking for her keys. It was the only thing she could think to do to save face. Any excuse, even a nonsensical one, allowed her to take the time and get her emotions in check. It wouldn't do for anyone to see the crushing hurt Michael's words had caused.

And how stupid was she, allowing her feelings to grow out of control in a matter of hours? What had she expected? For someone like him to suddenly fall head over heels in love? A tearful snort rose up and escaped. God, she was an idiot.

"Sammy? Can I apologize for what I said?"

The gentleness in his tone wasn't lost on her. Because he sounded contrite, tears welled up and burned the back of her lids. A lump formed in her throat and made it impossible to respond. Embarrassed beyond reason, she furiously blinked back the evidence of her upset. She continued to make an active search for the non-existent lost keys in the grass. Regaining her composure was difficult, but she managed.

"Found 'em," she lied with forced cheer. She straightened and shook her keys in the air.

Turning, she nearly jumped out of her skin. She hadn't expected Michael to be so close. His presence sucked all the air from her lungs. As of yet, she couldn't look at him. How did he not feel their bond as strongly as she did? How could he think she was little more than a child?

"I'm sorry, Sammy," he said softly.

His velvety Southern drawl created butterflies in her stomach. Kindness was the one thing she didn't need right now. Knowing she had to steel herself against the pull of his charm, she shifted to go around him only to have him reach out and stop her progress. Image after image of their potential futures flashed through her mind, throwing her off-kilter. She couldn't keep them straight, and they eventually all ran together. A massive headache was forming. She swayed, and he brought up his other arm to steady her. Envisioning a solid metal shield between them, she was able to block out most of the visions.

Before he could speak or ask her if she was okay, she said, "I don't know what you're talking about, or what you have to be sorry for, but no problem." She fake-smiled. "We should get going before Margie decides to join us."

Let him believe it didn't matter. With any luck, he would. Perhaps she should tell him they needed to stage a "break up" at the bonfire. It would give him an out instead of forcing him to hang around her. But if he didn't want to be with her, why had he backed her up in the kitchen? Why perpetuate her lie? Answers were impossible to find. Later, when she was alone in her bed, she would be able to replay what she'd seen and, hopefully, make sense of it all.

MICHAEL DEBATED PUSHING THE ISSUE OR ALLOWING HER TO SAVE FACE and bluff her way through the awkwardness. The best course of action was to smile, to let her think he believed her, and so he went with it. With a gesture for her to precede him, he fell into place behind her. It was an effort, but he managed to keep his eyes from wandering down to her shapely ass. She had only taken two steps before his conscience reared its ugly head. It was impossible for him *not* to apologize once again. Hurting her killed him.

"Wait, Sammy. Look, I know you heard me tell your sister you were just a kid. I... the thing is... I didn't mean for the words to sound harsh. I just wanted to get across to Annie that there's nothing between us."

Sammy focused on a point beyond his shoulder without speaking. Inside, he cringed. He'd made the situation even worse. Why couldn't he leave well enough alone? Of its own volition, his mouth opened again. "Please, forgive me. I know you see yourself as a grown-up, but... damn, I..."

Words failed him as she turned her furious, eerie eyes on him. The urge to slap himself on the forehead washed over him. But Jesus, she was gorgeous in her anger. If she were only three years older, he wouldn't care that she was James's baby sister. He'd pounce before she could blink.

"I appreciate you continued to play along to get rid of Rob. But you are *so* not my type. I can promise you, you did not hurt my feelings in the least. Rest easy, okay?"

Maybe if she hadn't reached up to condescendingly pat his cheek, Michael would've let it go. *Or maybe not.* Her refusal to accept his apology, as well as her superior attitude, was enough to raise his ire.

He prevented her escape by grabbing the hand that patted his face. If he pondered why, he was sure to blame it on a throwback to a caveman ancestor. But Michael was damned if he could stop himself from doing what came next.

Icy blue eyes clashed with his searching look a second before his lips found and savaged hers. The kiss sparked to life a passion he didn't know he possessed. Sammy moaned and pressed her body against him. His hands found the firm little ass of hers that he'd spent the entire day so enamored with. Her hands wound their way up from his chest to hook around his neck. She wove her fingers in the hair at his nape. Reaching down past the curve of her hip, he caressed the back of one smooth thigh before he hoisted her up higher against him. He sighed and delved deeper into her mouth as she wrapped her legs around his waist. Heaven couldn't taste as sweet. As she pressed and rubbed against him, he moaned his frustration into her mouth. Most assuredly, if they weren't in her parent's side yard, he'd have her on the ground, sinking into her willing warmth.

CHAPTER 3

$\mathcal{A}$nnie, round-eyed and shocked, let the kiss continue. It wasn't as if she had much of a choice either way. She was over-heated by their display—such was the result of her empath curse—and until she heard James stomping to where she stared, undecided on a course of action, she let Sammy experience the joy of making out with the man she'd already developed an affection for. When Annie's "pssst" failed to part the two, she briefly considered the garden hose. Luckily, Michael seemed to come to his senses before she was forced to take drastic measures.

Reaching up, he ripped Sammy's hands from their exploration and shoved her none too gently away. Annie was no great judge, but if anyone had bothered to ask her to describe his expression, she would have said shell-shocked.

"Are we leaving any time tonight?" James snapped.

The hard look he directed at Michael left no room for doubt that he expected an explanation later.

As one, they all moved to the driveway. Sammy tossed her keys to Annie, instinctively knowing she would understand Sammy was way too shaken to drive. Annie couldn't blame her. She was a bit shaken herself. The heat they were putting off rivaled the hottest summer day in Florida.

To the best of her knowledge, her younger sister had never been interested in anyone the way she was currently with Michael. Annie only hoped the two of them could wade through the sea of emotions surrounding them and come together. Michael seemed to carry some heavy baggage, based on what she could sense, but deep down, he was the best sort of guy. Her little sister needed someone like him in her life. As the Holt family member gifted with psychic abilities, Sammy was in for a rough road. Nothing in their family's history had ever been easy. It stood to reason nothing going forward ever would be either.

THE BONFIRE WAS IN FULL SWING AS THE FOUR OF THEM WALKED UP. Sammy ran off to greet her friends before Michael could talk to her about a plan to shut down Rob's persistent advances if the need arose. He watched her flee then turned to grab the beer James offered him. Because they had things they needed to discuss, the two of them distanced themselves from the partying crowd.

Stopping twenty yards or more away from the bonfire, James faced him. "What's going on between you and Sammy?"

Ah, the question of the hour.

Michael stared out over the moonlit water. How could he tell his best friend that Sammy had him twisted in knots?

"I don't know, man. I truly don't. Meeting her was like a shockwave to my system. I know she's your baby sister, but I... there's just something about her that gets to me."

"Look, I know you wouldn't ever dream of hurting her. That's not your style. But I don't want you encouraging her. She's innocent."

Michael snorted in derision before he could stop himself. "Don't all brothers think that?"

"What the fuck, man? You're really going to say something like that about my *sister*?" With a balled fist, he took an aggressive step toward

Michael. "You keep your fucking distance. I mean it. I don't want to hate you or have to fight you."

Complete honesty was needed. Michael didn't see any other way to placate his buddy. "James, man, come on. You *know* I don't think of her that way. You also know I have no intention of sleeping with her." Michael ran a shaky hand through his mussed hair and tried to salvage the moment. "I'm attracted to her. I'm not going to lie about that. But I promise you, I won't give her any encouragement. Does that satisfy?"

A brisk nod from James and a tap of his beer to Michael's closed the issue. Both men paused to inhale the salty sea air and let the calming effects of Mother Nature smooth this small ripple in their friendship. When they were in silent accord once more, James shifted to head back to the party.

"Now let's go find some girls our own age, huh?" suggested James.

"I can't. I'm supposed to pose as your sister's boyfriend, remember?" Michael reminded him with a wry smile.

"Oh, shit!"

"Yeah, my thoughts exactly." Michael sighed. "You go. I want a few minutes to myself anyway. I'm not used to being surrounded by so many people all the time. Only child, remember?"

With a slap on his back, James was gone, leaving him to his own thoughts. Michael wondered, not for the first time, how he was going to get through this week with his sanity and friendship intact. Not to mention surviving a serious case of blue balls. Christ, he was only on day one. He'd never make it the full trip.

"If he's your boyfriend, why haven't I seen you kissing? I think you just want me to believe he is," Rob's nasal voice came from close behind Sammy.

She raised her face up to the sky, silently berating the Heavens for not sounding thunder or some other warning before the Devil's spawn walked up.

"You're trying to make me jealous. But I don't like your little games, Samantha."

"Rob, get it through your head; I am not now, nor will I ever be, interested in you. *Stop stalking me, you freak!*" His constant sneering presence grated on Sammy's last nerve, and she lost her shit. "I mean it. If you don't leave me alone, I am going to get a restraining order."

He grabbed her arm in a punishing hold.

"Don't think I'm not going to teach you a lesson soon, you little prick-tease. We all see you walking around here like you're all that. You are just another little—" The remainder of Rob's words turned into a gurgle and were cut off by a shove to his throat. He lost focus on Sammy and became alert to the angry, hulking beast that was her brother.

"One more word and you are going to seriously regret it. I don't know what it's like to try to eat with a jaw wired shut, but you are about to find out," snapped James. "You stay the fuck away from my sister."

"You can't be around her all the time, asshole. Remember that."

James was an enraged bull, and Rob had just waved the red flag. The younger guy never stood a chance as James tackled him and rained down one punch after another. It required Michael and two other guys to pull her brother off, but one touch from Annie was enough to penetrate his rage. "Jamie, you need to stop."

"He threatened her, Annie. I could kill him for that alone. He..." Words failed to express how livid he truly was, but the fury in his face said it all. Annie's small hand covered his heart and worked its magic. "Okay, okay," he muttered before he stomped off, followed closely by their sister.

"You okay, darlin'?" Michael's concerned voice reached Sammy.

She hadn't been conscious of her own body shaking, but he had. She shot him a beseeching look, and he recognized her need for contact. Sweeping her up in his arms, he strode along the dark beach some distance, not stopping until he found a secluded area that offered up the privacy they needed. He settled onto the warm sand with her in his lap, and they tuned out the residual noise created by the party. His primary goal was to comfort her, and she adored him for it.

The intent to kill had been on James's face. Rob brought something ugly with him wherever he turned up—usually wherever Sammy happened to be. She didn't know how to vocalize what she was feeling. In the end, she just clung to the man holding her. The closeness was something she'd never experienced before. Michael's spicy smell and warm touch brought to life a wanting she would never have thought possible. Feeling breathless and twitchy, she combed her brain for a distraction. If she wasn't diverted from the riot of emotions she was feeling, she was likely to rip his clothing in her need to burrow closer.

"Will they arrest Jamie for assault?" Although she could see glimpses of the future, this particular worry brought with it no foreseeable vision.

"I don't see why they would. That sonofabitch grabbed you first."

Both inspected the place on her arm where a dark bruise was already forming. The ugly mark was visible even with little light.

MICHAEL HAD TO SWALLOW DOWN HIS OWN FURY. WHEN HE SAW THAT bastard Rob manhandle Sammy, rage such as he'd never known rose to the forefront. Had James not arrived first, Michael was afraid he would have done far worse damage than her brother.

Not sure how to deal with his new out-of-control emotions, he tuck her against his chest and rested his cheek atop her head. Gradually, the sound of the water rolling against the shore and receding relaxed them both.

He became aware of Sammy on a more physical level. Her tight, compact body felt too right against his. More than once, he had to stop the hand rubbing large circles on her back from traveling south to cup her shapely ass. God, he was enamored with her ass. He'd be the next one James beat to a bloody pulp.

Sammy lifted her head from his chest to study his face. A stray lock of hair had fallen across his brow and caught her attention. It seemed to hold her transfixed as the breeze tossed around the rest of his unruly mop. Unable to resist the urge, she reached to brush it back. Her simple gesture caused him to flinch. He caught and lowered her hand. It was time to be frank with her.

"Sammy..." He cleared his throat. "...You and me, it's not going to happen. You're my best friend's sister. Even if I disregard my friendship with James—which I'm not going to do—you are way too young and inexperienced for my tastes. I would feel like a perv. You think you are all grown up, but I promise you, nineteen is still a kid."

He paused to collect his thoughts because, honestly, her sitting in his lap was quickly causing him to forget all the reasons not to touch her.

The lack of reaction on her part disconcerted him. Why wasn't she angry at this point of his speech? Any other woman would view the rejection as a personal affront. Instead, Sammy stared without expression. Maybe the hard ridge of his dick resting against her hip made her skeptical. With a long list of reasons why the two of them wouldn't work, he stated them one by one. A frown darkened her forehead, but otherwise, she remained silent. He only felt marginally better as she appeared to listen and understand.

As HIS EXCUSES PILED UP, SAMMY WANTED TO HOWL HER OBJECTIONS. His logic was sound, and he'd clearly made up his mind. She allowed him to continue without interruption, but her heart ached. *So much for love at first sight!* Apparently, her feelings were all one-sided. But how? How could one person feel a connection so strongly while the other felt nothing but a passing desire? Yeah, she might be innocent when it came to actual sexual encounters, but she was wise enough to know that was no banana in his pocket.

She swallowed down her protest and sighed heavily. Why did the idea of never seeing him after this week make her want to weep? Out of the blue, a deep-seated knowledge gripped her. A *knowing* that one day they would be together. They were meant to be. She trusted the message. Her gift rarely failed her.

She pasted on a serene smile, causing Michael to pause in the long list of reasons as to why they could never be together. She leaned in to catch his wary gaze.

"We're inevitable," she stated. Before rising and walking away, she gave him a soft, lingering kiss. "Remember this long after you go home."

In her wake, she had no doubt she'd left a very confused and shaken man.

CHAPTER 4

THREE YEARS LATER...

*S*ammy twisted around in her seat to peer behind her for what had to be the hundredth time in her hope to locate Michael in the massive crowd.

As far as the eye could see, colored caps were bobbing here and there in the excitement of this special day. Why she searched in vain was beyond her. Michael had failed to respond to her invitation. It was doubtful he even remembered—much less cared—about her graduation. And who could blame him? She'd gotten tipsy and practically mauled him this past Christmas. Not her proudest moment.

"Tonto, sit still," Renee hissed from beside her.

"I'm sorry, Kemo. I just thought he would be here, ya know?"

There was no need to clarify who "he" was. Renee knew very well she referred to Michael. He had been the topic of Sammy's every conversation their entire summer after her first year of college. By the time fall rolled around and they were once again back at the University of Florida, Sammy was determined never to speak of him again. The failure on his part to respond to her not-so-subtle overtures had finally sunk in. Still, she refused to form any lasting relationship with anyone else. The torch she carried for Michael had never been extinguished.

"I thought you had moved on. It's not like there was ever any real relationship there, right?" asked Renee.

Sammy's tight expression was answer enough. Renee wisely remained silent.

The row in front of them stood and cut off their discussion. The time had come to receive their diplomas. Sammy breathed a sigh of relief. Renee could be relentless with her questions, and although she'd taken the hint, Sammy didn't expect her friend to stay quiet for long.

After her name was called and just as Sammy received the rolled document, a piercing whistle rang out. She'd only heard a whistle like that once before. Michael possessed a *very* distinctive whistle.

Sammy's smile couldn't be contained. She strode to her seat, impatient for all the hoopla to be over. At times like these, having a last name starting with a letter in the first third of the alphabet absolutely sucked. Williams, Young, or Zahn would've made her much happier about now.

Sammy spent the rest of the ceremony plagued with questions. Would she come across as adult enough to him? Did he even find her attractive? Was she delusional? Had he brought his girlfriend, Paige, with him? *That* sobering thought brought reality crashing back.

No one could see Paige for what she was except Sammy—and most likely Annie, although her sister had never said. Annie had avoided the other woman at every opportunity.

Regardless, Michael had shown up today. That had to count for something, right? She sighed and shook her head. Who was she fooling? Not herself. *God, the friend zone sucked.* But there was no point dwelling on negative thoughts. The probability was high she wasn't the only woman on the planet dealing with unrequited love. Others survived. She would, too.

"What has you so moody? One second your expression looked like you won the lottery, and now you look like you lost your best friend. What the hell, Sammy?"

Renee could always be counted on for brutal honesty. The least Sammy could do was return the favor.

"Michael's here. I'm positive that was his whistle when I was up there." With a hard swallow, she continued, "I'm thrilled he showed, but then my mind switched to devil's advocate mode and taunted me with the real possibility he brought his bitch girlfriend." She groaned. "What is it about him that throws me into such emotional hell? I've never cared about another guy enough to spare them a second glance."

Renee paused to formulate the proper response. She eventually settled on, "Maybe he is just the first person to tell you no and mean it. You know the old cliché 'the one that got away'? I think it could apply to your situation. You've become somewhat obsessed."

"You could be right, bu—" The rest of what Sammy would have said was cut short by the celebration of cap tosses, indicating the conclusion of the graduation ceremony. "Catch up to me later," she shouted over the din as she hugged her friend.

Locating her family in the massive crowd wasn't easy, but Sammy eventually managed it. Overcome with love, she halted about twenty feet away to watch them laugh and joke with another student's family.

"They're great, aren't they?" That smooth, yummy voice never failed to cause the nerve endings in her body to stand at attention.

Pure soft, sexy Southern goodness. Damn, his voice turned her on. She needed to get over her feelings for him. Facing Michael was impossible because her absurd joy wasn't easily contained. Her face, always an open book, would give her away. Instead, she croaked out "yes" and let him believe it was her family who made her so emotional.

"No hug for an old friend, Sammy Darlin'?"

The whisper of his breath on her ear caused a shiver. No mean feat as she sweltered in her ceremonial garb under the hot Florida sun. Because looking at him hurt too badly, she studied her brother instead.

"I'm surprised you came. After what happened during the Christmas break..." Sammy trailed off.

. . .

MICHAEL SWORE UNDER HIS BREATH AND GENTLY SPUN HER TO face him.

"I wouldn't miss your big day, Sammy." The truth was, he almost *had* missed her graduation because Paige had destroyed the invitation before he could see it. If James hadn't messaged him a few days ago, Michael wouldn't be standing here now. But none of that mattered. Not when he looked down into those stunningly blue eyes of Sammy's. "As for your kiss, well, in all honesty, it's all I've thought about for the last five months."

Her eyes flew wide at his admission.

He chuckled softly. "I wanted to kiss you back so badly, and it took everything I had to remember Paige was in the next room."

At the mention of his girlfriend, Sammy stiffened and attempted to dislodge his hold. Michael refused to allow her to escape what, for them, amounted to a crucial moment. His grip on her arms tightened slightly as he leaned down to catch her complete attention.

"Sammy, I need you to actually listen to what I'm saying here."

"I get it, Michael, okay?" Her lips tightened, and her bright eyes dulled. "You have a girlfriend, and I crossed a line. I'm sorry."

"No, I don't have a girlfriend. Not anymore. And as for that line, I'm hoping we can cross it together."

"Are you s-serious?" she stuttered.

Michael grinned and pulled her close as he murmured against her lips, "I'm tired of pretending I'm not crazy about you."

When he would've kissed her, Sammy placed a hand between them. "Michael, I'm sorry, but I can't. I've… I've met someone, and we've gotten pretty serious."

Her words were like a blow to his solar plexus. Heart pounding an erratic tattoo, he couldn't quite catch a breath. Why had he never considered she might have fallen for someone else? Hadn't she been the one who said they were inevitable? What the hell?

A small chirp from her drew his attention back to her face. As she erupted into giggles, her game became obvious. Thank Christ, she'd been messing with him. Relief warred with anger. Relief won. He wrapped a hand around her neck and pulled her in close to rest his forehead against hers.

"You little wench," he growled. "You about gave me a heart attack. Props to you. Well played. But I *will* get you back for that." With that said, he did what he had been fantasizing about for a very long time. He kissed her. His lips hungrily devoured hers, and she matched him kiss for kiss. The taste of her was so much better than he remembered. It felt like coming home, and nothing had ever felt so right.

PART II

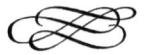

CHAPTER 5

*A*s Sammy finished adding the last touches of makeup, she heard the front door slam shut. Slamming doors were the unfortunate result of living close to the beach if you had other windows in the house open. The wind had a mind of its own.

Sassy barked a greeting to the intruder.

Michael was home from work.

Joy infused her. In almost six years together, their love hadn't diminished. Each day brought a deeper caring and understanding of one another.

"Sammy Darlin', where are you?" Michael called out in his deep, Southern drawl.

"I'll be right out."

She surveyed her reflection in the mirror and searched out her few, more obvious flaws. As she leaned forward to closer inspect her under-eye concealer, the image in the mirror morphed into a haggard woman resembling her in face shape only. The hollowed-out planes of her pale face and the dark circles under her dull, sorrowful eyes made Sammy gasp her shock.

She reached out to touch her future self and encountered cold glass. The image changed once more. This time, she saw the ghost of her former self. The lank-haired woman with the gaunt face on the hospital bed simply stared, registering no emotion whatsoever.

"Sammy? You okay?"

With a shaking hand, she threw down the makeup brush and fled the bathroom. She needed Michael's warm embrace to chase away her demons.

"Hi!" When Michael flashed his dimpled grin, her knees went weak.

"Hi!" She tried to offer him a cheeky grin in return.

Next came the tight hug and the soft, lingering kiss. Their unique way to say hello and goodbye. In these gestures, the love they shared could be felt the most. Plus, it didn't hurt that he smelled so divine all the time. To hug him, to breathe in his clean, fresh scent, made her content and deliriously happy.

His sharp-eyed stare missed nothing. "What's up?"

"Nothing."

He narrowed those warm-honey eyes and raised a brow to show his disbelief.

"Really," she assured him. *If only she could assure herself as easily.* "How was your day, babe?"

Michael studied her another moment before he shook his head and grinned ruefully. "I suppose you'll tell me when you're good and ready, huh?"

"Maayyybe," she teased.

Later, when she was alone, she'd take the time to process her vision.

They shared a second lingering kiss and parted. "I have news for you," they both said in unison and burst into laughter.

Talking over one another happened frequently. They communicated on a different level than the rest of the world and often completed each other's sentences. It had to appear odd to anyone witnessing their exchanges. Their mental link afforded them the ability to read each other's thoughts and, on occasion, share each other's dreams at night. This ability might've frightened anyone else, but not the two of them. It came as natural as breathing, and she never questioned it.

"Are you reading my mind again, or do you actually have news, too?" he asked as he snuggled her close.

"No, I have a surprise for you." She wiggled against him. "I got a promotion."

He pulled back to stare. "Seriously? That's great, darlin'."

She did an abbreviated version of the cabbage patch, using only her arms. "You are looking at the newest manager of our Palm Coast branch. It's going to be nice not to drive forty-five minutes one way anymore. I'm stoked."

Michael laughed at her antics. He didn't seem surprised she'd blurted her news. Even had she wanted to, she would never have been able to contain a secret long enough to last through the dinner date they had planned, and he knew it.

"That's wonderful!" His genuine happiness was like a warm blanket wrapped around her shoulders.

Her announcement made, she waved a hand in dismissal. "Okay, what's yours?" She skipped downstairs behind him on the way to their kitchen.

Again, his laughter boomed.

"Well, I have good news, and I have bad news," he taunted as he strolled to the refrigerator. Because he had the power to, he teased her and made her squirm.

"Don't eat anything. You won't be hungry when we go out," she ordered.

As was standard, Michael ignored her to root around for something to snack on. "Nag, nag, nag," he teased.

Cold washed through her, and she had a mental image of him boarding a plane. "You're going away," she said tonelessly.

Surprise lit his features as he glanced up from the tuna casserole he'd been studying. "What made you ask that?"

"You are, aren't you?" she demanded.

. . .

MICHAEL SIGHED. SAMMY HAD MADE HER FEELINGS PLAIN. ON A DEEPER level, he recognized it terrified her when he left town and it triggered her nightmares, but life couldn't be put on hold for a few bad dreams. Why she feared his leaving, she could never truly say. In the past, they'd discussed Michael's desire to travel for business, if only to break up the tediousness of every day at the same job. However, Sammy's standpoint was always the same. Most times, her anxiety made him back down. Once the fear took hold, it was difficult for her to let go.

There were times he wondered if her fear was jealousy or insecurity based. And, because he had never given her any reason not to trust him, her irrational behavior set his teeth on edge. Of course, the occasional fight would ensue, and the two of them would be stuck trying to deal with residual anger, neither understanding how it had transpired in the first place. These were probably the only true arguments they ever had.

"When Pete and Roger cornered me, I said yes," Michael informed her. He closed the refrigerator and braced himself for the storm about to be unleashed.

Sammy surprised him and didn't say a word. She wanted to. That much was obvious from her mutinous expression. Instead, in an effort to control her hair-trigger temper, she nodded and rushed from the room.

With a frustrated sigh, Michael followed her up the stairs. When he walked into their room, he found Sammy staring at the wall, stony expression in place.

"Well, aren't you going to say anything?" Anger struggled to the surface. He was hurt she'd stalked off without trying to discuss the issue at hand. He was also damned tired of it being Sammy's way or the highway.

"No, you've made up your mind. Without ever asking me—*as usual.*"

"Come on, Sammy. Don't make me feel like an insensitive jerk. I'm always the bad guy, aren't I? I just found out today and needed to make a snap decision. Besides, I knew how you felt about it. Why did I have to ask you?" As the words left his mouth, he realized his mistake. *Wrong, wrong, wrong, wrong, wrong!* Of course, he should have discussed it with her. Now he'd done it. He would've been better off to stay in the kitchen by himself. *Oh, Christ!*

Sammy shoved back her thick dark hair none too gently.

He winced on her scalp's behalf.

"Are you *kidding* me right now? You're saying you knew how I'd feel and didn't care?" She placed her hands on her hips. Her temper sizzled. *And didn't that turn him on?* A feisty Sammy appealed to him on every level.

"Of course I care."

"You couldn't offer up enough respect to come home and say, 'Honey, Roger wants me to go with him on a job. I know you don't want me to, but I feel a few days would do me good. I thought we should discuss it'?"

She inhaled deeply, ready to unleash hell on him. He remained quiet and braced for the fiery impact.

"At the very least, you could've called or shot me a text." Sammy dug a finger into the wall of his chest. "*How hard is that, Michael?* Whatever happened to consideration?"

"Darlin'—"

"We've been together close to six years, and you *still* don't consult me on anything." She shoved his comforting hands away. "*What. The. Fuck?* Why is everything solely *your* decision? I thought we were a couple. My mistake."

He understood her behavior, and sometimes it was justified. But there were times, like now, when she made him crazy.

He threw his hands up. "Seriously? You want to go there right now? You are being totally irrational—*as usual*," he snapped, using her words against her. "I already knew how you felt, and I thought to save an argument. That makes me an asshole? Right!"

Her tears welled up. They shimmered and emphasized the light blue of her eyes. One lone tear escaped down Sammy's pale cheek, and Michael's heart went to mush. Those damned tears were his kryptonite.

"Honey, it's only for three days. We are going to Dallas to meet with a client. It's a simple sales call. I design the machines, and they want to talk to me in person. That's it. And after we close the deal, we hop on another plane and come home. No big thing."

He tried to pull her into his embrace, but Sammy, stubborn wench she was, shrugged him off. He tried a second time. The feel of her cold, clammy skin sent a shockwave through him. What in the world had caused this type of reaction in her? Dread followed and clutched his heart in its meaty, little fist. How terrified must she be, and had he made a huge mistake for her emotional well-being by agreeing to go?

"Sammy, listen to me. I want you to take a few deep breaths, okay?" He smoothed back the sweat-dampened hair on either side of her pale face. "It's going to be fine. I promise."

"You can't promise," she croaked. "You don't know."

"Then explain it to me. Please. It hurts to see you like this and not know why."

SAMMY WANTED TO RAGE, BUT MICHAEL WAS SINCERE IN HIS DESIRE TO understand. How was she supposed to relay how terrified she was that something could, and probably *would*, happen to him? Even she knew she sounded off her rocker. The likely culprit? The recent nightmares plaguing her.

Likely, hell. They *were* the culprit.

Sammy was hesitant to provide her real reasons for wanting him home where he was safe. Whenever she spoke in depth about her psychic gift, he got spooked. He'd look for logical explanations for her visions and dismissed them accordingly. It was one thing to have the same thought now and again. He wrote that off to the years they'd been together and their like-minded beliefs. His lack of understanding was the one bone of contention in their relationship. He couldn't grasp how much she needed for him to believe her.

When Sammy remained withdrawn and silent, unsure what to say, Michael threw up his hands in frustration and left their room. She flopped back onto the mattress and stared at the knockdown pattern on the ceiling. On a deeper level, she understood she was being unfair to him. He hadn't lived with the gifts as she and her family had. He still didn't get how it all worked. However, ignoring her gut reaction in this manner cost her a lot.

Most people would ask why worry about things that couldn't be changed. If it was meant to be, there wasn't anything anyone could do to change it anyway. Sammy didn't believe that. She believed in fate, destiny, and little pink bubbles sent up to the universe. *And* the fact that fate could play cruel jokes on people. Just when you were happy —*BAM!* That capricious bitch would throw a monkey wrench into the works.

Pessimists viewed these setbacks as obstacles. Optimists viewed them as challenges. Sammy was an odd mixture of both. If she could work around whatever popped up, they were challenges, and if she couldn't, they became obstacles. But either way, migraines followed when things didn't play out according to Fate's design.

The sounds of Michael making his own dinner carried to her. He wasn't the neatest of cooks. For that reason, she primarily prepared their meals. While not as OCD as her sister Annie, Sammy preferred a spotless kitchen. That meant not letting Michael within ten feet of the stove.

She sighed, pushed off of the bed, and went to find him. When she saw he intended to cook spaghetti, she grabbed the pot from his hand and slammed it on the stove. *Oh, hell no!* Marinara sauce was a bitch to clean up.

"I thought we were going out to dinner," she said.

"I'm not taking you anywhere, cranky pants."

MICHAEL REACHED INTO THE CABINET FOR THE SAUCE. HE WOULD BE damned if she was going to make him feel guilty over doing his job. When Sammy's signature stubborn look appeared, Michael placed his hand on an open box of pasta. At that exact moment, she latched onto it. Both refused to release their hold. Their tug of war ended with an explosion of dry spaghetti all over the stove and floor.

The humor of the situation struck Michael.

Sammy, on the other hand, didn't appreciate his hilarity. Because he was laughing so hard, she shot him the stink eye. In a fit of pique, Sammy threw the remaining spaghetti at his head. *"Asshole!"*

To prevent her from stalking away, Michael wrapped his arms around her. He tucked her into his chest, still rumbling with laughter. "Darlin', you have to admit that was funny. Each one of us racing for the ingredients. You should've seen your face."

All the while, Sammy struggled to dislodge his embrace. Futile. He was too strong, and she knew it. All humor faded away when she knocked him in the shin with her heel.

"I'm not letting you go until you talk to me," he said, dead serious.

She just clamped her lips tighter and stuck up her chin. The struggle to keep his humor in check was real. *What a stubborn little wretch she could be.* He had ways of melting her resistance, and he employed them now. Trailing his lips ever so softly along her ear, he played with the lobe, pulling it between his teeth to tug. When she shivered, he fought another smile and shifted to nuzzle her throat. At the same time, he glided his palms under her shirt and cradled the fullness of her breasts.

Her soft moan brought him satisfaction. If Michael had to use sex to soften her up and to open the lines of communication, then that's exactly what he intended to do. She stopped resisting his advances. What was the point? She adored his lovemaking, and they both knew it. According to her, Michael thrilled her in ways no one ever had or could again. After being a couple for so long, he found that level of intensity incredible. What they had together was powerful. Although she refused to show his seduction was working, her body had a mind of its own. Pebbled nipples and the wetness at the junction between her thighs gave her away. Aroused, she turned to him and captured his mouth in a kiss that nearly melted his brain matter.

Again, he teased, nipping at her bottom lip. Holding back enough to make her burn for him. Toying with her most intimate parts, never quite giving what she wanted. He wouldn't carry through lovemaking if she was still angry. It went against his personal code of right and wrong. He took her face between his hands and kissed her ever so gently on the mouth.

"Please don't be mad, my Sammy. I can't stand to see you unhappy," he whispered, his voice husky with passion and something more emotional. He touched one fingertip to the dampness on her cheek. He leaned in to feather a kiss on each closed eyelid. "The time away can only make us appreciate what we have even more, right?"

He wanted to hold her forever. To prevent any type of sorrow from ever touching her. An impossibility, he knew. All the same, the desire was strong.

Sammy's shoulders dropped as if she was giving up the fight, and she wrapped her arms around him in a fierce hug. Emotion clogged his throat, blocking the words he longed to say. He knew she needed to express her fears, just as he needed to ease them. He didn't need her to impress upon him those fears were valid.

She cradled his face within her hands. "I just love you so damn much."

"Ditto," he whispered back.

He, too, felt the sting of tears. Her mood must be rubbing off.

Dinner forgotten, he swept her up in his arms and made his way to their bedroom. On the staircase, he paused every few steps to taste her lips. She was his greatest addiction. Reaching his destination, Michael carefully laid her on the bed, treating her like the finest porcelain. He took his time and unbuttoned her blouse. With each button he unfastened, he rained kisses down upon her exposed flesh and skimmed his tongue along her smooth skin, tasting every available inch.

After he had her undressed, he stood to remove his own clothing. Sammy knelt on the bed and replaced his hands with hers. She had none of his finesse as she tore at the offending material blocking her access to his body. After depositing his shirt onto the heap of clothes piling up on the floor, she wasted no time pressing her chest to his. He luxuriated in the contrast of hard against soft. She was always so silky smooth to the touch.

Neither rushed their lovemaking. They knew the pleasure

involved in going slow. In savoring each skim of their fingers. Michael used his mouth and hands to worship her body. Her whimpers filled the room as he took first one breast into his mouth and then devoted equal time to the other. With his tongue, he teased the tight buds of her nipples. Pausing to admire the perfection of her chest, he blew on the tip then dove back in to suck harder. He caressed her body everywhere. Up one side and down the other. Created heat with every stroke. His fingers, long and lean, resembled those of a musician. And just like a musician, he strummed her body like a finely tuned instrument.

She begged for him to enter her. Her breath came in little pants.

Ignoring her demands, he explored her most private area. Using his thumb, he made little circles. He inserted first one finger then a second into her drenched core, stretching her to prepare for his entry. She arched up to meet his palm. Wanting. Needing. He could feel it build within her, fueled as his lips joined in the slow torture. His tongue teasing. Tantalizing. How well he knew her body. It was as if she'd been made especially for him.

Michael brought Sammy to the point of ecstasy, only to stop and start a different lovemaking technique. One designed to torment her longer. In her annoyance, she struck out, kicking him lightly. His deep chuckle filled the air even as his very touch marked her as his. This time, there was no stopping the scream that welled up in her throat, bursting forth.

"Oh, God! Oh, God! I love you... Oh... *God!*"

Bucking in the throes of her orgasm, she tried to throw off his hands. He laughed and touched her again.

"Stop! I'll die. Are you crazy?" She tried to squirm out of his reach.

Her words turned into another groan as he shifted their positions and thrust inside her. He gripped her hips and filled her, driving forward as she thrust back. Their joining was a primal, erotic dance. Moaning and thrusting. Emotions swirled around them and engulfed them. She climaxed, the walls of her vagina tightening around him, and he followed her over the edge, her body milking him dry.

After he collapsed on the bed, Michael wrapped her in his

embrace and spooned her body. He stroked her silky hair and feathered light kisses across the smooth, satiny skin of her shoulder and neck.

Both were spent.

"I FEEL LIKE A GIANT MARSHMALLOW," SAMMY PANTED.

His chuckle came out a bit broken through his own pants. He'd once said she always did the cutest things after sex.

"Where did you learn to do that thing with your tongue, babe? That's new."

"Mmmmm. Yeah, I read it in a magazine recently. You like?"

"Oh, *hell yes*, I like! You have my permission to do that any time."

She could feel the vibration of his laughter against her back. She smiled. "Your turn to get the washcloth."

"Your turn," Michael murmured, half asleep.

"Nope, I got the last one." Listless, she shifted to her stomach.

"I'm almost sure *I* got the last one." He gently stroked, then smack her ass.

"Ouch!" Sammy grumbled from underneath the pillow. "If my legs weren't jelly right now, I'd make you pay for that."

"Yeah, right."

"Are you *trying* to pick a fight?"

Michael snorted. "No, I'm just saying the day you could beat me or make me *pay* for anything will be the day I eat my socks."

Never one to resist a challenge, her head poked out from its hiding spot.

"Oh yeah?"

"Yeah," he said, incorporating his best Jersey accent.

She utilized her toughest gangster voice. "You talkin' to me?"

"You'd better believe I'm talkin' to you," he retorted as he got into their game.

"I know you're not freakin' talkin' to me, because if you was freakin' talkin' to me, dat would mean I'd have to get Guido to break your freakin' legs!"

"Oh yeah, tough guy, where's your freakin' Guido now, huh?" He pounced and tickled her neck before going for her sides.

She tried to act tough, to prevent her giggles. Of course, her resistance made him tickle her harder. Soon, she was hysterical. "Stop, *stop!* I'll get the stupid rag."

"And be quick about it, wench."

Sammy rolled out of bed, removed a washcloth from the linen closet, and turned on the water. After she warmed up the water and washed herself, she turned the tap from hot to cold. Barely controlling the wicked laughter bubbling up, she strolled in with the frigid cloth. Michael held out his hand to take the rag, but she pulled back.

"Let me," she purred.

He lay back like an indulgent King to grant her access. Smiling and batting her eyelashes, she placed the freezing cloth on his groin and held it.

"You little brat!"

He lunged for her, but she danced away. The hilarity she fought so hard to contain burst forth.

"I think I'll go get those socks for you to eat. Want some ketchup to make them more palatable?"

CHAPTER 6

Four days later, Sammy and Michael were snuggled in their bed under the down comforter. He was scheduled to fly to Dallas that morning, but each was loath to start the day.

"I wish I could go with you." Her head rested above his heart, and she allowed the steady rhythm to soothe her. Absently, she wove an aimless pattern on his right pec.

Michael was hesitant to say the same. Instead, he said that knowing her, she'd be on the next plane out if she thought she could get away with it. He tried not to encourage her impulsiveness in any way, shape, or form. While Sammy loved him for being the one constant voice of reason, she also felt he could stand to bend the rules on occasion.

"It's only three days. What's with you, Sammy? Are you crying again?" He contorted to see her face, a frown forming to indicate his confusion. They both knew it wasn't like her to be so weepy. He dropped a kiss on her temple before lying back down. "You'll see, you won't even miss me. As a matter of fact, you'll probably like it so much you'll want to get rid of me."

"I know," she choked out. "I'm concerned, is all. Knowing Pete and his shit scheduling, you'll get stuck in Dallas until January." She half sat up and stared down at him. "I couldn't handle that, Michael. I really couldn't. I would die or go nuts with you gone all the time."

"Sammy, you know I won't allow Pete to abuse my position. So don't worry about it," Michael stated firmly. "As a matter of fact, I tried to get out of this trip, but it was too late."

She lifted her head to better check his expression. "You did? You actually asked them not to send you?" She gave him a quick kiss and lay back down. Her favorite spot was any position in which he was holding her close. "Thank you, babe." She took a deep breath. "I just feel... I don't know the right words. How can I explain I sense some great, impending disaster and I can't do a freaking thing to prevent it? It all sounds so stupid and melodramatic."

She paused for the space of eight heartbeats before she confessed, "Bad dreams started up again last week. I went so long without having any, and now, well..." She trailed off. The words once again refused to come. Explaining her dilemma was pointless. Sammy didn't want to be that needy girlfriend. Michael deserved the freedom to come and go as he so chose. But together, well, together they were safer somehow. This was a belief she held close to her heart.

"I know you feel your dreams mean something, and I'm not doubting them. Or you. But what could possibly happen? I don't think your fears are based on anything substantial this time around."

He tried to appear nonchalant for her sake, but he couldn't fully hide his own apprehension. Tension was in every line of his body this morning. He'd witnessed enough of her premonitions and couldn't be blasé about them. However, once he'd volunteered for this job, there was no turning back as far as his boss was concerned, or so Michael had told her.

"Sammy Darlin', you are going to be late for work if you don't get going, and I'm going to miss my flight."

"I really do love you, Michael," she told him, tracing one deep crevice in his cheek. "I wrote you a letter, and I want you to read it every night. It's to remind you how much you're going to miss me."

His beloved dimples flashed in response, and he tightened his arms around her for a brief hug. "Your procrastination is at an end!" He patted her ass, and rolled off the bed, dragging her with him.

"When I get back, there's something we need to discuss."

"What?"

He flashed a mischievous smile and lightly pushed her in the direction of the bathroom. "You'll see."

CONCENTRATING ON HER WORK WAS A CHORE IN THE DAYS FOLLOWING his departure. When his call came that particular evening, Sammy felt terrible for Michael. The low rasp in his voice indicated weariness, and it very nearly broke her heart. She sensed more bad news on the horizon.

"Honey, there is a problem. I'm afraid our stay is going to be longer than we anticipated."

Of course there was a problem. It was inevitable with his stupid-ass company. If it continued this way, she doubted he would be home in time for Thanksgiving next week.

"How long is the expected delay? A day or two?" Sammy held her breath against the anxiety gripping her heart. With each passing minute, the feeling of impending disaster grew, nearly suffocating her in its intensity. If he were home, he would be safe. Or at least that's what the irrational side of her believed. If he planned to be gone any longer, she'd have to hit Margie up for her stash of Xanax.

"There's a problem with one of the other machines we sold them last year. It's still under warranty, and I need to fix it. Unfortunately, this particular place closes down on Saturday and Sunday. Roger wants to try to get permission for us to work the weekend. The thing is, if we don't repair this now, it affects their production and puts us in a bad light. We really need that new machine deal."

"Will you be home for Thanksgiving?"

"Yes, unless Roger doesn't get the go-ahead. But even then, we may have to come home and go back. It's four days' work at best. I can't see them granting permission on a holiday weekend if they don't for a standard non-holiday one though."

"When will you find out?"

"Probably not until tomorrow. They have to get approval from Corporate." His deep sigh sounded through the receiver. "Sammy, I honestly believed everything would run smoothly this time." This was his way of apologizing.

"I realize that." This was her concession.

"I have to go. Roger and Bruce are waiting on me."

"Bruce?"

"He's the GM of the shop. He intends to take us to dinner."

"Call me when you get in, okay?"

"We may be late."

"Why?"

"It's guys blowing off steam and drinking beer, darlin'. But if you want, I'll call you when I get in from the bar, okay?"

MICHAEL'S CALL CAME IN THE WEE HOURS OF THE MORNING, WAKING her from a restless sleep.

"Hi!"

"Hi, yourself. Are you guys just now coming in?" she asked, groggy.

"Yep!"

"Babe, do you realize what time it is?" Sammy glanced at the clock.

"Yep."

"Did you have a good time?"

"Uh huh."

"Michael, are you okay? You sound strange."

"Fine. I'm reading your letter."

"Could you do that when I'm *not* on the phone, trying to have a conversation with you? After all, it's only three in the morning here. Not like I have to get up in a few hours or anything," she complained good-naturedly. "Why were you out so late if you have to work another twelve tomorrow?"

"Just eight tomorrow. We may be coming home, remember? I love you, too."

"What? Oh, the letter. Michael, I think you should go to sleep now. Call me tomorrow before you leave for the airport, okay?"

"No, want to talk now. Got a s'prise for you. Early Chrissmsss present. Never wait. Not with you," he slurred.

Sammy really couldn't be mad. He rarely got drunk, but he was so stinking cute and affectionate during the times he was. She only had herself to blame. Who was the idiot who wanted him to call when he got in? She shook her head and smiled. "What's your surprise?"

"Not tellin'. It's for Chrissmss. Can't you ever wait?" he demanded with mock outrage.

"Michael, I'm going to bed, and so should you. You are *blitzed*, my friend."

"Nope. Just a slight buzz."

A grin played on her lips as she hung up the phone. He called back immediately.

"Why'd ja hang up?" he sounded hurt.

"Because we are having one of the stupidest conversations of our relationship."

"I'm tryin' to tell you about your love present."

She laughed at the ridiculousness of his comment. "*Love present? What the hell's a love present?"*

"A present you will *love* because I got it with my love for you in mind," he explained, sounding as if he'd confused himself.

Again, she had to force down her amusement.

"Okay, so what did you get?"

"Steak. We had a bottle of wine with it."

"I meant my present," she exclaimed in exasperation.

"Not telling," he sing-songed.

"I really need my sleep, Michael. I love you. Call me tomorrow."

"Righto! Cheers!"

"Michael?"

"Hmm?"

"You do a terrible Englishman when you're drunk!"

She clicked off the phone on his outraged protest.

Jolted awake, Sammy looked at the clock face. Five-fifteen. She lay still, listening and trying to figure out what had disturbed her. Sassy's soft snore was all she heard. Careful not to make a sound, she swung her legs off the bed and tiptoed to the door.

Nothing.

She crept her way to the living room then turned on lights to inspect the locks on all the windows and doors. After a check of the alarm, she headed back upstairs. But her unease refused to be dismissed. It took another fifteen minutes before she felt comfortable enough to turn off the light.

As she dozed, her nightmare started. It began as a low hum and rose to deafening, high-pitched ringing in the span of seconds. She covered her ears in a vain attempt to ward off the noise. She desperately wanted to shake free of the sound but couldn't.

He had her under his spell again. Unable to break free. Unable to scream.

"Samantha," the eerie voice whispered, cutting through the static.

His evil cackle echoed around her and cloaked her in terror. He called to her again, his voice coming ever closer. Mist oozed into the room and grew larger into the distinct shape of a man. The dark form materialized in her doorway and wormed its way to where she lay paralyzed on the bed.

Her throat closed and refused to allow any sound to escape. She tried to swallow past the lump. Sweat broke out on her upper lip and along her hairline as she trembled. Trembled? Hell, her whole body practically convulsed in her fear.

She knew he was only a specter, some made-up entity from her own mind—or so she liked to believe. Trepidation flooded her. It caused her heart to thump rapidly against the wall of her chest. The heavy thud reverberating in her ears until it was almost all she could hear.

Sassy's guard mode engaged. The dog's hackles rose, and Sammy felt more than heard Sassy's vicious barking. The dog refused to budge from where she rested against Sammy's leg.

"This time, Samantha… *this* time, I win," the voice taunted cruelly.

"No," she pushed past frozen lips.

Nearer and nearer, he drifted. If she could raise a hand to touch him, it would pass straight through. He was a phantom. Never quite corporeal in form. The fog swirled, enveloping the room until it was all she could focus on. It flowed upwards, like serpents slithering, and attempted to encircle her.

"You're not real," she screamed within the confines of her mind, unable to force out the words.

"Michael is not coming home, Samantha," he revealed, delighting in her torment.

"No! Please, not Michael! *Please!*" she begged. These words, too, were in her mind because her vocal cords were as incapacitated as the rest of her.

Night terrors.

She'd read about them once. They make movement and speech impossible when one was locked in the state between sleep and wakefulness.

The ghostly presence had one hand stretched toward her. Fright pushed Sammy's heart into overdrive, and the pressure in her chest bordered on painful. Just as he was inches away from stroking her cheek, the phone rang.

The music of Michael's ringtone broke through to her consciousness and shattered the spell holding her transfixed. It took another few seconds before she could move.

Her harbinger of bad news disappeared as if he'd never existed. Sammy strained to see, but she no longer felt his presence. Breathing harshly, she answered the phone. "Hello?" she shouted.

MICHAEL WAS TAKEN ABACK BY THE BORDERLINE HYSTERIA IN SAMMY'S voice. "Sammy? Are you okay?"

"Oh my God, Michael!" She burst into tears. "He almost had me! He was only a foot from me. He almost had me."

"Darlin', calm down. I need you to tell me who. Who almost had you? Sweetie? Please, calm down." He tried to sound calm, but inside his brain was scrambled. The residual buzz from drinking earlier was fading fast. He had to fight down his own unease. "Sammy, I need you to listen to me. Is someone in the house? *Samantha!*"

"Y-yes… n-no… I d-don't know," she stuttered.

"Listen, you need to lock the bedroom door and call 911. Can you do that? Sammy?"

Michael was ready to go out of his mind. That she was in danger and he couldn't get to her caused his gut to clench. He was thoroughly rattled.

"He wants you now, Michael," she croaked.

"Who? *Fuck!* Okay, calm down," he ordered. It finally dawned on him who she was talking about. The dark man from her dreams. Every time he reared his nasty little head, something tragic happened. How she knew he had targeted Michael this time stumped him. "We're both going to calm down." Yeah, it was definitely do as I say, not as I do, because Michael's stress level was through the fucking roof.

In the past, preceding an incident, Sammy would have a horrific nightmare. Tragedy would happen. *Always.* As much as he preferred to ignore these things, to pretend she didn't really have a gift, he couldn't.

Her phantom never clarified a person, and the date was anyone's guess. Best they could calculate, an incident would take place within a week's time frame. Michael and Sammy never had anything specific to go by. Just enough information to have them scrambling for answers when these premonitions popped up. They would be left with a mystery to solve and prevent if at all possible. Thank God she didn't have them all that often, or he was sure he would lose his freaking mind. As it was, he continually strove to be the voice of reason.

"What's going to happen, Sammy? How do you know it's me this time?" He had to find a way to calm her down, the best he could come up with was to keep her talking.

"He said your name!" She was perched on the edge, ready to lose her mind.

"Sammy, you have to get a hold of yourself. Please, darlin'."

He tried to appear cool for her sake, but inside, he was scared shitless. In his recollection, there wasn't one time that she'd been wrong.

"What exactly did he say? Can you tell me? Try to stay calm."

She took deep breaths and struggled for control. "He said... he said, 'Michael is not coming home.'"

The air was sucked right out of Michael's lungs, and his heart rate shot up to stroke level.

"Michael?" she croaked.

He had to answer. He knew he did. But what the hell could he say? How could his demise be any plainer? "I'm here," he finally managed.

"I'm scared," she whispered.

"Me, too."

He heard her sniffling. Briefly, he wondered how much time he had left. He shoved that thought away. This was insanity. What about changing destiny and Sammy's little pink bubbles? The same thought hit her at that precise moment.

"I have an idea."

"Believe me, I'm all ears," he said dryly.

"Come home. Catch the next flight, or better yet, the next bus."

"How is that going to stop fate, Sammy?"

"After every one of my dreams, whatever is going to happen usually takes a few days. We could beat the time frame if you come home right now." Her electrified voice told him she was happy with this new plan of attack.

"Yeah, well, tell me when he's ever said anyone's name before. I don't think this particular premonition is following a pattern here." He sounded testy even to his own ears. "Besides, who's to say that whatever is going to happen won't happen at home."

"He did! He said, 'Michael is not coming home.' If you return today, you would beat the time frame."

"Okay, so tell me how I explain to my boss I had to jump on a plane because you had a dream. And that is *if* I can find a flight coming home this late." He released a ragged sigh. "Sammy, this is so ridiculous."

"No, Michael, you're ridiculous," she snapped. "Why can't you see this is serious? Make something up. Family emergency, just come home. *Please.*"

The seriousness of the situation wasn't lost on him, and he didn't feel like dying anytime soon. Still, he refused to let fear rule them. "Maybe the dream meant I wasn't coming home because of the work delay. Maybe your fear was triggered by what I said earlier tonight about needing to stay longer," he rationalized.

Sammy lifted a hand to her mouth to hold back the angry words working their way to the forefront. *Michael didn't want to believe.* If he could rationalize the premonition, he believed it wouldn't happen. The thought pounded through Sammy's brain, demanding to be heard.

"Maybe," she replied in a soft voice.

Her tears dried up. Everything else within her did, too. Numbness settled in its place. She shivered against the cold seeping into her soul. Her attention was caught by Sassy, who rested her tiny head on her paws, anxiety written all over her fuzzy little face. Poor pup was picking up on her mama's energy. Sammy patted her lap, hoping the dog would understand the gesture to come cuddle. The two of them needed the mutual comfort. Her fluffy buddy complied, and Sammy snuggled her close.

"Sammy, please understand I'm not trying to hurt your feelings. Truly. I know you want to protect me from whatever you believe this to be, but it's impossible. I have a job to do. I just can't pick up and leave because of a possible fluke."

Her sudden anger verged on rage. "A *fluke?* You know damned well it's not a fluke." Sammy paused to catch her breath and control her temper. "You know I could list at least ten occurrences, Michael. You could say all of those nightmares were flukes, but to have them happen within a week of each incident is pretty fucking coincidental, don't you think? Not to mention preceding each dream, Mr. Gruesome happened to make his presence known."

Mr. Gruesome was Sammy's nickname for the specter who haunted her during the worst of her night terrors.

Michael remained quiet, and Sammy understood why. How could he argue? She was right, and he damned well knew it. How else had he sensed to call her tonight? He'd felt her need of him through their special link. He had to have.

"Michael? How did you know to call me?"

"I dreamed I heard Sassy barking and you were trying to scream for help. I woke up and had to be sure you were all right."

They both felt the heaviness. It was in the air around them although they were over a thousand miles apart. The helplessness clung to them like a bad fragrance that wouldn't wash off.

"Okay, listen. I am going to see if I can make a flight out this morning. Screw working the weekend."

"But I thought you said—"

"I know what I said," he barked his irritation with the whole mess. "I'm going to have to think up a really good excuse."

He'd made a decision, one Sammy appreciated to the very marrow of her bones. She hoped like hell it wouldn't cost him his job.

"Michael, I realize it's hard for you to go against what you feel is right. But this is different. I wouldn't ask you to return if I didn't think it wasn't a real threat. *You know that.* If you lose your job, we'll find you another."

"Yeah, well, I wonder how I'm going to pay for your gift if I'm unemployed."

"What gift? Oh, the love gift. Tell me what you bought me." She strove for a brighter note.

"I don't know what you're talkin' about." Michael's gangster act was back.

"All right, tough guy. But when I get you here tomorrow, I'll beat it outta ya."

He snorted. "Yeah. Yeah. You and what army?"

"I love you, Michael," she said, unable to joke anymore. Unable to pretend.

"Ditto. I'll call you later so you know what time to expect me. I may need you to be my taxi service. Will that be a problem?"

"No, of course not."

"Try to go back to sleep. I don't want to come home and see some baggy-eyed, messy-headed, breath-smellin'—"

"All right, already. I get the picture, you bar-hopping, beer-drinking, party-loving, bad-attitude—" She'd cut his speech off only to have him do the same. "Hello? Michael? What a punk!"

She cleared the screen on her cell then dialed his hotel.

"Room two-twenty-five."

As soon as Michael answered, she yelled loudly into the phone and disconnected. As she drifted back to sleep, she recalled his laughter. Holding the memory close to her, she used it to ward off any lingering evil.

CHAPTER 7

*W*ork was hectic the next day. Sammy reasoned that all the weirdos must be out. She shook her head as she hung up the telephone. She'd been on the receiving end of a tongue-lashing from a normally cheerful customer, and it had ruined her morning.

Michael had texted her earlier to say he was unable to get a morning flight, but the airline had him on standby for later today. His call came during her lunch break when she most needed a pick-me-up.

"Hi, you."

"Hi, you."

She smiled. His voice had the ability to warm her from the inside out.

"You sound relieved. What's up?"

"I just had the thought that if one more cranky customer called me, I intended to quit on the spot. You saved my job," she said, ending on a groan.

"That bad, huh?"

"That bad. But enough about that. Did you call to offer me raunchy phone sex?"

"That depends."

"On what?"

"Do you have the door to your office locked? If we are going to do this thing, we are going to FaceTime so I can see you."

Sammy went from irritated to overheated in a split second.

"You don't play fair, Michael."

Hearing his deep chuckle, she changed the subject. "You'll pay for that when I see you again. Were you able to solidify the flight for tonight?"

His heavy sigh said it all, and Sammy closed her eyes.

"No. Also, we were unable to get into the building for the weekend. Of course, that means coming home, but our original seats got bumped. Fucking airlines with their over-booking. Although, they offered to put us on standby if we want to wait around at the airport. Otherwise, we fly out tomorrow night."

"I guess Saturday will have to do." She struggled not to reveal her disappointment, but her voice betrayed the apprehension she sought to keep at bay.

"I tried, darlin'." He attempted to infuse a chipper note. "It's just one extra day."

"I know. It's probably soon enough." Inside, Sammy knew it wasn't, but for Michael, she could pretend. Tears clogged her throat and made it difficult to respond to the idle chitchat that followed. She rubbed the center of her forehead. Where were these crazy emotions coming from?

"I'll let you get back to work. I can hear the other line ringing. Must be those mean, rotten customers again." His attempt to lighten her mood failed miserably, and she suspected he knew it. "I love you, Sammy Darlin'."

"Ditto."

"Hey, that's my line," he protested.

"I believe it was Patrick Swayze's line first."

"I don't know what you're freakin' talkin' about."

"Is that Al Pacino I hear?"

His chuckle sounded as she hung up the phone.

His call came just after six o'clock that evening. They talked of what went on in their daily routines and of the plans she had made for Thanksgiving. Both pretended nothing out of the ordinary would happen. Eventually, their attempts at casual conversation ran dry. Each one sick of the pretense.

"Why don't you wait at the airport tonight?" she asked.

"So I can get mugged and murdered? No, thank you. I thought you wanted me home."

"Michael, I'm serious. If there isn't a standby flight, then get a bus ticket. I can't explain it. There's an urgency about this whole thing."

She couldn't change the topic, and it was getting old even to her. Yet if there was a chance he might listen to her, might catch the first available transportation, then she'd nag him to hell and back.

His impatience came through in the form of a huffed breath. "Sammy, *stop*. Don't you think I'd return this minute if I could? It's not possible. I will be home tomorrow night, and that's just going to have to be soon enough."

His anger startled her. It shouldn't have. She would have reacted the same way. To blame him for being irritable would have been unreasonable on her part.

"Okay. Not another word," she promised. "Can I pick you up at the airport tomorrow?"

"Well, let's make a deal. You can pick me up at the airport, but then you'll have to wait on the present. Quite frankly, I don't think you'll be able to wait until Christmas though."

"What are you saying? I can have you tomorrow at the airport or my present? No contest. I'll take the present."

"That stung." He chuckled. "No, really, Roger's truck is already at the airport. You can meet me at his house so he doesn't have to go out of the way to drop me off. Melanie won't mind if you wait with her."

"Yeah, but when do I get my present?"

"Mercenary woman."

"I'll have you know I'm doing a major search tonight. If it's here, I *will* find it."

"Uh huh." His warm laughter was like sunshine on a dreary day. "It's in a safe place."

"Where?" she demanded.

"You really are cute when you get pushy."

"And you're a wiseass."

"Okay, potty mouth. I believe that's my cue to cut this call short."

"Yes, there is still one more room I have to search before you get here tomorrow," she sassed, causing more merriment on his part.

"Ask your mom."

"You mean mom has it? Then it can't be very big because she doesn't have much room at the condo. Did I ever tell you my mother can't keep a secret any better than I can?" Victory was within her grasp. She did a happy dance.

"I can hear you dancing around. What have I told you about counting your chickens?" He tsked. "I didn't say your mother has it. I said, *ask your mom*. She may know who does." The doorbell pealed, and Michael heard it through the phone. "I'll let you go. I'll see you tomorrow."

"No! Are you crazy? It could be a serial killer or something. Just hang on a damned minute."

"What am I going to do a thousand miles away?"

She ignored him to answer the door.

"Hi, I'm back. Miss me?"

"Oh, yeah. Sure, in the whole fifteen seconds you were gone." His sarcasm was in top form. "Who was that?"

"My new boyfriend. He decided to stay with me tonight since you weren't home," she teased. At his snort, she clarified, "Actually, it's Mom. I asked her if she wouldn't mind staying the night. I figured in all probability I'd have another nightmare, and I don't want to be alone."

"Sammy, I want you to know if I thought my going to Dallas would have this kind of an effect on you, I would have said no the day Pete and Roger approached me. I never want you to have to go through this uncertainty ever again."

"That means a lot to me. I guess I shouldn't have told you about the dreams either. It doesn't do you any good to have that constantly in the back of your mind when you should be concentrating on your work. I'm sorry."

"I don't know how to prove exactly how much I love you. I may not have always shown it, but these have been the best years of my life."

"Mine, too."

"All I could see was darkness after my mom and dad died. You taught me how to feel again. You make me stronger in every way." He gave a self-deprecating laugh. "I know it sounds corny, but I'm whole with you." He blew out a breath. "I really do miss you, Sammy. I love you so damned much." This time, he couldn't manage to stop the break in his voice.

She couldn't speak for the intense emotions suffocating her. Love and major anxiety warred for dominance. She tried to shove aside the worry and savor the poignant moment. But the very real fear their time together was at an end persisted.

"Me, too," Sammy rasped, her throat aching from suppressing the threatening sobs. "I... ditto." She tried to vocalize what was in her heart, but she was overcome. Michael was her everything.

Understanding all the same, he cleared his throat and said, "I've got to go. I haven't eaten yet."

She wasn't surprised he was discomfited by the sappy turn in their conversation. He'd always been ruled more by action than emotion.

"Don't."

"What?"

"Don't be ashamed of what you feel. I hear it in your voice. Never be embarrassed for filling someone's life with the type of happiness you've given me. I could never love anyone as much as I love you. *Never.* I sometimes wonder how I will ever live without you in my life if anything were to happen to you, or if you didn't love me anymore. You're my other half too, Michael."

Baring one's innermost thoughts made a person vulnerable. Uncomfortable. She experienced her own awkwardness.

"Don't," he said.

She knew what he meant. He didn't want her to hide from embarrassment any more than she did him. "Okay, I won't."

"We have to end this mushy stuff. Roger is going to make fun of me for having puffy eyes."

In reality, they had an enviable bond. True soulmates.

Neither Michael nor Sammy wanted to break the connection.

"You better go get some food in that bottomless pit you call a stomach. You'll get a headache."

"The pounding in my head indicates that ship has sailed." He groaned. "I ordered a pizza forty-five minutes ago. This is the slowest delivery on the planet. Roger is supposed to join me. We didn't want the hassle of dressing up to go out."

"You really should get some sleep. You sound tired, babe."

"I will. Good night, darlin'."

"Good night, Michael."

They both still seemed hesitant to hang up. For her, the need to prolong their time together was strong. She fished for something to add so they wouldn't have to hang on to dead air.

Michael beat her to it. "Oh, before you go. Do you know how to get to Roger and Melanie's new place?"

"No, let me get a pen."

The instructions only took a moment. They were needless because she had GPS on her phone, but she loved listening to him. His velvety voice with its slight Southern twang always sent a silent thrill through her.

"What time is your flight arriving tomorrow night?"

"We leave here at five forty-five your time. We should be there at Roger and Melanie's by roughly ten-fifteen, taking into account the drive from the airport." Sammy heard a knock on his hotel door. "Hey, babe, I think my pizza finally got here. I gotta run. Love you."

"Right. Cheers, mate."

"Cheerio, luv," he said, joining their accent game.

"Better Englishman."

"Been practicing since your last insult," he retorted.

"I love you, Michael."

"Why do you suppose people always have to keep saying that phrase all the time? Oh well, who am I to question the love of a beautiful woman?"

"Did I ever tell you how cheesy you are?"

"Now, Sammy Darlin', no need to draw blood here."

MICHAEL ANSWERED THE DOOR AND USED HIS FOOT TO PROP IT WIDE. Fishing through his billfold, he found enough to cover the cost of the pizza and a tip. He paused in his actions, taken aback by the sight of the man in front of him. The resemblance between them was uncanny. They were enough alike in height, build, and coloring to be brothers. He had a doppelgänger. Who would've guessed? Wouldn't Sammy's sister Annie, with her genealogy background, have been curious. However, the delivery guy paid no attention to him. He seemed fixated on the wallet instead.

Unease filled Michael. All he needed to end his crappy day was to get mugged in his hotel room. He quickly closed the billfold and shoved it into his back pocket, then he placed thirty dollars into the other guy's hand.

"Keep the change."

As Michael toyed with questioning the guy about his lineage, Roger came sauntering up and grabbed for the box.

"Damn, son. This is just what the doctor ordered. I'm starving. So much for delivery being thirty minutes or less."

Michael tried to peer around Roger as their delivery man hustled down the hallway. Maybe he'd feared being rebuked. With a shrug, Michael followed the smell of the pizza and the man who now held the key to his happiness. Ah, food. His stomach complained it was past time.

CHAPTER 8

*I*t was after three a.m. when the dream started.

SAMMY DOUBLE-CHECKED HER BAGS ONE LAST TIME, MAKING SURE everything was packed. As always, she felt as if she were leaving important items behind and did one more sweep of the room. A glance out the window showed Roger waiting by the taxi. The irritation on his face spoke of his eagerness to be off.

She hurried across the parking lot, but before entering the vehicle, she looked at Roger. He checked at his watch, impatient as always. When he glared back at the hotel, Sammy whirled to see what had caught his attention. Michael waved to her, anguish on his face. His ravaged expression triggered Sammy's anxiety. Turning back toward the vehicle, she screamed at the chilling new scene: plane carnage.

The aircraft appeared almost torn in two. A gaping hole in the fuselage resembled the jagged edges of shredded paper, curled back and burnt. A woman rested in her seat, mouth agape, her throat severed. Blood coated the rows of seats Sammy could see and pooled on the floor at her feet. Waves crashed into the opening and rushed to fill up the fuselage and drag the aircraft down into the icy blue depths. Roger sat unconscious but still breathing.

As hard as she searched, there was no sign of Michael. Panic nearly suffocated her. She heard the buzzing and the sinister voice that followed closely behind. "I told you, Samantha. In time, you will learn to listen."

The whispered words blew through her brain like wind whistling through the slash pines surrounding their house. Her torment at being unable to find Michael was real. Sammy had to ignore Death's dreaded voice. Concentrate on finding him, she told herself. Warn him. But where was he? Desperately, she tried to recall if she had seen him sitting next to Roger. Surely she would have noticed him first.

She sifted through the bodies, turning them over one by one. Trying to shut out the horror of their lifeless eyes. She needed to find the face so dear to her. She repeatedly called his name, hoping beyond hope that he would respond.

Sammy fought the rushing waters, the sea of bodies, and her fear. Hands gripped her ankles and attempted to pull her down with the rest of the lost souls. She came upon Roger, now a corpse with sightless eyes. Bile rose up, choking her. She concentrated on inhaling, exhaling, and inhaling again. Each breath was labored and painful.

The search became fruitless. She didn't know how long she could continue. Her lungs burned, and before long, she would be sucked down into the ocean's inky depths with the wreckage. Cold crept into her whole being. No Michael. No survivors. The time had come to give up the search or drown. Sammy almost chose the latter. Without Michael, she didn't care to exist.

With no warning, she popped to the surface like a cork. The darkened sky surprised her. Searchlights were overhead now. What remained of the plane was ablaze. It would soon find its final resting place at the bottom of the unforgiving sea.

SAMMY FOUGHT TO WAKE UP, BUT THE NIGHT TERROR HAD HER IN ITS clutches, trapped inside a loop of grisly images. She fell into another nightmare.

.   .   .

Sammy packed her bags and finalized her hotel check out. A strong sense of déjà vu struck. Why did it seem like she'd done this exact thing before?

Knowing something was off, she told Roger to go ahead to the airport. This was after observing him check his watch for the third time in less than one minute. Though there was plenty of time, Roger obsessed about being early wherever he went.

"Seriously. Go on. I need to call home, and my cell is dead. I'll catch another cab."

"Come on, Michael. Christ. I have never seen someone call their girl-friend as much as you. Use my phone," Roger grumbled.

"Just go. I'm checked in online, so there's time."

"It's like you can't stand to be away from her. For fuck's sake, man. We're on our way home, or would be if you got your ass in gear."

The attitude angered her.

"What the hell? I said go already. I'll meet you at the terminal."

Sammy walked into the hotel room and dialed the phone. The call confirmed everything at home was well. Still, an uneasy feeling niggled at the edges of her consciousness. As she stepped from the hotel, hard hands shoved her against the wall. A familiar-looking man grabbed her duffle bag and darted toward the highway.

"Hey!" she yelled. "Motherfucker!"

Sammy gave chase. She had no choice. That bag contained all her essentials: phone, ticket, wallet, iPad, and keys. Without a second thought for her safety, hyped up on adrenaline, she plunged into the oncoming traffic. A squeal of brakes was the last thing she heard. The impact to her body propelled her upon the hood, shattering the windshield with her head. The heat of an explosion seared her skin. Making her cry out in agony. She was aware of little else as blackness beckoned. Then blessed nothingness embraced her.

Sammy woke with a silent scream on her lips. Sweat covered

every inch of her shaking body. The room remained dark, and Sassy shifted and whined anxiously by her feet. Taking deep gulps of the air around her, she struggled to regulate her breathing. It must be how marathon runners felt. Not that she would know, because she avoided exercise at all costs, but still.

Slowly, she stroked Sassy's head and murmured sweet nothings to ease her stress. When they were both calmer, she lay back against her pillow, marveling it had all been a dream. Even knowing it hadn't been real, she had a difficult time getting herself together.

Her fear was well founded. The nightmare had told her as much. Now, she knew what was going to go down, had seen it from Michael's perspective when it would eventually happen to him. In the past, the clarity hadn't always been there. Often, she had a hard time differentiating who the targeted subject was in her dreams. And always, she experienced the dream vision from the perspective of the victim, or in this case, victims.

Sammy wanted to call Michael, but the clock showed it was only four a.m. Her hand hovered over the phone. Should she? *No.* There would be time to warn him without having to wake him up in the middle of the night. She closed her eyes and struggled to regulate her pulse. Maybe she would luck into a few more hours of sleep before she had to start her day.

LATER THAT MORNING, AFTER SAMMY SHOWERED AND DRESSED, SHE made her way to the kitchen. She bussed her mother's soft cheek. The delicious smell rising from Violet's mug taunted her. Because of the tempting aroma, Sammy decided a hot chocolate was just the thing instead of her usual coffee. The sugar boost would give her more of a kickstart than the caffeine.

"You okay, honey?" Violet studied her through concerned gray eyes. "You look a little rough for wear."

"Yeah, just a little tired. I had another dream last night, and it's left me a little drained." She went on to highlight the worst parts and voiced how terrified she felt. "I've tried calling Michael, but I haven't been able to reach him."

She set her mug on the table and sat next to her mother. "Mom, what do I do? If there is a factor here I'm missing, please explain it to me. I've thought of everything. If Michael gets on the plane, it crashes, and he dies. If he doesn't, he gets mugged, hit by a car, and dies." The edge of hysteria crept into her voice. Sammy rested the right side of her face on her folded arms and stared out the window at the early morning sunrise. "I'm so scared."

Violet rubbed a hand in small circles on Sammy's upper back. "I think you may be overreacting here."

"What?" Sammy's head popped up.

"Michael's in Dallas, and your lack of sleep has made you a little loopy. The dreams could be manifestations of your fears. The explanation could be as simple as that."

"Mom, I can't believe you said that. *You,* of all people, know better. Whoever Mr. Gruesome is, he used to haunt you, too. You told me as much."

As Sammy stared in astonishment, her mother shrugged. Distraught, she dropped her eyes to her mug. It took her another moment to firm her resolve.

"Remember the first time I told you about the night terrors? You told me you had experienced the same thing. You told me I had to learn to control my dreams so they didn't control me. Was it all bullshit?"

"I remember, but this *is* different. How many times have your dreams revealed anyone in particular?" At Sammy's reluctant shrug, Violet continued, "That's what I thought. The dream you had last night was very specific. I believe it's fear, plain and simple." She sipped her coffee. "I used to have the same type of dreams when your father was gone on business. *Nothing happened.* In a way, even though our family has rotten luck, I've always felt we were protected. If you're honest with yourself, I think that's the way you see it, too."

WHEN HER CELL RANG LATER THAT AFTERNOON, SAMMY FEARED answering. Should she mention the newest dream to Michael?

"Hello?"

"Hey, Darlin', are you all right?"

She infused false cheer into her voice and said, "Fine."

"You're lying, Sammy. I can hear it in your voice. What's the matter? Is your mom okay? I tried calling earlier, but I didn't get an answer on your cell or our home phone. Were you out?"

"Mom's fine. I'm sorry. I must not have heard my phone. I was out for a couple hours for last-minute shopping. Remind me never to shop within five days of Thanksgiving, okay?"

"Will do. But you're sure you're all right?" he asked, sounding troubled.

"Fine, I tell ya. Jeez. Pushy man," she joked.

"I know you're fine, you sexy thang, but how are you feeling?" he returned.

"If you were here, you could feel me and find out for yourself."

His delighted laughter sounded so good and warm. So alive.

"Later tonight I'm going to feel you."

"Is that a promise?"

"Bet on it."

She laughed lightly. "You know my luck. I never bet anymore. You saw what happened last time we went to the race track. I bet on a sure thing. The damned dog got bumped and ran the opposite direction." She paused for his laughter. "Although, to give him credit, he did catch the rabbit."

"Yeah, maybe you should keep your money. I *do* know your luck!" She heard a shuffling on his end of the phone line. "Look, sweetie, Roger already went on ahead to the airport. I can't delay any longer. I have to catch a cab."

Sammy's heart skidded to a stop.

"What? What did you just say?" Perhaps she heard wrong.

"I said I have to catch a cab. Or maybe they have a second shuttle to the airport. I sent Roger on ahead and decided to call you one last time. But I'm really late. I have to go."

"Michael, listen to me. I—"

He cut her off. "Honey, I know you want to warn me to be careful, but I have to go. I love you. Okay, gotta run."

"Michael, listen. I—" The line died. "Michael?"

What were the odds he would cut her off mid-conversation? He *never* did that. Terrified, she frantically tried to redial the number he'd called from. Based on the caller ID, she knew it hadn't been his cell. When Michael didn't answer, Sammy tried his iPhone. It immediately went to voicemail. Sammy growled aloud and tore through the kitchen, trying to find the main number for the hotel. Where the hell had she been when she jotted down the details of his stay?

He still had to check out. She had time. She found what she was looking for in the bedroom, but her hands shook so badly, she misdialed—*twice.*

"Dammit!" Sammy was ready to pull her hair out. Hysteria, raw and ugly, flooded her. She finally connected with the front desk clerk.

"Sir, when Michael Anselin in two-twenty-five checks out, please tell him to call home. It's an emergency. He should be on his way there now."

"Sorry, ma'am, he checked out twenty minutes ago. He did say he had to run back to the room. I could try to ring him for you," the clerk offered in an attempt to be helpful.

"Yes, please."

After ten rings, the call returned to the switchboard.

"I'm sorry, ma'am. No answer. Would you like me to try again?"

CHAPTER 9

S ammy dreaded the drive to Melanie's. To delay her
departure, she meandered from room to room. Michael was
in every aspect of their home from the design to the decorating to the
beat-up recliner in the corner.

Walking into the bathroom, she looked at herself in the mirror.
God, she was pale. Maybe even a little gaunt. Had stress done that this
last week? She hadn't realized she lost weight. Regardless, it was time
to make herself presentable. Switching to autopilot, she applied her
makeup and dressed.

There could still be the slightest chance her premonition wouldn't
come to pass. Sammy prayed that would be the case. The probability
these flashes of the future *would* happen was too terrifying to contem-
plate. She stayed lost in her thoughts until she arrived at Melanie's.
The knock on the driver's side window jerked her back to the present
and to reality.

"Sammy?"

As her surroundings came into focus, incredulity took over.
Apparently, her autopilot mode had bled into her driving. The idea of
driving in such a daze sickened her. She could have hurt other drivers

or pedestrians and been totally unaware, such was her distracted state of mind.

"Sammy? Are you okay?" Melanie's concern helped Sammy focus.

"Fine. I hope you don't mind me waiting here with you."

"No problem. Our kids are at a sleepover. I could use the company."

They conversed about Melanie's children for about twenty minutes. Their antics never failed to entertain. When Melanie suddenly became morose, Sammy asked, "What is it, Mel?"

"I'm not sure if Michael told you, or if he even knows, but Roger and I are going to separate."

Unsure what to say, Sammy sat back against the couch cushions, breathless from the wind being knocked from her lungs.

"No, he didn't." Sadness crept in and settled for a long visit. Mel and Roger had been married for about fifteen years. They were one of the good couples. The ones who stayed together, not for the kids, but because they honestly loved one another. Sammy hated to see her friends dissolve their marriage.

"I don't know why I'm telling you this. For whatever reason, I've been feeling overly sentimental today. Maybe my hormones are out of whack. Still, I need someone objective to talk to. Of course, Roger doesn't want to split up, but I can't stand the arguing anymore."

"Do you still love him?"

"I'm not sure what love is this late in the game."

"Yes, you do. It's that warm fuzzy you get when the person you care about has done something considerate. The passion both in bed and out. Overlooking their morning breath for a kiss. That particular one helps if your partner is hot, and it's not like Roger's a troll."

"Oh, Sammy." Melanie's laugh ended on a choked sob. "That type of closeness has been long gone in our relationship."

"Okay, maybe. But do you want it back? Or do you look at Roger and feel nothing?"

"I want to be loved like everyone else. I can't stand the anger anymore. Mine toward him and vice versa. Along the way, we forgot how to talk to each other. We agree on nothing. Not even how to raise the kids. I'm sick to death of the fighting."

"Do either of you *try* to sit and talk? Are you both thoughtful and considerate of the other person's feelings if you have a legitimate complaint, or is it more of a war zone?" Sammy fought to ease her friend's mind. Perhaps to give her hope even when she herself had none. "If you don't agree on how to raise the children, maybe you can compromise. Just think of the disagreements you are going to have if one gets custody and the other doesn't." She tried to force Melanie to see it would take both parties to make the marriage work.

If fate allowed Roger to live, sneered the ugly voice in her head.

"You're right. I know you're right." Her friend wiped shaky fingers below her eyes. "We can't say a word without hurting one another. Not a day goes by without an argument. I have to wonder, where did we go wrong?"

Before Sammy could respond, Melanie's cell rang.

"I wonder who that could be at this time of night." Melanie frowned as she stood and headed for her phone.

From her spot across the room, Sammy heard the screaming and sobbing through the receiver. While she couldn't make out the exact words being said, she had a damned good idea. Panic closed her throat.

"What? No. No, I can't remember. What channel? There's only one flight from Dallas that I know of. Hold on." Melanie looked worried. "It's my sister-in-law. She was watching TV and said she saw the breaking news on CBN. A plane crash in the Gulf of Mexico. Barb thinks it's the Dallas flight. Channel forty-three."

After a frantic, unsuccessful search for the remote, Sammy rushed to the television and flipped it on. The television screen showed the view from the angle of the station's news helicopter of a plane on fire, half-sunken. Searchlights veered left and right, front to back. "Fire rages out of control as Coast Guard workers and divers struggle to locate survivors. The cause of the crash has been undetermined. Search and rescue..."

The newscaster droned on and on, but Sammy couldn't process

the words. The scene resembled her dream. *So much for the idea of her premonition being only a manifestation of her fears.*

Her chest constricted. Bile rose in her throat and sweat beaded her brow. She rushed to the hall powder room and dislodged the contents of her stomach. After waiting a minute to make certain she wasn't going to vomit again, Sammy rinsed her mouth and hurried back out to the living room.

Melanie sat, deathly pale, with the phone face up in her lap. Barb's shouting echoed out of the receiver. Sammy snatched up the device. "Barb? Barb, listen. Please, calm down. *Barbara!*"

The hysteria continued coming from the other end. Sammy stared at the screen, helpless and unsure what to do. She looked at Melanie, who seemed to be heading toward shock. Once more, she tried to calm Barbara. With no recourse, Sammy hung up the phone and dialed nine-one-one. She explained the circumstances, gave them Barb's number, then Melanie's address. After apprising them of her friend's condition, she requested a policeman or paramedic to be sent for Melanie. She didn't know what else to do.

Once she disconnected the call, she rushed to the nearest bedroom and pulled the comforter off the bed. She was sure she'd read somewhere it was important to keep a shock victim warm. After wrapping up Melanie mummy-tight, she headed for the liquor cabinet. Sammy poured a finger of Fireball whisky, eyeballed the amount, and added another finger or two. She held the tumbler to Melanie's lips and encouraged her to drink. But her friend sat sightless, refusing to acknowledge her in any way. Sammy touched her face and found it was ice cold.

Tears gathered in her own eyes. What the hell was she supposed to do?

"Dammit, Mel. Please snap out of it." Sammy endeavored to rub warmth back into the other woman's hands. "What's taking them so fucking long?" she ranted as she tried to ignore the newscast, not wanting to hear how they had, at this time, found no survivors. If she could have located the goddamned remote, she would have muted that monotonous dialog.

Last night's dream flashed back to her. Silent tears continued to stream down her face, though she struggled to remain calm. Tried not to wonder whether Michael had caught that flight. How long she sat there, she couldn't say. It could have been a minute or thirty. Her goal was to keep Melanie as warm as possible, so she held her and rocked. All the while whispering nonsense phrases like "It's going to be all right." "We'll get through this." "Maybe there was a second flight." None of it helped.

A knock sounded at the door.

"Ma'am, this is Deputy Daniels of the Sheriff's Department. We received a call from this address. Could you please open the door?"

Thank God! If she had to sit there another moment with Melanie in her unresponsive stupor, Sammy would lose it, too. She flung open the door to admit the officer and the paramedics, then hung back and hugged the wall as they hovered over Melanie. As she watched, they took her pulse and checked the dilation of her eyes.

"She's in shock," one of the men said.

No shit. Sammy rubbed her arms and stomped her feet. She hadn't noticed the temperature drop.

"Ma'am, what exactly happened here tonight?" Deputy Daniels asked. "Ma'am?"

It finally registered that he was talking to her. She looked into his eyes. Oddly enough, although they were a slightly different shade, they reminded her of Michael's. Unable to take her gaze away from those warm brown eyes, she waved her hand to gesture at the television. He seemed to understand.

"Did it have something to do with the news? Ma'am?"

"Yes, our... her... they were... the plane."

She barely made sense, but it was enough.

"Ma'am, are you trying to tell me she knew someone on that flight?"

Her teeth started to chatter, and she clamped her jaw tight.

"Yes, h-her husband," she acknowledged. "R-Roger. May-maybe Michael, t-too."

Trembles wracked her body. *When did it become so cold?* It was her last thought before her knees buckled.

SOUND WAS THE FIRST SENSE TO RETURN. FOLLOWING CLOSELY ON ITS heels came light as Sammy cracked open her lids. Confused, she stared at the ceiling a moment to absorb the noise and people moving about the living room. A squawking radio reminded her what had transpired.

She sat up with great care, taking inventory of all her parts. The deputy must have caught her as she fell because nothing felt bruised. That same deputy now spoke to Melanie and Roger's children, Cory and Penny. They saw Sammy shift and ran into her arms. As the only familiar person in the room, they were looking for comfort. She didn't know what she had left to offer.

"They took Mom away, Ms. Sammy. That man said she was sick. Where's my dad? Mom said when we got back from the party tomorrow, Dad would be back from Dallas." In that moment, Cory seemed more grown up than a ten-year-old child should've. "We were supposed to spend the night, but Mrs. Connor saw the cop cars and brought us home. Where's Mom and Dad?"

Sammy stared at him, helpless to formulate the words. How did one tell a kid, his dad was never coming home or that his mother was just carted away in shock?

Penny, at seven, could only cry and bury her head in the crook of Sammy's neck. "I want my mommy."

"I know you do, baby. Mommy had to go..." Sammy struggled to soothe the children, a task beyond her ability. She shifted to address the cop. "I... I don't know what to say to them. Did you hear anything else? Where did they take Melanie?"

"They took your friend to the Flagler Memorial Hospital for observation."

He gestured to the hallway with a head tilt. Sammy nodded her understanding and settled the kids on the sofa to follow him the short distance away for a private conversation.

"Their aunt Barbara called while you were out. She's calmer now and is on her way to care for the children. Is there someone we can call for you?"

"Yes... no... I... how do I find out if someone was on that plane?" she questioned numbly.

He offered to have dispatch contact the airline to find out about the flight manifest. "What's the name of the person you are trying to locate?"

"Michael... Michael Anselin. He... he may have missed his flight. He was on the phone with me and worried he wouldn't find a ride to the airport." She looked up at him, hopeful. "I came to pick him up when they got in. But maybe he missed the flight?"

Pity was reflected in the deputy's face, and Sammy died a little inside.

CHAPTER 10

A pounding on the door disturbed Sammy's sleep.

"Michael," she murmured. The knock registered a second time, and she threw back the covers. She raced down the steps as if all the demons in hell were after her, all the while praying to God that Michael had returned. Just shy of the door, she stopped, afraid to answer. He had a key and would never need to knock. If she opened the door right now, reality would set in, and she wasn't sure she wanted to face facts just yet.

"Samantha? Honey, are you there?" Violet called out.

A sob gathered in Sammy's chest, and she choked it back. She wanted to scream. To rage at the uncertainty of it all. Where the hell was Michael? With a glance skyward, she tried to get a grip, or maybe it was a search for guidance from a higher power. She wasn't certain of anything at this point. Struggling for composure, she opened the door.

"Honey, we were so worried about you." Violet wrapped her in a tight embrace. After a long minute, she pulled back to look at Sammy. Lines of strain were etched around her eyes and mouth. Tears seeped from her mom's beautiful gray eyes. "We heard what happened. Is there any additional news yet?"

Sammy indicated no with a simple shake of her head.

"Sammy, we are all so sorry about Michael," Margie said, giving her sister the first genuine hug of their relationship.

If it had been any other situation, Sammy would have appreciated and returned the embrace. Right now, she just wanted to be left alone. It wasn't to be.

Most of the Holt clan crowded through the open doorway: Mom, Dad, Margie, Annie, Annie's husband, Charlie, and even Great Aunt Aggie. Sammy was still unsure how they were related, but she loved the old curmudgeon. The woman had to be eighty if she was a day.

The only person missing was James, who was wrapping up a home-rebuild project for their uncle up in North Carolina.

Sammy bit her lip. "Why are you all here?"

From the range of shocked expressions, she'd say everyone was flabbergasted.

"We didn't think you should be alone at a time like this." Martin gave her a tight hug and a pat on the back. "We were worried."

"A time like this?" She couldn't stop the bitchy edge to her tone. "Michael's not gone."

Again, her words paralyzed everyone. Margie got snippy in return. The underlying animosity they'd always shared came to the forefront. "What the hell's the matter with you? We love you. We came here to offer our sympathy and support." She sighed and made a concerted effort to control her temper. "I know you're hurting and it's a bad time for you, but we're here to help you through it."

"When Michael gets back, he can help me just fine."

No one could believe she refused to accept the situation. Granted, the crash had only happened a few hours ago, but based on their blank expressions, none of them expected this reaction from her.

"Sammy, Michael's dead," Annie said quietly.

Sammy shot her a look that would melt stone. "No."

"You saw the news report. You had to have seen the wreckage. It's all they've talked about for hours. Samantha, no one survived," Violet insisted, moderating her tone so as not to set her daughter off.

"No. You're wrong. Michael wasn't on that plane," Sammy argued, her voice hoarse. "When the sheriff's office calls, I'll prove it."

"It was a horrible tragedy, but it's real, honey." Violet attempted to embrace her again.

Sammy rejected a second hug and dodged to the side. She didn't want their grief to cloud her mind. Having them here was torment enough. "Can you all leave? Please? I don't want anyone around me right now. Please understand."

"We aren't leaving Sammy. Deal with it," Margie snapped.

Her sister's attitude set off the spark of fire that had been brewing just below the surface, ready to ignite. "You are in my fucking house! Don't you ever tell me to 'deal with it' again! With anything for that matter, do you understand? I... I..." Her anger dissipated as swiftly as it had come. Her sister meant well even if her delivery was clumsy as hell. "I'm sorry, Margie. I..."

What could she say? She was one gaping wound, and they were the salt. Sammy darted up the stairs, stopping on the landing just out of their sight but within hearing.

Heavy sorrow filled the air. Her family huddled in a section of her hallway, helpless to figure out why she'd just freaked out. They spoke amongst themselves, but not one of them knew what to do or say to ease her pain. A comment from Aunt Aggie sent them all into action.

"You don't think she'd take her life, do you?"

"*Aggie!*" Violet exclaimed her shock.

"All I'm saying is that it could be a possibility. You always read about these things on Facebook."

"Samantha would never take her own life."

Sammy overheard her mother defend her from where she huddled against the wall. Her mother's faith in her was the one thing to be grateful for, she supposed. It wasn't as if she were mentally unstable or anything for fuck's sake. All she desired was not to be inundated with do-gooders and mourners. Her family could learn a thing or two about privacy.

Her dad decided they should take temptation out of her path. "Vi, we should still take away any medications or guns she may have in the house. You saw her. She's not rational."

Tired and heartsick, Sammy had heard enough. She slipped into her bedroom and closed the door with a near-soundless click.

VIOLET SEARCHED THE FACES OF THOSE AROUND HER TO SEE ALMOST everyone in agreement with her husband. "Annie? What do you feel?"

Annie, who had been carefully watching her mother, knew the question would turn to her. She gazed up the stairs, no longer sensing Sammy's presence on the landing. "I think you are all overreacting. Sammy may be right. I think she should be alone right now. It's how I'd feel."

"Well, I don't think she should be alone," Margie stated, marching up the steps toward the bedroom.

"Of course not," Annie muttered under her breath. "Saint Margaret to the rescue."

Within a minute, her older sister returned.

"Dad's right. I think we should get rid of anything that might hurt her. Maybe we should even pack Michael's stuff up for her this week. Sooner rather than later. She is in bed with a bunch of his clothes piled around her. It's so pitiful." Margie sat down with her head in her hands, allowing her own sorrow to break free. "Why Michael? Poor Sammy."

Annie hugged her sister. Margie often felt the need to be the strong one. If she had to guess, Annie would have said Margie, being the oldest, felt she had to cloak her emotions and hide any weakness. Maybe because she was a mother herself. On the outside, Margie was a hard shell, but on the inside, she was a big softie.

Violet took command.

"Let's shelve the suicide discussion. It's not going to happen. Samantha just needs time to rest. You all go home for tonight. I'll stay here. In the morning, I'll make the family breakfast and we can discuss funeral arrangements." She paused to take a breath. "James should be here by then. He'll want a voice in this since Michael was his best friend. He is probably the perfect one to comfort her."

Funeral arrangements, while not a priority, were a necessity. The world wouldn't stop for a lost loved one. There was too much to think about, too much to do. However, Violet decided it could all wait until her daughter was ready, and Annie silently agreed.

FROM HER BEDROOM, SAMMY HEARD THE LOW MURMUR OF VOICES. Soon enough, the front door opened and closed. Except for the muted sounds of someone moving about the kitchen, silence filled the house.

Sammy drew Michael's shirt to her face and inhaled. His spicy scent still lingered on his favorite pullover. Her eyes burned with unshed tears, and she closed her lids against the salty sting.

"You're not dead. I'd know it if you were," she whispered aloud to him. "I'd know."

The shirt triggered another vision, but this one was of the past. It was of the two of them walking hand-in-hand on the beach as their beloved Sassy chased the sandpipers running along the shoreline. It had been a lovely Saturday morning the week before he left for Dallas.

A cold nose nudged her neck from behind.

Sammy turned to cuddle Sassy to her. "He's not dead, Sassy. You believe me, right?"

Her pup showered her chin with canine kisses, either to say "yes" or "get me some food." Distinguishing between the two was never easy.

Feeling every one of her twenty-nine years, Sammy rose to her feet and padded to the door. She opened it enough for Sassy to get out before she closed it again.

Without a doubt, she knew it was her mother who had stayed. And maybe it was an arrogant assumption on Sammy's part, but she also knew Violet would care for the dog for the time being. Violet Holt couldn't bear to see any living thing suffer. Sammy imagined it was why she was downstairs, piddling around in the kitchen. Odds were she was making a meal fit for a king.

"Thank you, Mom," she murmured as she rested her forehead against the closed door.

CHAPTER 11

"Sammy, you are being completely ridiculous. I can't believe you refuse to discuss Michael's funeral arrangements." Normally the quiet sister, Annie gave in to frustration and shouted, "Get up and get dressed! You *smell!*"

It had been three days, and although she hated to admit it, Annie feared for Sammy's mental health. All her sister did was lie around in the same clothes she'd had on since the day of the crash. If Annie hadn't known where Violet stored the spare key, she would probably still be pounding on the door. For sure, Sammy wouldn't have let her in. Her sister's refusal to accept the situation weighed heavy on Annie's mind. She tried to soften her voice, to add reason to an already unreasonable discussion.

"Sammy, please. Michael wouldn't want to see you this way. He loved you. Do you think he would've wanted you to mourn for him the rest of your life or waste away like this?"

Sammy was alert to her presence. Annie could see the tell-tale tension in her sister's body. Whenever anyone said Michael's name in the past tense, Sammy would stiffen up and become enraged. With her gift, Annie could physically feel her emotions, and it was uncomfortable as hell.

The last to admit it, she concluded the rest of the family might be correct. Sammy needed an emergency therapy session. Tomorrow, Annie intended to make a few phone calls. She doubted scheduling an appointment would be very successful since the Thanksgiving holiday loomed, but she needed to do something. She had to hope for the best and hold on to the belief a professional might reach her sister. Anything else was unthinkable. Sammy was her bestie. Without her, Annie might not get through the roughest parts of the day—dealing with actual people.

Over the last couple of days, each family member had taken a turn and stayed to watch over Sammy. After a search for Michael's handgun came up empty, no one wanted to leave her alone for long. Annie had a sneaking suspicion Sammy had perceived their intent and hid the weapon. Most probably under the mattress she refused to budge from. But from what she could determine, Sammy's actions screamed grief and not self-harm.

Annie studied her sister's set face. She looked gaunt and as if she hadn't slept for days. With her hair matted and sticking up in every direction, Sammy resembled a homeless waif. Dark circles emphasized her haunted blue eyes. She'd never looked so pale in all the time Annie could remember.

She feared Sammy had eaten little to nothing since she holed up in her room. If she'd gotten up to go to the kitchen, she did it in stealth mode while her houseguests were sleeping.

In an effort to get a read on her sister's emotional status, Annie sat on the bed and gripped Sammy's hand. She hadn't said two words to anyone since the first night, and she'd left Sassy's care to whoever happened to be present, so she could wallow in her grief and despair.

Annie observed Sammy a bit longer before bending to lift Sassy to hug her close. The little dog refused to leave her mama's side. They were all forced to carry her outside to complete her business. Once done, she made a beeline right back to Sammy on the bed.

"Oh, Sammy," Annie whispered, forlorn and afraid. "Come back to us."

A light bulb went off in her brain. Determined to make a difference, she rushed to the bathroom and turned the shower tap to the coldest setting. She then made sure the central heat was on a comfortable setting. Their mother would kill her if Sammy caught pneumonia. Annie grabbed her sister and pulled her into a sitting position. When she attempted to remove her clothing, Sammy went into fight mode. Belligerent as always, she refused to give up her possessions.

Deciding it was no great tragedy if Sammy's clothing got wet because they stunk, too, Annie let Sammy keep them on. Next, she dragged her to the shower stall and shoved her under the icy spray. Sammy's outraged cry and shocked expression caused Annie to wince. Hopefully, she was doing the right thing.

She picked up the soap and a washcloth hanging from a nearby towel rack, then got to scrubbing. Although Sammy never said a word, Annie was singed by the heat of the glare she cast her way. Feeling remorse, she adjusted the temperature of the water.

"I love you, Sammy. Whether you like it or not, you are getting a shower and a bite to eat in that stomach. Maybe when you feel more human, you'll feel up to planning the services."

Annie talked as she struggled to peel through layers of material. She scrubbed any available skin. Shampooing her sister's filthy hair came next.

"Jeez, Sammy. Doesn't this itch?"

Annie talked of nonsensical things in an effort to penetrate the shell surrounding her sister.

"I'll do it."

The sound coming out of Sammy's mouth resembled a croak. Annie wasn't quite sure she heard correctly and continued to scrub.

"I said, I'll do it!" Sammy tried to shout, but it came out as no more than a hoarse whisper.

Exhausted from the emotion as well as the chore of caring for her sister, Annie slapped the washcloth into Sammy's hand, toweled herself dry, and went back to pick out more appropriate clothes for her sister to wear. Yoga pants and a hoodie would be good enough for now. All she needed was to get Sammy downstairs to consume food and discuss arrangements. Afterwards, she could hand her off to another family member while she detoxed from the emotional overload.

Leaving Sammy to her privacy, Annie left to shoot off a quick text to her mother and siblings.

"Meet here ASAP. Sammy is back in the land of the living."

She returned to the bathroom to find Sammy sitting on the floor, wrapped in Michael's wet shirt. Most days, Annie's anger was slow to boil. She couldn't afford the expense of energy. But today, in this moment, she erupted. "Sammy, I can understand what you must be feeling, but you have to *stop it*. You can't curl up in a ball and die. How do I get through to you?" She threw up her hands in frustration. "Michael wouldn't want this. He'd—"

"Fuck you! You don't have a *clue* what Michael would want." Sammy's voice was raspy and sore from disuse, but the edge of her fury was obvious. "Tell me, Annie, who have you lost? Hmmm? No one? Then don't presume to tell me how to feel."

While the words coming from Sammy wounded, relief flooded Annie.

"Well, that's a start. You can be angry; I think that's supposed to be healthy," Annie muttered.

"AND STOP CLEANING MY FUCKING BATHROOM," SAMMY GROWLED. "YOU always put things away wrong."

As Annie bustled around and straightened up the mess they'd made from the forced shower, Sammy rolled her eyes. Her sister was OCD about her surroundings, and deep emotions—hers or anyone else's—kicked her tendencies into overdrive.

"No, you have the bathroom set up wrong."

It was an old argument. Annie had a desire to rearrange everyone's house wherever she went. Sammy would lay odds she'd even gone so far as to straighten cans in their pantry while she stayed here, alphabetizing and shifting them so they all faced forward. If she could drum up an ounce of give a shit, Sammy would be full-on irritated.

The kitchen was sacred in her house. Her siblings knew that. Her kitchen setup was not to be disturbed if anyone visited.

Within a half hour, the entirety of Sammy's immediate family were gathered in the dining room. Sammy sat and stared at her half-eaten sandwich. When had she eaten it? She couldn't recall anything other than the muted buzz of people entering her home. God, she was exhausted. Why wouldn't they let her sleep?

The doorbell rang, and she welcomed the distraction.

Margie elected to answer the door, and when she returned, Deputy Daniels followed her back into the room. Sammy vaguely remembered him from the night of the plane crash. But now, a slow, sinking sensation hit her. His presence was indicative of bad news.

He nodded a greeting to everyone then leveled all his attention on her.

"Ma'am, I'm following up on your request from the other evening. I'm not quite sure how you knew, but you were right. Your boyfriend never got on that flight."

The words he uttered weren't as unexpected to her as they were to her family.

"What? Then why haven't we heard from him? Where the hell is he?" James demanded.

But Sammy knew. The dream had told her. She continued staring at the deputy, her eyes locked with his. At least until his next words. His handful of sentences had her slamming her lids shut, picturing the scene as she remembered it in her head.

"There was a major accident on a Dallas freeway." He seemed hesitant to go on, but eventually did. "I spoke with the officer who worked the scene. He emailed me the report along with the witnesses' statements." He broke off to consult his notepad. Continuing, he said, "It seems two men ran into oncoming traffic. It resulted in a multi-vehicle collision. A gas tanker crashed at the scene and created one helluva explosion. Excuse the expression."

Daniels paused, and Sammy opened her eyes. She nodded for him to continue.

"There were five casualties." Once again, he stopped. This time to soften the blow of the news to come. "Mr. Anselin's body was one of the deceased identified at the scene." He paused to clear his throat. "I'm sorry."

Deputy Daniels answered the handful of questions her family directed toward him. Sammy had none to ask. She was too numb. Before he left, he squatted in front of her, took her hand, and offered his condolences. With a nod of acknowledgment, she offered him a whispered thank you. He really was a kind man, and she hoped his future was as bright as the brief vision she received.

She returned to picking at her sandwich as her family discussed the circumstances surrounding Michael's death. Sammy slowly shifted her gaze to them, studying each one after the other, detached from it all. They could have been bugs under a microscope for all the feeling she had in that moment. Without a word to anyone, she stood and walked back to her bedroom. She had nothing left in her and, for that reason, had nothing to contribute.

THANKSGIVING WAS A SOMBER AFFAIR. SAMMY WENT THROUGH THE motions of eating, but she mostly only managed to push food around her plate. The smell of meat turned her stomach. Odd how nausea had become her constant companion in recent days.

Plans had been made to retrieve Michael's charred remains for a funeral. She left all the details to James and her mother, not caring about any of it. Michael was gone. What did it matter what color the casket material was? Who cared if it was to be roses or calla lilies at the service? None of it was going to bring him back to her.

The whole discussion made her weary. All she'd managed since the confirmation of the accident was sleep. It was all she cared about. Because when asleep, dreams of Michael would come to comfort her. The ability to touch his face or hear his whispered words of love brought her joy. She wasn't a coward, but Sammy just couldn't find her way back to giving a crap about the rest of the world. Not as long as she could spend her sleeping hours with her lover.

James had tried to talk her into boxing up Michael's items and donating them to those in need. He'd suggested selling the house, or at the very least, redecorating might help her with her grief. Violet stepped in and shushed him, informing him Sammy would do all this in due course. Their mother felt it was too soon, and they all needed the closure of the memorial first.

Sammy had no intention of selling their home. She needed to keep Michael close to her until she had a chance to be with him once more.

CHAPTER 12

he morning of the funeral dawned, clear and bright. A typical Florida sunrise. Margie was Sammy's designated babysitter for the day. At least, that's how Sammy considered it. The two of them had argued again about Sammy's refusal to attend the service.

She didn't want to go. Why should she if none of this was real? She had to be living an alternate life, right? Michael didn't feel gone. Sure, he wasn't exactly present, but he wasn't deceased. She couldn't say why she still believed this. She just did. Why should she attend this farce?

"Michael is not dead," she insisted for what felt like the thousandth time. "No one has shown me any proof. And if he had died, I'd feel it. I would know it *here*." She pointed to her heart. Sammy looked at her sister, comprehending Margie's need to try to help in a helpless predicament. "He didn't die in that wreck, Margie. Don't ask me how I know. I just do."

"If he didn't, Sammy, how come he hasn't called? It's been two weeks," Margie tried to reason.

Sammy shied away from that line of inquiry, unable to answer the one question plaguing her. Compliance was easier than arguing, but she wouldn't participate. She wouldn't sit on the pew like a sad widow. No, if she had to attend to appease her family, it would be under protest. She walked toward her closet, praying her intuition wasn't wrong. Praying the numbness would leave.

"Could you get me a bite to eat? Maybe the chocolate ice cream in the fridge would be a good start," Sammy requested with an attempt at a smile.

Nothing stayed in her stomach for long. She felt as weak as a newborn kitten. However, feeding her seemed to make them all happy, so she went with it. Also, the excuse gained her privacy. She wanted to be alone at least long enough to dress.

She heard her sister leave the room but didn't bother to look up. Going through her clothes, Sammy decided at some future point a shopping expedition was in order. Her wardrobe was sadly lacking. She pulled out a deep-sapphire dress and put it back. If she wanted to wear it again, she didn't want it as a reminder of today.

Nothing suitable to wear popped out at her. With a deep sigh, she shifted to look through Michael's things. Methodically, she worked her way through the clothes she hadn't previously used as her nest. A small smile played around her lips. Sammy recalled the various occasions she'd purchased shirts or slacks for him. Shopping for Michael had been a chore. He hated to dress up and did it only under duress. Because he was comfortable in his shorts and t-shirts, most of his good clothing still had the tags.

She half suspected the playful arguments he'd caused allowed him an excuse for great make-up sex afterwards. Not that either of them needed an excuse for great sex. A sharp pang of loss hit, but she shoved it aside, reminding herself once again he wasn't dead.

Her mind came back to the task at hand. Perhaps she should treat this funeral like the farce it was? With renewed determination, she pulled on a pair of her black jeans and Michael's new, red flannel shirt. Sammy had no desire to go to this service, and she sure as hell wouldn't dress up for it. She reached for her black boots and slipped them on as well. Satisfied, Sammy went and added little makeup touches here and there, then ran a comb through her tangled mass of hair. She didn't bother to dry it. What did she care?

"Sammy, I've fixed bacon and eggs. Come eat," Margie called from the kitchen.

"Be right down."

Taking a long, hard look in the mirror, Sammy noted the dark circles and pale complexion. She bore an uncanny resemblance to the haunted woman she'd first seen in the mirror a few weeks back—the night Michael told her he was scheduled to go to Dallas. For someone living in Florida, she certainly needed a tan. Again, she told herself she didn't care what she looked like. With a deep, resolved breath, she went to join her family.

Margie and her youngest son, Aaron, were already seated. Sammy walked to where Aaron sat with his face turned up for a kiss. At eleven, Aaron exuded charm like no other kid of her acquaintance. Unlike most boys his age, he always wanted a hug or kiss, accepting nothing less than total devotion from his relatives. Complying with his wishes, she wondered at the love and innocence of children. She wanted to be that free again.

The moment Margie saw how Sammy had dressed, she exploded in anger.

"You cannot be *serious!* I thought you had decided to go to the service."

"I agreed under duress. And Margie, before you say another word, I already told you I thought this was a joke. I refuse to dress up for something I don't believe in. If you are going to argue with me, I can go straight back upstairs and go back to bed." Sammy effectively cut off any argument from Margie. "Do we have any egg bagels?"

Shaking her head in anger, Margie was astute enough to grasp if she offered another word of protest, Sammy would do just that. "The bagels are in the freezer. You're the only one who eats that kind." A few minutes passed, but Margie being Margie had to try one more time. "Listen, Sammy. I think you should change out of respect for the other mourners. You may not care, but other people will."

All she received in return was an icy glare. Sammy refused to budge an inch.

SCORES OF MOURNERS WERE MAKING THEIR WAY THROUGH THE DOUBLE doors when they pulled into the parking lot. The sea of black clarified to any passersby that it was a memorial service.

Margie exited the car and buttoned up Aaron s suit jacket.

"You go ahead. I'll be right in."

Her sister snorted her disbelief. "You're cracked if you think I'm leaving you alone so you can take off."

"And if I promise to stay, will you leave me the fuck alone for a few minutes?"

"Fine. You have three minutes, then I'm sending Jamie out to get your ass."

Margie cast one last frustrated look at Sammy before she led her son to where her ex-husband waited with their daughter, Kaley, and oldest son, Scott Junior, or Scotty as he was known in the Holt clan. Once Margie reached the group, Sammy saw Scott Senior gesture in her direction. Viewed from a distance, his anger was obvious. Poor Margie. She'd really picked a winner when she chose that one. Another man, much broader and taller than Scott, strode up and directed them all inside with a mere nod of his head. It brought Sammy up short. Someone able to silence Margie that easily? Impressive.

Sammy leaned against her sister's vehicle. The small hairs on her arms lifted—a clear indication she was the recipient of curious stares from the local gossips. She rubbed her arms, rolled her eyes, and looked away. What did she care what they thought?

The parking area outside the church was now close to deserted, minus the automobiles. Yet, she continued to hold back, unable or unwilling to step into God's domain. Unease wormed its way throughout her body. Her palms were clammy. Mouth dry. Head aching. Tension or avoidance? Sighing, she straightened.

Out of the corner of her eye, she spotted a press van. To the locals, the man who was supposed to have died in a plane crash but who had actually died in a multi-car pile-up was big news. Perhaps it should have surprised her they would intrude on a family in mourning at this time, but it didn't.

Sammy took deep, gulping breaths and cast about for a means to escape the heaviness settling in her chest. If she kept this up, she'd hyperventilate, but she couldn't seem to stop. Churches and grave-yards all had the same effect on her. It was as if the weight of those who had passed were all clamoring for her attention. She had to find a way to center herself.

She delayed entering the building a little longer, knowing that once she walked through those church doors, people would expect her to follow all society's mourning dictates. She'd be expected to accept Michael was gone for good, and she wasn't prepared for the finality by any stretch of the imagination. Tilting her head back, she looked up through the canopy of trees at the brilliant sky. Shouldn't it be the dull gray of her life? Shouldn't rain pour down to mingle with her tears that were never far from the surface?

Sammy sucked in a deep breath and attempted to gather what remaining strength she possessed, then headed for the church entrance. The opening strains of the service could be heard from outside the doorway. "We are gathered here to honor the memory of Michael Anselin. As I look out among the faces…"

Sammy lounged in the opening and observed the crowd of mourn-ers. It was quite the turnout, but then everyone had loved Michael. Dispassionately, she watched the pastor. He spoke of Michael's life—someone he'd never met—as if they'd been great friends. Did they use the same sermon at all funerals for the deceased? Similar to weddings?

Her gaze touched on the front pew where her family sat. Was this really a comfort to them? It wasn't to her. She turned her attention back to the pastor, her eyes never really seeing him as a messenger of God, but as an entity who tried to make Michael's disappearance a finality. Nope. She refused to accept that.

Slowly, Sammy pushed away from the wall and ambled toward the podium. With each step, she gained the confidence she needed to confront him. It took an effort, but she ignored the gasps and whispers flying around her. Giving a half shrug to dispel their negativity, she stretched and ran her hand along the top of the casket resting in a place of honor at the front of the room. That single touch firmed her resolve and cemented her decision.

As she got to the podium, Sammy asked, "May I say a few words about Michael?"

By cutting the pastor off midstream, she once again surprised the crowd lining the pews. He, too, appeared taken aback but recovered quickly and stepped away with a lukewarm smile.

Mustering her courage, she turned a calm face to the crowd. One by one, she examined their faces, not knowing exactly what she searched for. She'd have sworn one of her siblings muttered, *"Oh shit!"*

Belatedly, she spotted the news crew in the back of the church. Their presence changed nothing. Things needed to be said. While she believed Michael was alive, it didn't make her any less emotionally raw. Because, bottom line, he was still missing.

Speaking softly at first, gaining momentum with each second, Sammy spoke the words from her heart. "You'll have to forgive me for going off script here. I didn't have anything planned, and I'm afraid I've hijacked this memorial service. But since it's for my boyfriend, Michael, I don't think this one indiscretion is too terrible." She paused to swallow. "You see, we lived together. Loved together. We worked to build our lives around our mutual goals. We shared our thoughts and our feelings. And on occasion, the same dreams."

She cleared her throat and avoided eye contact with her family. "Some of you who know us will understand what I mean. Just two months before Michael left for Dallas, we closed on our new house. More recently, we made plans to vacation in London and then Paris." Sammy took another cleansing breath. "We knew everything there was to know about the other. So, I believe I speak with the utmost authority when I say Michael's not dead. You all need to understand there has been a grave error. I don't know whose body is in that casket, but it's not his."

Gasps and wide-eyed stares met her declaration.

The pastor was the first to react. "See here, young woman! You cannot come into my church and interrupt a service for the bereaved."

Barely sparing him a glance, her eyes finally sought out and found the faces whose familiarity should have warmed her but, in reality, left her quite cold.

"Don't you see? I would know." Sammy felt righteous indignation flowing in her veins. "He's not there. That's not Michael's body in that casket. I would know. *I would know!*"

The pitying looks of the attendees fueled her irritation.

Fleshy arms seized her from behind, and Sammy struggled free. When she whirled, she found the pastor in all his outraged glory. He scowled at her with something akin to hatred on his face. For a moment, she was taken aback by his rage. Where was the compassion and understanding?

"You will leave my church at *once*," he snapped.

"You hypocritical little bastard," she snarled into his pudgy little pig face. "You never even knew him. He's never set foot in this church. *Not once.* Yet there you stand, the actor you are, and you perform your laughable little sermon for all these poor saps who don't know any better."

If anyone else stood in her place, she would have been appalled on their behalf. But it was *her* lover and *her* life. Indignation ruled her actions. She twisted in time to see the camera crew shift forward in their attempt to catch the unfolding scene. Disgust rolled through her. *How dare they prey on other people's pain?*

Picking up the closest candlestick, she hefted it up and tested its weight.

"*Sammy, no!*"

Sammy ignored her mother and flung the metal stick at the nearest camera. With shocking accuracy, it hit dead center and cracked the lens. Something wild but justified unfurled inside. She smiled with grim satisfaction as the cameraman jumped backward. She tried to muffle her laugh. She truly did. But the one thought playing in her mind was Michael would be proud of her throwing arm. He had always said she threw like a girl.

Once again, the pastor made a grab for her. Sammy swung her fist without thinking. All the fury at the fates, all the pain of her loss, all the worry that she was wrong and Michael might really be dead were behind that balled fist. When she connected with the side of the man's face, he dropped like a stone. Who knew there was a glass jaw under those heavy jowls?

The paralyzed air that held the mourners still broke loose, and pandemonium ruled. Friends and family tried to reach her all at the same time. What they hoped to accomplish when they did, even they probably didn't know.

Claustrophobia clawed at her. Its tentacles curled around her ribcage, squeezing. Sammy struggled to gulp in enough air and, unable to do so, fainted dead away.

CHAPTER 13

The continuous beep of a machine penetrated Sammy's fog and annoyed her to the point of waking. A blood pressure cuff on her arm filled and released.

Hospital.

Even if she hadn't known what the sound and feel of it was like, she certainly would have recognized the scent. Antiseptic overpowered her nostrils and sent her stomach into rebellion. She rolled and distributed the contents of her stomach on the floor by her bedside. Helpful hands urged her back against the pillows as a cup of water was thrust at her for a rinse of her mouth. A kind voice asked how long she had been experiencing nausea.

"Samantha?"

For a moment, Sammy debated the merits of pretending to be passed out. The need to hide from the world was strong. With a huge sigh, she opened her eyes to focus on the small group of people in her room: Mom, Dad, and a nurse. "What day is it?"

Her father glanced nervously at her mother. "Do you not know?"

"No. And not because I have forgotten. If I haven't slept for more than a few hours, this is the day you scheduled for the service. But I really don't know because I couldn't give a crap," Sammy delivered in a leaden voice. Her give-a-shit meter was busted.

"It's Saturday," Violet informed her as she fluttered around Sammy and fluffed the pillow behind her head.

Sammy's heart spasmed.

Two weeks. Michael should have returned home two weeks ago.

"I've been sick for a little over a week and a half," Sammy finally answered the nurse's original question.

"Honey, why didn't you tell anyone?" The concern in her mother's voice triggered a small kernel of guilt.

Sammy watched as her father stepped in to rub Violet's back with a soothing word or two. The burning moisture behind her lids forced her eyes closed.

Michael. He would have done that for her. Always conscientious of Sammy's needs, Michael would step up to take care of her in every way. God, she missed him. Missed his smell, his warmth, his laughter.

"When was your last menstrual cycle?"

The nurse's question disconcerted Sammy enough that her eyes popped open to stare in shocked wonder. The increase in her heart rate was clearly visible on the large-screen monitor unit next to her bed. With a swift mental calculation, she came up with a date. Her breath hitched, and the reality of the situation hit her. She looked down at her stomach as if she could see through her clothes to the life that would be smaller than a peanut in her womb. Placing both hands on her abdomen, she turned tear-bright eyes to her mother, who stood with her hands cupped over her mouth.

Michael hadn't left her completely alone after all. *A baby.* She was going to have a baby. *His* baby. And for the first time, true sobs hit her. Body-racking sobs. Pulled from so deep within her, she couldn't catch her breath, couldn't do anything but give over to sorrow.

Multiple arms surrounded her and offered comfort where none could be found.

A BLOOD TEST CONFIRMED WHAT SAMMY KNEW: SHE WAS OFFICIALLY

pregnant. By her calculations, she would be about five weeks along. She liked to think she remembered the day. It was a beautiful Sunday morning, the first weekend of November. Beautiful because it had been raining, and Michael had brought her breakfast in bed. French toast. The only thing he could make, besides scrambled eggs or oatmeal, although she strongly suspected he'd snuck out to a local restaurant to pick up the food. They'd shared one plate, trading bites and kissing off the syrupy goodness from each other's lips. After a leisurely morning of lovemaking, they had snuggled down into the comforter and binge-watched a season of Game of Thrones.

They had come to the series a few years late but were completely hooked. Wrecked by the "Red Wedding" episode, Sammy could only rant her shock. Of course, Michael had laughed at her. It was his favorite pastime—laughing at her rants. He'd told her how cute she was when she became indignant over such things, right before he tackled her onto the pillows for another round of earth-shattering sex.

Boisterous voices brought Sammy back to the present.

Over the next hour, she dealt with family members who offered her congratulations on the baby and rebuked her for her "tantrum" at the church. They all assumed the news of the baby changed the situation. What did they expect? That she would suddenly return to the happy-go-lucky Sammy from before Michael's disappearance?

She wouldn't.

Let them all believe what they will. In due time, she'd make her own plans to find Michael. Sammy was quick to avoid eye contact with Annie. Although, how she ever expected to hide anything from her all-knowing sister was anyone's guess.

"Sammy…"

Annie was cut off by the arrival of the nurse.

She stated the doctor intended to admit her overnight due to dehydration from a condition known as hyperemesis gravidarum. "A standard pregnancy doesn't bring the severe nausea like you've been experiencing. The fainting is concerning, too. We need to get some fluids in you."

Her family was encouraged to make their way out for the evening. Of course, they all ignored the order. Such was the stubbornness of the Holt clan.

Just when Sammy thought she couldn't take another second of the attention, the well-wishing and happy plans were interrupted by an unexpected visitor. Dread overrode her numbed state when Deputy Daniels walked into the room she had been assigned.

"Ms. Holt."

"Deputy Daniels. Do I need to ask to what I owe this pleasure?"

It was never good when the Po-Po sought a person out.

"I suspect you already know. Pastor Simms filed charges of assault against you." The police deputy didn't look happy. "After having met him, I can sympathize with you. However, you did strike him."

He stood at the end of the bed, commanding attention in his dark forest-green uniform with its yellow-lettered badges sewn on the sleeves. His hands were hooked on the service belt resting on his hips as his radio squawked out numbered codes from a faceless dispatcher. He disregarded the sound and concentrated all his attention on Sammy.

"Also, the news station is pressing charges for destruction of property and assault with a candlestick."

"Sounds like a game of clue," James said. "It was Sammy, in the church, with the candlestick."

Although she wanted to, Sammy curbed her impulse to laugh. She bit her lip and refused to look at her warped brother.

"A *valuable* candlestick as it turns out," Daniels stressed. "Not only did you shatter the camera lens, you cut open the camera operator's nose with the impact."

The room erupted with protests from her family. The deputy ignored them and maintained eye contact with her.

"How does this work? I've been admitted for the night." Sammy picked at the edge of the blanket and straightened the seams of the sheet.

"Well, since you're the worst criminal element I've come across, I went out on a limb and talked to my lieutenant before coming here.

He said you can come by the station tomorrow after you're released from the hospital. You'll be booked, bonded, and released on your own recognizance afterwards. Of course, you'll have to show for the court date when it's scheduled."

Sammy sought her brother out. "Jamie, will you take me over? My jeep is at the house." At James's brisk nod, she shifted her attention back to Deputy Daniels. "I'll be there. Please leave the address with Jamie. I imagine it will be closer to the afternoon. In my experience, you can't blow this joint much before eleven or twelve."

James collected the information.

"If you are going to keep turning up like a bad penny, can I at least get your first name?" Sammy requested with wry humor. She saw the matching amusement light the deputy's face.

"Eric."

"Okay then, Eric. I suppose I owe you a big thank you for foregoing the handcuffs-and-patrol-car routine. So, thank you. I do appreciate it."

"I think that's the longest speech I've heard from you." His lips twitched before he sobered. "You're welcome, Ms. Holt. I am sorry for your loss."

"Please, call me Sammy. You've seen me at my absolute worst more times than I care to count. It's like we're old friends now."

"Sammy, it is." He leveled her with a stern look. "Be sure to show up tomorrow, Sammy. I would hate to arrest you. You've been through enough."

"I'll see that she gets there." James offered Eric his hand. "Thank you."

———

THE BOOKING OFFICER TREATED HER WITH KINDNESS, AND SAMMY WAS grateful she wasn't being viewed as a hardened criminal. Most likely, Eric Daniels had spoken up on her behalf. It took roughly three hours, but they bonded and had her at her mother's home for the evening meal.

Once again, the family gathered ranks in an effort to comfort and protect her. She grimaced. Being the baby of the family brought out their protective instincts.

The discussion that night centered around local attorneys who might be beneficial to her case. Martin was confident the charges would eventually be dropped. Violet wasn't so sure. Margie put in her two cents, as usual, and promised to make some calls in the morning.

For once, Sammy was happy to let her. Her sister excelled at organizing and scheduling appointments. As a single mother of three, Margie ran a tight ship. She made lists and got things done. Sammy was convinced her sister would have made an excellent CEO of some Fortune 500 company.

Eventually, the conversation ran to the pregnancy. Violet almost danced with excitement for a new grandchild to spoil. Totally inappropriate to Sammy's way of thinking.

"Have you thought about names?" Violet asked as she gathered a forkful of chicken.

Sammy hadn't had a chance to process the events of the last day, but she paused to think about it. "I would like to name him or her after Michael. He'll like that."

Her refusal to use the past tense wasn't lost on her family. The clatter of forks rang out as they dropped to plates. The verbal silence only lasted a few seconds before everyone started speaking at once. Violet held up her hand to quiet the masses so she could be heard.

"Honey, I think maybe you should reconsider naming the baby after Michael."

"Why?" Sammy asked.

Everyone jumped when Martin's hand slapped the table, rattling all the plates and glasses.

"This is going to stop, Samantha. Right here, right now," he shouted. "We all loved that young man. And it's very sad, but the truth is Michael is gone. *Gone!* You have to face facts. You are not doing yourself or your baby any favors pretending he isn't. Stop the nonsense and the harmful behavior. You need to grieve, have your baby, and move on. That child deserves a parent who lives in the present."

How could they not understand? How many times did Sammy have to prove herself? It didn't matter. She'd defy them to the bitter end if she had to, anything to make them see the truth.

Nodding her head, more with the conclusion she had come to and not in agreement, Sammy left the dining room, heading for the foyer to retrieve her purse and go home. One thing was correct: she needed to start living. For her baby, if for nothing else. If Michael returned, she would prove them wrong on that score. In the meantime, she needed a break from family gatherings. They were suffocating her, and she needed a breather.

Margie rushed after her. "Sammy."

Sammy turned, bone-weary and sad. "What is it, Margie?"

"I still want to help with the lawyer. I know one I think may be good. He's my neighbor. Do you want me to discuss this with him on your behalf?"

"Sure. Thanks."

As Sammy turned to leave, Margie stopped her once more. "What about an OB/GYN? The one I went to for my pregnancies was excellent."

She raised her eyes to meet Margie's, taking the time to see her sister without resentment. Margie truly meant well and had good intentions. Love or something like it blossomed in Sammy's chest, and she took the three steps to reach her sister, wrapping her in a fierce hug.

Nonplussed, Margie hugged her back.

"I appreciate all you're doing. Thank you, Margie."

CHAPTER 14

S ammy's appointment with the lawyer rolled around the early part of the following week. Margie had even offered to go with her to speak to him. Sammy hoped her refusal wouldn't be viewed as a rejection. Her relationship with her sister couldn't take many more hits. However, she needed to do this on her own. Find her own footing again. Achieving a balance was more difficult than anyone could imagine because her family was suffocating the life out of her.

As she walked into the reception area for the offices of Gabriel James, attorney-at-law, Sammy felt nerves start to flutter low in her abdomen. She'd never been in trouble before and was clueless as to how any of this worked. She prayed Margie had picked a good lawyer and not some shyster who would take what little money she had, then do nothing when her ass got sent up to the big house. *The big house.* Did anyone really call it that? Regardless, her temper was going to get her shanked on the inside. *Shanked* was a word. She was pretty sure she saw that on Sons of Anarchy.

An administrative assistant introduced herself as Jenny and ushered Sammy through the doors of the main office. A Greek god in a business suit rose from behind the mahogany desk.

She froze in her tracks and cast an *"Is this guy for real?"* look at the attorney's assistant.

Holy hell, he had to be at least six-feet-four if an inch and built like a brick shithouse. His chestnut hair contrasted sharply with piercing pale gray eyes. Yet the combination was breathtaking. Yes, he would cause fear in the hearts of mere mortals and something a little more primal in any woman who happened to meet him. He definitely wasn't hard to look at. Sammy suspected that might be the true reason Margie had wanted to come with her today and not sisterly affection.

Sammy loved Michael, but she wasn't without eyes in her head or a little vanity in her heart. Currently under Gabriel's cool regard, she felt damned uncomfortable and out of her depth. "I wonder how many women he's bent over that desk."

Jenny's horrified laugh-snort rang out.

Sammy's filter had apparently malfunctioned yet again. Her ever-ready, full-body flush chose that precise moment to engage. She shot a quick glance at the god and realized he had been too far away to hear her remark—*unless* he had superhuman hearing, and then all bets were off.

A frown marred Gabriel's movie-star good looks. Sammy cringed. He'd heard the inappropriate snicker from his assistant but not the reason for it. She hoped he didn't reprimand Jenny once she was gone.

He offered up his hand to shake in greeting, nodded his dismissal to Jenny, then gestured to the leather armchair across from him. He perched on the corner of his desk, one muscular leg swinging, the movement straining the seams of his slacks, while the other leg supported his weight. Gabriel got right down to business.

"Ms. Holt, I've read through the charges against you, and I'm convinced we can plead this down, if not get it dismissed altogether."

"What's the catch?"

"No catch. I need to run this by the DA's office. However, I think there is something you can do in good faith that will help me get this settled."

"I believe they call that a catch, Mr. James," she said sardonically.

Sammy waited for the other shoe to drop. That was the way her life was going lately. Shoes were dropping so fast and furious, it felt like a torrential downpour.

As he sat, silent and waiting, Sammy decided, if anyone could help her, Gabriel James could. The man intimidated the hell out of her. Under that piercing silver stare, Sammy was ready to confess to all of her sins—and cop to a few she hadn't even done yet.

"What do I need to do?"

His smile, when it came, resembled a cat who had caught its prey. Satisfied. Triumphant. She was surprised his tail wasn't twitching.

When his eyes narrowed, a shiver chased down her spine.

"You need to see a mental health specialist. *Today.* My assistant has set up an appointment for you for this afternoon. His name is Dr. Stephen Montgomery, and he's one of the best in his field."

"I don't need a damned shrink!" Sammy snapped as she jumped to her feet.

She was halfway to the exit when Gabriel's next words halted her in her tracks. "If you walk out that door, I can promise you no lawyer in a hundred-mile radius is going to touch your case."

"Oh? And how do you know that?"

"Because I will see to it," he smiled.

Sammy decided that uber-white, toothy smile was far more shark-like than cat-like.

"You can't do that!"

"Oh, but I can."

The rug had been pulled out from under her, and once again, she experienced a sense of falling. "Why? Why are you doing this?" she croaked.

GABRIEL LOOKED AT THE BRISTLING YOUNG WOMAN STANDING IN FRONT of him. He wasn't sure what he'd initially expected when Margaret told him her story. Perhaps someone with a nose piercing and pink hair like her daughter, Kaley? The Samantha Holt who'd arrived at the memorial service last week was decidedly not who he'd pictured. Neither was the woman facing him now. Yes, defiance lurked underneath the surface, but Gabe suspected it held her together during her grief. Or what should be her grief.

Her sister had informed him Samantha refused to accept her lover's death. None of the Holt family knew how to get through to her. The stunt she'd pulled at the church wasn't normal for her, but they feared it would happen again if she didn't deal with her frustration and rage over the loss.

He'd met with her family in private before agreeing to represent her. Gabe wanted a good grasp on his client's mental state. The Holts cared a great deal and appeared to want the best for Samantha. It had been a unanimous decision to get her help.

"Your family is worried about you."

Gabe knew he had made a mistake the second the words left his mouth. Her expression said as much.

"*My family.* Nice. When did you meet with my family?"

It was Samantha's turn to be cold. Gabe had to admit she did it well.

"Yesterday."

"Go fuck yourself, asshole," she spat.

He should have been ticked off by her attitude, but she amused him. It was similar to watching a tiny kitten get its back up and jump sideways. "Don't you have the potty mouth?" Not expecting her to turn pale and drop into a faint, Gabe reacted too late to catch her as she fell. "*Jesus!* Jenny! Get in here!"

By the time his assistant rushed into the office, he'd already scooped up Samantha and settled her on the sofa along the far wall.

"Call 911 and find some ice to put on her head. She fell pretty hard."

With phone in hand, he dialed Margaret and was giving her the specifics when Samantha awoke.

"What the hell?" she yelled.

Gabriel never saw the fist coming.

"*Son of a bitch!*" He held his nose—correction, his *bleeding* nose—with one hand while he stared at her in stunned disbelief. He'd been at the service for her boyfriend as a friend to Margaret and knew

Samantha was quick with her fists. Why he was surprised she'd socked him was anyone's guess.

"Gabe? Gabriel?" Margaret's frantic voice could be heard over the speakerphone. "What's going on?"

"Your crazy-ass sister just punched me in the fucking face is what's going on."

"Seriously?" Margaret's sputtering laughter was the last thing he expected.

"Seriously. Get here," he barked and disconnected the call.

SAMMY CRAB-CRAWLED BACK THE LENGTH OF THE SOFA, OUT OF Gabriel's reach. The man had been looming over her when she woke up, and seeing him so close had startled her to such a degree that she reacted badly—*again*. She tended to physically strike out in her fear, and poor Gabe's nose was the unsuspecting victim this time around.

"I'm sorry. Truly. I just... you... yeah, well you can't scare me like that."

"No shit," he grumbled, looking from the blood on his hand to the blood on his shirt.

He tipped his head back to stem the flow. "Christ! Save me from damsels in distress."

She noted his vexed countenance, and an inappropriate giggle escaped. It was a twisted side effect of going from terrified to horrified. Sammy struck, then she would break out in nervous laughter. It happened *every single time*.

"Michael always says I'm not great to have around in a crisis for that very reason. I tend to find things inappropriately funny," she explained when he gave her a disbelieving look.

At his frown, she threw her hand over her mouth, hoping to stem any more hilarity. Old Gabriel James didn't appear as if he were the type to appreciate it.

It was the scene Deputy Eric Daniels walked in on.

"Jeez, Sammy. You are causing me serious paperwork lately."

"You're on a first-name basis with the cops?" Gabriel asked, stunned.

"I can explain…"

As Sammy proceeded to tell them she hadn't been expecting Gabriel to use "potty mouth," which was a frequent endearment of Michael's, she experienced a pang of loneliness. *Michael.* The faint could only be blamed on a lack of food mixed with the stress of the situation concerning his disappearance. As for hitting Gabriel, well, who lurked over someone like that? He was a beast of a man and scary to a disoriented woman who was only five-three.

After the paramedics checked out his nose and Sammy's head, Gabriel had Jenny reschedule his appointments for the rest of the day. Apparently, his nose wasn't as hard as her head, and he needed to have it reset.

Gabe muttered about having a bone to pick with Margie when she showed up just as the first responders were leaving and greeted Deputy Daniels like an old friend. Unsure why this aggravated Gabriel more than being punched by her, Sammy waved him off.

Daniels left when Gabe assured him no assault charges were necessary. Once the room cleared of everyone but Sammy, Margie, and himself, Gabe seemed to decide it was the perfect time to light into Margie.

"You didn't tell me your sister was looney tunes," he ranted as he paced. "She broke my damn nose! *My nose!*"

Margie's snort triggered Sammy's giggle. It was no great family secret the Holts were a passionate, bloodthirsty lot. They were all reactive to a large degree. Before long, both sisters were hugging their stomachs and each other as tears of mirth rolled down their cheeks.

"Are you two honestly going to sit there and laugh at this situation?" Gabriel asked with icy disdain.

"Oh, Gabe, get the stick out of your ass."

Three heads whipped around to gaze at the man who leaned against the doorframe. He had dark hair, with twinkling mocha eyes to match, and he was grinning from ear to ear, doing nothing to suppress his own amusement.

"Stephen." Gabriel gave a brief nod in greeting. "Impeccable timing, as usual."

The sarcasm wasn't lost on his best friend, because his grin widened.

"So which one of you is my new patient, and which one is the neighbor?" Stephen asked.

Margie had the nerve to raise her hand.

"I would be the neighbor," she stated with a residual giggle.

Gabriel shot her a heated look.

The sparks between him and her sister weren't lost on Sammy. At first glance, they were an unlikely pairing, the lawyer and the soccer mom. Upon further reflection, they might just be what the other needed. Their unfolding relationship would be interesting to watch. Margie would lead Gabe on a merry chase.

"Stephen, may I introduce you to Margaret Holt, my pain-in-the-ass neighbor." At Margie's dirty look, he pointed to Sammy. "And this is Samantha Holt, your new patient. Watch that one; she has a wicked right hook. Ladies, this is Dr. Stephen Montgomery. Margaret and I will leave you two alone for the evaluation."

Any leftover amusement Sammy felt, quickly vanished. Resentment filled its place. She was extremely tired of everyone assuming they knew what was in her best interests. She understood her family cared, but forced therapy was a massive step over the line.

Lips sealed, she sat back on the sofa with her arms crossed. Dr. Montgomery took the seat directly opposite her, reached into a computer bag, and pulled out a pad and pen.

They remained in relative silence for two or three minutes before Sammy told him, "I didn't agree to this."

"No? Then why am I here?"

She shrugged. "Busybodies?"

"You and your sister were having a nice laugh at Gabe's expense. Do you frequently go around bloodying people's noses?"

"Don't try to make small talk. Ask your damned questions, and let's get this over with."

He noted that with a simple scratch of his pen and moved on to the main questions he needed to know.

"Tell me about Michael."

"What do you want to know?"

"It's my understanding you don't believe he's dead. Why is that?"

She paused. How did she explain it in terms that didn't make her seem completely mental? She sighed heavily. Regardless of what she said, he wouldn't believe her, and she'd come out of this looking like a head case. But in for a penny, in for a pound, right?

"Because he isn't."

"Care to elaborate?"

"I would know," Sammy stated confidently, secure in her abilities since the details Deputy Daniels had provided matched those of her dream.

He made another notation and asked, "Wasn't his body shipped back to you for burial?"

"*A* body was. *Not* Michael's."

"How can you be sure it wasn't his?"

"Michael and I have a connection. We are bonded in a weird metaphysical way..." Sammy paused and tried to formulate the correct response. How did she explain the difference in touch from what was important to her to what wasn't? The body in that casket didn't have the right vibe. Giving up, she stressed, *"I would know."*

Sammy watched as Dr. Montgomery scribbled more in-depth notes. Initially, she hadn't intended to tell him a single thing. He had such a compelling way about him that she found herself opening up. It would probably be to her own detriment. But oddly enough, he was the only one so far who hadn't looked at her like she *was* crazy. She smirked at her own thoughts and saw his eyebrows shoot up in question. Sammy shook her head, having no intention of going there.

"Do you believe in the paranormal, Doc?"

She could see her question caught him off guard.

"No."

At his blunt answer, she merely nodded. She almost wished Annie was present so she might decipher his energy. Sammy would delight in his reaction to her sister's findings. Without a doubt, Annie's gift would shake him up. It usually spooked anyone subjected to it.

"Do you believe people can have precognitive images or dreams about an event?"

"Do you?"

"I asked you first."

She tried not to be testy, she really did, but the whole avoidance thing, where psychiatrists tossed questions back at you to delve deeper into your brain, annoyed her. Sammy had to get him to see things from her perspective. An open mind was essential. She hoped like hell he had one.

"Fair enough. I can't say that I do. There have been patients during the life of my career who believed they were psychic. They weren't. Each of their 'visions' was either a blatant lie or disproved."

"How?"

"How what?"

"How did you disprove them? What were their visions about? Maybe the timing was just off."

"What are you trying to say, Ms. Holt? Are you telling me you believe you are psychic?"

"No. I don't believe I am," she said with a wry smile. Sammy knew her next words would cut her own throat. "I know I am."

"Have you ever been wrong?"

His question was legit. Why it bothered her, she didn't know. Or maybe she did. If she were being honest with herself, she couldn't claim she'd never been wrong. Because for all the times she'd predicted events, there was the odd occasion or two that it hadn't happened. Rare, but nonetheless, she *had* been mistaken. She was in deep trouble. This she sensed with every fiber of her being.

CHAPTER 15

Three days later, Sammy strolled up the drive to Margie's house. The usual cast of characters gathered there with the added bonus of Gabriel James and Dr. Stephen Montgomery. She sensed she wasn't going to be thrilled about the outcome of this little shindig. It reeked of intervention. Sure, they'd all tried to hide the fact it was a let's-save-Sammy-from-herself party by making it look like a family luncheon. Only a complete idiot would be blind to the real reason for this impromptu get-together. Good grief, they were a relentless bunch.

She caught the eye of her niece, Kaley, and saw the younger girl gesture to the group huddled together with a nod of her head and roll of her eyes. At least one person was still on her side.

Sammy grinned at the girl with pink hair and nose ring. She decided then and there to make Kaley godmother to her child. At only fourteen, she had it going on. Not only did she have a genius IQ, but she embodied mellow, down-to-earth qualities. Definitely a good influence for Sammy's baby. Hopefully, Kaley would never have to step up into a role of caring for her child other than in the capacity of favorite cousin. Making a face at her niece, she strode over to the table where the food was laid out. Might as well stuff herself before things got ugly and her appetite abandoned her.

Distracted by triple-chocolate brownies, she hadn't paid attention to Dr. Montgomery's approach. It wasn't until Sammy felt the touch at her elbow that she became aware of him.

She held up a hand. "You are going to have to wait until my lil' peanut has had some sustenance. Today is the first day I've felt hungry in weeks, and I plan to make the best of it." She took a huge bite of brownie. "*Ohdeargod!* You have got to try this."

She shoved the other half of the dessert into his mouth. Giving him no choice but to chew or choke. Preferably choke.

"Am I right?" she demanded, walking off before he answered.

A snickering Kaley met her by another table. Maybe a little fun could be salvaged today after all. She scooped up a huge helping of macaroni salad as her niece laughingly proclaimed Sammy her hero.

Stephen liked Samantha Holt. Sure, at first glance, she appeared a little mentally off, but she retained a certain spark for life, and it made her all the more entertaining. And she was right; the brownies *were* divine. As he chewed, he thought perhaps she wasn't as delusional as he'd originally surmised. After leaving her on Wednesday afternoon, Stephen took to the internet, googling all the events she had described to him. He perused the notes he'd taken and compared them to the articles he found.

Explaining them all away had been fairly simple *until* he talked to her sisters. They corroborated her story. She did indeed have dreams in the week prior to each incident. Still unable to completely buy into Samantha's precognitive abilities, he put all thoughts of anything beyond the scope of normal on the back burner. The real issue here was her refusal to accept the death of her lover. That, at least, the family could agree upon.

Samantha would be displeased with the agreement Gabriel and the DA had settled on to appease the news station employee and Pastor Simms. Stephen worried what effect the ninety days in Brookhaven

Mental Health Clinic would have on her. Without a doubt, she needed therapy, but Stephen disagreed with having her admitted. Her personality would rebel against the confinement. It might even be detrimental. He had tried to explain his reasoning, but the DA, a close friend of Simms's wife, had been adamant. No amount of arguing would budge her. The choice had been between Brookhaven or Samantha spending one hundred twenty days in jail along with paying a hefty fine. Personally, he suspected the District Attorney was a hardass because of the upcoming election year.

"Are you ready to talk to Samantha?" Gabe's sharp tone gave him a start.

Stephen had been concentrating on his new patient and lost all sense of his surroundings. He frowned. Because he worked at a mental hospital, attention to his environment was a must.

"Sure. Is the rest of the family already in the living room?"

"Yes. We are waiting on the two of you."

With a nod, Stephen followed him to where Samantha lounged, talking to her niece. She stiffened. Upon seeing their approach, she leaned in to whisper something to Kaley. The girl grinned, wicked delight lighting her face. Whatever Sammy had said about them was not favorable. It didn't take a psychiatrist to figure that one out.

Sammy looked at Gabe, a hint of challenge in her eyes. "How's the nose?"

SAMMY LOOKED AROUND THE TABLE AND QUICKLY REALIZED EVERY member of her family was waiting for her explosion. Her mother eyed her with apprehension. The wary expression caused Sammy to reflect on her actions from the time the dreams had started until today. She couldn't say they were wrong to insist on therapy. Perhaps she was a bit off the rails, emotionally speaking. It did hurt, however, that they had so little faith in her. None of them had believed her in the beginning even though she was proven right, and none of them had confidence in her ability to run her own life now.

Sadness and a sense of isolation swept her. She wanted so very badly to cry. The burning in her nose and throat almost choked her. It was likely the pregnancy, but Sammy felt highly emotional and exhausted.

"Can I have a week to make arrangements for my dog and resign my job? I have some other things to finish up as well."

She almost broke, thinking about Sassy. Three months was an eternity to abandon her fuzzy baby. With Michael gone and now with Sammy forced to spend time at a hospital, her poor pup would think her pack had deserted her.

"You have until noon Wednesday to voluntarily check yourself in," Gabe informed her.

"But that's a week before Christmas. They couldn't wait until after the holidays?" Violet asked, visibly upset. Christmas and family were important to her.

"I'm afraid the justice system doesn't recognize Christmas as a reason to put off incarceration." Gabe's sarcastic response annoyed the ever-loving hell out of Sammy. He shot her a warning look as if he discerned her desire to punch him in the face again. "If you don't show up, a warrant will go out for your arrest."

"You have got to be kidding me! *Christ.* It isn't like I'm a career criminal." She shook her head in disgust. When he would have commented, she waved him off. "Whatever. Wednesday will be soon enough."

"Why would you have to resign your job?" Stephen asked quietly.

"You're joking, right?" At the negative shake of his head, she continued, "Although I've been with my current company for a few years, I've only just started the job as manager. With this company, starting a new position requires a new probationary period. They can dismiss me for any reason during that time. I would think missing the *entire* probationary period might be a red flag. I've already missed a good portion of the last month due to Michael's disappearance, and the... *situations* associated with it. My television debut didn't reflect favorably on me either. I will see what might be covered under the FMLA, but I'm not hopeful."

Gabe had the grace to look embarrassed by this. Sammy glanced at Annie. Her sister seemed to be fascinated by him. She must have detected something off in his energy. The woman was a human lie detector.

"What do you feel, Annie?" she asked, clearly startling her sister. Sammy had never put her sister on the spot or spoke of her ability to outsiders.

"Guilt. He feels guilty."

The attorney's expression froze. He regarded Annie as if she had two heads.

"Hmmm. Makes one wonder what he has to feel guilty about," Sammy said snidely, causing him to shift his cold, gunmetal-gray gaze to her. "Didn't try so hard to get the charges dismissed, did you? Is that why you didn't cash my retainer? You felt guilty for not doing your job, Mr. James?"

Mainly, she'd said it to needle Gabriel. His cloak of arrogance made her feel the need to poke at him. A flash of hurt came and went on his face before it settled into an icy mask. Maybe she'd crossed a line by insulting his work ethic. The man had pride. Perhaps too much of it. One thing he would not do was sandbag a client.

"I'm sorry. I'm sure you did your best."

Graciously, he accepted her apology, but not before he clarified a few things.

"I didn't cash your retainer for reasons of my own, which have nothing to do with you." His eyes flicked to Margie's. A hot light flared in them before he tamped it down. He returned his gaze to Sammy's face. "As for feeling guilty, I was mainly embarrassed by how poorly I judged you. I try never to do that. Your situation has made me realize I've much to be grateful for."

Sammy rose to her feet and patted him on the shoulder. "I'm sorry for being a bitch, Gabe. I appreciate all you've done for me," she said before turning to Dr. Montgomery and offering up a slight smile. "Doc, I guess I'll see you Wednesday at Brookhaven."

James jumped up. "I'll walk you out, Lil' Bit."

She gave her parents a quick hug, then made her way to the car with James beside her like a silent sentinel.

"What's up, Jamie?"

"I wanted to be sure you were okay."

"Why wouldn't I be? My boyfriend went on a business trip and disappeared. My family thinks I'm crazy and need to be locked away. There is a huge probability I am going to lose my job. And oh yeah, I'm pregnant. I'm just fan-freaking-tastic. No worries." Sammy was sarcastic and bitter. She couldn't find it in her to be anything less. "At least my stay at the funny farm will allow me to get away from all of *you*. Do you think it's any great picnic, being smothered to death by well-meaning family? To be pitied or made to feel like the proverbial problem child all the time?"

"Sammy, you're being overly dramatic. We're all worried. Michael has been a large part of your life. I get that it's hard, but by refusing to accept his death, you are scaring everyone. None of us know how to help you."

"*I don't want your goddamn help!*" She inhaled deeply and shook her head. "Not if it means letting go of him. Don't ask that of me, Jamie. I can't do it. I just can't," she ended on a broken whisper.

James gave her a gentle shake, trying to penetrate the wall she'd erected around her mind and heart.

"He's dead, Sammy. Time to face some fucking facts. Don't you think I miss him, too? He was my best friend. I miss him every damned day. But he's *gone*." He gave her another small shake to emphasize his words.

She tore out of his grasp and shoved him hard. He grunted but never budged.

"You don't know what the hell you're talking about," she snarled. "He *isn't* dead. I would know. Jamie, I swear I would know."

CHAPTER 16

*W*ednesday arrived and brought with it a monstrous thunderstorm. Extreme even for Florida standards. *A portent of things to come?*

Sammy shuddered. Sure, everyone had bad things happen to them, but ever since Michael left on that cursed trip, Sammy's life had tilted so far off-kilter, she feared she'd never find her balance again.

It was fitting that today would be the day she started her stint in the psych ward. Four weeks ago, Michael had left for Dallas. Wednesday would be her new hated day of the week and not just because it was hump day. Now, she could add the mental hospital to the list of reasons why Wednesdays sucked.

Brookhaven was a bit more upscale than a state hospital, but the stigma of this would continue to follow her throughout life. She would be forever known as crazy and weak. Strong individuals didn't have breakdowns, or so most people wrongly believed. Her family would handle her with kid gloves from this point on, always wondering if or when she would snap again.

Sammy wanted to hop on a plane to another country and leave this mess far behind. But if Michael returned—and she desperately prayed he would—he wouldn't know where to find her.

James whipped into the driveway right on time, effectively destroying her half-baked plan to flee. He'd been volunteered by the Holts to see she got to the clinic by the designated hour for Sammy to avoid jail time. He'd also relented to the pressure to house-sit for her. As he didn't have so much as a plant to worry about killing, and she had a whole jungle in her house that needed constant care along with sweet little Sassy, Sammy appreciated his sacrifice. James, savvy businessman he was, sublet his two-bedroom condo to a couple of snowbirds for the next three months. He had figured he might as well make a quick dime for his inconvenience, and she admired his financial smarts.

Sammy clutched Sassy to her one last time and rained kisses down on her adorable, fuzzy head. Goodbye was difficult. Rulebreaker she was, she debated the idea of smuggling her pup into the facility. She squashed the thought.

"Come on, Sammy. We have to go." James picked up her bag and scratched Sassy behind one ear. "I promise to take good care of her."

The admission process was fairly simple and over quickly. Sammy's toiletry bag had been thoroughly searched and a few items, like her razor, disposed of. Although she hated hairy legs, she had no one to impress. She could also understand the need to keep sharp objects out of the hands of the patients. It might be too tempting to self-harm or slash their way to freedom.

James left Sammy in the foyer after delivering a bear hug and making her promise to call if she needed anything. She shrugged off his assurances that the family would be there on visiting days. She honestly didn't care anymore. All she wanted was to do her time and vacate the premises.

An orderly named Dale showed Sammy to the private room that would be hers for the duration of her stay. He instructed her to change into the light blue scrubs at the foot of the bed and said her first meeting with Dr. Montgomery would be in fifteen minutes. She kept reminding herself this was better than a jail cell. It became her mantra. Dale returned in precisely twelve minutes to take her to her appointment.

Following him down the corridor, Sammy made a concerted effort to stare only at his back. She refused to look around or acknowledge the stares of the other patients. It was bad enough she could feel the shift in the energy of those around her. Some were curious. Some were cold. And some were downright menacing.

STEPHEN WALKED OUT OF HIS OFFICE TO FIND SAMANTHA PACING THE waiting area. Originally, he thought her agitation might be nerves, but she rubbed her back as if it ached. Leaning against the doorframe, he took the time to unobtrusively observe her. Something was definitely off. Perhaps meeting her and seeing her as more than just a patient for their first two encounters had made him more in tuned to her. He quickly dismissed that line of thought.

"Did your check-in go smoothly?"

His question startled her. After her initial surprise, she answered, "Yes, thank you."

"Good. Shall we get started?" Stephen shifted and gestured to the interior of his office.

Once they were both seated, he went over the requirements of her stay and what was expected of her based on the DA's guidelines for her release. General Admission would have addressed the same items of behavior, but Stephen always liked to reiterate the rules and take note of a patient's reaction. Samantha seemed impatient going through the routine again but said nothing. Which was mostly progress on her part from what he could tell. She wasn't the type to keep quiet.

After he crossed those items off his list, he told her what he hoped to achieve with each session. He wanted her on board with the plan. Through it all, she remained distracted, sometimes shifting in her chair.

"Ms. Holt? Are you feeling all right?"

"It's nothing. I must have slept wrong last night. My back is a bit sore today." When he remained unconvinced, she said, "Really. I'm fine."

Accepting her words at face value, Stephen moved on to the next order of business.

"If you are feeling up to it, I would like to give you a tour of the facility and show you what amenities are available. We can start with the cafeteria if you haven't eaten lunch yet."

At her nod, he escorted her to the lunchroom. As they ate, Stephen asked her general questions about herself and avoided any serious topics that might trigger her or make her defiant. One thing he'd noticed the day of their family barbecue, the Holts were all quick to rile. The amazing aspect of their family dynamic? Everything was taken in stride as one of their own raged. All was forgiven in a matter of minutes. Stephen could make it his life's work to study that crew.

During the time they spent talking and viewing the facility, he noticed Samantha trying to hide her discomfort. "What are you not telling me?"

"Nothing." When he lifted his brow, she confessed, "I'm feeling a bit warm and achy. I must be coming down with something. Do you mind if we continue this tour another time?"

"Not at all, but I am taking you to the on-site medical center first. I want to have you checked out."

"I don't—"

"Stop fighting me at every turn. You're going. This isn't open for debate."

ALTHOUGH PIQUED BY DR. MONTGOMERY'S INSISTENCE THAT SHE BE examined by the resident general physician, Sammy was also too tired and sore to protest his high-handed attitude. With a baby in the mix, she would rather not take any chances.

After an initial exam by Dr. Monroe, both doctors concluded it was best to put her on bed rest for the next twenty-four hours.

"Ms. Holt, have you seen a gynecologist yet?" Monroe asked.

"There wasn't time. Is something wrong with my peanut?" Dread settled deep in the pit of her stomach. She became queasy. If she lost her baby, she'd lose her last link to Michael, and fear turned her blood cold.

"I want to run bloodwork to get a few preliminary tests out of the way. We have a specialist on call for female patients. I'd like to go ahead and schedule an appointment for you with her for tomorrow morning. Her name is Dr. Darah Talbot. She has office hours here on Fridays, but I don't want to wait. You are in your first trimester, and spontaneous miscarriage can happen for any number of reasons."

"Is that what's happening now? Can I do anything to prevent it?"

The moisture built behind her lids. It sounded as if he was preparing her for the worst-case scenario. Any moment, she would begin weeping copious amounts of tears and embarrass herself.

"It's why I want you on bed rest until Dr. Talbot can examine you. She's the best, Ms. Holt. If anyone can figure out what is going on with your pregnancy, she can. Until you see her, I don't want you on your feet. You can use the restroom, then it is back in bed with your legs up. Understood?"

The kindness in his old faded-blue eyes spoke to Sammy. He reminded her of the grandfather she'd lost when she was a young teen. She still missed him terribly. Without a second thought, Sammy threw herself into the arms of the older doctor and hugged him tight. Awkwardly, he patted her on the back. Quite possibly a bit uncomfortable by her spontaneity.

"Thank you."

"You're welcome, dear. Now relax for a bit. The nurse will be in shortly."

AFTER SEEING SAMANTHA WHEELED TO AND SECURE IN HER ROOM, Stephen stopped by the nurses' station to provide detailed instructions. He encountered Rob, the one Brookhaven employee he disliked.

Stephen stalled in hopes another nurse or orderly would appear at the desk and he wouldn't have to deal with the guy. Taking his time, he wrote up his notes for the day on his laptop. Finally, with no real choice, he addressed the lazy bastard who annoyed him to no end. He really needed to discuss the hiring of new staff with HR. Rob wasn't cutting it.

"The patient in room two-twenty-eight is Samantha Holt. She's a new arrival today. I want her checked every two hours by the RN on duty. No excuses. If Ms. Holt pages this station, she is to get emergency care ASAP. I don't care what anyone is involved in; she's a priority. Her situation is precarious, and she is on bed rest for her pregnancy until further notice."

The sparkle that lit Rob's eyes made Stephen uneasy. He appeared gleeful to hear the news of Samantha's condition.

"Is something amusing?" Stephen's hard tone quickly wiped the expression off the orderly's face. Quite possibly, the stony countenance the orderly now possessed disturbed Stephen even more. *Hate.* It had flashed for an instant before Rob could hide it. There was something seriously wrong here. Stephen was sure of it. This guy required watching, and that's just what he would do.

A CHILL SWEPT ACROSS THE EXPOSED SKIN OF SAMMY'S ARMS AS THE lock to her door disengaged. To say she was surprised when Rob Marks stepped into her room early that evening would be a gross understatement. The chill turned to body-wracking shivers, and all her internal warning bells began to clang. She swayed as she stood to face him.

Not good.

He was dressed as one of the clinic workers.

Who the hell would put such an evil twatwaffle in charge of mentally ill people?

When the second orderly stepped in, real panic began to rear its ugly little head.

She recognized him as the same man who had directed her to Dr. Montgomery's office earlier. It didn't take a psychic to know these two intended a sinister act. The darkness surrounding them was as black as their hearts. One man she might have fought off, but two? This was not going to turn out well for her.

Her hand instinctively went to cradle her abdomen.

"Rob. Long time no see. Looks like you survived my brother's beating."

Flippant apparently wasn't the right way to go if his purple, enraged face was a true indicator. If Sammy possessed one serious flaw next to laughing when nervous, it was sarcasm when cornered. A switch would flip, and trash talk just poured out of her mouth.

She shot a furtive glance toward the call button on the wall by the bed. She lunged for it only to be jerked to a halt mere inches from her goal.

"You little bitch. You are seriously going to pay for the humiliation your family caused me," Rob ground out.

"You caused your own problems, Rob. Your obsession and refusal to accept no were your biggest issues. Apparently, they still are."

His body radiated with fury. "Hold her, Dale."

An involuntary scream escaped her as Dale forced her arm up between her shoulder blades. The excitement he felt from holding her was clearly evident in the budding erection he pressed against her backside. The hand not pinning her left arm had found its way under her shirt. He gripped her right breast, squeezing hard.

She gasped and tried to headbutt him, but the top of her head wasn't anywhere close to his chin.

Dale's grip brought with it image after image of all the despicable acts he had perpetrated on patients. He didn't appear to be selective in his victims. Male or female, anyone weak enough would do.

Violent shudders of revulsion shook Sammy, and her teeth began to chatter. Blinking back hot tears, she tried to reason with the man holding her. It might be futile, but it was worth a shot.

"You d-don't have to do this, Dale. D-Dale's your name, isn't it? Whatever Rob t-told you, promised you, however he hoped t-to hide this, you *will* get in trouble. How do you expect to c-cover it up? My family will..."

A vicious twist of her nipple disrupted her speech and gave her a clear indication of his answer.

"You don't have a boyfriend or brother to stop me this time, Sammy," Rob taunted.

She spit in his face. Better to go down fighting than quietly submit to what these two planned for her. The blow to her stomach was unexpected and excruciating. Breathing became impossible as agony ripped through her entire torso. Her vision went dark, and she lost all awareness.

Upon regaining her senses, she registered Rob had her top ripped almost in two and currently worked the knot on her bottoms. His rancid breath was doing nothing to stop her from gagging. Nausea threatened with a vengeance.

She couldn't even bend to protect her belly, or her shoulder would be dislocated. Sammy inhaled a deep breath to scream only to be thwarted when Rob anticipated the action and cuffed her on the chin. Her teeth rattled in her head. She began to struggle in earnest. Kicking, biting, and scratching whatever she could reach. If Dale tore her shoulder from its socket, so be it. Not trying to save herself wasn't an option. She almost connected her knee with Rob's family jewels, but he dodged to the side with a few choice words for his partner in crime. He followed it up with a "Hold her still, goddammit!"

Stephen had worked later that night to make up for the time he lost taking Samantha for her exam. He intended to check on her once more before he left for the night. An incoming text had him pausing outside her door.

If it hadn't been for working past his normal hours and for that text, he would never have heard her muffled exclamation of pain or the barked words to "Hold her still, goddammit!"

He rushed to a landline and placed a call to security, then he hauled ass back to her room to scan his ID badge. He hauled Rob off Samantha and followed with a fist to the orderly's face. Rob's eyes rolled up into his head as the floor rose up to greet him. Dale shoved

Samantha directly in Stephen's path and ran for the door. Unfortunately for him, security entered at that precise moment and halted his escape.

"Call the police. I want them both cuffed and in custody. See that the officer charges them with assault and attempted rape. Also, get some *trustworthy* staff to fill in for these two tonight," Stephen barked the orders as he covered Samantha with a blanket. "It wouldn't hurt my feelings if they resisted arrest and obtained a few bruises in the process of being subdued."

"They've done it before," Samantha croaked. "I saw... many times... many patients..."

He stared down into her paper-white face. Her blue eyes looked almost black and were nothing short of haunted.

Over his shoulder, he addressed the remaining security member. "I want you to pull all the tapes for whenever these two have been scheduled to work. If there are any complaints from patients or co-workers, I want those as well."

Taking one look at Samantha's hunched form, he whipped out his cell and called Dr. Monroe, hoping to catch him before he left for the day.

Monroe promised to call Dr. Talbot after he heard what had taken place. Stephen scooped her up and headed for the in-house clinic.

THE MISCARRIAGE HAPPENED WITHIN TWO HOURS AFTER HER ATTACK. Devastated, Sammy was too empty to cry. It seemed as if the last of her life left her at the same moment her baby did. Now, if Michael never returned, she had nothing.

She listened to the doctor's assurances that the miscarriage probably would have happened anyway. Her body had been trying to spontaneously abort the baby since earlier in the day. Deep down, she knew the attack on her person had been the final straw.

Dr. Montgomery must've contacted her parents because her mother hovered next to her bed, grief written all over her face as she held Sammy's limp hand. She couldn't form the words to communicate her desire to be left alone. All she could do was stare at the dull white ceiling tiles. Even blinking was too much of an effort.

Dimly, as if from far away, she heard her mother speak. "What's wrong with her? Why is she just lying there like she's frozen?"

"She's suffered a shock, Mrs. Holt. Time to heal is what she needs most," Dr. Monroe kindly explained. "We'll monitor her closely and notify you of any changes."

If any of the rest of her family visited, she didn't know or care to acknowledge them. Retreating into her own mind proved safest. Nothing bad could touch her in that world She welcomed the oblivion brought on by the pain medication.

Sammy dreamed of Michael that night.

He was smiling as he always did when he came home. "Hi, darlin'," he said in his warm Southern drawl.

She wanted to respond with her usual "hi." Wanted to fling herself into his arms and never let go. Wanted to find out why he hadn't visited her dreams since the first few nights after he was declared dead. Seeing him standing there, so real, so alive, brought forth the loneliness she'd suffered since he went away. No words would come. How did she explain all that she'd been through?

"Are you not going to talk to me, Sammy Darlin'?" he teased, breaking through her reticence.

"Michael," she said on a sigh. "Oh, Michael."

They embraced. His arms were warmer, more welcoming than she remembered. Or maybe she'd yearned too long, too desperately, for his touch. Hugging him was like coming home.

"God, I missed you. What the hell is going on? When are you coming back?"

Her eyes traced his features and soaked in all the rugged handsomeness. It became impossible to keep her hands to herself. The need to touch him, to prove to herself he was real, prevailed.

His countenance turned grim. "I don't know."

"What does that mean? Where are you? You're alive. I know you are. You are, right? I don't want this to just be a dream." What had started as demanding, ended on a weepy whisper. "Please don't let this just be a dream."

"Does it matter if it is? We're both here. Together." Michael's words were tender, and they broke her heart.

Sammy didn't answer. Couldn't. All she could do, all she had energy for, was to cling to him. To listen to the sound of his heart, steady and strong. They stayed like that for what seemed like hours. Neither speaking. Taking comfort in each other's presence.

After a time, the words poured from her. Not dissimilar to a runaway train. Those words, they refused to be stopped. She told him about her forced hospital stay. Of what had led her to be there. Of Rob's attack. Finally, of the loss of their baby. He held her and cried with her. Rocked her and soothed her as nothing and no one else could. More time elapsed. Sammy was exhausted. A deeper sleep beckoned.

"Sammy, I have to go."

"No," she growled.

Michael chuckled. Ah, she remembered that beautiful sound well. She cherished it above all others.

Gently, he disentangled himself from her. Raising both hands to cradle her face for one last tender kiss. His lips clung to hers. The kiss of a reluctant goodbye.

"I have to go, love."

"No." This was more tearful, fearful. "If you go now, you won't come back to me."

"That's not true, darlin'," his voice sounded distant, fainter. "Be strong. You'll find me, Sammy. I know you will."

CHAPTER 17

*J*ames was reclining in the downstairs guest room of
Sammy's house when he heard a door slam. It startled
him from a light doze. It wasn't the first time. It had been
happening for the better part of the month he resided here.

He didn't rush to get up. He knew what he would find if he did:
Michael's spirit.

The strange scene played over and over every evening like a
broken record or a never-ending movie. It didn't disturb him as it
should have to see Michael return to his home each night. After all,
Michael had been happiest here when he was alive.

What *did* bother him was seeing Sammy's spirit run to embrace
Michael's.

The first time it happened, James had called Brookhaven and
demanded they check on his sister. He'd never seen a ghost while the
host body was still living. After the nurse reported the all's well, he sat
down in disbelief. He'd quickly dressed and headed to the clinic to see
the truth for himself. Sure enough, Sammy rested peacefully in her
room. More still than he had ever seen anyone sleep, but sleeping
nonetheless.

He shook her and attempted to wake her. His sister had always crashed like the dead. But now, it brought unease. It was imperative he speak with her. If only to convince himself she was okay. He shook her again, a little rougher this time. A peep of protest escaped the nurse.

"What's wrong with her? Is she drugged?" he demanded when he failed to wake her.

"No." At his look, she raised her hands as if to defend herself. "No, I swear."

The apprehension in the nurse's eyes forced him to check his temper. James could be foul when the mood struck.

Yet spirits were spirits for a reason. They had abandoned their bodies. Sometimes it was spontaneous, as in death. Other times it was done deliberately, during deeper, darker practices. James hadn't thought his sister knew of such things. Maybe she'd learned tools over time to help deal with her premonitions. If she practiced this, he intended to put a stop to it. There were consequences to dabbling in the darker arts.

"Sammy, I need you to wake up. Come on, Lil' Bit. Wake up for me," James tried to cajole. Her lack of response alarmed him. "Dammit, Samantha. Wake up! *Right now!*"

From the corner of his eye, he caught the nurse backing toward the door. Why the hell did she look so guilty?

He stalked to where she stood. "What aren't you telling me?"

"Nothing," she chirped in her fright.

"You're lying. *Out with it, woman!*"

"Your parents didn't want you to know. They…"

His eyes burned into her. He silently promised retribution.

The nurse, helpless and beyond afraid, confessed. "Ms. Holt was attacked by two of our orderlies. Then she… she lost her baby," she squeaked out.

The air was sucked from his lungs. He glanced back at his sister, noting the pale, almost translucent look of her skin. "I don't care what time it is, you get Dr. Montgomery here. *Immediately!* Or I'm taking her out of here."

With a mumbled "of course," she hurried from the room to do as he bid.

James moved to the foot of the bed. Sammy hadn't so much as twitched. Sagging against the wall, he took deep breaths and worked to regain some semblance of control. The vicious desire to kill somebody swamped him. How could his parents keep something of this magnitude from him?

While waiting for Dr. Montgomery, James tried to get through to Sammy. He spent the remainder of the time pacing, waiting for answers. By the time her doctor finally arrived, James had worked himself into a fine frenzy. He charged over and gripped Stephen's collar.

"What the fuck is going on with Sammy? *No bullshit!*"

"Mr. Holt, I need you to calm down. I understand your concern, and I'll tell you everything, but not if you are going to threaten me or my staff."

Dr. Montgomery was stern and no-nonsense. James respected his cool demeanor. With great effort, he reined in his excess of emotion. He stretched his neck to his chest and inhaled deeply. A little less agitated, he cast the doctor a rueful look.

"This is as calm as I'm going to get, Doc. Spill."

"All right but not here. My office."

As James followed Dr. Montgomery through the hallways, the beige-papered walls expanded, contracted, and pulsed with the spirits of the past. They threatened to close in on him. Patients had died here. Their souls lingered and waited for a justice that never came.

Jesus! What the hell did Sammy feel if he experienced this after only seconds in these haunted halls? Was she hiding in a self-induced-type of coma to avoid the constant waves of sensations she must have received from this wretched place?

He rubbed the tiredness from his eyes. After he was seated, the doctor explained the circumstances surrounding Sammy's attack.

"*Rob Marks?* Who the hell hires a weasel to guard prized hens?"

"We do extensive background checks on all employees. He had no priors, and all his references were glowing," Stephen told him stiffly.

"Was that son of a bitch the reason she lost the baby?" James asked, his voice hoarse and tight even to his own ears.

"It didn't help, but no. She had been having problems earlier in the day. It is the medical opinion of both our staff GP and specialist that there was a high probability she would have miscarried anyway. Spontaneous abortion is what it's called. It happens when conditions in the womb are not ideal. Genetically, something was off with the fetus."

"To clarify, this happened the day she checked in?"

"Yes."

"When were my parents notified?"

"Within a half hour of the incident."

"*Incident?* That's rich. So they knew, and for the last week, they lied to me."

Dr. Montgomery said nothing. He didn't need to.

James sat forward, hands steepled over his nose and mouth, and attempted to control his fury. Yesterday had been Christmas. The whole family had gathered for an early dinner. His parents had acted as if they didn't have a worry in the world. He replayed the day in his mind. Annie might know. She had been quiet through it all. Although to be fair, it wasn't unusual for her to be subdued at large family functions. A negative side effect of trying to stave off other people's energy. He was glad he hadn't received that particular curse, because it had to be exhausting. For sure, Margie did *not* know. His older sister didn't have the ability to hide something so huge. She was the type of person who would lead the villagers to stone the miscreants who attacked her sister.

Dr. Montgomery cleared his throat. "I know it's no consolation, but your parents have already talked to Gabriel James about filing a lawsuit against the hospital. He'll see your sister is taken care of."

"Money isn't going to bring back her child, is it?"

"I wasn't suggesting it would, but Samantha can use the settlement to tide her over after her release." The strain around the doctor's mouth and the regret in his eyes spoke volumes. He wasn't a bad man, and he truly cared about Sammy's welfare.

Dialing back his anger, James tried to understand why Sammy's spirit wandered at night. He couldn't imagine the energy it took. Like a sledgehammer, it hit him.

"What is she like during waking hours?"

The sharpening of Dr. Montgomery's gaze confirmed a suspicion.

"Why do you ask?"

"Answer the question, Doc," he bit out.

The long pause made James wonder if Stephen intended to say anything at all. However, James would wait all damned night if he had to.

With a sigh, Dr. Montgomery gave in.

"Her behavior disturbs me. She wakes up every morning and eats the food put in front of her. That's it. She doesn't look at anyone. Doesn't interact with anyone in the room. Not doctors, staff, or other patients. After breakfast, Samantha will walk to the sunroom, find an empty chair, and ignore everything happening around her. She's on a type of autopilot."

"Is she cold?"

"Yes. We keep her dressed as warmly as possible, but her skin is always cold to the touch. How did you know?"

James was now positive Sammy dreamwalked while asleep. Nothing else explained her behavior. The dangers involved in dreamwalking made him fearful. James scrambled his brain to find a way to stop her.

"Just a guess, Doc."

It wasn't. Without a doubt, Sammy left her body each night to meet Michael. Was Michael somewhere, leaving his body, or was his friend calling to Sammy from beyond?

Chilled, James rubbed his arms.

His sister would follow Michael to hell if he asked her to, but that wasn't a subject to discuss with good old, staid Dr. Montgomery. If he did, James would find himself in the room right next to Sammy's.

At present, James stood in the doorway of the guest room and silently watched as his sister embraced Michael. She was happier than he ever remembered her being. The two of them moved to the couch to cuddle and whisper their sweet nothings to each other.

James had a bit more studying up on her condition to do. He didn't have much longer to figure out how to save her. Sammy's essence was strong here, as was Michael's. Soon, maybe a month or two at the most, she would stop returning to her body in the mornings. He'd done enough research to be certain of the outcome.

And really, what did she have to return to? All she wanted was with her in the dream state.

He ruefully shook his head, belatedly realizing Sammy had assigned the right person to house-sit. Anyone else would have a freaking coronary if they heard the doors opening and closing at all hours of the night. The murmur of voices would set anyone else over the edge.

James glanced down at his sister's dog, who watched the whole interchange between her two masters with her shiny blond head tilted. Longing was in her big brown eyes. His heart hurt for the little beastie. She must feel abandoned.

"Go on. Go hang with them. Tell your parents to keep it down so I can sleep, okay?"

SAMMY WENT THROUGH THE MOTIONS AS SHE DID EACH DAY. SHE WOKE at 7:30 that morning. Dressed in the required patient uniform of scrubs, added a zip-up hoodie to ward off the constant cold, and headed to breakfast. She sat through group therapy. Spent a half hour subjected to Dr. Montgomery's attempt to pierce her fog, then wandered into the sunroom to spend the day observing dust dance on sunbeams. In her mind, she compiled all the subjects she intended to discuss with Michael that night. When it was time for bed, she went through her nightly ritual: wash her face, brush her teeth, change into pajamas. Excitement ran through her veins, and she curled up on the bed to welcome sleep and, with it, Michael.

Sammy arrived at their house first, as she frequently did. She greeted their Sassy. A smile twisted her lips at the memory of Michael naming their little pup on the day they'd first brought her home from the shelter. He said she liked to talk back, like his Sammy. He'd pretended the light punch she gave him was no peskier than a bug bite and had wrestled her to the ground. Much to the delight of Sassy, who, living up to her name, barked and gave them hell.

Grinning at the memory, Sammy continued to wander the house. It shouldn't be long. Michael usually showed up within a short time of her arrival. Of course, time differed in a dream state, but she was certain it would be mere minutes.

She took multiple walks throughout the house, becoming more unsettled with each passing moment. Most of the night flew by with no Michael. Something was wrong.

"Michael?" she called out. "Michael, are you here?"

Silence was her answer.

"Michael? If this is a game, it isn't funny!"

Frantic, she ran through the house, opening and slamming doors.

"Michael?"

"He's not here, Sammy."

She whirled around to find James standing in the middle of her living room. He stood there, rumpled and sleepy. A deep furrow marred his forehead.

"It's almost dawn. You need to go back."

"Where is he? What did you do?" she demanded.

"Sammy, you need to listen to me. You've been gone from your body too long. You have to go back."

She backed away with a violent shake of her head and ran from room to room, screaming Michael's name.

"What did you do, Jamie? *What did you do?*" When his head moved in denial, she raged. "*You did!* You had to have. Michael wouldn't leave me without a word like this."

"Lil' Bit." The nickname cut through her rising hysteria like nothing else could. "I've watched you and Michael meet for the better part of two months now. His spirit was growing dimmer. You didn't notice, but I did. He's gone. It's time for you to come back."

. . .

JAMES WATCHED HIS SISTER'S EYES GO DEAD AS SHE ACKNOWLEDGED THE truth. Perhaps she *had* noticed.

"I want to go with him," she whispered. "Why won't anyone let me go?"

A lump formed in his throat and prevented him from answering. He'd never experienced a love like theirs. Powerful. All-consuming. He wasn't sure he ever wanted to if it brought such destructive behavior as hers. He would have hugged her if she was corporeal, but at the moment, he felt completely helpless.

"Go then." James shocked his little sister along with himself. Wouldn't it be better if she died and moved on than wandered around like a damned wraith? At times, he thought so.

Oddly enough, his words pissed her off instead of offering release. Or maybe not so oddly. It made sense she'd get riled. Sammy was a fighter—at least she had been until Michael died.

"What?"

"*Go!* Just fucking go already, Sammy!" James shouted into her outraged face. He hoped like hell he could provoke her out of this apathetic state she'd settled into. "Do you honestly think anyone wants you to stay if this is what we're left with? This pathetic shell of who you were?"

"You don't get to talk to me that way. Not *you*, Jamie. You don't know what I've been through," she cried.

"Who else if not me, Sammy? No one else knows you've been dreamwalking to meet him. You got your goodbye. It was more than most people get. But now he's gone." He watched her face crumble in grief. James gentled his tone. "Oh, Lil' Bit. Come back to us now. We all miss you."

SAMMY JERKED AWAKE. THE CLOCK SHOWED SIX-FORTY-FIVE A.M. IT WAS the absolute latest she'd ever been gone. Her eyes were gritty, and exhaustion weighed heavily on her. Maybe she would rest for a bit longer. Today she didn't have the will or the energy to dress. What did it matter anyway? Jamie's harsh words washed over her but were soon forgotten. Sleep claimed her.

When next she woke, Sammy spotted James dozing in the chair on her left. If she had the energy, she would have smiled at how ridiculous his big body looked, stuffed into such a tiny chair. Light poured through the blinds, and she blinked in confusion. How long had she been sleeping? The growling of her stomach spoke of her many missed meals.

She shifted to sit up. Dizziness assailed her and laid her flat again. Damn, she was weak and achy. Deciding rest was her best option, Sammy rolled onto her side to silently observe James, curious as to why he was in her room. Had something happened to one of the family? Had he discovered what happened to Micha—No! She couldn't let her mind wander there right now. To think their connection was severed upset her too much.

Focusing all her attention on her brother, Sammy noted the tired lines of his face even at rest. Dark purple shadows under his eyes indicated little to no sleep. How long had he been able to see spirits? Why had he never said anything to any of them? Was this something else her mother had swept under the rug in her effort to not disturb their father's peace of mind?

As if sensing her regard, James opened his eyes, took a deep breath, and rubbed his palms over his face. His gaze sought hers, and his worry showed just below the surface. Sammy tried to convey that she was fine with a quick twist of her lips. Siblings had a type of body language all their own. What they felt was easily established with micro expressions.

"Good to see you back in the land of the living, Lil' Bit. You had me worried," James's voice was rough, packed full of emotion.

"Whe... when... did you...?" Sammy's voice was rusty with disuse and lack of moisture. She swallowed and tried again. "When did you start seeing spirits?"

"Seven."

"Seven months ago?"

"No. I was seven."

"How did I never know this?" she whispered, hand to throat.

James jumped up to pour water into a cup. He handed it to her and perched on the side of her bed. He took his time forming the words, and Sammy didn't push. While she waited, she guzzled her drink. The water was cool and refreshing. She could have downed a gallon, but a more pressing need was the bathroom. Not until she got answers first.

"You know we weren't encouraged to talk about our gifts growing up. When I needed someone to speak with, well... then it was no longer a big deal. I learned to control it for the most part. There are still some disturbances, and I avoid places that contain multiple spirits if I can help it. Annie knows."

Sammy snorted. "Why doesn't that surprise me? That chick is like a one-way vault. Things go in and get locked up tight, never to see the light of day again."

James laughed. "Yeah, that's our sister."

"Do you suppose Margie inherited something we don't know about?"

She could see her question intrigued James.

"I honestly never thought about it. Wait, inherited? What makes you say inherited?"

"Seriously? You don't know about Mom and Pop Pop?"

"Are you trying to tell me they both have gifts?" James was indignant.

"Not cool when family has secrets, is it?" Sammy taunted. "Anyway. Yes, Mom is like me. She gets premonitions by way of dreams. Though not as consistent or as strong as I get them. Pop was an empath, like Annie. Until now, I've never heard of anyone seeing spirits or ghosts. Though I suppose if anyone did, it would probably have been Pop's brother. Do you remember Uncle Tommy? He always had a haunted look about him, didn't he?"

"You're right. I'll have to ask Mom."

"Ya know, it doesn't make sense that Margie wouldn't have anything if we all did."

"Unless she got most of Dad's DNA."

"I suppose there is that. So seven, huh? That must've been frightening when it first happened."

"You have no idea."

JAMES NODDED, RECALLING THE FIRST TIME. THE FRIGHT HAD CAUSED him to wet his pants. "Terrifying. Since then, I've been able to see spirits. Any and all that happen to be hanging around," he told her.

"So, it wasn't just a dream? Me and Michael? We were there, in our house, these last weeks?"

Her expression was wrecked. Grief pulled at her mouth, and sadness clouded her eyes. He drew her tightly against him, remembering the paralyzing fear of initially seeing her wandering her home, and believing she'd died.

"Yes. I saw you both. When it first happened, I freaked and called Brookhaven and yelled at some poor nurse to check on you. I broke every speed record to get here and see for myself that you were all right. We're lucky they didn't take out a restraining order on me. I may have been a little aggressive."

She tried to smile, but it dropped away just as quickly as it appeared. "Is he truly gone, Jamie?"

"I think so, Lil' Bit. I'm so sorry," he said, voice breaking. He hurt for her. Hell, he hurt for himself. His best friend in the world was gone. Coping with loss didn't come naturally to him. It was easier to take out his feelings on a home build or reno.

"What if he isn't? What if, like me, he was coming from a dream?"

It was something to think about. Perhaps Michael *was* somewhere alive. For Sammy's sake, James wanted him to be. The probability was low. He just couldn't fathom Michael not returning to Sammy. They had been too close. Too in love. Not to mention, there would've had to have been a hell of a mistake. Shaking his head, James couldn't see where it was possible.

"It doesn't explain his spirit fading, Sammy. Where did he go? Why hasn't he come back? Why only haunt your home? If he was dreamwalking, like you, he could have gone anywhere. He wouldn't be tied to the house."

"Yeah, I don't know."

"Did you ever ask him?"

"Yes. He didn't have answers. You know Michael. He laughs off anything he doesn't want to deal with."

It was the closest Sammy had ever come to criticizing Michael as far as James knew. One thing *did* bother him about her answer. "He didn't *know?* Did he remember the accident at all?"

The negative shake of her head caused James serious misgivings. While some spirits became confused in the afterlife, it took years and years before that happened. Centuries even. In his experience, most ghosts quickly assimilated. They were aware of everything past, present, and often future. It didn't make sense that Michael wouldn't know the specifics surrounding his death.

His sister's rumbling stomach distracted him. He would delve into the circumstances surrounding the crash. If he had to, James would fly to Dallas himself to get to the bottom of it. For right now, he needed to guide his sister on her path to getting well.

"I don't have answers right now. But I intend to find them. Tomorrow I'll make some calls. Do you trust me, Lil' Bit?" At her nod, he instructed her to take care of herself. "You've worried a lot of people. I need you to work on recovering. Mentally and physically."

Though her eyes were drooping with her need to sleep again, Sammy gave one slight inclination of her head. James hoped like hell that meant she intended to fight. Losing his favorite sister would destroy him.

"Let's get some food in you before you go back to sleep."

CHAPTER 18

*T*here were brief glimpses of Michael throughout Sammy's dreams over the next five weeks. One day, even those were no more. He was well and truly gone from her life. Sammy thought it a bit ironic that he'd disappeared for good on the day she'd been initially scheduled to leave Brookhaven.

That day dawned bright and beautiful. It came and went with nothing to mark it but frustration and a middle finger to the world from Sammy. Had she followed the program, had she not held so tightly to the belief Michael was alive, she would've been released. Apparently, sleeping the day away, not participating in group, not talking to your therapist, and completely avoiding family on visiting days didn't make you appear too stable. To meet the guidelines of what the DA and Gabe had mapped out for her, she needed to show improvement before being released. She hadn't.

The worst part was the constant ache she felt for Michael never diminished. And, if she wasn't mourning his loss, she mourned the loss of their baby. The doctors diagnosed her with depression. She didn't doubt they were right, because some days it sure seemed easier to curl up and die. Too bad the body didn't work that way. Those stories of people dying of a broken heart? Yeah, bullshit. If it weren't a fallacy, Sammy would be gone now. Gone to spend eternity with their child.

In her mind, it was their *child*. No longer a baby. She envisioned a little girl with dark ringlets. Always messy, the way her father's hair was. Their daughter would've had dancing warm-honey eyes. She would have laughed delightedly at the world and everything in it, just like Michael. Yes, on Sammy's more alive days, she thought about things like picnics at the beach or the park. Visions of Michael teaching his daughter to fly a kite and pushing her on the swing while she squealed, *"Higher, Daddy! Higher!"* clouded her mind.

Sammy would be pregnant with their second child by then. Sassy would be lying on the blanket next to her, tongue lolling about outside her mouth. A big canine grin would take over her face as she watched her girl with her papa. Then, they would stop for ice cream on the way home. Of course, it would drip down her daughter's hand onto her cute pink outfit. Sassy would make a grab for the cone when it dipped her way as their little girl's attention drifted to whatever fascinated her.

It was a beautiful dream. One she never wanted to let go of. Then there were the days when all she could see was darkness. Her beautiful fantasy refused to take her away. Even music couldn't help her escape. It was the one luxury item she was allowed: an iPad to read and to listen to her tunes. Sammy guessed she could thank the Universe for small favors. She refused to thank God, because she was a bit on the outs with the Almighty at the moment. They ignored each other for the most part. That was cool. Sammy had nowhere to be. Nothing to prove. She had her music and three square meals per day. For now, this half-life was enough.

STEPHEN WATCHED SAMANTHA SHUFFLE BY HIM FOR THE THIRD TIME that day. He had observed her heading to breakfast, then again for group, where she refused to participate and stared off into space. She meandered her way to the sunroom and curled up in her favorite plush chair, legs over the side, eyes shut tight, and earbuds in place.

To the naked eye, it was easy to see she'd lost weight. There were permanent dark circles under her eyes. Eyes that had previously sparkled with light and intelligence, were currently lifeless.

His inability to help Samantha frustrated Stephen. He'd become a doctor to help people cope with the tragedies in their everyday life. Samantha Holt wasn't going to allow him to cure her. She didn't want to move forward. To do so, she'd have to accept her boyfriend's death. It hadn't made a difference when James sat her down and said the phone calls to Dallas yielded nothing. In fact, James's revelation proved detrimental. Samantha retreated further inside herself.

Stephen had only failed in treating one other patient. He had been too close to that one. His frustration level escalated. Again, he found himself drawn in, caring too much about a single patient to the exclusion of all others. If it were anyone else besides himself, Stephen would have labeled it obsession. Definitely not a healthy emotion. The time to remove himself as her doctor had long since passed. Developing a special attachment to a patient was taboo. He decided to assign Samantha to Dr. Sheridan Jones.

Sheridan and Stephen had been colleagues for three years. She was exceptional in her work. Perfect for Samantha. Stephen picked up the phone and dialed her extension.

"Sheridan? Hi, it's Stephen. Listen, I have a favor to ask."

———

Dr. Montgomery appeared in Sammy's line of vision. She did what anyone who desired to avoid another person would've done. She cranked up the volume of her tunes and closed her eyes. Points for maturity weren't going to make her report card, but so what?

He surprised her when he ripped the headphones from her ears.

"What's up, Doc?"

Uh oh. He didn't look too thrilled with her. A bubble of laughter worked its way up. Just when it had became amusing to her to make

Dr. Mild-Mannered Montgomery mad, she didn't know. It had been her goal for some time. Nearing thirty, Sammy still had traces of a rebellious teen inside her. She had never gone through the defiant phase growing up. Better late than never? Doubtful.

She was elated she'd succeeded in ruffling his feathers. Doc always gave the impression of superiority, as if he were well above everyone else. Possibly, it was just her perception. Still, he was too damn starchy. Not at all fun-loving like Michael. The thought sobered her. Damn. Why the need to compare the two?

A MISCHIEVOUS EXPRESSION FLASHED ACROSS SAMANTHA'S FACE AND disappeared as fast as it had appeared. It was the first sign of life Stephen had seen from her since her brother's intervention five weeks ago. Observing them on the video feed made him feel like a voyeur, but the interaction between the two gave him insight on Samantha. Or at least he thought it would. After her brother's departure, she'd shut down again.

"Ms. Holt, I need you to come with me. We need to talk."

Stephen cursed his professional tone when she rolled her eyes. What was it about this one woman? She could reduce him to insecurity in mere seconds. He worked hard to advance his career and was proud of his accomplishments. Stephen now understood how Gabriel felt and why he referred to her as a menace.

Once they were seated in his office, Stephen explained he'd assigned her a new doctor. One who might be able to actually guide her through her recovery. Samantha's display of disappointment knocked him for a loop. He would have bet good money she wouldn't care either way. She'd wallowed in an apathetic state for months.

"Why? What's wrong with you staying on as my doctor?"

"You aren't getting well under my care. Dr. Jones is exceptional. I believe she will see you through your grief and help you be stronger on the other side."

"No."

"No? No, you don't want another doctor, or no, you don't want to get better?"

"No, I don't want another doctor poking around in my head. It's bad enough *you* are. I won't talk to her."

"Ms. Holt…"

"Jesus, you're Ms. Holt-ing me to death. Please, stop already. My name is Sammy or Samantha."

"Okay, Samantha it is. But regardless of your desires, you *will* be assigned to Dr. Jones."

SAMMY REGISTERED HIS DETERMINATION AND SERIOUSNESS ON THE subject. Arguing now would be pointless. Time to admit defeat. She conceded with a brief nod and stood to leave.

"Samantha?"

She turned at the question, her hand on the doorknob.

"Dr. Jones is on her way here. Please stay and meet her. We can talk for a bit."

The smile he offered was similar to the first time she'd met him when he was teasing Gabriel James. Engaging and open. She found herself somewhat drawn to his smile. He used it so rarely around the clinic. Always the professional was Dr. Montgomery.

"Do you play poker, Doc?"

She watched as his smile bloomed into a full-blown grin. He said nothing more as he rose and removed a deck of cards from his desk. Strolling to the round meeting table to one side of his office, he pulled out a chair and gestured for Sammy to sit down.

The next twenty minutes were spent in battle. Sammy was ruthless at cards. Her father had taught her poker at a young age. Martin had also taught her to cheat by shuffling and dealing from the bottom of the deck, but she reserved her tricks for playing with family. The probability was always high they were going to be a bit underhanded during a card game.

She was sweating the possibility of losing to Dr. Montgomery when the most exquisite female she'd ever seen, drifted into his office.

Her soon-to-be-ex therapist's face lit up with admiration. He ran appreciative eyes over her well-trimmed figure.

Was Doc having a relationship with this woman? She'd never seen him so animated. His hand rested low on the back of the woman she assumed was Dr. Jones. He guided her to one of the two guest chairs across from the sofa. They fit perfectly together. He had to be at least six foot two, and Sammy would have put the beautiful doctor at around five-eight or -nine. That didn't count the four-inch heels bringing her eye level with Doc.

Feeling positively grubby and stubby after seeing the other woman, Sammy was determined not to like her. Needing time to adjust to having a jaw-dropping amazon as her new psychiatrist, Sammy gathered up the cards. Why was it that these doctors always looked so classy and put together? She glanced down at her scrubs and sneaked a sniff of her armpit. With a last glance over her shoulder to see the two absorbed in each other, Sammy checked her reflection in the mirror over the table and attempted to smooth her hair. What she hadn't expected was to catch Doc's amused gaze in the mirror. A flush rose from somewhere down at her feet and warmed her whole body. It was good to see she hadn't grown out of *that* particular trait.

She pasted on her standard I-don't-give-a-shit expression and strode toward the door.

"Samantha," Stephen's voice halted her in her tracks. "Please, come meet Dr. Jones."

Sammy would rather stick pins under her fingernails, but she joined them and offered her hand like the good little patient Brookhaven's staff preferred she was. Surely, this canceled out her rudeness from earlier today. She avoided looking at Dr. Montgomery. If she saw adoration for the perfect Dr. Jones on his face, she might vomit.

"Please, sit. Now then, Dr. Montgomery tells me you're having a difficult time coping with the death of your boyfriend." Her new doctor's superior tone sparked off a fire inside Sammy, to say *nothing* of her words.

"I'm not having a difficult time coping with anything except being kept prisoner in the looney bin," Sammy sneered and curled her hands into fists. The desire to punch that perfect nose was a compulsion she found difficult to curb. She tried to moderate her tone as she continued. "I'm sure Doc filled you in, but no, I don't believe he's dead."

Dr. Jones ran her shrewd golden-brown eyes from the top of Sammy's head to her feet encased in flip-flops. Self-conscious, she curled her toes. She was in terrible need of a pedicure. It drove her batty not to have her feet groomed. Sammy choked back a snort of amusement due to the irony behind that thought. She surmised if the good Dr. Jones withdrew her feet from her expensive red pumps, her toes would be flawlessly done in shades of pale pink. Okay, now Sammy was just being petty, but she hated feeling inferior to other people. This new doctor made her feel small without even trying.

"First, let us address something. Mental health is no joking matter. Your reference to 'looney' is inappropriate. Almost half of the adults in the United States alone will deal with some type of mental illness in their lifetime. For every time I hear you crack a joke at the expense of the residents here, I'll add a week to your time."

Sammy nodded. In no way was she trying to be disrespectful to those dealing with legitimate issues. She simply believed she wasn't one of them. Dr. Jones was right to call her out.

"Now, back to the subject at hand. What insight do *you* have on Mitchell's death that anyone else who's investigated it doesn't?"

"*Michael!* His name is Michael," Sammy snarled through clenched teeth. She bound to her feet, pissed off to her core. "I'm done here. Call me when you've actually had a chance to read my file and know what the fuck you're talking about."

"Sit *down*, Ms. Holt. I have read your file. *Thoroughly.* If you ever expect to leave this facility, you need to get one thing straight. *I'm* in charge now. You will *not* walk over me the way you have the rest of this clinic's staff. From here on out, you will keep your appointments with me. You will be on time, and you will contribute to the discussion. Group therapy and participation are also mandatory. If—and that is a big *if*—you start showing progress, I will make my recommendations to the district attorney and Mr. James in regard to your release. Do I make myself clear?"

Sammy felt frozen in hate. Disdain had to be written all over her face. It didn't sit well with her to give in to demands. Dr. Jones sensed it, based on her smug mug. Sammy asked herself if she cared one way or the other.

No.

Maybe down the road she would, but she wasn't there yet.

"Kiss my ass, Dr. Janes."

A flash of amusement flared in the other woman's eyes before she quickly tamped it down.

"Touché," Dr. Jones acknowledged with a clapping of her hands. "Tomorrow morning at eight forty-five will be our first appointment. My office is two doors down from Dr. Montgomery's, on the right. I expect we'll have some very interesting conversations, Ms. Holt. Good day."

The good doctor dismissed her, and it suited Sammy just fine. Offering up a middle-finger salute, she made her way toward the door. She heard Dr. Jones murmur something to Dr. Montgomery. He chuckled in response.

Always sure of her place in the world before Michael's disappearance had turned it topsy-turvy, Sammy felt a keen sense of insecurity and humiliation from this encounter. In spite of everything, Doc had always seemed kind to her. *Until this instant.* It was beyond cruel to treat a patient this way, even one as argumentative as herself. Doc's behavior hurt in some small way. It didn't take her long to close down that line of thought. She wouldn't let anything hurt her anymore. Losing Michael and their baby had been too painful. She couldn't let herself care again. Staying detached remained her best course of action.

Sammy cut her gaze to Dr. Montgomery as she opened the door. She locked onto Stephen's warm mocha eyes. A look of disquiet flashed across his face before he smoothed his features. A ping echoed around the area where her heart used to be. Jerkily, she yanked open the door and ran for her room. It seemed as if she were channeling her sister Annie's abilities. Her senses were open and exposed. That shit needed to be shut down. She wanted no part of emotions again, not in this lifetime. Not if she couldn't have Michael back.

For the longest time, she lay on the bed and stared at the ceiling. The distinct sensation of being watched brought goosebumps to her skin. Maybe the doctors were entertaining themselves by observing her through the camera feed. The lack of privacy nearly drove her mad. Funny, because the thing that could honestly make her crazy and want to harm someone was the tool they used to make sure she didn't. Rolling on her side, Sammy presented her back to the camera, effectively shutting them out.

CHAPTER 19

Sammy entered the theater doubling as the group therapy room. It would be a stretch of the imagination to say she arrived on time. Luckily, patients were usually given a few minutes' leeway to let everyone collect their refreshments and find a seat. A quick glance showed Drs. Jones and Montgomery standing by the front, closest to the stage. Sammy stopped just inside the doorway to process her surroundings.

"Move, bitch! You gonna stand there all damn day?" a woman growled, behind her.

Most people here at Brookhaven were considerate of one another. Even so, a select few were eerily similar to playground bullies. Standing before her happened to be the ringleader and most troublesome of all. *Ronni Thompson.*

Everyone knew the rules of confrontation. You either stood up to a bully, or you were going to be a target of their aggression for the remainder of your time. Sammy didn't want a confrontation, but never one to back down, she decided to put a stop to this singular threat.

"Look, chick..." she began. The shove came out of nowhere and effectively aborted her cutting remarks. Ronni's touch triggered a premonition like Sammy had never experienced.

Fueled by her fury, Ronni shouted directly into Dr. Jones's face. The doctor actively worked to calm her, which only served to enrage Ronni further. Her arm shot up, and a weapon dropped from her sleeve to her fist. In the blink of an eye, Ronni laid open Dr. Jones's throat. Shock and pain flashed in the doctor's eyes before they were filled with nothingness, only death. All life extinguished.

Ronni stalked toward Dr. Jones as Sammy recovered from the movie inside her head. Sammy noted the setting. *Yeah, this was happening in real time.* The conflict was about to go down.

Scrambling to her feet, she rushed to intercede. She unceremoniously shoved patients and staff out of her way. In a split-second decision, Sammy calculated that tackling the doctor would be easier than stopping two hundred pounds of enraged bull, aka Ronni.

Ronni's weapon caught Sammy across the shoulder and sliced a long diagonal gash from shoulder to spine. The burning in her back was excruciating, but until Ronni was contained, Sammy wasn't safe to just lay sprawled across Dr. Jones. The psycho would be out for more of Sammy's blood now she'd interfered with Ronni's objective.

Flipping on her back with only seconds to spare, she brought her legs up to her chest and pushed out. The impact to Ronni's abdomen slowed the other woman down but only marginally. The bloody knife waved wildly back and forth in front of Sammy's face. Spittle peppered her from Ronni's snarling mouth. As Sammy's legs started to give out and the wicked edge of the blade inched ever closer to her own throat, two orderlies along with Dr. Montgomery manhandled Rabid Ronni to the floor.

Once the weight lifted, Sammy flopped, spread-eagle, panting and spent. Heart hammering harder than any workout could achieve. "Well, that was scary," she said to no one in particular. "Anyone got a tranq gun?"

Dr. Jones scrambled to her side. "My God, Samantha! Are you all right?"

"Um, no. No, I'm p-pretty sure I'm n-not. My back. She c-cut my b-back."

With the initial adrenaline rush over, Sammy began to feel the pain tenfold.

"Okay. Stay calm. I'm going to turn you toward me to have a look. Just breathe in and out in controlled breaths. Three in and three out," Dr. Jones counseled while she slipped on a pair of nitrile gloves she pulled from her lab coat.

"Sure, no w-worries. Can you d-do me a f-favor? S-stop giving that ch-chick steroids, okay? She n-needs Xanax or lorazepam, ya know."

Dr. Jones's lips twisted into a semblance of a smile. "I promise to review her med list as soon as we've treated you, okay?"

Dr. Montgomery joined them, pulling on gloves of his own. He helped prop Sammy on her left side while Dr. Jones peeled back the jagged edges of her scrub top. Sammy cast a worried glance at Stephen, who looked white around the mouth, as if he were holding back some deeper emotion. His reaction puzzled her, but it was a question for another time.

WORDLESSLY, STEPHEN LIFTED SAMANTHA IN HIS ARMS AND HURRIED for the door.

The click of Sheridan's impossibly high heels echoed behind them as she trotted to catch up and apply pressure to Samantha's wound. More attendants flooded in to offer their services or to take her from his arms, but he plowed on, ignoring them as he rushed with her to the medical center.

"Get Dr. Monroe on the phone. Tell him to set up a tray. She is going to need stitches to close this wound," he called over his shoulder.

"Stephen, let someone help you carry her."

"I've got it. Just do as I say, Sheridan," he ordered, tone harsh.

Once they had Samantha in the care of their co-worker and his staff, Sheridan cornered Stephen, hoping for answers.

"What the hell, Stephen? Is there something between you and this woman?"

"Jesus, Sheridan." He scrubbed his palms up and down his face.

He'd made his affection for Samantha obvious with his actions.

Sheridan became a dog with a bone. "Answer the question!"

"What do you want me to say? I find her attractive? Hell, who wouldn't? But is there anything inappropriate going on? *Hell, no.* You know me better than that."

"Is your attraction to her the real reason you turned her care over to me?"

He knew his body language answered for him. His agitation, the rubbing of his hand along his neck as he looked anywhere but at her—they were all classic signs of avoidance, and a woman of Sheridan's intelligence wasn't likely to miss them.

"How long have you been in love with her?" she asked quietly.

"What difference does it make? I told you there is nothing going on. She's still in love with a dead man. She's also a patient in this facility, and I have shifted her care over to you. Short of shipping her to a different clinic—which I won't do, because this one is by far the best—and short of me taking an undetermined leave of absence while she's here, nothing more can be done. Please, drop it."

The topic of conversation was a difficult one for Stephen. Here he stood, talking with his occasional lover about a patient he'd developed feelings for. If that wasn't enough, he'd always worry Sheridan would feel compelled to report him to the board. Technically, she had to acknowledge he hadn't once stepped out of line. His integrity shouldn't be in question.

They stared at one another; he in fear of reprisal, and her torn as to what she should do.

He could see Sheridan wanted to continue interrogating him, but if she was being honest with herself, she didn't have the right. He'd never given her any romantic encouragement. He'd been careful to keep their relationship on a strictly casual sex/friendship basis. Refusing to stay the night had been a hard-and-fast rule of his. If it became more than sex, more than fun, or when it turned to cuddling or confidences in the dark, boundaries became murky. Or so he'd told her.

"Let's discuss something else," Stephen suggested. "How did she know you were about to be attacked? I saw Samantha get pushed to the floor. I wasn't that far from you and still didn't have enough time to react or anticipate the knife."

"Maybe she put Ronni up to it and then had second thoughts."

"No. Not Samantha. I don't buy it. You don't believe it either. At best, she overheard something and came to the meeting to stop it, but there is no way in hell she would hurt another human being. Not purposely."

"Honestly, I thought the same thing. I just wanted to throw the other theory out there."

He was surprised she agreed. If he would have said anything more, it was forgotten as Dr. Monroe wheeled Samantha out of his office.

"Here she is. The hero of the hour. It seems I'm forever patching her up. Her pain medications have kicked in. She won't feel anything for a good long while," he told them. The next sentence he directed at Samantha. "Try to stay out of trouble, dear."

With a nod to the two doctors, Dr. Monroe went whistling off.

"I like him," she said with a small smile. "He reminds me of my grandfather."

"Pfft. Just don't get on his bad side," Stephen quipped. At the questioning look from both women, he proceeded to tell them an amusing story of the doctor, a troublesome patient, and a syringe full of tranquilizer. "Dr. Monroe gave Hector enough to bring down an elephant. The guy was drooling and wetting himself for days."

Stephen glanced down into Samantha's sparkling blue eyes, knowing he could get lost in them if circumstances were different. It lightened his heart to see her genuine laugh. He'd felt an urge to protect her from day one. He loved her and could now silently admit it to himself.

Samantha held his gaze overly long. He didn't dare hope her attention meant anything. The moment was broken by Sheridan. Which was probably intelligent on her part. She helped break Samantha's spell over him, to once more reel in his professionalism. His control had taken a serious beating after he'd witnessed Samantha get assaulted for the second time since she was admitted to the hospital.

"Ms. Holt, I need to start off with a thank you. How did you know what she was planning?"

Samantha shifted in her seat. Sheridan's question clearly made her uncomfortable.

"Sammy?"

The tentative voice had all three of them turning to see the lone woman in the hallway.

"Annie? What are you doing here?" Samantha placed a shaky hand to her lips.

"It's a long story. I flew in last night. Jamie is getting ready to head out of town. I thought I would house-sit for you."

Samantha rose and limped to where her sister hovered in the hallway. Dr. Monroe's nurse must have contacted her family. Stephen felt more than a little guilty that he hadn't thought to do so.

"No, I meant here at Brookhaven."

"I got a... call."

SAMMY FLUNG AN ARM AROUND HER SISTER AND HUGGED HER. IT TOOK seeing Annie's hesitancy, unsure of her welcome, to make Sammy realize how much she'd missed her.

"Oh, Annie." She pulled away to meet her sister's concerned blue eyes. "Not that I'm not thrilled to see you, but why did you come? This place is too much for you."

She recognized Annie's warning look for what it was. While Sammy never really cared if anyone knew of her precognitive abilities, Annie tended to be much more reserved.

"You needed me," Annie said simply.

The sisters had always been able to sense if the other was in trouble, not very different from identical twins. The frisson of danger was the call referred to.

"I do need you."

"You're struggling. You should tell the truth. He'll listen this time."

Stephen met Sammy with the wheelchair and ordered her to sit down. She wasn't in any doubt he'd overheard their conversation. His next words proved it. "What truth? What do you need to tell me, Samantha?"

"Rabid Ronni pushed me down when she walked into the group session..." The only reason Sammy paused was because her sister snorted and fell into a fit of giggles.

"Rabid Ronni? *Really?*" Annie choked out.

The ridiculous name set both sisters off. The more they tried to contain their hilarity, the less control they had. Sammy wasn't the only family member with an inappropriate sense of humor.

"Why don't you and your sister spend time catching up? Dr. Montgomery and I will meet with you later, Samantha," Dr. Jones offered.

Surprised out of her laughter, Sammy clasped Dr. Jones's hand before she could turn away. Her intent was to explain, but the force of the next vision slammed her back into the chair with a painful cry.

Ronni hid behind Dr. Jones's office door. In her hand, she held a glass trophy or award of some kind. The second the doctor cleared the opening to the room, Ronni slammed the weapon down on the back of Dr. Jones's head. The doctor fell to the ground, eyes staring sightlessly, her body landing next to Dr. Montgomery's still form. Their blood intermingled on the carpeted floor.

Sammy held Sheridan's wrist in a punishing grip, unable to let go. Her hand convulsing along with her body.

"Get Dr. Monroe back here immediately," Sheridan ordered Stephen.

"*No!*" Annie stopped Stephen from reaching for his phone. The doctors looked to each other in confusion. As Sammy returned to herself, she loosened her hold and let go of Sheridan.

STEPHEN LOOKED BETWEEN THE TWO SISTERS. "WHAT THE HELL JUST happened here?" He was never informed Samantha had a history of seizures. She'd never listed it on the intake form.

"It's not what you think, Doc," she whispered.

"How do you know what I think?" he demanded.

Samantha's gaze sought and held Annie's. Both women shared a grim look.

"What did you see, Sammy?" Annie questioned.

"See? What do you mean *see*?" Sheridan asked harshly, nerves obviously still strained from her earlier attack.

"If everyone could calm down, that'd be great," Annie urged. She closed her eyes and inhaled deeply before continuing. "Sammy had a premonition. My guess would be that it was about you." She tilted her head toward Sheridan. "Sammy, what did you see?"

Samantha outlined the events of the vision.

Dr. Jones squatted in front of her. No easy feat in the four-inch stilettos and pencil skirt she wore. Stephen noticed she was careful not to touch Samantha.

"Samantha. I don't know what to say. The scientist in me..." she trailed off, shaking her head.

"It's all right. You don't have to believe. You just have to be careful for a while."

"I'm not saying your... premonitions... are real or not real, but how is the timing so vague?"

"I don't know. I never have. But in this last one you were wearing the same outfit you have on right now. It seemed later in the day. Maybe closer to six or seven." Sammy shrugged. "The lighting was dimmer in your office."

"How often do you wear the same thing twice?" Annie asked.

Sheridan cast an unreadable look at Stephen as she gracefully rose to her feet. "Not often. Certainly not in the same week because I drop items off to be dry-cleaned."

She barely finished before Stephen pulled out and dialed his phone. His eyes never breaking contact with hers, he barked, "Get me the head of security." Stephen ordered heightened security measures put in place. "Where is Ronni Thompson now?"

"We're searching for her, sir."

"She's on the loose?" Stephan was mad enough to swallow his own tongue. "Jesus Christ, when did that happen?" He listened to the stammering explanation and wanted to fling his phone down the hallway.

"Find her!" he bit out before hanging up.

"What's going on?" Samantha asked.

"Rabid Ronni got loose."

Both sisters snorted their amusement at the name.

Rolling his eyes, Stephen ushered them all into the medical center's waiting room. "We can't loiter in the hallway. I want the three of you to remain here while I go help with the search for Ronni."

As he turned to leave, Samantha caught his lab coat and held firm. "Doc, don't go into Dr. Jones's office. At least not alone. Promise me you'll take security with you and send them in first. *Please.*"

Stephen wanted to sweep her up in his arms and kiss her like a soldier going off to war would his sweetheart. Any action on his part would likely earn him a hard slap from Samatha and give Sheridan a heart attack in the process. He settled for a half smile instead. "Promise."

THE THREE WOMEN SAT IN RELATIVE SILENCE FOR A TIME.

Dr. Jones was the first to speak. "I should go. I should go check on Stephen. He's been gone too long."

Sammy wanted to hold Dr. Jones's hand to offer comfort. She seemed to really care about Doc. But the contact might cause another premonition, and Sammy had experienced enough for today.

"No, ma'am. Ronni targeted you for whatever insane reason, and you aren't safe out there. You'll stay here with us until Doc returns with the news that wackadoo is caught."

"Not a bad idea. Will you tell me about your visions, Samantha? I didn't believe before. I'm not sure I do now, but..." Dr. Jones shrugged, not finishing the sentence. It was implied. Twice Ronni had intended her harm, and twice Sammy had staved off tragedy.

Because she expressed clear, non-judgmental interest, Sammy agreed to tell the doctor all about her abilities. She explained how, in the last few months, they seemed to have morphed into something stronger. Clearer, where they had never been as crisp or as detailed before. When she received one now, it was with the force of a freight train slamming into her body and affected all her senses at once.

Dr. Jones plagued her with questions until they were both wrung out, and Sammy answered as openly and honestly as she could, secure in the knowledge her explanation wouldn't be used against her as it might've been in the past.

"Do you have any... gifts?" Dr. Jones stumbled over the question.

Sammy shot her sister a sharp look. For Annie to open up and reveal what she could do would be like exposing the most intimate part of herself.

Finally, her sister gave a reluctant nod. "I'm an empath. A person able to read and feel other people's energy."

"What does that entail?"

Annie sighed and closed her eyes. "You care about Dr. Montgomery in a very non-professional capacity. If pressed, I'd say you two are lovers. The sexual energy you put off when he's around is powerful."

Dr. Jones grimaced, and Sammy knew what she was thinking; Annie had proved nothing so far.

"No, not a guess, Doctor. You love him. *Very much.* He doesn't love you, because he's fascinated with another."

Dr. Jones's complexion shifted to a deep, dark red. Uncomfortable didn't begin to describe her feelings on the subject. Even Sammy could feel her discomfort.

"Ah, you know who. I suspected you did," Annie said. "Often, if I accidentally touch someone, I feel their physical issues or ailments."

"This is incredible. How does it not drive you mad? I mean you have to be deluged constantly. And as a child? I can't fathom what you must have gone through."

Her understanding and compassion touched both sisters. She believed them.

"Thank you. It wasn't easy."

"On a different subject, how do you suppose Ronni got that knife?" Sammy asked, trying to deflect attention from Annie and ease her uncomfortableness.

CHAPTER 20

The next several months brought with them healing. Every hour of every day, Sammy learned to come to terms with the loss of her child a little bit more. It helped to know Rob Marks was going away for his crimes against her and the other patients he and Dale had harmed during their reign of terror.

Stephen had devoted endless hours and poured over files, interviewed patients, and reviewed security tapes. In short order, he was able to uncover the atrocities Rob and Dale had committed. It came to light that Rob, along with his cohort Dale, had been molesting patients, which resulted in a harsher sentence. While her own interview with Stephen brought painful memories, Sammy was thrilled those asshats were on their way to receiving their just desserts.

On occasion, like today, Stephen sought her out to play cards. They had developed a real bond of friendship. And since that was the case, Sammy felt it was okay to implement the family-only cheating rules. They extended to friends when the poker competition was fierce.

"Are you cheating, Samantha Holt?" he demanded when she won her third hand in a row.

"Why, Doc, whatever gave you that idea?"

He snorted at her innocent act. Throwing down his cards, he stood and gestured to his office door with his thumb. "Go find someone else to terrorize. I have a patient in five."

"Sure thing, Doc." Standing on her tiptoes, she rumbled his perfectly coiffed hair and ran for the door.

At times like these, she liked to tease him when he became too stodgy. In return, he helped her temper her overly sensitive nature regarding the necessary questions Dr. Jones asked.

Sammy understood the doctors truly wanted to help her through her emotional turmoil. The sticking point came when they talked about acceptance of Michael's death. Sammy still wasn't there yet.

Michael had crept back into her dreams. It was rare, but it renewed her hope that he was alive and waiting for her, out there somewhere. What disturbed her the most was how much he'd changed. There was also a distance she couldn't breach. Touching and holding him was impossible. He would lurk in the shadows and stare, his expression forlorn.

"Come find me, Sammy," would drift to her just before she woke crying and once more alone. Those were the days that made it difficult for anyone to penetrate the barrier she'd erected around herself. Not Stephen, not her family, and certainly not Dr. Jones. Getting lost in her music as she vegged out in the sunroom seemed to be the only thing that soothed her. She decided if she ever got sprung from this joint, she was taking the oversized armchair with her.

Sammy sometimes wondered if she shouldn't tell Stephen and Sheridan what they wanted to hear. Tell them she believed Michael was dead, so she could leave this place. But there was a comfort here. A routine that soothed her. Visiting days were fun now since she'd received permission for her family to bring Sassy. Yes, for Sassy, she needed to lie. To tell them she accepted Michael's death.

———

EIGHT MONTHS AND FIVE DAYS AFTER MICHAEL HAD DISAPPEARED, Sammy was scheduled to be released. All the charges against her were dropped. Gabriel James had convinced the district attorney she no longer posed a threat to society as a whole.

She'd already exchanged farewells with the staff members who'd been kind to her. Leaving today was essentially a done deal. She only waited for Dr. Jones to sign off on her official discharge papers. The signature was a technicality. Sammy was free.

She wandered over to stare out the main window in the reception area, wondering if she could spot anything to indicate the storm would end soon.

Lightning flashed. On its heels, a boom of thunder shook the panes of glass in front of her. Involuntarily, Sammy took a step back. The storm raged out of control and made her nervous.

Stephen's words woke her from her preoccupation with the elements. "Just a few short steps and you're free. Free to be whoever you choose to be from this moment forward." Stephen continued to try to encourage her to find herself, to let go of the past and start fresh.

Sammy thought back on the events which had brought her to this exact moment. And, as the memories faded, she peered at Stephen, who stood before her. She met his intense mocha eyes. Those eyes held a deeper message. One she failed to decipher. But she *would* take his encouraging words to heart. She *would* believe in herself.

"Okay. You're right. I need to start believing in myself again. But do you mind if I just hang out until the storm passes? I need to say goodbye to my favorite chair."

"I have a better idea. Karaoke starts in ten minutes. Why don't you stay for a last round? We can sit in the back, and you can make fun of the screechers for old time's sake."

She grinned. "Sure. Lead on."

The shouts of *"Surprise!"* threw her when she entered the entertainment center. She registered the banner and multicolored balloons then turned to Stephen in disbelief. When had they set this up, and why were so many people in attendance? It wasn't like she'd collected friends here. The sea of faces held excitement and wariness. They all waited with bated breath.

"Thank you." She graciously offered up a smile. "This means a lot. Seriously, thank you."

A cheer rang out, and the party began in force. A few braver patients patted her on the shoulder.

"Who knew I was so scary?" she murmured in an aside to Stephen.

"I did. Anyone who would take on Rabid Ronni is a full-on badass."

She snorted her amusement and bumped her shoulder into his arm.

"What's with the *'Bon Voyage'* sign? You couldn't find one to say 'We're Happy To See Your Cranky Ass Go'?"

Stephen's laughter triggered her smile. She'd cut one more chink out of his professional armor. This was the man she liked, not the uptight doctor who made her feel out of her depth. He could be fun when he let loose. She liked these little moments when his real personality emerged.

"Let's get this party started. I need some champagne. Wait, we only have sparkling grape juice, don't we? Dammit," she swore without heat.

Stephen flung an arm around her shoulders and led her to the refreshment table.

"Quit yer bitchin'," he ordered in a low voice.

"Why, Doc, did you just swear? Here, in a facility where there are vulnerable minds to be shaped? I'm tellin'. You gonna be in *trou-ble!*" she sang out the last little bit.

When he would have said more, someone across the room caught his attention, and his smile flashed. Sammy caught her breath. He had such a wide, engaging smile. Unexpectedly feeling warm, she decided to ask about the air conditioning. You always had to be on top of the a/c in Florida. It was absolutely brutal if a system went on the fritz in August.

"Lil' Bit."

She spun with a squeal. "Jamie! You're back in town!"

She was referring to a reconstruction project he had taken on for a third-world cause. Her brother possessed a heart of gold. Once a year, he spent roughly two or three months on charity work in other countries who needed a hand up.

"I returned earlier this week. I wouldn't miss your homecoming for the world."

James opened his arms, and Sammy stepped into them. She'd missed her brother terribly. Words and tears clogged her throat.

"Yeah, okay, enough of that. You're going to make her a mental case again."

"Smooth, Margaret. Real smooth," Gabriel James said as he emerged from behind Margie.

He appeared to be fighting laughter. His eyes met Sammy's who, upon seeing the wicked silver gleam, was the first to snort. Her family's laughter couldn't be contained after that.

Gabe leaned down to whisper into Sammy's ear. "Your family is twisted."

She couldn't argue. They really *were*.

He had referred to the whole family but had eyes only for Margie. Interesting development. Sammy caught Stephen's gaze, nodded, and made the universal "something's going on there" face which consisted of huge, sparkling eyes and a hopeful smile. Stephen rolled his eyes, but his grin said it all.

Her name was called by the karaoke hostess, and she went cold inside. Everyone shouted good-natured encouragements and tried to get her to participate. She treated them all to her now-infamous death stare and made her way to the stage.

"Sweet Serendipity," she told the karaoke hostess. To the audience, she said, "It seems most fitting. But I have a special request. I need someone to help me out here. Dr. Montgomery?"

The surprise and discomfort Stephen felt was obvious. His narrowed eyes promised retribution. It only pleased Sammy more. She offered up a challenging grin and reached out her hand to jerk him up on the stage.

"Come on, Doc. Can we get a round of applause to help encourage him to overcome his shyness?"

Gabe let out a piercing wolf-whistle, earning Stephen's glare and Sammy's grin.

"Payback is hell," Stephen told her, hand over the mic.

"Do your worst, Doc."

The music started, and their playful little skirmish ended. They followed the highlighted words for the remainder of the song, only slightly off-key. After they finished all of the verses, the crowd went wild with cheers and applause. They weren't that good, but she decided to let the crazies have their fun. And by crazies, she meant her family, who were hooting and hollering the loudest. To be honest, she'd had a blast. Stephen radiated embarrassment but also wore a satisfied air. Sammy laughed when he threw Gabe and Margie under the proverbial bus for the next song.

She didn't want to remember when she'd last had that much fun, and tried not to think of Michael. Of how much he would have enjoyed this. Or of the times he'd sang so lovingly to her during their own karaoke days.

Dammit, she went there. Right after she swore to herself she wouldn't. The party would probably continue for another half hour or more, and Sammy figured three-quarters of the attendees wouldn't miss her. She snuck out to find Dr. Jones and her release forms. The fierce storm traveled on to wreak damage on another part of the state, and the perfect time to leave Brookhaven arrived. Sammy found it somewhat fitting that she'd started her stay on the day of a monster thunderstorm and was now ending it the same way.

WALKING INTO HER HOUSE AFTER MANY MONTHS SEEMED SURREAL. THE smells were the same. Clean and lemony. The same family pictures rested on the shelves. The same filmy curtains gently swayed from the air forced through vents. The same comfortable couch sat in the same spot. And Michael's same old recliner, which he'd dragged with him from location to location throughout life, held a place of honor, angled just so in the living room and facing the flat-screen TV from the best vantage point. But mostly, the same pain she'd experienced the day he disappeared struck her with the force of a ton of cinderblocks.

She wanted nothing more than to rewind her life to the day Michael had boarded the plane to Dallas. To beg him not to leave her. To chain him to their damned bed if she had to. It was nothing but wishful thinking.

Had she told him she loved him enough? Told him how much she treasured all he was, inside and out? How complete he'd made her feel? Had he known just by looking in her eyes he alone held her heart in the palm of his hand?

Tears worked their way down her cheeks and dripped on that same old recliner. Sammy caressed the leather as she recalled making love in it for the first time. Her personal mission had been to distract Michael from whatever sporting event he was watching on ESPN that long-ago day. Her matching lace bra and thong had worked exceedingly well.

God, she missed him. A single, hot tear hit her hand and bounced off. Coming back to herself, Sammy knuckled her eyes and struggled to pull herself together.

Strong arms wrapped around her from behind. A dark head found a spot on her shoulder, tucked right in next to her own. "I miss him too, ya know. If something happens at work and I need to vent, I dial his number without thinking. Football season is coming around again, and I don't know how I'm going to enjoy a game without him. Without seeing him in that big POS chair, drinking a beer and eating chips while you bitch at us for being too loud for you to get work done. The end of last year was hell."

Sammy sniffed and smacked one of the arms encircling her.

"I never bitched. I strongly suggested you keep the noise down."

"Sure you did," James said as he ruffled her hair. "You keep telling yourself that."

"Bite me," she retorted without heat.

Walking into the kitchen, Sammy decided to try something normal like making a sandwich. She opened the refrigerator and eyed the condiment shelf. With a disgusted sigh, she noted the disarray of her fridge.

"*Dude, seriously?* Are you sure you weren't adopted? Who did your OCD gene go to? This was organized when I left. And why the hell is there no strawberry jam?" Sammy glared at her brother where he sat at the kitchen counter, pissed she didn't have the makings for her standard PB&J.

"That's my beloved Lil' Bit. Always a beast if she wants to avoid being in touch with her feelings," James quipped. "Check the bags on the counter by the stove before you yell next time. And you were gone eight months for Christ's sake. How was anyone supposed to maintain OCD-ville for you that long? Really?"

"You're an asshole. But thanks for shopping."

"You're welcome. Make me one too, will ya?"

"Where's Sassy? How come she's not here?"

"I dropped her with the groomer before the party. They should be calling any time." As if on cue, James's phone rang. After he hung up, he snatched up a sandwich and made for the door. "I'll go get her. Oh, Renee called this morning. She wants you to come by the CBW tomorrow. She and Skye plan to have a girls' lunch. Her exact words were *'Tell Tonto I'm not taking no for an answer. One o'clock sharp.'* She's scary, Lil' Bit. I want you to know that chick frightens me."

"Wimp."

"No argument here."

CHAPTER 21

With no small amount of nervousness, Sammy met her friends at the coffeehouse in Palm Coast. After Renee's failed marriage, she and her sister, Skye, had pooled their resources and opened The Cool Beans Way, aka the CBW as it was known to locals. Combining the faux-brick wall, the off-white paint, the old-world lighting fixtures, along with a scattering of local artists' paintings, they'd created a lovely European atmosphere. It helped they offered up the best in gourmet coffee.

Skye refused to divulge the name of her roaster. She'd only say she would never go anywhere else. Incredibly enough, although she received samples from all over the world, she had settled on a company in Florida as her main source. Renee had sworn Sammy to secrecy when she told her. She said a real threat to her life existed in the event her sister ever found out she'd said a word.

When Sammy entered the shop, she was surprised to see so many of her friends. She'd only expected Kemo and Skye, so she felt decidedly uneasy to face the curious stares of the others. She wasn't sure she could deal with questions about herself or condolences about Michael. She doubted any of them knew about the loss of her baby, and she was probably in the clear if she decided she wasn't in the mood to share. Pausing for a long moment, frozen with indecision whether to join the group of laughing women, Sammy gasped and jumped as the door she had been blocking opened.

"Samantha?"

Sammy turned to see Stephen. A slight frown etched his features.

Working to get back to a state of calm, she took a deep breath and smiled. "Hey. What's up, Doc?"

He favored her with a look of mock disgust.

She grinned in the face of his irritation and found comfort in the normality of it. "Are you stalking me?"

"Not today. That's on schedule for tomorrow." Stephen held up a list. "I'm just here to pick up refreshments for a staff meeting."

"Thank you, Stephen." It helped Sammy shake off the remaining unease about lunch with her group of friends. She stretched up and kissed his cheek.

His brows rose in question.

"You've been good to me even when I was a total shit to you. You deserve a major apology along with that thank you. So here goes… I'm sorry for all the hell I've put you through. I know it was mostly your job, but you were kind to me. You didn't have to be. You only had to do the bare minimum and be my doctor."

"It was my pleasure." A wry smile tilted his lips, but the sharp watchfulness in his gaze made her heart beat faster.

"I doubt that, Doc."

"How did you handle being on your own last night?"

"Are you asking as a doctor or concerned friend?"

"A concerned friend. Was it difficult?"

"Not really. Jamie was there, and it helped some. But sleeping in my own bed again was still surreal, ya know? Going back home after all those months. It was as if time hadn't caught up yet. Well, minus the mess my brother made of my kitchen." She scowled.

"I know what you mean. I lost a friend and mentor a while back. I was the one who offered to clear out his office. At the oddest moments, I would find myself overwhelmed. Being there, touching his things, it almost seemed as if he would walk through that door at any moment. Like I would look up to find him standing in the doorway."

"Yes, exactly. Thank you for sharing that. I'm sorry for your loss."

"It was quite a few years ago, but thanks. I appreciate it."

Their conversation was interrupted by a shout of *"Tonto!"*

Sammy felt the first real tug of belonging in a long while. It could never be an act with her bestie. Renee was truly happy to see her.

"Do I want to know why she is yelling 'Tonto'?"

"Probably not."

"Tell me you don't have a propensity for scalping people."

"Why, Doc, how un-PC of you!"

"I have Native American ancestry. I'm allowed to make references like that."

Sammy wasn't sure why she'd never seen it before, but the truth was in his nearly black hair and dark eyes. She laughed and sauntered away to join her friends.

"Who in the world is that tall, delicious drink of water?"

Sammy turned to Renee and noticed the lustful look in her eyes. Eyes that tracked Stephen from the counter to his black Lexus. Unsure why she suddenly felt snappish, Sammy tried to shake it off. Stephen was her friend, but it didn't mean other women couldn't find him attractive. He was downright gorgeous, yet she never allowed herself to actively think about it. No, his sex appeal didn't matter, because there would never be more than friendship between them in any regard. The idea of moving on from Michael wasn't something she was ready to entertain.

"That, my horny friend, is Dr. Stephen Montgomery. He's a psychiatrist at Brookhaven."

"Damn. Seriously? I may have to get myself committed."

"Oh, Kemo. I missed you," Sammy laughed.

For the next hour and a half, her group of friends ran the gauntlet of conversations. No subject was sacred. Sammy told them of the near-rape, of losing the baby, and of working to find the will to live again. She spoke of Rabid Ronni and how she had helped prevent a tragedy with her premonition.

She didn't have to worry about her friends thinking she was off her rocker if she talked about precognitive things. They had all been recipients of her warnings at one time or another while they were growing up.

The one thing she didn't speak of was the dreamwalking. The subject made her uncomfortable, and she planned to hold her secret moments with Michael close to her heart.

"Earth to Sammy!"

"I'm sorry. What'd I miss?"

"Skye just asked what you planned to do for work? We have an opening here until you're ready to delve into a more substantial job," Renee said.

"That would be great. Are you sure? I don't want to push the boundaries of friendship if you truly don't need the help."

"Oh, we need help, all right. Jem took off for maternity leave and plans to be gone for the next three to four months." Skye paused, realizing what she'd said. Sammy and Jem would have been due at the exact same time. "Oh, Sammy, I'm sorry. You... I... Oh *shit!*"

"Don't. Seriously, Skye. It's okay. I've had time to deal with it." Sammy had had time to deal, she just hadn't completely let the dream of Michael and their child go. But if she didn't want to go back to Brookhaven, she needed to find a way to hide her feelings on the subject.

Skye's concerned gaze swept her face. *She knew.* Yet Sammy desperately wanted to pretend everything was okay, if only for one lunch. She needed something in her life to be normal. She pasted on a bright smile. "Have you had the baby shower for Jem yet?"

"We did. Just last week in fact."

Sammy sent a silent thank you up to the universe. If she was forced to sit through a baby shower, she thought she would lose her stinking mind. "I'm sorry I missed it. Does she know what she's having?" she asked.

Linda told her a girl and waxed on about all the cute gifts.

Sweat formed on Sammy's upper lip, and she flashed her teeth in an attempt at a pleasant smile. She swore to herself she was happy for

Jem—and she truly was—but she couldn't chase away the images of the beautiful little girl she'd dreamed about.

When the subject moved on to another friend's upcoming vacation, Sammy excused herself and tossed up her lunch in the bathroom toilet. She wanted to smack her head against the sink repeatedly. Anything to force away her memories. Wasn't the frontal lobe responsible for memories? She should have asked for a lobotomy while at Brookhaven. Did doctors even perform those surgeries anymore? One could only hope.

She rinsed her mouth, then dug in her purse for a stick of gum. She washed her face and reapplied her makeup. Looking and feeling almost human once more, she made her way back to the table.

"Where can we get some chocolate around here?" she broke through the chatter.

"I have just the thing." Skye jumped up and offered her a hug. "I'm so sorry," she whispered.

Heat crept up Sammy's neck and warmed her cheeks. She patted Skye's back as she broke the hug. "Really, it's okay. I just need some chocolate. STAT!"

She watched as her purple-haired friend went running for the kitchen.

The door to the cafe was jerked open by the most insanely hot man Sammy had ever seen. All the women stopped talking to stare.

"Holy shit!"

Sammy wasn't sure who'd said it. It could have been her. The man was a work of art. He strolled in like a hungry panther, each move sensuous without trying to be. His eyes scanned the group staring at him, seeming to look for one person in particular. Frowning in puzzlement, he cast his eyes around the rest of the cafe.

"I'm interrupting, aren't I?" he said, voice smooth and warm, with a hint of wry humor. "I apologize, ladies. I was looking for Skye. Renee, will you let her know I stopped by and to come see me next door if she has time?"

The women remained silent, eyes locked on his retreating ass until Skye brought back the dessert.

"What's going on? Did I miss something?" she asked.

"More like someone," Linda offered up, practically wiping drool from the side of her mouth.

"Greyson James," Sue sighed in a reverent tone.

Linda and Sue were sisters and happily married, but they weren't blind. They were, without a doubt, the funniest duo in their group of friends. It was rare to see either of them without a smile. A more bubbly and naturally beautiful pair of women, both inside and out, Sammy had yet to see.

"Okay, spill," ordered Sammy as she picked up a fork. She could use the distraction. "Wait, Greyson James? His brother wouldn't be Gabriel James the attorney, would he?"

"You know, Gabriel?" Linda eyes widened like an eager puppy wanting a treat.

Sammy started to laugh. A deep belly laugh that came from her core. When she could catch her breath, she told them of breaking Gabe's nose during their first meeting.

"Oh, Sammy, the craziest things happen to you. You should write a book."

Clarity came to her along with a vision of the future. Sammy knew exactly what she needed to do. She'd toyed with the idea while at Brookhaven, had even felt the need to keep a journal. But she never in a million years would have pictured herself as a writer. However, once the suggestion was thrown out there and the idea took hold, Sammy latched on to it.

Yes, she was going to become an author!

PART III

CHAPTER 22

FIVE MONTHS LATER

"For Christ's sake, Lil' Bit, Sassy has her legs crossed. Take a break and walk your dog, will ya?"

The interruption almost made her lose her cool. She was just about finished with the current chapter and didn't need the distraction. She scowled at James. More and more lately, she'd become so absorbed in her writing she failed to see or hear anything going on around her. As a result, poor Sassy went to her brother for her basic needs. Instead of taking care of them, James would disrupt Sammy's artistic flow. She couldn't understand why he didn't get she needed complete concentration for her work in progress.

"You know, Jamie, if you are going to live here, you could stand to take the dog out when I'm working."

"It doesn't matter I pay rent? Now I have to walk your damned dog? I did enough of that while you were vacationing at Brookhaven."

"Take that back. You've crossed a line, buddy. You will not—I repeat not—call my sweet Sassy a damned dog." Sammy leaned down to kiss and cuddle her pup. "He didn't mean it. He's a mean butthole, Sassy girl. Don't you listen to him. Mommy will take you out."

"Seriously? No wonder she looks for me. I would hunt out anyone else who didn't baby-talk me."

"Oh, shut it. I'm just soothing her since you hurt her feelings."

"Whatever. But can you please pay attention to your dog? Since I am the breadwinner in this little household, I need to be able to do my work without Sassy begging me to let her out, play ball, or feed her."

"Pfft. As if redesigning and rehabbing old houses is work," Sammy teased, snatching the leash from her brother's hand as she pushed past him in the doorway. "We're going to the beach. Hold my calls."

"I'm not your secretary. Take your phone. Oh, and Mom wants us to come for dinner tonight. Annie's in town and has some pretty important news, I guess."

Sammy shot Jamie a questioning look. "Do you think she's ready to talk about her divorce? Wouldn't it be great if she is moving back to Flagler? Maybe that is what tonight's dinner is about."

"I don't know, but if I ever see her asshole of an ex, I am going to beat the shit out of him. I can't believe he cheated on her. *With his fucking assistant!* How cliché can you get? Every time I think about it, I get pissed off. He moved her to Virginia—away from our family, I might add—and then took up with someone else? What the fuck?"

"I know. I won't be long. Do you want to ride together, or do you have plans after?"

"We can ride together."

"Good, we can devise ways to do away with that fucktwat Charlie and feed him to the fishes."

Sammy zipped up her hoodie and headed across the street with Sassy. A1A was busy this time of day due to people heading home from work or to late-afternoon errands. As another car zipped passed, she sighed. She certainly didn't miss the rat race. Writing suited her personality. Already, she had lucked on to a terrific mentor with the help of Gabriel James.

Gabe had turned out to be a better person than she'd initially thought. She supposed she only had herself to blame for his initial hostility. Although, it could be argued he was more handsome now that his nose wasn't as perfect or straight. Women liked a rugged-looking man—or at least that is what she told him whenever she saw him and felt guilty for rearranging his face.

Fifteen minutes of ball play was enough for Sassy. Her attention was soon caught by sandpipers running along the shoreline, sticking their heads in the sand. Once the closest bird chirped at her in outrage, it became game on. Sassy tore up and down a short section of beach, chasing them as fast as her little legs would carry her. Unfortunately for her, the birds were faster. It didn't stop the dog from trying, causing Sammy no small amount of amusement.

Sassy noticed the man jogging toward them well before Sammy, and raced over to throw herself at his legs. She only did that for one other person besides James. *Stephen*. It turned out he lived three blocks north of her. Why she and Michael had never encountered him on the beach was an odd twist of fate.

"A guy can't get a jog in on this beach without being accosted by a wet, sandy dog. I don't know why I bother to come to this stretch," he joked as he plopped down in the sand next to her, panting and sucking in air.

"Yeah, they let anyone come here," she returned, bumping his shoulder with her own. "How've you been? I haven't seen you for a while."

"Vacation. I went to Europe with my family over the Christmas holiday." He paused to check his heart rate on his monitor. "Did you manage all right with James?"

Stephen referred to the anniversary of Sammy's miscarriage. It had been a tough day, without a doubt. She'd spent it with a bottle of wine and her laptop. Losing herself to her writing had been cathartic.

"Actually, I sent him to spend time with my mother. He was hovering and driving me crazy. Did you put him up to it?"

"The truth?" At her nod, he confessed, "Yes. I was worried it would be more than you could deal with. I should've known you'd prove me wrong."

Scanning the horizon, Sammy tried to piece her words together carefully. In the end, she came up with nothing to relay her upset from the constant interference of others. Everyone still treated her as if she were broken, and it was annoying as fuck. You'd think she wasn't a thirty-year-old woman with a mind of her own.

Whistling for Sassy, who had begun to get too close to a suspicious blob, Sammy abruptly stood and brushed the sand from her jeans.

"Samantha? Are you angry with me?"

"No. Not really. I'm sure you can't help being a doctor. It's your job after all." She smiled tightly.

"I wasn't being a doctor. I was being your friend."

"Excuse me if I find it hard to tell the difference," she snapped. She doubted he could tell the difference either. His caring nature was ingrained in his DNA.

"If you want to see it that way, fine. But I'm not going to apologize for caring about you. Catch you later."

Sassy whined as her favorite friend ran off without showering her with affection. It was a clear sign of his agitation. Stephen never left without paying homage to Sassy.

Sammy mentally debated following him but decided to let him get over it on his own. They each needed to find a balance between friendship and the ex-doctor/patient relationship. As she trudged through the sand back to her little house, she thought about all the things he'd done for her and felt like a total bitch. Just as she was lifting her phone to call him, his number popped up on her screen.

"I'm sorry," they both said it at the same time, talking over one another.

"Stephen, I really am sorry. I always feel like everyone thinks I'm fragile, and it's my trigger. Not to mention, I like you better as my friend than I ever did as my psychiatrist."

"I get it. Believe me when I say I was only looking out for you, *as a friend*. Knowing what you went through after the miscarriage worried me. When no one could get through to you, it was frightening. I didn't want you to have a setback and no one be there to help you. I called your brother, figuring since he lived with you, he was the best candidate for the job." He sighed heavily. "To separate the doctor from the friend is impossible to the degree you want, Samantha. But I'm not analyzing you when we're together. If you understand nothing else, please understand that."

"Okay."

"Okay? That's it? No 'fuck you, Stephen, you're an asshole'?"

Sammy had to laugh at his disbelief. There was a time those would have been the first words out of her mouth.

"Thank you, Stephen. *For being such a good friend.*"

"You're welcome, Samantha. How about dinner tonight?"

"I'd love to, but I can't. Something's going down with Annie. Mom called a family dinner. What about tomorrow?"

"I have a shift at the hospital. I'm off Wednesday. Do you think you can take a break from your rewrites?"

"Yes. Call me Wednesday around lunch to remind me. I have no concept of time anymore."

"Deal. And give Sassy a kiss for me. Tell her when I pick you up on Wednesday, I will bring her a special treat."

"Good, because she's quite cross with you at the moment. You stormed off without treating her like the princess she believes she is."

"My bad."

Sammy giggled. There was something about such a GQ man using slang like "my bad" that tickled her.

"Bye, Doc."

"Bye, Samantha."

"I INTEND TO MOVE TO A PLACE CALLED STONEBROOKE, NORTH Carolina. It's a laid-back and stress-free lifestyle. I can also work from home. Then, if I do go out, I'm not overcome with people's overworked and aggressive energy."

Annie didn't need to explain further. The whole Holt clan knew how difficult everyday life could be for an empath of her level.

A pang of sadness caused Sammy's heart to glitch. She wanted nothing more than to have Annie return to Florida for good. But Annie had always loved the mountains of North Carolina, and her sister claimed she loved the cooler weather better than the heat. As a result, she'd be much happier in her intended location.

Personally, Sammy couldn't understand why anyone would give

up the beach. What she could understand was Annie's need to start over. Most days, she wanted the same thing. Regardless, she was going to miss her.

The distance Sammy had created over Michael had damaged her relationship with Annie to a small degree. She owed her sister better. The second they had a quiet moment alone, Sammy pulled her to the side. "Annie, I want to say I'm sorry. I could've been a much better friend to you this last year. I was so wrapped up in my own problems, I failed to see what you were going through."

"Oh, Sammy. Thank you, but I think the fact I was blind to my marriage failing is a hell of a lot different than you losing both Michael and your baby." Annie hugged her tight. "Please know this has nothing to do with you and me. I simply want a fresh start." She swallowed hard and stared out the slider door. "If anyone's to blame here, it's Charlie. He could've come to me. I sensed something. Anytime I brought it up, he made me think I was going crazy or intruding in his mind."

"You weren't." Without a doubt, Annie wasn't the type to pry into another's thoughts, even if the other person was her husband. If Charlie had made her experience doubt, he'd done it deliberately. "Obviously, he was gaslighting you, the prick."

"Yep, and I never suspected a thing. I feel like such an idiot."

"Stop it. He's the idiot. He threw away the perfect woman."

Annie scrunched up her face.

"He did," Sammy stressed.

"I love you, Sammy. You know that. Besides, now that you work from home, there is nothing stopping you from coming to visit me, right?"

Wordlessly, she nodded her agreement. Today had been a day of changes. Annie's decision to relocate to North Carolina was one, and Sammy's new three-book deal heralded another. She wanted to share her good news, but waiting was best.

"What aren't you telling me? Something great happened. What is it?"

"You know it's creepy when you do that, right?" Sammy teased, not finding it creepy at all. Sammy'd had a similar connection with Michael. "My new agent called earlier today. They've landed me a traditional publishing deal for a series I plan to write. Can you believe it?" She inhaled deeply. "I'm not going to lie, I'm terrified. It's a lot of work."

"*Ohmygod, Sammy!* That is incredible. I'm so thrilled for you. *Wow!* My sister, the author. You'll hit the New York Times bestsellers list."

"Wouldn't that be great? Although, I highly doubt that will happen with my second book." She clasped Annie's hand. "I didn't know how much I loved the whole creative process until now. I haven't dared call myself professional, even after Hannah signed on as my agent. This makes it real though. I'll be a hybrid author." Sammy couldn't contain herself and squealed her excitement. "I was trying to hold off because I didn't want to eclipse your news."

The greatest thing about channeling other people's energy was the excitement and laughter they provided. Even if you were feeling your worst, if someone else was in a great mood, it became impossible to be upset. In that regard, Annie was as ecstatic as Sammy, both from absorbing her emotions and from being honestly happy for her good fortune. Seeing her sister's smile brought joy to Sammy's heart.

Annie arched a brow and gave her a no-nonsense look. "I demand the first autographed copy."

"You got it. Can I tell the rest of the family tonight?"

"After that scream? They'd ferret it out anyway," Annie said dryly.

"Sorry. How are the eardrums?"

They laughed and headed back to the dining room where they stumbled upon their oldest sister setting the table for dinner. Because Margie was humming, they stopped to watch her in disbelief. Squinting one eye and tilting her head, Sammy tried to make out what was causing the glow radiating from Margie.

"Think she got laid?" she asked.

Annie snorted and choked in an attempt to contain her laughter. Even after the long months in Brookhaven, Sammy hadn't developed much of a filter. When Margie glanced up at the noise, she flushed red, and it told Annie and Sammy everything they needed to know.

"*Go, Margie!*" Sammy cheered. "Who's the lucky guy?"

Both sisters had been so caught up in teasing Margie, they failed to notice the fourth person in the room until he chuckled. *Gabriel James.* Margie studiously avoided looking at Gabe as she turned the color of a beet.

"My children are present," she hissed.

Sammy looked at her niece and nephews in the next room. The two boys were battling it out on the latest video game craze, and Kaley was engrossed in her iPhone with headphones dangling from her ears.

"It's not as if they're even paying attention. Spill," she egged her on.

Gabe's bark of laughter rang out and caught all three women's attention. He was sitting in Martin's favorite seat, tilted back on two legs. As they watched, he landed the chair on all fours and strutted over to Margie. He leaned down and whispered in her ear. If it was possible for Margie to blush any brighter red, she did. With a wicked grin, he winked at Annie and Sammy, then headed into the kitchen, proclaiming something smelled delightful.

"If you're hitting that, Margie, you better be sharing the high points. We need to live vicariously through you."

Once again, Sammy's outrageous comment caused Annie untold merriment.

"You two are seriously ridiculous, you know that?" Margie retorted.

"Not good, huh? That's a damned shame. I had such high hopes for Old Gabe," Sammy teased.

"You told them I was bad in bed?" Gabriel stepped back into the dining room with drinking glasses sandwiched between his large hands. His tone, dark and dangerous, caused a shiver to chase down Sammy's spine. He set the glassware down with such force, Sammy feared they'd need to search for cracks. Without another word, he clasped Margie's hand and proceeded to drag her from the room. A promised "we'll see about that" echoed in the space around them. He paused in the doorway and spun back with a pointed glare at Sammy.

"And you... stop calling me *old*." With that, he continued out the door, tugging an indignant Margie along behind him.

"Oh, someone's going to get it."

"Ohmygod, Sammy!" Annie doubled over in her hysteria. The effort to breathe through her laughter was too much, and she collapsed against the wall, weak and gasping for air—much to Sammy's own amusement. Fanning herself with one hand, Annie wiped away tears with the other. "You are too much. If she comes back in with a satisfied smile on her face, promise me you'll set me up the same way if I ever start dating again."

"Done. Let's finish setting up the table before Mom suspects the trouble we've caused."

"We've caused? How about *you've* caused?"

"Yeah, you're splitting hairs. Grab a plate. Oh, and check those glasses. We don't want to be the cause of Gabe's murder if he broke one."

CHAPTER 23

Winter turned to spring, which heralded the looming deadline for Sammy's first novel and the rough draft of her second. She'd only registered for a small handful of book-signing events throughout the Southern states she thought might be beneficial for sales.

As Sammy perused her upcoming itinerary, Stephen spoke to her from his favorite chair in her home office. "Are you even listening to me?" he complained good-naturedly.

"Not really. Last I tuned in, you were bitching about my sister breaking your friend's heart."

"So you *were* listening."

"Tell Old Gabe to man up. Margie needs someone forceful." She waved a hand in dismissal, more than a little distracted.

"I think his forcefulness started this whole issue."

Sammy's head came up. *Finally!* Something interesting. "Really? What did Gabriel do this time?"

The truth was, Margie always found fault with her neighbor. For a brief moment in time, Sammy had thought her sister and Gabe would make a match of it, especially after the favor she'd done for Margie back in January. A more satisfied expression she had yet to see on anyone's face when they came in to dinner. Gabriel and Margie couldn't keep their eyes off each other throughout the rest of their meal, and Annie couldn't keep the smirk off her face. Sammy assumed Annie had picked up on all those crazy, hot vibes between the two.

"He tells me it boils down to Margie's fear of commitment. She doesn't think he can possibly be serious about her, because he's younger than she is, and he dated 'supermodels' in the past. Her words, not his."

"Oh, good grief! It's only a six year gap between them. It isn't like he's young enough to be her son or anything." Sammy rolled her eyes. "My sister's insecure because of the previous jerk she was married to. Gabe has his work cut out for him."

"That was my opinion, too. I think he was looking for something more profound from me. Some solution I didn't have to give." Stephen changed the subject. "What has you so distracted today? It's not like you."

"My signing schedule. I went ahead and booked a few smaller venues, and I need to decide whether I want to only do local one-day signings or add weekend conventions. My first one is in three months, and I'm terrified."

"Book signings? I'm surprised those are a thing anymore. Don't most people use e-readers?"

"Actually, you would be surprised how many still buy paperbacks. But yes, promo tours are dead. Usually, authors register for signing events to connect with fans and only for a handful of bigger cities." She flared her eyes. "Being that my budget for travel and lodging is so low, I will probably need to rule out a few here or there. The hotel costs are a killer." She avoided his penetrating gaze and studied her on-screen list. "A new author friend told me about a smaller event. She said they get a decent turnout, so I added it for later in the year."

THE THING SAMANTHA BRUSHED OVER AND THAT STOOD OUT FOR Stephen was the addition of a new city. For a relatively unknown author to go to book signings didn't make much sense. Dread filled him.

"Tell me you aren't going where I think you're going."

Samantha clammed up, confirming Stephen's suspicions.

"Why are you doing this to yourself? It's been a year and a half. You can't still believe he's alive? It's preposterous."

Would he ever hold on this tightly if someone he loved died? As a psychiatrist, he was well schooled in the stages of grief. He also knew some individuals refused to let go. To heal completely. They clung to the memory of their loved one like a life preserver. Without that faith, they felt adrift. Perhaps past success made him so much more upset now. He was invested in Samantha's recovery for reasons of his own.

"I'll find out the truth and be able to put this all to rest—or I won't. But either way, I owe it to Michael and myself to try."

"I want to understand, Samantha. I really do. But how is it going to help at this late date?"

"You can never understand."

"Try me," Stephen offered, careful to keep his tone neutral. To make her defensive would mean she would shut down and refuse to give an explanation.

Closing her eyes, Samantha sighed.

"I let him down." Swallowing hard and forcing back tears, she tried again. "When he first disappeared, I was in a daze. I rejected the idea he was lost to me. Of course, anyone who suggested differently pissed me right off." She met his concerned gaze head-on. "You saw the result. I was a train wreck. Jesus, Stephen, I assaulted a man of God! *In a church!* Who does that?"

She cleared her throat. "Then my stint in Brookhaven took longer than it should have. In the end, I could—*and should*—have searched sooner. I did everything wrong from the get-go. But now it's been so long, and I'm starting to question my own certainty. I need to do this."

Her wide blue eyes begged him to understand even if he didn't agree. He was no match for the pleading look she directed his way.

"Okay. I get it." At her disbelieving gasp, he said, "I do. And I think you should go."

"Really?"

He was deeply troubled by Samantha's insistence Michael was still alive, but Stephen nodded all the same.

"Oh, Stephen! Thank you. Thank you for getting it. Thank you for being so supportive." She launched herself at him and wound her arms tightly around his neck. "You are such a great friend."

If Samantha could've seen his face, Stephen was sure she would've noticed the grimace her words caused. He fought the urge to pull her closer and confess he desired so much more than friendship. No, he'd bide his time until she was well and truly past all thoughts of Michael. The trick would be getting her to see him as a real contender for her heart and not as a buddy. She'd thrown him into the friend zone, and being relegated to friend status seriously hurt a man's chances at a relationship with a woman.

"I have a stipulation. When it comes time for you to go to Dallas, you take someone with you. If you find out some ugly truths, you will need support. Promise?"

Samantha pulled back, a frown on her face. He watched the play of emotions as she debated the pros and cons of what he suggested. It went against her nature to ask for help. Finally, she nodded.

"Will you go with me?"

"Me?" He was stupefied she'd even asked. "I have to work."

"Never mind. Forget I asked."

Stephen could almost believe he'd disappointed her with his answer. It wasn't like he couldn't get time off. He had vacation days piling up, and he hadn't taken leave in over a year.

"No. I'll go. Just get me the dates as soon as you can."

"You mean it? Seriously?"

"Yes. But no sex. No matter how much you beg. I'm not your boy toy." Stephen basked in the light of her laughter. Michael had been a very lucky man while he was alive.

CHAPTER 24

FOUR MONTHS LATER...

Sammy sifted through the clothing she had brought with her to Dallas. Nothing seemed to suit her mood this evening. She wanted to look her best but discarded dress after dress. Nothing she'd brought felt right. A check of her watch destroyed her hope that there might be enough time to run out and shop. There wasn't. Nerves ate at her stomach, tying it into tight knots.

Why the need to be so picture-perfect tonight? This dinner would be the same as any other dinner she'd shared with Stephen over the past year. She couldn't figure out why she was so edgy.

After mentally scolding herself and a debate of the merits of each outfit, she settled on one of her favorites. The dress was made of a shimmering deep red silk. It was backless, and the hem came to just above the knee. The thin spaghetti straps allowed the bodice to dip just shy of revealing an indecent amount of cleavage. The skirt flared out and was given fullness by another layer of dark red material. The perfect outfit to make a woman feel feminine and sexy.

Stephen had insisted on taking her to one of Dallas's finest restaurants for their first night in town. While it was a nice gesture on his part, Sammy couldn't work up the enthusiasm to go.

Wouldn't it be better to research and see what she could find on

Michael, if anything? Stephen shot down her plan. He pointed out they'd have difficulty reaching anyone this late in the day. Though he had a valid point, Sammy needed to be productive. Being this close to her objective after almost two years made her itch to find answers. She exhaled in frustration and turned her attention to the finishing touches of her outfit for the evening.

Her stockings came last. She attached them to the garter belt to complete her underwear set. She scrutinized her body carefully in the full-length wall mirror, taking the time to admire her figure. She still couldn't believe how such a dramatic change could happen with a little exercise and proper diet. Not that she'd been too terribly overweight before. No, maybe a little out of shape would be the better description. Now, as she took in the muscle tone and definition, Sammy had to admit it was worth the effort to run on the beach in the mornings. All her hard work deserved expensive underwear. It was her newest obsession and made her feel as if she had a secret all her own.

Those first weeks of exercise about killed her, but she'd persevered, mainly because Stephen was a damned workhorse. When she'd added squats to her workout routine, the difference to her body became pronounced.

Sammy turned to get a better look at her perky ass. *Definitely not bad.* Michael would love the difference. She winced. Yeah, she had to stop letting those pesky thoughts of Michael constantly sneak up on her. The trip to Dallas was to find answers so she could let go of the past and forge a new future for herself. She also needed to figure out why her gift had let her down. Had the man she'd known and loved been alive and well, he'd have returned to her. But one way or another, she needed to get a grip.

Nerves ate at her, and she decided to change from her current underwear to something a little more sedate. A knock on the connecting door interrupted her.

"Yes?" she called out.

"Samantha, it's Stephen. Are you about ready?"

"Give me another two minutes, please."

She gave her reflection one last rueful look. *So much for changing into practical underwear.* She carefully slipped the dress back over her head, slid her feet into the red shoes, and grabbed the matching purse. Once she'd transferred the contents of her everyday purse to the pretty red bag, she was good to go.

One last time, she examined the woman in the mirror. Something was missing, but what? *Earrings!* She walked to the small safe located inside the closet and worked the combination. Taking out a small velvet box, she opened the lid. The diamond and ruby earrings winked as they caught the hall light. She'd always loved this set. They were a present from Michael.

Fresh pain filled her heart, causing her to wonder if she dared to wear them. The day she'd received them—Christmas morning three years ago—was emblazoned in her memories. Her mind drifted back to that wonderful day.

"Hurry, Michael! Hurry!" Sammy urged, jumping up and down on their queen-size bed like a small child.

"Uh," he moaned, rolling onto his stomach before saying, "Not now, love. I'm too worn out to be your sugar daddy."

"What?"

His muffled laugh told her he was playing her. "Michael, you get up this instant."

"Ah, darlin', I told you, I just need five more minutes then I promise I'll be your sex slave. Whatever you want." He heaved out a heartfelt sigh.

She nailed him in the back of the head with a pillow and laughed when he yelped.

"What the...!"

"Get moving!" she growled, realizing his game.

He rolled over and gave her a look of such hurt, it gave Sammy a moment's pause.

"Why did you do that? You really couldn't wait a few more minutes for sex?" His grin gave him away.

"You ass," she laughed as she swung the pillow at his head a second time.

Their playful tussle turned into a wonderful session of lovemaking.

Later, they sat next to the Christmas tree, listening to Giovanni's talent fill the room with classical carols. They opened all their gifts, none of which were any great surprise to her. She'd found and steamed open most of the packages earlier in the week and was careful to tape them back exactly as she'd found them.

"Oh, wait! There's one more I forgot to bring in." Michael grinned in the face of her shock. "What? You missed one in all your digging?"

"How did you know?"

"Oh, Sammy Darlin', I can read you like a book. Be right back."

He came in, pretending to struggle with a large gift-wrapped box.

"Where were you hiding that?" she asked. She'd made a thorough search of the garage the night before, and she'd have sworn under oath there wasn't a stone left unturned, or in their case, a bin left unsearched.

Michael dropped the box as if it weighed two hundred pounds, panting and wiping non-existent sweat from his brow. "This little thing?" he questioned.

"Yes, that little thing, you nerdy butt," Sammy retorted with a smile for his ridiculous antics.

"Well, I had James bring it over this morning while we were otherwise occupied."

"No way! You had absolutely no idea our fight this morning was going to happen," she protested. "Besides, I would have heard the garage door."

Michael's delighted grin widened. It turned into full-fledged laughter as she blushed. Okay, he had a point. She never would have heard the door.

The suspense of the gift was killing her, and she decided to go for the prize. She tore at the wrapping paper, not unlike a kid expecting to find Santa had brought her favorite toy. As she opened the plain cardboard box, she was astonished to find another gift-wrapped package inside. This went on for at least five more. By the time she got to the bottom, not just a little frustrated, she got down to a small jewelry-sized box. Holding her breath, she opened the lid, unsure what to expect. Resting there against the black velvet was a pair of exquisite earrings.

"Michael, you shouldn't have. We really can't afford these."

She felt a catch in her throat as he focused on her stunned face. He loved her so much. It was obvious in his every look and touch. The sheer force of his adoring gaze made her want to weep.

"Aren't you going to try them on?" he asked with a husky catch to his voice.

She readily complied.

"Stand up," he commanded.

Again, she complied.

"Hmm, something's not quite right."

His frown gave her the impression there must be some flaw in one of the beautiful ruby stones. Her hand came up to touch one of the earrings.

"I know." He snapped his fingers, stood, and closed the distance between them. "They don't match your blue robe."

Tugging at the knot holding it in place, he untied her robe. Gentle hands pushed the material down her shoulders, letting it pool on the ground at her feet. His honey eyes hypnotized her.

Sammy stood trembling, exposed.

"Much better. Much, much better."

The deep, husky timbre of his voice left little doubt of his desire. It ignited a fire low in Sammy's belly. It blazed out of control as it raced to her lady parts. Her breasts tightened with want.

"Oh, Michael."

A SECOND KNOCK JERKED SAMMY FROM HER MEMORIES.

"Samantha?"

Sammy looked from the door to the diamond and ruby earrings. How could she move forward when it was so beautiful in the past? With a deep sigh, she let Stephen into her room.

"I'm sorry, Stephen. Just one more second."

She fastened the jewelry to her lobes. With a smile for Stephen, she scooped up her clutch and wrap from the bed. When she would have passed him to go to the door, Stephen grabbed her shoulders from behind.

"Samantha, wait."

Tension locked her in place.

"Your zipper is not quite all the way up," he told her stiffly.

He pulled it up the remaining distance and closed the clasp at the back of her dress.

Shame coursed through her. Clearly, she'd insulted him with her withdrawal. His touch, however innocent, had come too close on the heels of her memories of Michael's lovemaking.

"Thank you." She rose up to kiss his cheek.

During the ride to the restaurant, Sammy's thoughts drifted to Michael again and again. Maybe it was the earrings. Or maybe it was Dallas. He lingered at the forefront of her mind and made it impossible for her to concentrate on the tale with which Stephen tried to amuse her.

After the cab stopped, she got out and offered him her arm so he could escort her inside. She paused in the foyer to wait for him to check their reservation and to admire the sheer beauty of the room. This was the fanciest place she'd ever been to in her entire life.

The marble floor was a rich chocolate espresso, almost black in color. The shine was so great, the room looked twice as crowded from the reflection of its patrons. Grecian-styled columns were topped with busts of Plato, Caesar, and other historical greats, each tastefully displayed throughout the foyer without seeming ostentatious.

As she watched, couples continued to enter the restaurant, young and old alike. They all seemed to be happy, without a care in the world. As she was about to turn away, another couple entering the restaurant captured her attention.

From behind, there was something almost familiar about the way the man moved. Perhaps without the limp he would have had a smoother gait. As it was, he reminded her of a wounded lion. Part grace, part awkwardness. He captivated her. It was there in how he stood, holding the hand of the woman he was with, tilting his head to listen to her. Smiling. Dimples flashing.

The object of her attention cast a glance in her direction as if he sensed her regard.

Her heart seized. Shock washed through her entire body. When her lungs refused to go another moment without air, she took huge gulping breaths.

He shifted to let his date follow the hostess.

Sammy bolted across the room and latched onto his arm. "Michael!"

He frowned down at her as if he'd never seen her before. "I'm sorry, do I know you?"

While his look was polite, as if he were addressing a stranger, the underlying curiosity he exhibited kept her going. Made her push for some response.

"I... y-you..." Sammy stuttered to a halt.

She'd finally found him. But in all the scenarios she'd created in her mind, his polite indifference had not been one of them. She stared, speechless. Helpless. With her focus intent on Michael, she ignored Stephen's approach and the ashen expression on the face of the young woman who clutched Michael's opposite arm.

"Joe, who is this woman?"

JOE SHOOK HIS HEAD AS IF AWAKENING FROM A DREAM. HIS GAZE shifted between each person in their group. The small, dark-haired woman who'd approached him seemed familiar. The nagging sensation that he knew her grew in intensity. Where from? How? His mind would not let him recall. Trying to recover the situation, he smiled at his date.

"Beth, I would like you to meet..." He paused for the dark-haired woman to fill in her name. His gaze lingered on her, and he couldn't tear his eyes away a second time.

Wide blue eyes flew to his. She stared at him as if he were an angel sent from heaven. Her look of adoration bothered him. Not because he didn't like the admiration of a beautiful woman, but because she seemed to think he was someone he wasn't. His next words unintentionally erased the delight from her face.

"Please tell me where we know each other from."

She'd started to reach up to touch his face, but jerked as if he'd struck her.

Unease curled in his chest, and the desire to apologize and recall his words nearly overwhelmed him. As he watched, the light died from those stunning eyes and tears shimmered in their depths. His urge to comfort this stranger was stronger than anything he'd experienced to date.

"I'm sorry," he whispered. His throat felt scratchy. His own eyes stung, and he rubbed his hand along the back of his neck to ease his building tension.

SAMMY REALIZED WHAT HAD BEEN NAGGING AT HER. *HIS FACE.* IT WAS different than she remembered. A scar ran from his temple to his jaw. Also, his nose looked as if it had been broken at some point. Even the cut and style of his hair differed from what she remembered. But his lips, his general face shape, even his eyes resembled Michael's.

A doppelgänger? Everyone supposedly had one. But she'd been so sure.

She placed her hand on his sleeve, an apology of sorts.

As she touched him, she opened her mind to receive whatever vision might come but shut it right back down an instant later. The future didn't matter now. The man she knew was gone. *What an idiot she'd been to come all this way for nothing!*

Panic and sorrow welled up inside her, so strong as to cause the air to stop flowing to her lungs. She struggled to inhale the oxygen she so desperately needed.

"No! No!" pounded in her brain. She whispered it repeatedly until Stephen gripped her shoulders and gave her a little shake.

"Samantha!" The forcefulness of his tone did the trick.

The heat of embarrassment swept up from her toes to her hairline. She had to be as red as her damned dress.

"I'm sorry," Sammy choked out. Pulling away, she rushed for the door and for the freedom escaping these people would afford.

"Samantha! *Wait!*" Stephen hollered.

But she couldn't wait. If she didn't get away, she would disgrace herself.

"Stupid! Stupid! Stupid!" played like a recording through her brain as she rushed away in mindless flight. It was imperative she keep moving. She didn't care where as long as it was away from here.

A cab paused to distribute a man and woman on the sidewalk outside of the restaurant. Sammy took advantage and jumped inside.

"Drive," she barked.

"Where to, lady?"

"Anywhere. Please, just drive," she begged, desperate to be gone.

The door was jerked open, and Joe jumped inside, startling them both and eliciting a scream from Sammy.

"Drive," he commanded.

This time the cab driver did as he was told.

"Dude, seriously?" she leaned forward to hiss at the cabbie. "You listened to him but not to me? *What the fuck?"*

"Ignore her," Joe ordered the driver before he shifted to face her. "Now, how about you tell me where you know me from?"

"Driver, stop the car, this man needs to get out," she commanded.

Once again, the cabbie ignored her. It might have had something to do with Joe's "Don't you dare." His dark tone brooked no argument.

"Man, I am *so* not paying your fare!" she muttered.

The cabbie glanced back at Joe from the rearview mirror. Joe nodded to indicate he had it covered.

"Where's Stephen?" Sammy searched through the back window.

"The guy you were with? Yeah, I'm afraid he was detained."

JOE WASN'T ABOUT TO TELL HER THAT WHILE HE HELD THE LEAD IN THE race to follow her, he'd shoved a trash can in front of Stephen, effectively slowing the other guy down. It had allowed Joe the advantage of reaching her first.

With gentle fingers, he clasped her chin and turned her face to his. "Samantha, right? Samantha, please. I want to know, how do you know me?"

In her apparent embarrassment and misery, Samantha missed the urgency and slight hint of desperation in his voice. She also missed the too familiar way he touched her. A touch no stranger should have taken liberties to perform. Joe was grateful for her distraction. He didn't want her to question his motives.

"Why? Why did you follow me?" She closed her eyes and thunked her head back against the headrest. "I've made such a fool of myself. I just wanted to leave you to enjoy dinner with your beautiful girlfriend."

Wordlessly, he studied her lovely, closed face.

How could he tell her about the accident that had cost his memory? How did he explain the fear associated with not knowing who he was? And how could he stress his need to uncover the past to a complete stranger?

Joe remained silent. What he did do was give in to the impulse he'd had since first seeing her across the crowded room, remote and alone in her sexy red dress. He kissed her. Hesitantly at first. A mere whisper of his lips brushing against hers, like a prince waking Sleeping Beauty. As he felt her mouth relax, deepening, devouring, and tasting became his only goal.

She latched onto him like a drowning woman. Her fingers laced through his hair, clutching his head in a death grip.

He took advantage of her acquiescence and drew her onto his lap to straddle him. His hand caressed her stocking-clad thigh, reaching up under her dress in exploration. He died a little as he came in contact with the garter belt. *Holy shit!* Was anything hotter?

She shifted her hips and rubbed against his building erection. He would have taken her right then and there if the embarrassed cough of the cab driver hadn't finally penetrated. It brought Joe crashing back to reality.

Good God! He felt as if he would burn to a cinder at any moment. An image of her in nothing but those damn lacy undergarments was going to haunt him the rest of the night.

Samantha took a while longer to come back to the present.

"Why did you do that?" she asked, her voice low and soft.

Her eyes bored into his, willing him to... *What?* He didn't know. The deep emotion he witnessed alarmed him and made his pulse hammer harder than it already was.

"I don't know," he responded, equally as soft. He tucked a lock of her dark hair behind her ear. Her left earring caught and held his attention. An image of her wearing nothing but these earrings came to him. He shoved it away. Wishful thinking on his part, he was sure. "I couldn't not do it."

She nodded and shifted back to her seat. After straightening the skirt of her dress, she stared into the dark night outside the window. Joe got the distinct impression he'd disappointed her.

After a brief time, whatever problem she'd been working out in her mind resolved itself. Samantha came to a decision with a swift, short nod. He was left to wonder what it was, until she finally spoke. "I think we better find Stephen and..."

"Elizabeth," he finished for her.

"Yes, Elizabeth."

"Are you hungry?" Joe stalled for time.

"Aren't you at all concerned you left your girlfriend alone to run after another woman? One you don't even rem... know?"

"No. She can be pretty resilient." He cringed inside. Beth was going to read him the riot act when next she saw him. "Are you hungry?"

"A little."

"Let's go find somewhere we can talk."

At her reluctant nod, he directed the cab driver to an Italian mom-and-pop restaurant on the outskirts of town.

CHAPTER 25

Samantha and Joe kept their conversation light and shelved any serious discussion until the food was ordered and served. Once the dishes had been placed on the table, Joe broached the subject at hand.

"Why did you approach me earlier? What was it about me that you thought you recognized?"

"You remind me of someone I knew a long time ago. The resemblance is remarkable."

"Who?"

Joe didn't want to acknowledge, even to himself, how important her response was. He refused to get his hopes up that she might have the answers he searched for.

"His name was Michael, and he… he…" She cleared her throat. "He is supposed to have died in an accident two years ago."

Joe's stomach dropped to somewhere around his big toe, but he showed no outward signs of his unease. He experienced the actual physical sensation of a large, invisible fist grabbing his heart and squeezing. His rapid pulse made him wonder if a bursting heart was imminent.

"What was he to you? Fiancé? Husband?"

"Boyfriend."

"But you don't believe he died," he stated flatly, knowing she didn't before she even answered.

"No."

"Please, explain."

She paused to draw in a deep, calming breath and exhaled audibly. "I'm not sure I can, or at least not without sounding crazy."

"Try."

Samantha set down her utensils and folded her hands in her lap. He wanted to squirm under her steady regard. Finally, she shrugged and took a sip of water.

"A few years back, I began having nightmares. Premonitions of a sort. They started a few weeks before my boyfriend was supposed to leave for a business trip." Her lips twisted in a bitter little smile. "I didn't want him to go, because I knew he wouldn't return home. He was adamant because his company had already made the arrangements for him to go."

Was she saying she was psychic? He didn't buy it. "If you suspected something was going to happen, why didn't you stop him?"

"I *tried*," she snapped. "He wouldn't listen. He thought I was being unreasonable. By the time he realized what I was experiencing was real, it was too late."

"What do you mean too late?"

"Exactly that. Too late." Samantha flung up her hands as if exasperated with the whole subject. Impatient to be done with this whole conversation. "I'm exhausted, and I want to head back to my hotel. Meeting you..." Her lips tightened and looked anywhere but at him. "I'm sorry I interrupted your evening."

She collected her purse and scooted to the edge of the seat.

Panic seized him. He had the sneaking suspicion if she left, he'd never find the truth to his own situation.

"What if you weren't? Wrong, that is. What if you weren't wrong?" he blurted.

Samantha cast him a sharp glance. He shifted and looked away, avoiding her probing gaze. He planned to keep his inner demons to himself as long as he could.

Joe risked another look her way.

She did a fast visual survey of the restaurant and leaned forward, her voice lowered. "Look, I spent eight months of my life in a hospital. Everyone, my family included, thought grief had sent me over the edge. There is only one person who knows the real reason I came to Dallas. That reason, come hell or high water, was to find answers about Michael. If anyone thought I haven't accepted his death, they'd put me away again. I can't let that happen. I *won't* let that happen."

"What kind of man was he that you refuse to let him go?" he asked. He found himself resenting Michael and his hold on her.

"He was everything. Kind. Caring. Strong, yet gentle when he needed to be. He read and understood me in a way no one else can. He was my one true soulmate—if you believe in that sort of thing. He did. Believed, that is. To anyone else, it sounds hokey. But we..."

SAMMY WAS UNABLE TO FINISH. SHE'D EXPOSED TOO MUCH OF HERSELF when she was never planning on saying anything. Joe's gentle understanding was hard to witness. It literally hurt to look at him. He resembled her Michael so damned much, and the ache in her chest was unbearable.

His hand enfolded hers. She tried to pull away, to hide, to stop her out-of-control emotions. He held on, intertwining their fingers. She raised her eyes to meet his beautiful, warm gaze.

For the first time in ages, she let down her barrier and allowed him to see into her heart. They sat silent and staring. Two strangers sharing a private moment, unable to break the connection they'd formed. He seemed to be searching for something. What? She wasn't sure.

As they sat there, a stray thought occurred to her. Michael had had a scar on the underside of his wrist from some childhood incident. Frowning, she turned his hand over. She examined the skin and smiled softly. Of course, she wouldn't be able to tell so easily. There was a burn mark on Joe's wrist in the location where Michael's mark had been. Disappointed, she withdrew her hand.

"I'm sorry."

"Don't."

"Don't what?" she asked.

"Don't shut me out because you are embarrassed, Sammy."

She sent him another sharp glance.

"Why did you just call me Sammy?" It required everything she had to remain calm.

"I'm not sure. It just seemed to fit. You look like a Sammy," he explained, a little perplexed himself. "Does it bother you?"

"Michael used to call me that. Most people call me Samantha now. I like it better because it's a lot less... painful. I don't have to remember what I've lost."

"Okay, fair enough. Samantha it is. Now back to why you are shutting me out."

"It's not just the embarrassment. It's the similarity. I find it difficult to get over how much you resemble him."

Neither said anything for a long, awkward moment.

Sammy sucked in a lungful of air and exhaled in an effort to center herself.

"Not to mention, I'm pouring my heart out to a complete stranger. It's weird. You must think I'm a basket case," she added with a grimace.

JOE SENSED HER VALIANT STRUGGLE TO BURY HER HEARTACHE. DEEP sadness assailed him. Part sympathy and part some other, more elusive emotion. A loneliness he, himself, couldn't shake. She had something special, this woman. Some tangible thing he wanted to grasp with both hands. A lifeline of sorts. The length of time she'd searched for her boyfriend astonished him. *Two years!* He shook his head in wonder. It seemed like an eternity to carry hope for a happy ending. He wished he could be her Michael. Wished someone would search for him the way she so selflessly searched for her missing lover.

He'd spent a long time hoping there was another person, somewhere, who cared whether he'd lived or died.

"I don't think you're a basket case, Samantha. However, I can't help but wonder, if Michael *is* alive, why hasn't he tried to get in touch with you?"

It was easy to see she disliked the question. Her whole body recoiled, and her lips tightened in response.

"I don't have an answer. At least one that makes any sense. Maybe he was hurt badly and didn't want to be a burden. Perhaps he thought he would ruin my life if he came back after all this time." She paused and looked him squarely in the eyes. "Maybe he lost his memory. Who knows?" She laughed softly and shrugged. "It must be the writer in me. I've made up a thousand different scenarios, convincing myself they all make sense."

"Fair enough. But I'm sure there are phones wherever he is. He could've at least called to break it off."

He didn't want to cause her more pain by pointing these things out, but they needed to be said. It bothered him to think she'd waste any more time on a guy who didn't have the decency to end their relationship properly.

"Stephen said much the same thing."

"Stephen? Ah, the guy you were with earlier." He didn't care for his curl of jealousy at the warmth in her tone. "I imagine he's out of his mind with worry by now."

"Yeah, he'll be worried."

"He loves you, you know."

"No, he's just a good friend," she denied.

How could she be so clueless? It was in everything about the guy. The way he had looked at her. The way he'd stood protectively by her side. Even in how he'd given chase after she became upset. Stephen was nuts for her.

Joe had observed it all in less than five minutes. How long had she been blinded by Michael that she couldn't see how much someone else cared?

"I know this is a strange question since you are on a mission to find this Mike guy and you don't know me from the next man, but have you ever thought about a relationship with Stephen? Exactly who is he to you? Because I can promise you, he sees you as more than a good friend."

Joe refused to question his motives for asking. What did it say about him that he found this woman more fascinating in one evening than he had Beth in the many months they'd spent combined? He'd shot his relationship to hell tonight and couldn't find it in himself to care. Not right then anyway.

"Michael," she corrected. "His name is Michael. Stephen was my doctor when I first arrived at Brookhaven."

"Doctor? As in *shrink*? Isn't there some law against a relationship with a patient?" he asked incredulously.

"No one calls them shrinks anymore. They're therapists. And yes, Stephen was my therapist. *Was* being the key word here. Besides, like I said, he's only a friend." Irritation heavy in her tone. She twisted a straw wrapper around her finger, winding and unwinding the paper in her agitation.

"What? Your family wouldn't let you come here without your own personal *therapist*?" he mocked. She looked as if he'd slapped her. Ashamed, he apologized. "I'm sorry. I don't know why I said that. It was cruel, and my behavior was uncalled for. We should be heading back."

His inner voice chimed up. *Jealousy. Pure and simple.* Joe wanted to shout back at the pesky green-eyed monster not to be ridiculous. He didn't even know her. *True, but he certainly wished he did.*

"Maybe I need a shrink," he muttered beneath his breath.

"What did you say?"

"Nothing." A flush started up his neck as she eyed him with skepticism. "Come on. Let's go," he said gruffly, throwing money on the table as he stood.

SAMMY SAT IN HER ROOM LATER THAT NIGHT, WITH THE LIGHTS OFF, AND stared out over the Dallas skyline. Had she dreamed the night's bizarre events? Lifting her glass of wine, she took a long sip. Everything had been so surreal.

The conversation with Joe replayed like a broken record through her mind. Something he'd said earlier tickled her brain. *Stephen loved her.*

Could it be possible? Joe had also asked her if she'd ever thought of starting a relationship with Stephen. Had she? No, not in all seriousness. Not when she lived and breathed Michael. He'd consumed her. To consider anyone else was preposterous.

Now, she began to realize just how selfish she'd been on her quest. How selfish she'd been all her life, really. When hadn't every moment been about her or her feelings? Had she ever stopped to care about someone else's thoughts or opinions?

God, how blind and immature she'd been in her relationship with Michael! He'd given everything, and she'd brought so little to their partnership. Holding her glass up in a toast to the stupid girl she'd been, Sammy gulped more wine.

Had she considered what would've happened if Joe had indeed been Michael? What would've happened to Elizabeth? Would her existing relationship with Joe cease to exist?

Sammy had assumed Michael would return to her, and it had been an arrogant assumption. Self-doubt rocked her. Maybe Michael had volunteered for his work trip to escape her neediness for a while. Maybe he had required a break from her constant dreams, demands, and all-around spoiled attitude.

Self-reflection was a bitch. As she would've taken another sip, she realized the glass was empty. Reaching for the bottle, she saw it was empty as well. Great. Now she could add wino to her list of faults.

For the first time, Sammy thought perhaps it was better to let Michael rest in peace. She'd wanted him back so badly, for so long, she never entertained any other notion. Would she finally be able to accept he was lost to her?

A soft knock interrupted her musings. She looked through the peephole and frowned at the empty hall. As she was about to park her ass on the sofa, a knock sounded again. When it clicked the tapping came from the connecting suite, she felt like a complete tool.

Stephen.

No one else knew she was here. Quieting the small part of her heart hoping her visitor was Joe, Sammy opened the door wide to admit Stephen.

"Hi."

"I came to see if you were okay."

Blinking twice to dispel her fuzziness, Sammy took the time to assess him. His handsomeness was the stuff of fantasies. The thick, wavy hair and warm brown, bedroom eyes of his would make any normal woman's heart skip a beat. Sammy continued to study him. His straight, perfect nose. Those full, generous lips. His features all came together to create a dark, brooding, yet sensual face. She'd always known he was on the tall side, but his athletic body was a bonus. His quiet strength enticed her. She felt her pulse quicken. Finally, she saw him as a real man and not only her doctor or buddy.

What an injustice she'd done him—treating him as if he didn't exist unless it was to cater to her needs. Had she ever thanked him properly? Or even wondered what it had cost him emotionally to follow her on this insane quest? He did indeed love her. Joe had woken her up to that at least.

"Samantha? Are you okay? Where did you run off to tonight?"

Her silence had carried on too long. Because she couldn't admit to being okay when she wasn't, and because she didn't want to address the issue of Joe, Sammy decided to apologize. Maybe in the future, she could stop doing things she needed to apologize for.

"Stephen, I'm so sorry." She threw her arms around his middle.

He didn't hesitate. He swept her close and returned her hug.

"Whatever for?"

"For not seeing you as a person with feelings. For only seeing you as my doctor to take care of my wants and needs."

"You don't know how long I have waited to hear you say that," he told her gruffly.

CHAPTER 26

*E*ventually, Joe found his way back to Elizabeth's condo, and now stood on her balcony, looking out over the city. Normally, she'd join him and he'd place an arm around her. But tonight, he kept his arms resting on the railing, effectively isolating himself. The rejection caused a pang in the region of her heart.

"Want to explain to me what happened earlier?" she asked, trying to keep the accusing tone at bay.

"I don't know that I can, Beth."

"Why did you chase after that woman, Joe?" Her heart had taken a beating tonight. Answers might help understand what took place and put to rest her uneasiness.

With a heartfelt sigh, he shifted to face her. His struggle to relay his inner turmoil was evident. "I feel like some part of me knows her," he stated hoarsely. "Do you realize what that means?" At the negative shake of her head, he said, "I'm not sure I do either. But Samantha said the guy she was looking for, Michael, was in an accident almost two years ago. *Here*. In Dallas."

He ran a shaking hand through his unruly blond hair. "On the ride home, I googled the accident. Imagine my surprise when I discovered it was the same one I was involved in, Beth. One of the deceased was

Michael Anselin. Now that may be a coincidence, and it may not. If it is, it's a mighty powerful one."

"Joe, I was there, remember? They identified everyone involved. Michael Anselin was the other guy. The one who died, *not* you. Granted, he was burned beyond recognition, but even if they didn't find his ID on him—which they did—DNA and dental records prove these things. You are not who she was looking for. She admitted she made a mistake."

"Do you think I'm not aware of that? But Samantha thought she recognized me. How can that be? I've had reconstructive surgery. I have to resemble her Michael an awful lot for that to happen."

JOE RUBBED HIS TEMPLES. A HEADACHE HAD FORMED IN EARNEST. IT happened whenever he tried to remember the past. Nothing would come to him for his efforts except a sharp, searing-hot pain followed by a raging migraine. Always before, he'd allowed the discomfort to dissuade him from delving into the truth. This time he couldn't. He needed to push through and discover what had really happened.

"What if someone dropped the ball, Beth? What if the Dallas police department was too busy with all the injured and dead to properly identify everyone? There was a plane crash that same night. I'm sure resources were stretched thin."

"Jesus, Joe! That only happens in made-for-TV movies. Not real life," Elizabeth scoffed. "Listen to yourself."

"Can't you understand my need to find out who I am? I had no identification on me. I have a made-up name, and according to you, I was chasing that poor bastard through traffic. If he really was Michael, then I caused the death of Samantha's boyfriend. I owe it to her to find the truth." His guilt was crushing. "I'll never be able to live with myself if I don't."

Elizabeth's anger evaporated, and she caressed his jaw. "Please, Joe, let this go. The doctors said your memory may never come back. Head trauma is tricky."

She put her arms around him, trying to offer comfort, but Joe didn't respond to her touch.

He shifted out of her reach and turned to face the darkness. The bustle of the city was lost as his worry consumed him. "I can't, Beth. Do you mind giving me some space right now? I need time to think."

"Don't do this," Elizabeth whispered. But he was already mentally too far away.

She wandered into her bedroom and viewed the space with new eyes. In the fading light, she could see very few traces of Joe scattered about. How had she failed to realize he'd actively steered away from committing to her? He refused to move in, to move their relationship to a deeper level, or even leave clothes at her condo so he'd have a fresh set if he happened to stay over.

Stephen would've lectured her about unhealthy dating habits if he explored this one too closely.

Elizabeth curled up on her reading chaise and drew her plush throw around her shoulders.

Stephen.

What a shock it had been to encounter him tonight! What were the odds after ten years and a handful of states between them? When he'd spoken her name, without any condemnation or censure, the anger she previously heaped on him had disappeared. All the pent-up hostility became a thing of the past. *As it should be.* Growing up allowed her to let go of the old wounds.

After Joe drove off with Samantha, Stephen had escorted Elizabeth back into the restaurant. He had listened without commenting as she explained why she chose to run away all those years ago. The made-up version. The one she told herself in the hopes she'd one day believe. She would die a thousand deaths if he ever discovered the truth.

At eighteen, losing her parents in a fire had messed her up. And because she had inadvertently started the blaze, she was unable to deal with the loss of her beloved family. Self-torture was her cross to bear.

Stephen had been her therapist through the worst of it. Together they'd worked through the guilt and pain. Elizabeth had come to the realization she loved him long before their sessions ended. Eventually, she'd concluded there was no future in loving a man who didn't, and who would never, love her in return.

"Beth."

Joe's voice returned her from the past in a blink.

"Yes?"

"Why are you sitting here in the dark?"

The question caught her off guard. She looked up at his silhouette lingering in the doorway, then glanced around the room. She hadn't been aware of time passing or of the lack of lighting until he mentioned it.

"I don't know," she said softly. "Old ghosts maybe."

When she didn't elaborate, he told her he intended to head back to his apartment.

"Okay." For once, she wanted him to go. Her need to be alone was stronger than her desire to repair their relationship. The things she thought she'd put behind her years ago swamped her. Haunted her.

"What? No argument?" he tried to tease.

"No argument," she agreed tonelessly.

Joe turned on the light to better see her face.

"I know you must be upset, but I promise to clear this up soon."

Elizabeth cast Joe a bland look. Her energy and want abandoned her. There was nothing left to give.

"Actually, tonight's events gave me a clarity I didn't have before." Joe remained silent but attentive, so she continued. "I love you, Joe. I hoped you loved me in return. You don't. Not really." He would have spoken then, but she held her hand up to forestall him. "Please, let me finish. I know you care about me. That isn't in question. However, it's not the type of love I want. Not the way I've always dreamed of someone loving me. I want... no, I need the passionate love you read about. The kind with dashing heroes. Someone who considers me first and himself second. Maybe I'm being foolish and asking for a lot.

Maybe unselfish love doesn't exist. And that's okay. But I won't settle for less. Not anymore."

"Beth, I care about you a great deal. I just don't know who I am. I could be a criminal for all either of us know. How the hell am I supposed to subject you to what I uncover? If I even uncover anything at all?" He raked a hand through his hair and shook his head. "I'd like nothing better than to give you the romance and passion you deserve. I want to be able to consider you first. I simply can't. But I do know I don't want to see what we've built so far be destroyed."

"What do you mean what we've built so far?" Elizabeth's temper boiled over. She hadn't realized it was simmering when only moments before she'd felt so drained. *"We have nothing, Joe.* Nothing but friendship. *If* that." She rose and stormed to where he stood. Without intention, she punched him in the chest. "You left me standing in a restaurant by myself, *at night,* to chase after a woman who may or may not know you. Who does that?"

He stared at her in tortured silence.

"After you finally found your way back here tonight, I didn't even get an 'I'm sorry I ruined your evening, Beth.' What the hell do I look like to you? *A doormat?*" she screeched.

Shame clung to every line of his body. Arguing was futile because he knew she was right. "I never considered you a doormat, babe. And I do love you. Maybe not the way you wish, but it's still love any way you look at it. I didn't spend this last year and a half of my life with you just for the hell of it. I wasn't just marking time. You mean something to me. It's why I found an apartment and a job to support myself."

He gripped her shoulders, but she shrugged him off. "Don't," she warned.

With a heavy sigh, he released her. "Not being able to give someone a name to call you, not having memories, and not having references to check out, made all of that a little more difficult, but I did it. I did it so I wouldn't have to feel I was using you. You, the only person I know enough to even care about. So, if that makes me a selfish asshole, then I'm sorry."

It was Elizabeth's turn to be silent. She understood. Even ached for him. She just wasn't budging or compromising any longer.

"I'm sorry I ruined your evening, Beth," he stated on a sigh.

Joe gave her one last long look before turning and heading out the door.

CHAPTER 27

*S*tephen let Samantha cry out her guilt and pain. He tried to tell her she had nothing to be sorry for, but she insisted she did. He understood the grieving process, and perhaps for the first time, she was experiencing the final steps to let Michael go for good.

There were so many things he wanted to tell her. To confess his love for her and ask her to marry him was utmost on that list. He held off. Timing was everything. Right now wasn't the perfect moment to tell her his heart's desire. They both needed to be on the same page when it came to future promises.

Perhaps he was a little reticent about proposing marriage because his first engagement had turned into such a disaster. The professional in him knew fear of the unknown could paralyze someone and prevent them from making a decision or moving forward. Stephen still wasn't sure Samantha saw him as anything but a friend, and he needed assurances. He was human enough to admit it.

"Samantha, I think we need to turn in. I just came by to make sure you were okay with everything that happened tonight. When you ignored your cell, I was worried. I figured I would see if you wanted to talk." She burrowed deeper against him. "Besides, your mascara is ruining my shirt."

The last sentence jerked Samantha's head upright. First, she glanced at his damp shirt and then to his face. She relaxed once she registered his teasing.

"Thank you."

"For what?"

"For being my friend even when you were my doctor."

"Just wait until you get my bill."

She smiled. "I'd gladly pay it, Stephen. No matter what the cost."

Even if it meant being my wife? he wanted to ask. Instead, he tapped her nose. "Okay, so it's agreed. You'll buy me breakfast tomorrow before the signing."

The book signing! Shit! Oh, Stephen, I forgot," she exclaimed.

"That's why I'm here, my dear. To not only be your friend, therapist, and fellow diner, but to remind you of the small things like your career and the book signings that go with it."

She smiled at him again but added rather seriously, "No. You came to help me find Michael, which is the real reason I'm here, and you know it. But I'm starting to have doubts that will ever happen."

"If he's alive, we'll find him. Right now, our game plan for tomorrow is simple. We get up, get dressed, eat a huge breakfast—because you're buying—and then we go our separate ways."

"What? You aren't coming with me?"

He grinned at her and gave a small shake of his head.

"What are you up to, Stephen?" A speculative gleam entered her eyes.

"You'll just have to wait."

"But I can't stand surprises."

"Really? Huh. And here I thought I knew everything there was to know about you."

He laughed and shifted to stand. Samantha tackled him against the mattress.

"What the hell?"

She had him pinned in five seconds flat.

Grinning down into his face, she told him, "Here is something else you may not know about me. I'm a sore loser."

As he gazed into her face, it occurred to him he'd never seen her look more beautiful. Or sexy. His body was sending him all kinds of signals, and his mind worked diligently to shut them down.

"No, I must say, I was not aware of that one." The huskiness in his voice belied their playfulness.

Without thought to anything else but the need to finally taste her lips, he tangled his fingers in her hair. He pulled her face down to a mere inch away from his, giving her plenty of opportunity to pull away. She didn't. Instead, she closed the distance and became the aggressor. Stephen rolled over to press her into the mattress as he ravaged her mouth. Tongue battled tongue. Pulling. Sucking. Never quite getting enough. They parted to gulp oxygen into their lungs. All they could do was stare at each other in awe and amazement.

Samantha recovered first. "I need to get some sleep. We have to get an early start tomorrow."

"Mmhmm."

He gazed into her pale blue eyes, lost in wonder. Even crippled by the riot of sensations she'd caused with her kiss, he didn't miss her sly look.

Leisurely, she trailed her fingers from the nape of his neck to the opening of his shirt. She wove her fingers into the fine hairs on his chest and tantalized him with her touch. Samantha lowered her gaze to avoid letting him see her intent.

"So what is on your agenda for tomorrow, Stephen?" she whispered, nibbling along his jaw.

He allowed a small amount of space between them to search her face.

"Well?" she insisted.

The hint of impatience in her tone gave her away.

Without blinking, he deadpanned, "We get up, get dressed, eat a huge breakfast—because you're buying—and then we go our separate ways."

He rolled to his feet and darted through the connecting door. Laughter erupted from him when he heard her cry of outrage. It served the little schemer right.

"Jerk!"

"Yep!"

CHAPTER 28

The sun rose, bringing with it one of the most spectacular displays of color Sammy had the good fortune to witness. The pink, orange, and purple hues blended to perfection over the metal and brick buildings littering the horizon.

She sat on the balcony and wondered when she'd last paused to consider the splendor of a dawning day? Quite probably long before Michael disappeared from her life. She decided then and there this sunrise would herald a new beginning.

Her baby was dead, and Michael... well, Michael wasn't coming back. Joe had stated it correctly. Her Michael would have been in contact. Recovering what she'd had was a pipe dream. A team of therapists, along with Stephen and her family, had tried to prove it to her over the last two years. A universal truth she'd refused to accept. No longer could it be denied.

A loud knock carried to her, heralding room service.

"I didn't order anything," Sammy protested.

"No, ma'am. Dr. Montgomery ordered it for you. He sends his regrets that he couldn't join you this morning."

What the hell was Stephen up to?

The hotel staffer set up the food on the balcony. It enabled her to enjoy the remaining few minutes of the glorious morning. She signed the room service slip—making sure to include a hefty tip—and poured herself a cup of hot chocolate from the heated carafe. She took the first sip and sighed her contentment. *Mexican chocolate.* Was anything more delicious?

Although there was a week left to her Dallas trip, there were only two actual signings over the weekend. She'd built in a few days to conduct her investigation into Michael's supposed death. Did she still want answers? Did it matter anymore? Perhaps to a small degree.

Maybe it was time to sell the house she'd built with Michael. Buy a condo on the beach somewhere. She had always liked the west coast of Florida with its white sandy beaches and clear aquamarine water. In no way did she think she could recapture the girl she'd been two years ago. But she could take the remaining foundation and rebuild from there.

She thought about what she had shared with Stephen last night. *Quite the wake-up call!* Before his fevered kiss, she'd naively believed she couldn't physically feel anything for anyone else. Now, she knew differently.

Figuring Stephen into her plans for her new life would be nice. He had come to mean a lot to her. Although, perhaps it was best to make a clean break. Stephen did love her. Hadn't he proved that with every action? He believed in her enough to follow her to Dallas. Countless times she'd sensed his reservations, and yet, in one simple, soul-destroying kiss, she felt all his yearning.

Who knew Stephen had it in him to be so passionate? *Certainly not Sammy.* Being self-absorbed for so long hadn't allowed insight and understanding into someone else's situation. It was well past time for her to be a better friend, sibling, and daughter.

Sammy picked up her cell phone and stared down at it. If she called her mother, what advice might she receive?

Sammy dialed Violet's number.

"Hello?"

"Mom, it's me, Sammy."

"Samantha," Violet sighed her name as if she'd been waiting for this particular call.

"Do you have a moment for your shitty, selfish daughter?"

"What's wrong?"

Her mother's perceptiveness surprised her. Why? She didn't know. After all, her mother was intuitive by nature.

"Nothing. Really." Sammy played with her butter knife, knowing she was stalling. Trying to work out the best way to continue, she asked, "Mom, what do you think of Stephen?"

She heard her mother's soft laugh on the other end of the line.

"What's so funny?"

"I wondered if you'd get around to realizing what a wonderful and sexy man he was."

"I've always thought he was wonderful," she defended. But in reality, she'd never seen him as a man before last night.

"Did you, Samantha? Be truthful. Or did you just take it for granted that he was your friend, willing to do anything for you, just as you always assumed everyone would."

It was disconcerting to have her mother echo her thoughts from the night before. Sammy couldn't suppress the urge to defend herself from that terrible time in her life. "Mom, I think that's really unfair. I've been through a lot these last few years."

"I'm sorry if I've hurt your feelings, but you have been completely obsessed about Michael. You shut down and guarded your feelings around everyone who loved you. You expected everyone to do for you. *And they did.* Without any gratitude on your part in return. The constant take wears on a person, Samantha."

"Why are you saying this to me now?" she asked, trying like hell to not break down blubbering from the sharp edge of her mother's words.

"Because you're finally ready to hear it. You've been a ghost of the woman you once were. You've been unreachable. Never laughing or enjoying life. We all missed the happy girl you used to be. But what's more, I missed my daughter." Sammy detected a catch in her mother's voice. Violet was trying her damnedest not to cry. "Keep in mind

Jamie lost a best friend, your father and I lost what would have been our grandchild, and Annie truly needed a friend she could talk to during her divorce."

Violet packed a verbal punch, and Sammy reeled under the blow. "I'm sorry, Mom. I didn't think. Didn't know," she whispered.

"I know. I was simply pointing out other people exist in the world. Don't be hard on yourself. You tend to do that, too. You go from one extreme to the other. But I'm glad you're on your way back. Your dad, brother, and sisters will be, also."

The silence between them wasn't uncomfortable. It was more meaningful than anything. It had always been like that with the mother/daughter duo. A shared closeness they both held so dear.

"So, Mom, you think Stephen is hot, huh?" she teased to lighten the mood.

"Very!"

"Mother!"

"What? I'm only human. But if you tell your father, I'll deny it to my dying breath. And back to your original question, I think he's perfect for you."

"I've decided to give up the search for Michael."

Sammy could imagine her mom's closed eyes as Violet sent a silent *thank you* skyward. She'd loved Michael, but apparently, she hated what his death had done to her youngest daughter. Her mom would want her to find happiness again.

"Why?" Violet asked.

They both understood the question was a loaded one.

"I ran into a man last night. Mom, I could have sworn he was Michael. The way he moved, how he looked. His voice..." She rubbed the area above her heart. "I found out differently. It occurred to me, I've been acting irrationally. Refusing to accept the truth of what is. The man from my nightmare was right, Michael isn't coming home." She swallowed a sob. "And yet, through it all, Stephen has been so supportive. Did you know Stephen loves me?"

Violet hesitated before answering. "Yes."

"I thought you might."

"Did he tell you?"

"No, Joe did."

"Who's Joe?"

"The man I believed was my Michael."

"This sounds like a long story."

"It is. I promise to tell you all about it when I get back. Have I told you what a great mother you are?"

"No, you're a rotten kid."

Sammy laughed. She had missed their banter. Suddenly, she felt like a kid again, insecure and missing her mom.

"I love you, Mom," she choked out.

"I love you too, honey. Have a safe trip back."

CHAPTER 29

*J*oe was unsure what force drew him downtown. Probably the need to escape his apartment, along with the usual doubts he felt about not remembering his past. He had just exited his favorite bakery when he spotted people flocking into the bookstore located a block away. Curious, he strolled closer. A distraction from his problems would be welcome.

He skimmed the sign in the window then did a double take. His heart skipped a beat and resumed at triple time. Samantha Holt, along with five other authors, was in attendance today. She had to be the same woman from last night. The coincidence was too great. He vaguely recalled her mentioning her book during their conversation, but he never suspected she was a professional author. Astonishment and something close to disappointment settled inside him.

Was it possible the reason she seemed familiar had nothing to do with recognizing her and everything to do with the advertisement? Maybe a part of his subconscious had pieced it all together. It was highly probable. He walked to this bakery most mornings for a cup of coffee and an egg bagel. The flyer announced a book signing.

For a moment, he toyed with the idea of fate. Why was she here, at this exact place and time? Coincidence? His feet led him by way of his churning thoughts. He loitered toward the back of the room and watched Samantha interact with her fans. She was incredible. Always smiling and upbeat when inside, he knew her heart must still be battered from all she had been through.

Joe perused the book display and picked hers from the authors featured there. As he read the back cover, an ache formed deep in the region of his heart. Her story. Or rather, hers and Michael's. Instinct told him as much. Yes, it was depicted as fiction, and the character names were different, but the cover portrayed the tragedy of love lost and found. Without bothering to second-guess himself, he joined the line with all her other would-be readers.

He glanced down at his wristwatch and discovered it was only a few minutes until noon. He was surprised he'd hung around for over an hour. The sign on the store's easel at the front indicated the session ended at twelve, and Samantha would only be autographing books for another five minutes. A handful of people stood between them, and he judged it would take at least a half-hour for her to get to him. There was plenty of time, and so he waited, watching. Trying not to feel like a stalker.

A low grumble from Sammy's stomach was her body's reminder it was nearly lunchtime. If she didn't get food soon, she was liable to turn hangry. No one wanted a mean Sammy on their hands.

Only two people remained—a middle-aged woman and a man. The bookstore's owner, Lauren, stepped in to enforce the time limit for the customer currently chatting her ear off. If it came from someone else, Sammy could offer a commiserating smile to her fan.

Two more and she would be home free.

She spoke momentarily with the next woman and wrote her name with a flourish, smiling and thanking her. Then she turned her attention to the last person in line and gaped at the man in front of her. Her body went cold all over.

Joe.

Sparkling, honey eyes met her cautious gaze.

"What are you doing here, Joe?"

"Would you believe I was just in the neighborhood?"

Abruptly, the day turned a little brighter. She smiled up at him with genuine warmth.

"Not for a moment. You probably say that to all the girls."

"Only to gorgeous authors."

"Do you stumble across a lot of gorgeous authors around here?"

"Some. It is hell on my schedule, hanging around until one shows up."

Sammy did a visual scan of the bookstore.

"How convenient you just happen to be the last in line."

"I let everyone getting in line after me go first. I was assured all your attention after that."

"What are you going to do with all my attention now you have it?"

"I thought I would steal you away for lunch. How does Subway sound to you?"

Joe startled a laugh out of her. He had a rare and wonderful charm about him that seduced her on every level.

"Subway, huh?"

"Sure, there is nothing more romantic than those hard yellow booths for two. Or we can take the sandwiches to the park and cuddle on a bench."

His grin did her in.

"Okay, I'll go to lunch with you—on one condition."

"Which is?"

"No Subway."

"Do you realize the gourmet creations you're giving up? Ham and turkey slices thrown on a doughy piece of baked bread? Fountain soda in paper cups? Tasty chips from a plastic bag? Any person in their right mind wouldn't refuse such delightful temptation."

"It's difficult, but I'll force myself."

"What are you in the mood for?"

"You." Where the hell had that come from? She fought back a blush and prayed she hadn't said it aloud.

His twinkling eyes met hers. Heat flooded Sammy's body.

"Italian," she blurted when she could find her wits. "I would kill for baked ziti or a calzone. Maybe even pizza, but it has to be New York style. Anything good around here?"

"We had Italian last night."

"What's your point?"

"I happen to know a great little place."

"Smart man. Let's go."

She jumped up to grab her purse off the back of the chair when he forestalled her.

"Aren't you forgetting something?"

Sammy looked around, uncertain just what it was she was missing. There were very few people left mingling about to talk to the remaining authors. Lauren was at the register, ringing up the last stragglers.

"The store owner! Joe, thank you for reminding me. That would have been a terrible oversight."

She left him to say her goodbyes and to express her gratitude for hosting their small group. After she joined him again, he stood in the same spot, one of her books in his hand.

At her puzzled look, he took pity on her and told her what he wanted. "I'd hoped you'd sign my book."

"Oh! Of course."

Laughing, she wrote an inscription and signed her name.

"Is this how you keep track of the gorgeous authors you steal away to lunch?" she teased.

His grin was answer enough. When he would have read what she wrote, she closed the cover and made him promise to read it after she'd gone home.

The quaint restaurant Joe knew happened to be two blocks from their current location. He escorted her the short distance and ordered a spinach-cheese calzone for the two of them to split.

"Why are we sharing?" she asked.

"The portions here are huge, and we need to leave room for dessert."

"Dessert is essential to an author's way of life. But what makes you think I can't finish a whole meal *and* dessert by myself?"

He ran his gaze down her body in a leisurely, appreciative manner. He never said a word. He just gave her a slow, sexy smile, flashing those dimples that never failed to make her overly warm.

Sammy ripped her gaze away and mumbled something about a good call.

"What's it like to be famous?" he teased.

"Hardly that. But having to smile and constantly be upbeat can be exhausting."

"Understandable."

"I'm new to this. I'm grateful to be here. Without question, I'm grateful. When it all started, I was excited and more than a little afraid. Possibly even a little overeager. Now, I just want it to be finished. I want to go home to my dog and my comfortable little house in Flagler Beach. I'm dreaming of curling up with some other writer's book for a nice change."

"You live on the beach? Nice."

"Actually, a block off the beach, but yes, it is."

Their food arrived, and with it, the light banter was back. Joe, decidedly secretive about himself, insisted on questioning her. It embarrassed her to talk about herself, but she entertained him with funny stories of her childhood. Sammy explained how she and her brother, James, were the terrible twosome who terrorized their sisters. They were huge fans of pranks.

WHEN THEIR MEAL WAS DONE, JOE TALKED HER INTO SHARING A SLICE OF mud pie. Her eyes dulled and took on a haunted quality. It disturbed him to think he'd inadvertently caused it.

"Did I say something wrong?"

A small frown played about her brows. "What do you mean?"

"I noticed you seem sad, where you weren't a minute ago. Was it something I said?"

"Oh. No."

"Then what caused it? Surely not the mud pie? I've never known chocolate to depress anyone, most especially a female."

She smiled at the sexist remark, knowing he intended it as a joke only.

"It's nothing," she said as she went for a forkful of the rich, mocha goodness.

Joe moved the plate out of her range.

"What are you doing?" she demanded with a light laugh.

"Liars don't get dessert," he stated primly.

"What makes you the authority on liars and the punishments they deserve?"

"I could tell you, but then I'd have to kill you. It's James Bond kind of stuff."

Her musical laugh caused heads to turn in their direction.

"I knew you were with British Intelligence," she exclaimed as she pointed her fork at him.

"What gave it away?"

"The hogging of the mud pie." At his puzzled look, she explained, "As an agent of The Crown, I would imagine you were trained to be a deadly weapon."

"Yes, exactly so." He gestured in a circle with his fork for her to continue.

"Well, I imagine deadly weapons, such as yourself, are on strict schedules, training regimes, diets, that sort of thing. It only takes one glance to see what the physical training has done for you." She smirked and continued. "You've already mentioned the variance from your normal schedule today. You're also guarding the mud pie with your life. I can only deduce that you are unused to these little luxuries. Hence, based on all the facts, *you* are a spy."

"Brilliant, my dear. Bloody brilliant. I can see now why you are one of the top writers of our time. So, even though you are a liar and should be punished, I am going to allow you a share of my mud pie for your astounding reasoning," he offered up with a horrible attempt at a British accent.

"You do a terrible Englishman."

The sense of déjà vu struck Joe with a vengeance. It was as if a sledgehammer had whacked him in the skull. The pain was excruciating as images of a phone call swirled through his memories and tried to gain a foothold. Impressions of laughter and teasing were in the background of his mind. He tried to force the memories forward. All he received for his efforts was white-hot agony.

Worry was written all over Samantha's face. "Joe? Joe, what is it?"

Slowly, he became aware of her calling his name and of her soft hand as it clutched his forearm across the space between them. That image mingled with another. One of a younger Samantha laughing up at him.

"Nothing, Sammy Darlin'. It'll go away in a minute."

Joe shut his eyes against the pain and leaned his head back against the booth cushion.

Sᴀᴍᴍʏ ꜰᴇʟᴛ ᴛʜᴇ ʙʟᴏᴏᴅ ᴅʀᴀɪɴ ꜰʀᴏᴍ ʜᴇʀ ꜰᴀᴄᴇ, ᴀɴᴅ ɴᴇʀᴠᴇs ᴀᴛᴇ ᴀᴛ ʜᴇʀ belly. She worked to regulate both. "Mich—uh, *Joe*, I don't like this. I want to take you home."

This man caused too many conflicting emotions. To look into his eyes or to hear him call her Sammy was to believe he was her Michael. Unfortunately, she knew differently.

"Sammy, I'm fine. I promise." He raised his head and met her eyes. "Jesus, I'm sorry. I did it again, didn't I? I didn't mean to call you by your nickname. It seems I can't help myself. It slips out."

"It's okay. Really. Are you sure you are going to be all right?"

"I will be if you promise to spend the rest of the afternoon with me."

Satisfied whatever episode he experienced had abated, she agreed. She didn't want their time together to end any more than he did. *What a freaking sucker for punishment she was!*

CHAPTER 30

*M*ost of Stephen's morning involved compiling a list of hospitals and calling all those within the Dallas/Fort Worth area until he found the ones that had treated the trauma patients from the multi-vehicle accident two years prior. Although James's calls all those months ago had yielded nothing, Stephen now had a suspicion Samantha wasn't off-base in her claim Michael was alive.

An overly talkative ER nurse provided the information he sought. Amazing how the staff opened up once they discovered it was another doctor questioning them. They probably wouldn't have told a stranger as much because of HIPPA rules. However, with one of their own looking to transfer to the area, they were more comfortable gossiping. His white lie yielded another ICU nurse willing to elaborate about the circumstances surrounding the accident and all that had occurred that particular night.

She explained about the patient who'd been struck by a car. A blonde woman visited him every day without fail and talked to him all the while he resided in a coma. Eventually, the female was the one who checked him out.

All the information Stephen obtained completely dumbfounded

him. It was such a complex situation. He needed to find the driver of the vehicle to verify the facts. That person was the key. If he or she had a clear recollection of the man they'd hit and could identify him as Michael, then all that remained was to find out where Michael went after leaving the hospital. Right now, it was anyone's guess.

"Did the blonde woman who checked him out leave a forwarding address?"

Oddly, the nurse drew the line at delving into the patient records for contact information. He wasn't deterred. A police report should provide the answers he sought.

Stephen glanced at his watch and saw it was half past noon. Since he wasn't far from the bookstore, he decided to check-in with Samantha to see if she wanted to catch a late lunch. Afterwards, he would head over to the police department to see if he could obtain a copy of the accident report. He was positive they would have the information he needed.

Only a block from the bookstore, he noticed Samantha exit with the man from last night. John? Joe? That was it. *Joe*. It was like a jolt to his system, and he didn't care for the flare of jealousy he experienced at seeing the two together.

Stephen trailed them at a safe distance and watched as they made their way down the sidewalk. He noted the carefree way she walked beside him, and the teasing way Joe leaned down to speak to her, causing her to laugh.

Fury seized Stephen. Sharp. Fierce.

How the hell could Samantha claim to be searching for her long-lost love, kiss *him* with a passion that sizzled his insides, and yet still share a moment so intimate with a stranger she'd met less than twenty-four hours ago?

He tamped down his wayward rage. He debated confronting her, but really, what good would it do? In the end, he headed back to the hotel. As he analyzed the events leading up to now, he struggled to gain a better perspective.

Seeing Elizabeth out of the blue after ten years had been a kick to the gut. She'd grown more beautiful with time. He wouldn't have thought it possible. Recalling their conversation, Stephen was disturbed he no longer held her trust. Where once she would have confided in him, now she kept her own counsel. He remembered the pretty, carefree girl she was. In her place resided a guarded woman with steel at her core. But one who held the weight of the world upon her shoulders. The Bethy he'd known was no more. That free spirit had died with her parents and younger brother.

Pensive and moody, he looked up Elizabeth's contact information in his phone and prayed she hadn't given him a fake number the evening before. Unable to check his impulse, he dialed.

"Hello?"

Hearing her voice gave Stephen pause. *What the hell was he doing?*

"Hello?"

"Bethy." It came out in a rush. Stephen hated to feel so unsure and timid.

"Stephen?"

"Bethy, have you had lunch yet?"

"No."

"I would like to talk to you. Do you mind if I pick up something to bring by?" After she had agreed, he asked, "How do I get to your place?"

ELIZABETH OPENED THE DOOR TO ADMIT STEPHEN. SEEING HIM IN THE flesh for the second time in less than twenty-four hours reinforced how damned fine she thought he was. As a girl, had she understood she was drawn by his undeniable sex appeal? Had he always been so manly and handsome? Good-looking, yes. But downright lethal to her system? Fuck-me pheromones oozed from his very pores.

What had she done by agreeing to lunch? Her brain flashed warning signals and screamed, "Mistake!" Yet still, Stephen stood in front of her and waved the bag of Chinese food under her nose while offering up a devastating grin with the potential to send her into a tailspin.

Idiot woman!

She hoped it wouldn't take her another decade to recover as it had the last time she fell for him.

As they devoured food directly from the cartons, Elizabeth manipulated all the topics of conversation to safer subjects. For reasons she didn't care to explore, she didn't want Stephen to remember her in a bad light. Finally, when the food and conversation ran dry, she found the nerve to ask him why he'd really sought her out.

"I want you to tell me about Joe," he said.

Of course, he wouldn't be here for old times' sake. She set down her fried rice with a heavy sigh. "Why?"

"Bethy, who and what is this guy to you? What do you really know about him?"

"You haven't answered my question, Stephen. Why?"

Indecision clouded his dark eyes, and his mouth twisted in distaste. "I saw him today with Samantha. I hoped you might tell me why he sought her out."

The jealousy in Stephen's voice was impossible to miss.

She shouldn't have been hurt, but she was. Joe had wasted no time after their breakup last night. It was also obvious Stephen cared deeply about the other woman, too. But that Elizabeth didn't qualify for a true visit from an old friend was the final blow. Stephen had come seeking information and *not* to see her to renew their friendship.

"Joe's a big boy. He can hook up with anyone he wants," she told him in icy tones.

"Last night, I got the impression you and Joe were together?"

"*Were* is the key word."

"As in no more?"

"Yes. Not that it's any of your business, but we broke up."

"Because of what happened at the restaurant?"

Unsure how to answer that question, she wandered to the glass doors by her balcony. She gazed, unseeing, over the bustling city she loved. The cork popped, and the story poured out.

"The first time I saw Joe was the day he ran in front of my car. He was chasing a guy. An idiot move, by the way. Who the hell runs onto a major highway? I never saw him until it was too late." She paused and gave a small shudder. "The accident was..." She shrugged. How did she describe the scene? She'd been there and still couldn't find the words. "I thought I killed him. At first, I was frozen in fear." She remembered the sickening thud and placed a hand against her abdomen to quell the residual nerves. It still got to her after all this time.

"It was like seeing everything from a great distance, and yet not. Through the cracks in the windshield, I saw the guy Joe was chasing turn. He must've heard the impact. He seemed paralyzed by the sight of Joe on the ground." She rubbed her arms in an attempt to chase the coldness away. "The guy didn't stand a chance. Not in oncoming traffic. An oil truck struck him. The semi driver couldn't stop in time, but because he tried to, the back end of the trailer swept around to the side. It tipped, and I knew we were seconds from being caught up in a multi-car pileup."

ELIZABETH PAUSED IN HER TELLING OF THE STORY TO BURY HER HEAD IN her hands. She pressed the heels of her palms to her eyes. Stephen presumed it was in an effort to block out the haunting memory.

"Joe was too close to the blast, and his clothing caught fire. I jumped out of my car and used my jacket to smother the flames. He suffered third-degree burns. Mostly, his lower legs and a small section of one arm. It could have been so much worse." She dropped her arms and faced him. "Things got quite insane after that. I have no idea to this day how many vehicles or people were involved. I do remember hearing, or reading, there were at least five dead. Because I still have nightmares, I found it too gruesome to revisit."

Stephen remained quiet as she lifted her glass of water to take a sip. He recognized she needed a minute to compose herself. His patience paid off.

"The guy Joe was initially chasing, didn't survive. Oddly enough, the duffle bag he carried was found intact. It was knocked out of range of the fire, I suppose. The poor man wasn't so lucky." She turned stark eyes on him. "He was burned so badly, Stephen. I still remember the smell of charred flesh." She tilted her neck back to view the ceiling, blinking rapidly to disperse the tears forming. Inhaling deeply, she resumed the rest of the story. "The police were able to salvage his ID from that bag. I confirmed it was his because I saw him carrying it. I was watching him since he entered the road, fearful he'd get himself killed. It was why I never saw Joe until it was too late. I was hyper-focused on the other guy."

Elizabeth stopped pacing in front of Stephen and searched his face. He wondered what she was looking for. He closed his eyes and rubbed a hand across his forehead. It was a crap effort to hide from her probing gaze, but inside, his mind was racing. Samantha's vision was eerily similar to Elizabeth's memory of the event.

"Do you know the name of the man Joe was chasing?"

"Somehow, I knew that would be your next question," she said wryly. "Michael Anselin."

Stephen's eyes flashed to hers. For a moment, their gazes locked together, each challenging the other to react. Elizabeth broke eye contact first.

"Isn't that the name your sweet little Samantha called Joe last night?" she taunted him. Bitterness seeped out in her tone and the small twist of her lips.

"Why do you dislike Samantha? You don't even know her. If you knew what she's been through these last few years, you might have a little bit of compassion for her."

His tone left no doubt Elizabeth's disdain had destroyed his patience. The desire to strangle her was strong, and Stephen was at a loss to understand why.

"I'm sorry, Stephen. Put it down to jealousy because she's succeeded in capturing the attention of the only two men I thought I loved."

"Thought?"

"What else did you want to know?" Elizabeth turned her back and began to gather the remaining food from the coffee table. "Oh, that's right. You want to know why Joe is hot after Samantha. For some bizarre reason, he thinks she may hold the key to his identity."

Stephen stormed to where Elizabeth stood, grabbed her upper arm, and swung her around to face him. "What did you say?"

"Stephen, you're hurting me."

Breathing deeply, he skimmed his palms up to her shoulders.

ELIZABETH HAD NEVER SEEN THIS FIERCE-WARRIOR SIDE OF STEPHEN. IN this state, he seemed dangerous and unpredictable. Heat raced through her at his touch. Her pulse quickened. Okay, so sue her. Dark, dangerous men thrilled the fuck out of her. And apparently, emotionally detached ones as well.

"I want an answer, Beth."

She toyed with remaining silent, but the commanding intensity in his gaze compelled her to tell the truth. "He doesn't know who he is. He told me last night he has a connection to her. I'm sure he intends to explore it. To discover if they actually knew each other. Joe is obsessed with recalling his past. Stephen, *let go*."

At her harsh command, Stephen's gaze dropped to where his hands gripped her shoulders. He eased the pressure but didn't remove them. Gradually, he lowered his head until their foreheads touched. A hand cupped either side of her jaw and locked her in place.

Elizabeth told herself she could have easily broken the hold if she wanted. Instead, she reveled in the closeness. His whispered *"Bethy, I'm sorry I hurt you"* curled around her heart. Made her yearn for the days before her innocence was shattered. For a short time, she'd still believed in fairy tales and happy endings. It was harder to with each passing year.

Stephen trailed his fingers from her jaw to her collarbone and caressed each sensitive spot in between. Outside, clouds parted and sent a shaft of radiant sunlight through the glass slider, illuminating the piece of jewelry dangling about her neck. He lifted the warm chain at the base of her throat to get a better look. The ray of sunshine vanished as if it had never been. As if its only job had been to point out that necklace.

"You still have it."

"Yes."

"I thought you would have pawned it or given it away."

Elizabeth remained quiet, but she suspected her silence spoke volumes.

"Bethy, what did you mean earlier when you said 'the two men you thought you loved'?"

"Stephen, I want you to go."

They were the hardest words she'd ever spoken, but she meant them nonetheless. She knew, if he didn't leave now, her pride would be damned, and she would beg him to stay with her. Beg him to love her forever. It struck her then that her feelings for him had always been stronger than her feelings for Joe.

He bent his knees to make them eye level. She shut her traitorous eyes against him. She'd been told they tended to reveal her every thought, and she needed to hide from him now. She wanted to bawl like a baby. Something precious was in the process of shriveling up and dying.

Stephen retrieved his keys from the table. He paused to pull out a pen and a business card, then circled one of the phone numbers.

"If you need me, Bethy, for any reason, please call. I know I've failed you in the past. But this time, I want to be there for you. No matter what. Okay?"

He laid the card on her foyer table and strode out the door.

A single tear slid down the cheek he'd just caressed. She swiped it away. Humiliation was all she felt. How could she be so weak? Where was the level-headed woman she'd grown into? She stalked over to the table, intent on ripping his card into a million pieces. Yet as her fingers were positioned to tear it, something beyond her power stayed her hands. Maybe her defective heart refused to let her sever the last tie to Stephen. With a sigh, she tossed the card in the bottom of her purse and went to pour herself a stiff drink.

CHAPTER 31

Stephen spent the rest of the afternoon in the hotel lounge. His life seemed to be crumbling down around him, and he didn't know how to stop it.

A long time ago, he lost a friend who had been like a father to him. Those memories had all been resurrected the second Elizabeth came back into his orbit. He held up a shot of tequila in a silent toast to Jonathan and Mary. He added a silent apology for allowing it all to go so wrong.

And now, he was in love with a woman who searched for a phantom. Although to be fair to Samantha, she'd never asked anything of him. The offer to help her investigate Michael's disappearance had been his brilliant idea. No, Stephen had decided to be her knight in shining armor all on his own in the hopes she would miraculously favor him with her heart. But she'd given that to Michael a long time before Stephen arrived on the scene.

And added to it all, he'd just discovered he still lusted after Elizabeth. Really, who wouldn't? She was a goddess in human form. When she initially ran away, it had been mainly due to him. Today, he'd shown up and poured salt on her wounds by informing her Joe was with Samantha. He wanted to slam his head down on the granite bar.

What the hell was wrong with him? This whacked out behavior wasn't him. Of course, he didn't need to think too hard about it. Deep down, he resented Joe's ability to so easily charm both women.

Signaling the bartender for another round, Stephen endeavored to drown the guilt, anger, and frustration taking hold of him. He lost track of the time and number of shots he consumed.

"WHAT TIME IS IT, JOE?" SAMMY ASKED.

He gripped her hand and twirled her around. "Why? Do you turn into a pumpkin if you're not home by midnight?"

The laughter died on her lips. "Stephen will be worried if I don't return soon."

"Didn't you text him to let him know where you were going?"

"No, I left my phone at the bookstore. What time is it?"

"Eight o'clock," he said after checking his watch.

"Ohmygod! How did it get so late?"

"Do you want the long, scientific version?" His dimples flashed, and she had the insane desire to lick the creases they created.

"Don't be an ass," she ordered. His poking fun helped her relax and enjoy the moment with him. "I guess I should at least call him to let him know where I am."

"I know the man who runs this joint. He owes me a favor. If we can smuggle a message out, you're gonna owe me big time," he teased in a gangster voice.

Sammy was delighted and a little saddened at the same time. He was easy to be around, but with each passing moment, he brought bittersweet memories of Michael to the forefront of her brain.

"I have to use the restroom. Take your time," Joe said as he handed her his phone.

She tried Stephen's cell phone first and then rang his room when it went to voicemail. *No answer.* She left a message to let Stephen know she would be back late and she'd see him at breakfast the next morning.

Sammy joined Joe by the bar. When he smiled down at her, she felt a warmth start at her toes and carry up throughout her body, causing a riot of emotions. Some good, some bad, and some extremely naughty.

"What's your poison?" he asked.

"Vodka and orange juice."

After the drinks were delivered, he gestured to the billiard tables.

"Do you play?"

"Yes."

She watched as he set up the rack and picked out two good sticks.

"You break," he offered. As she scattered the balls across the table and sunk two more, Joe looked at her and grinned. "Where did you learn to shoot so well?"

"Michael taught me," she told him with a soft smile. For once, the terrible pain of loss didn't overwhelm her.

JOE WONDERED IF HE SHOULD CONFESS TO THE ACCIDENT THAT HAD taken her lover's life. He'd hoped just being with her would trigger his recall of the past or at least parts of it. Doubts crept in that it would ever happen. He remained silent. It would kill him to see the happy light in her eyes fade to hate.

Heaving a hearty sigh, he demanded, "Tell me about Michael."

She lifted a brow in his direction. "What do you want to know?"

"How did you meet?"

"Do you want the truth or some fantastical made-up version?" she joked.

"Isn't the truth always stranger than fiction? Let's go with the real thing."

Samantha concentrated as she lined up her next shot.

He detected a hesitancy in her. He almost told her she didn't need to rehash the past if it caused her pain, but she started to relay the story.

"We seemed destined to be together from the first time we met. Or so I believed. Laugh if you want," she told him when he rolled his eyes.

"I know it sounds corny, but it's true. Michael and my brother, Jamie, were college roommates. Jamie brought him home for Spring Break, and I fell in love at first sight. It sounds like romantic nonsense, but I did. Butterflies and all."

"Did he feel the same way about you?" he asked.

"No, or if he did, he didn't say. I don't think he wanted to damage his friendship with Jamie in the event something went wrong. I honestly never knew his reasoning. We didn't get together until a few years later—after I graduated college. He moved to the little beach town where I lived and took a job my brother offered him. Later, he found what he thought would be his dream position as an engineer."

Sammy chalked the tip of her pool stick. Shooting Joe a thoughtful look, she continued, "Michael never complained. But there were times, over the years, I sensed his dissatisfaction with his job. Maybe with me. Anyway, getting back to our hooking up; it didn't take us long to move in together. We were inseparable." She offered up a hint of a smile in remembrance. "Somewhere in there, he taught me to play pool. We were a little competitive and would bet on everything. The first bet I remember was a vacation destination."

At his questioning look, she explained. "If he won, we'd head to Barbados for a dive trip. If I won, he'd take me to France. I wanted to eat croissants with a view of the Eiffel Tower."

"And he won," Joe laughed.

"What makes you say that?"

"You had a wistful quality to your voice as you mentioned France. I suspect you never got around to going."

"Nope. We ended up in Barbados. I scratched on the eight ball the first time. I insisted we played double or nothing. That's when he won. Ran the damned table."

"Sounds to me like he won the first game."

"No, I lost. He didn't win."

"It's the same difference," he argued, feeling compelled to defend the absent Michael.

"No, it's not! I scratched. He did not beat me. Technically, I beat myself. So I lost, and he did not win."

"Come on, darlin', you're splitting hairs. You didn't win, hence he won."

"Bullshit."

"What did you say, potty mouth?"

SAMMY COULD ONLY STARE AT HIM. HOW COULD HE HAVE MICHAEL'S voice, his mannerisms, even utter the same phrases, and yet, not be Michael? But he wasn't. The man standing before her was Joe. She needed to remember that.

"Nothing. For a moment, I was transported back in time. I think you and Michael must have been twins separated at birth," she tried to joke, falling flat. "Maybe that's why I like you so much," she whispered. Dropping all pretense of humor, she asked, "Do you think a person's personality can change to a drastic degree?"

"I suppose it depends on the person. Why?"

She shook her head. "No reason."

"Whose shot is it?" he asked, taking a gulp of his drink.

"Yours. I need another drink. Are you ready for a refill?"

"Let me shoot, and I'll go get them."

"No. You have been paying for everything all afternoon. It's my turn to treat you. What are you drinking?"

He watched her closely as he said, "Seven and seven."

She closed her eyes and ruefully shook her head. He suspected she was with him because he reminded her of Michael, and he'd be right. Maybe part of her needed the closure.

"Be back in a sec." When Sammy returned, it was to find he ran the table except for the eight ball. She studied the ball placement. "Did you cheat?" she demanded.

"No. I don't need to cheat to beat you," he stated smugly.

"Well, I think you cheated."

"Okay. I'll prove to you I didn't, next game. *After*, I win this one."

"Yeah, right. What are you gonna do, send me off for drinks again?"

"How would you like to place a little wager?" he asked slyly.

"Fine. What do you want to bet?"

"What do you have to lose?"

She suspected her heart, but saying it out loud would spook him. Instead, she said, "Fifty dollars."

"I don't bet for money."

"What do you bet for?" she asked, already anticipating the answer.

"Sex. Hot. Steamy. Sex."

The way he drew out the words sent a shiver of longing through her. One man shouldn't have the power to turn a woman on with his voice alone. As far as the wager, she shouldn't go there. She really shouldn't. Talk about your danger zones. She guzzled down half of her drink before she agreed. Two drinks were starting a nice buzz. Maybe three or four would help her forget for a bit.

When he won, she was shocked.

"*Dude!* Double or nothing."

He looked at her, a mysterious half-smile on his face. "Rack 'em."

"You're a damned shark, and I feel like chum in the water," Sammy complained good-naturedly.

After she lost again, she resigned herself to her fate. She was tipsy. That much was obvious. She had to be because she felt too good. Elated in a way she hadn't felt in years.

The only blight was the thought of spending the night with Joe. The perceived consequences wreaked havoc on her mind. Sexual desire consumed her even as doubts assailed her. But she didn't intend to renege on the bet. *Hell, no!* No one would call Samantha Holt a welsher. The Holt family honor was at stake. The cynical part of her brain chided her and offered up a snarky *"You keep telling yourself that, Sammy."*

"Shut it," she muttered to herself.

"Excuse me?"

Embarrassed to have been caught talking to herself, her full-body flush worked its magic, making her glow bright red.

"Nothing, I… um… yeah, I was talking to myself," she stumbled.

Her face heated up more when he shot her a delighted grin. She didn't know why that made him so happy, but she'd go with it.

"Your place or mine?" he asked.

"Mine."

He took the drink from her hand, set it on the table, and dropped an arm around her shoulders in a friendly gesture. Sammy sighed and smiled up at him. He chose that moment to look down at her and smile.

Her heart stuttered.

Joe's combination of dark blond hair, honey-brown eyes, and dimples reminded her of the first time she'd met Michael on the boardwalk in Flagler Beach. Minus the current setting, and about twelve years, it could have been the two of them.

"You're sad again."

"Nope. I'm just admiring how freaking hot you are."

"Nice! You think I'm hot?"

"Fishing for compliments, Joe?"

"You bet."

After they had found a taxi and gave directions to the driver, they found it impossible to stop touching one another. The kisses were steamy, the caresses electric. One of Joe's roaming hands dipped past the waistband of her lacy panties.

"*Jesus!* Have you always had this sexy-panty fetish?" he whispered, pausing to drag down the V of her shirt and peer at her breasts encased in a black and pink lace demi-bra. He growled, "Your fucking underwear is killing my state of mind."

The driver broke them out of their little world with the loud clearing of his throat. "Excuse me, but didn't I have you two last night?"

Sammy giggled helplessly. He was indeed the driver from the night before. Her nervousness ebbed, and with it, welcoming warmth took hold and eased her conscience. *Fate.* It had to be.

The ride to the hotel took no time at all. Sammy paused by the main reception desk to check for messages. Except for one from Lauren to say she had Sammy's cell phone, there were no other missives.

Joe nudged her toward the elevator. As the doors opened, he

pressed her inside, his body crowding hers until they hit the elevator wall. She jumped, and he caught her with one hand under her ass and one arm locked around her waist. Lips interlocked. Her hands explored whatever they could find.

Joe couldn't seem to get enough of her taste, and she felt exactly the same. He cupped her neck as he pressed her into the wall. His mouth claimed hers again and again. Sammy whimpered as she ground her hips against his.

"God, Sammy, I want you."

"Yes," she breathed.

When they arrived on her floor, she fumbled with the key as Joe kissed her neck and caressed her breasts underneath her shirt.

"Hurry, Sammy."

"I'm trying. The stupid thing won't open. It's like the deadbolt's in place."

"Screw the bed. Let's find a linen closet," he said in frustration.

They exchanged another kiss. This one, more leisurely, where their tongues stroked and tasted, tempting one another to delve deeper.

This man shook her to her very core.

"Be patient," she scolded.

Again, she tried the lock.

"Dammit, do you have the right room?"

Sammy looked at the number on the door and then to the key envelope in her hand. Her eyes went back to the elevator to ascertain they were on the correct floor. A giggle bubbled up, and she started to laugh.

Joe looked at her as if she had lost her mind. "Do you mind telling me what is so funny?"

"Where am I going to hide you while maintenance lets me in?" she asked, pointedly looking at the front of his jeans.

It was the tension breaker he needed to put everything back into perspective.

"You've got a good point."

"No, I'd say you do," she sputtered and giggled.

"But I want to share my *point* with you," he whispered against her lips.

Those words should've been a joke, but Joe's delivery made them sexy as hell. Sammy wasted no time as she pushed him against the door and pulled his head down to hers. She had his shirt unbuttoned and off in record time.

Joe shifted their positions and pinned her in the corner between the wall and door. Sammy climbed up his body and wrapped her legs around him like a spider monkey. He was within an inch of taking her right there in the hallway, and she wouldn't have minded one bit. Their need for each other was ridiculous.

"We have to find a place to go. Quickly, or I can't be responsible for my actions," he murmured into her ear just before latching onto her earlobe.

Neither bargained for the door swinging inward. Sammy expected the sheer shock on their faces would have been comical in any other situation. She almost snorted. *Almost.*

Stephen's pissy attitude doused her humor along with her desire. "What the hell's going on?"

Sammy and Joe faced an enraged Stephen.

"Where the hell have you been, Samantha?"

"Didn't you get my message?" Sammy asked as she slid down Joe and straightened her skirt with shaky hands.

"What message? The one that said you were out and would see me tomorrow? *That* message?"

He bobbed a little before he leaned against the doorframe. Sammy frowned as she noted his disheveled appearance.

"Yeah, I got it. What the hell, Samantha?" he demanded, belligerent and combative.

Her back went up. He wasn't her keeper anymore. "Stephen, I don't like your tone. And I certainly don't answer to you. What are you doing in my room?"

"Waiting for you. I thought we were here to find Michael. But I'd have to say, it doesn't look like you've been doing much investigating beyond this bastard's bed."

. . .

ANGER WAS SLOW TO STIR FOR JOE IN NORMAL CIRCUMSTANCES, BUT with a few drinks, frustrated sexual desire, and Stephen's surly tone, it took no time at all to have his blood boiling.

"She's a fucking adult. And to the best of my knowledge, you have no claim on her," Joe's steely tone threatened even though his words didn't.

"Who the fuck do you think you are? Isn't one woman enough for you?"

"You son of a bitch!"

Joe drew back to throw a punch to smash Stephen's arrogant face. Sammy grabbed his raised arm with both of hers.

"Stop it, both of you," she growled low and sent a quelling look at a passing hotel guest who eyed them with avid curiosity.

She stormed through the open door to the small balcony.

Joe swept his shirt from the floor and was halfway to her when he heard her say he should go. The smug look on Stephen's face caused him to seethe. His was a face Joe severely wanted to pound. Helpless rage filled him. He turned his back on Stephen and whipped on his shirt, furious with the entire situation. What hold did this asshat have on Sammy? She'd shut down in a way Joe had never seen another person do. One moment, she'd been passionate and animated. The next, she was cold and distant. Polar opposite to the woman he'd gotten to know. Her high color attested to her embarrassment.

As he spun back around, he saw Stephen perched on the edge of the bed with his head in his hands. Joe frowned at the abrupt change. What the fuck was this guy's problem? Jealousy, he understood, but the harsh judgment when Sammy deserved neither set Joe's teeth on edge.

Joe dismissed all thoughts of Stephen and approached Sammy. "Are you going to be all right?" he asked in a hushed tone.

"I don't know," she whispered, a catch in her throat.

His arms came around to gather her close. He breathed in the scent of her. *Lemons.* His new favorite fragrance. Holding her was as familiar to him as breathing. Comforting almost. He wanted to hold her forever, but how could he tell her he was nuts about her after only two days together? He felt a burning behind his lids and inhaled deeply to regain control of himself.

"Sammy, have breakfast with me tomorrow."

"I can't." She sighed heavily but didn't shrug off his hug. "I think it's best if I don't see you again, Joe."

"I understand."

"Do you?" she asked, a hysterical note in her voice. "I'm glad, because I sure as shit don't."

"Don't torture yourself, Sammy. Please, don't," he ended on a gentle whisper.

He shifted her in his arms, putting a hand under her chin to urge her face up. It was important she look at him and take to heart his next words.

"Listen to me, darlin'. You did nothing wrong. You have absolutely no reason to feel guilty."

She burrowed into his embrace and hugged him as if she never wanted to let him go.

Her tortured expression and odd behavior bothered him to a huge degree. "Are you okay to be alone with him?"

"Yes. Stephen would never hurt me."

Sammy pulled back one last time to gaze up at him. He took that time to memorize her beautiful, tragic face.

"Goodbye, Joe."

"Goodbye, Sammy Darlin'."

After he had gone, Sammy crossed to where Stephen continued to sit, head cradled in his hands. She knelt and pulled his arms down to scrutinize his face. "Why, Stephen? Why did you act like that?"

The torment in his eyes answered her question. An ache started in her chest, swelling in proportion. Having been in love and understanding what a lost cause it could sometimes be, she could empathize. She sat down next to him and pulled his head to her breast. Trying to soothe him, she stroked his thick, wavy hair, absently noting its silky feel. His arms came around her back.

"I love you, Samantha," he finally confessed.

"I know."

"I'm sorry."

"For what? Looking out for me? For making sure I didn't make a mistake that would haunt me and cause me endless grief?" She sighed and rubbed her cheek against his soft mop of hair. "Tomorrow we'll talk."

They held each other in silence. Eventually, they shifted positions and dozed off to sleep.

In the early hours of the morning, Sammy woke to fingers lightly tracing her shoulder. She looked over to find Stephen resting on his side with one hand propping up his head. He hesitated for a brief second before he leaned over her, asking silent permission to kiss her. She nodded her agreement. No words were necessary.

STEPHEN'S MOUTH SETTLED OVER HERS. THERE WAS NO SOFTNESS AS HIS lips took hers. He was a man on a mission. Tasting her was essential. His tongue swept into her mouth, dancing with hers. His hands tore at her clothes. The need to possess her was greater than his need to show finesse.

He pulled back and admired the sweet, soft perfection of her body. Hoping if this was a dream, he'd not wake up. All his fantasies were nothing compared to this one exquisite moment in time.

When Samantha took him inside, he was sure he'd died and gone to heaven. Making love to her was more than he'd hoped or imagined. So much more. He rubbed a nipple to a hardened point, then bent to claim it with his lips. He showered his attention on each of her lovely breasts before slowly tracing the delicate curve of her neck with his lips. He caught her lobe with his teeth, causing her to moan softly. She abandoned all to him right then. With each hard thrust, he arrived one step closer to bliss. The climax shook him to his core and had him proclaiming his love for her.

She didn't answer, and he worried he'd pushed too hard too fast. Eventually, her arms tightened around him, and she buried her face in his throat. He released a ragged sigh. It would all be okay. It had to be. Her happiness meant all to him.

———

SAMMY LAY IN THE DARK, LISTENING TO THE STEADY, SHALLOW breathing that told her Stephen was sleeping. Quietly, she extracted herself from his loose embrace and tugged on the robe she kept on the bedside chair. She cast one last glance at Stephen to check she hadn't disturbed him. For the second time that night, she strolled over to the window.

Grief and sorrow welled up in her. The room triggered a claustrophobic reaction. A need to breathe fresh air. After inching the glass doors open to minimize the noise, she stepped out on the balcony and sat on the deck chair. Silent tears trailed down her cheeks. It was a well-worn path.

Today had been such a whirlwind. Thoughts of Joe and Michael intermingled and made it difficult to tell one from the other. Stephen's behavior wasn't so strange either, but the guilt she felt regarding both of them nearly cut her in half. She couldn't commit to either and had used them both abominably. First Joe because of his resemblance to Michael, then Stephen to assuage her never-ending guilt over Joe.

It was well past time to get her shit together. Even for her fucked-up head, this behavior was over the top. The dream of what used to be was harder than hell to let go, but she intended to do it. She *must* if she wanted a moderately normal future.

"Goodbye, Michael," she whispered.

The time had come to sever the invisible thread that bound them. And after twenty-two months of holding out hope, of refusing to let go, she did. Her heartbroken sobs couldn't be contained. It felt as if she wept for hours. She cried, remembering the day they'd met. Their few stolen kisses. She cried for the good times and the bad. She cried over their bittersweet goodbyes by phone. She cried for their baby. And lastly, she cried for the very real hole he'd left in her heart. What it would take to fill it, she didn't know. It was doubtful anything or anyone ever could. But she had to try. A half-life was no real life at all.

SILENT AS SAMANTHA WAS, STEPHEN STILL HEARD HER. HE DIDN'T MOVE a muscle, not wishing to disturb her. She'd sought solitude to grieve and had to face the mourning process on her own.

He'd never experienced such a level of self-loathing as he did just then. He'd thought when the time came to tell her about Michael, it would be a simple decision. All he had ever wanted was her happiness. But try as he might, he couldn't bring himself to do it. Instead, he'd practically forced himself on her. With what he'd done, she was left little choice but to say goodbye.

Listening to her muffled sobs very nearly destroyed him. Was he being fanciful to believe he could hear the cracking of her heart in two? Reaching up, he knuckled the moisture from his own eyes. He fought the urge to confess his sins, and instead, he lay there in the darkness, holding the truth back. Silent. Guilty. Miserable.

CHAPTER 32

*T*he next morning brought with it a somber mood for both Sammy and Stephen. They sat over breakfast in an uncomfortable silence, their first in over a year.

Stephen broke the ice. "Samantha, I want to talk to you about last night."

She stiffened, unsure how to comment. If this was about the incident with Joe, she would rather they didn't speak of it ever again. Hot coals applied to her palms would cause less clamminess. However, if the topic was about the sex, well, she supposed it was unavoidable.

"I've turned the words over and over in my mind. Trying to figure out what I wanted to say. I'm not sure this will come out right, but I need to try." He paused to clear his throat. "I know you can be stubborn and steadfast. However, I also know you tend to make rash decisions. I don't think you would knowingly cause yourself pain or anguish."

Still, she remained silent. Where was he going with this, and why did it begin like a lecture on her stupidity?

"I need to know. Why did you make such a quick about-face? Why did you go from never giving up on the hope Michael was alive to almost sleeping with a total stranger to sleeping with me?"

She glanced down at the half-eaten egg bagel in her hand. Slowly, and with great deliberation, she set it down. Sighing deeply, she bit her lip. When she finally looked up at Stephen, she witnessed the shutters dropping down to conceal his emotions. Normally, Stephen's face reflected openness. A willingness to listen.

He's hiding something.

The intuition that served her without fail screamed with the knowledge. These last few years she'd thought Stephen was professional and reserved. After last night, she wondered just how much he'd bottled up inside and for how long. She wasn't used to viewing Stephen as a flawed individual. But he was human, and humans were fallible.

"It was a number of things. First, my initial mistake was assuming Joe was Michael. He said something you and I had once touched on in a session. He asked why, if Michael was alive, he hadn't tried to contact me. I heard how far-fetched and lame my answers sounded. Not true reasoning at all." She ripped apart the last of the bagel and dropped it back on the plate. "Second, Joe was the one who told me you loved me. I never saw it before or how badly I was hurting the people around me." She paused to take a sip of water. As Stephen remained watchful, she continued. "Another reason was the kiss you and I shared the other night. I thought I wouldn't feel anything for anyone but Michael, and yet, I might be able to. For you. And lastly, I called my mother yesterday morning. She read me the riot act. She told me it was about time I got on with my life. Also, she thinks very highly of you."

She shrugged. What else could she say? She'd laid it on the line and was as honest as she could be. Stephen paused a few beats to absorb and process her words. She could see the wheels spinning in his mind and held her breath. If he got confrontational about Joe, it would piss her right the hell off.

"I saw you with Joe yesterday before you walked into the restaurant."

And there it was. Sammy glared at him, lips compressed in a thin line. Suppressing her angry attitude was an exercise in restraint.

"Samantha, I want to know what attraction he holds for you. I don't want to commit myself to a relationship that is doomed to fail. If you have this attraction for anyone that reminds you of Michael, we are going to have a problem."

"Don't you think you're mighty assumptive, Stephen? I never said I wanted a relationship with you," she snapped, stung by the accusation in his tone.

"I see." He snorted in disgust. "But what I don't see is why the hell I bother with you at all."

Stephen tossed down his napkin and marched out of the hotel dining room.

Sammy sighed and buried her head in her hands. She'd have to find a way to apologize and mean it. Perhaps it had been the word *relationship*. Although she had a guy as awesome as Stephen interested in her, it was all too much coming on the heels of this trip.

The seat creaked as Joe slid into the booth across from her.

She squeaked her disbelief. "Joe! What the hell are you doing here?"

"I'm not really sure. I guess I wanted to convince myself you were okay."

"Well, I'm not," she snapped.

"What happened after I left?"

His gentle question caused her to look away. She couldn't bear to see accusation or disapproval in his eyes.

"Sammy?"

"Please don't call me that," she cried.

"Did he hurt you?" he demanded to know. "I swear to God, if he did, I'll kill him."

"*No!*" She looked around and lowered her voice. "No, of course not. I told you the truth. Stephen would never hurt me."

"Then why won't you look at me?"

When she didn't answer, he figured it out. "Ah, you slept with him, didn't you?"

His tone was so understanding she wanted to die of shame. All she could do was nod. While Sammy watched, Joe picked up an uneaten piece of her bagel, inspected it, and bit into it.

"You weren't eating this, were you?" At her negative response, he finished the food and went on to say, "You feel like you betrayed Michael, don't you?"

"I do. But, more importantly, I feel like I betrayed you, Joe. Tell me why. Please."

JOE GOT THE IMPRESSION SHE HOPED FOR SOMETHING SPECIFIC FROM him. As if there might be magic words he could utter to fix all that was broken in her life. He couldn't. It frustrated the devil out of him to always feel he was disappointing her.

"I can't say. Maybe it was the same reason Beth and I broke up the night I met you. You and I, we have something, don't we? Chemistry. A connection. Call it what you will, but it's there and very real." He wiped his fingers on a napkin then entwined his hand with hers. Although he hated the jealousy he was experiencing, he didn't have the right. She'd been friends with Stephen far longer than with him.

"You didn't betray anyone, Sammy. Michael's dead. You don't owe me anything. Because the bottom line is we only shared a short span of time together. Well, that and a few incredibly hot kisses, which I refuse to apologize for." He cast her a wicked smile. He sobered again to add, "You've shared almost two years with Stephen. Don't tie yourself up in knots."

"I can't seem to help it."

They fell into a silence. She purposely removed her hand from his and sipped her water. Her eyes looked everywhere but at him.

"Another reason I'm here is to whisk you away for the day. What do you think?"

"Are you insane?"

"What do you mean?"

"I just told you I slept with another man last night. Right after you and I shared 'incredibly hot kisses.' You act as if it's a run-of-the-mill situation. How can you be so understanding and blasé? How can you even want to see me again? For that matter, *why?*" She finally managed to meet his warm regard.

"It doesn't change the way I'm starting to feel about you, Sammy."

"Oh, Joe, don't." She sounded weary, on the verge of tears.

"Don't what?"

"Don't do this to me. To us. We can't have anything together," she insisted. "You bear an uncanny resemblance to Michael. Your speech and mannerisms are almost exactly the same. Will you ever be able to look at me and not wonder if I'm only with you because you remind me of him? Will you wonder if I need to hold on to some part of the past, and you might just be that part with your beautiful eyes and voice that sounds so much like his?"

She fought valiantly, but he could see her tears welling up. "Are you willing to be a substitute? Because that's what you'd be, Joe. I don't want you, and I don't want Stephen. I want Michael. Would I settle because he's lost to me? Probably, but not without resentment. Yours. Mine. Stephen's. Who knows? But it would eventually surface."

"I care about you, Sammy. I don't know when it happened or why, but I do. I can live with a resemblance."

"I *can't.* I can't live with it at all. I die all over again every time you make a gesture similar to his. I can't do this, Joe."

"What about what we shared over the last two days? Do you think our chemistry isn't real? All because I look like someone you used to love?"

"*Yes, damn you!*" She slammed her hand on the table, causing the dishes to rattle and heads to turn. She glared at the couple closest to them but lowered her voice. "Do you honestly believe I was seeing *you*, Joe? *Do you?* Don't be so damned self-delusional."

"You are determined to drive away anyone who cares for you, aren't you?" he asked, unable to keep the edge of bitterness from his voice. She was set on destroying the bond he felt so keenly, and it hurt like hell. He rose to his feet and stared down into her furious face. "Michael's death should've taught you the one thing you seem to be missing—life's fleeting. You need to grab hold of anything that looks like happiness and hang on for all you're worth. Wake the fuck up before it's too late, lonely girl."

Joe stormed away, leaving Sammy at the mercy of every curious gaze in the hotel restaurant. She drew what little dignity she had left around her like a cloak, finished her water, and signed the tab the waiter brought to her. The looks of pity cast in her direction flayed her. Everyone in the restaurant must now know her whole life story. Humiliation burned from the inside out, but she lifted her head and walked from the restaurant as if she didn't have a care in the world.

She found herself in front of Stephen's door. Before she could allow herself to back down, she knocked. The door swung open on a glowering Stephen.

"What do you want?"

"May I come in, or should I stand in the hallway while I bare my soul to you?"

"Samantha, I don't know what game you are playing this time, but quite frankly, I'm tired of it."

"I would like to have an adult conversation and not trade insults. Are you up to it right now, or should I come back?"

Stephen bowed low and waved her in the room.

"Cut it out, Stephen. It's not like you to act this way."

"What do you really know about me or the way I act, Sammy?" he asked snidely.

"I know you."

"Really? What is my favorite color? How about my favorite food? What's my favorite movie of all time? What's my family like? Where was I raised?" He paused to let her flounder because he knew damned well she didn't know. "What's the matter, *Sammy?* Feeling bad? I can see from your expression you've realized you never once bothered to ask."

He was being ugly, but she couldn't say he was wrong. Her nerves were live wires, and her head was pounding. Not a great combination for her to retain any semblance of calm.

"What about you, Dr. High and Mighty Montgomery? What do you really know about me besides some trauma I experienced?"

Stephen stalked to the connecting door of their rooms and flung it open. He waved her over and pointed to the purple variegated roses scattered across the bed.

"Purple is your favorite color." He shoved a huge box of bonbons into her hands. "Your favorite food, if you can call candy a food, is chocolate, so I had this sent up while we were at breakfast." He crossed to the nightstand to lift a gift bag and upend the contents on the bed. "I know how much you love lemon everything. I know you love old movies. Each new romantic comedy is your favorite. I know your family and what you were like as a child growing up. I know you are close to your brother and youngest sister, but you and your oldest sister can often be like oil and water. How do I know all this? *Because I cared enough to ask!*"

She flinched at the volume of his voice. He stared at her, his anger palpable. "What's the matter, sweetheart? Did I strike a nerve?"

Stephen didn't wait for a response. He stalked back to his room.

Sammy looked around her. All the subtle, romantic nuances he'd arranged while they ate breakfast tugged at her heartstrings. She'd seriously misjudged him earlier. Although she'd initially believed he was acting jealous and possessive, all he really wanted was to protect his own heart from being crushed. She could appreciate the need to protect himself from pain.

She selected a rose from atop the comforter and entered his room. A half-packed suitcase rested on the bed. While Sammy knew she wasn't prepared for a new relationship, Stephen's departure from her world wasn't an option. She placed the rose on top of his neatly stacked clothes.

"Please don't go, Stephen."

"Why?"

"Because I need you."

"No, *Sammy,* you don't need anything but your fucking memories of Michael."

"Why do you keep saying my name like that?" she asked, ignoring the Michael comment. He wasn't mistaken. Until this point, she'd felt exactly that way. His swearing was a testament to how deep his emotions ran.

"After your snarky comment at breakfast, I made it all the way to the elevator before I went back. I intended to lay my heart at your feet. I hadn't been gone two minutes before Joe was filling my seat."

She flinched.

"My point? I'm sure it will take half that time for you to have him fill my spot in your bed. I can only guess it's his resemblance to Michael, and the way he calls you 'Sammy' that has you so hot and bothered."

With those words, he flung the rose on the floor and crushed it beneath his heel. He presented his back to her and zipped his suitcase. All she saw was her best friend leaving. Another loss. Another heart broken. Her eyes stung, and the room went blurry. She could feel her nasal passages fill and burn. God, she was about to cry the big ugly and beg him to stay. But did she have the right?

As STEPHEN TURNED TO SAY SAYONARA, HE SAW HER STANDING THERE like the brave little soldier she was. Silent tears streamed down her face. He'd never wanted to cause her the kind of turmoil she was experiencing, even now when his own heart was ripped open and bleeding.

"Samantha," he choked out.

It was enough. She raced the few steps into his arms and held on as if she never wanted to release him. And he didn't think he could let her go, even if she wanted him to.

"Stephen, please stay."

"I must be insane."

"Join the club," she retorted with a watery chuckle. "I know a great clinic you can visit."

He ignored her joke. "Before I commit to stay, I need to know about Joe."

"He came to make sure I was okay. I sent him away."

Stephen closed his eyes in relief. If he could keep her away from Joe, he might stand a chance.

"Will you spend the day with me in my beautiful room, Stephen? I want to learn your favorite color and foods, and maybe watch movies. I also want to hear about your family and where you were raised."

He swept her up in his arms and carried her into the adjoining suite. For a split second, he acted as if he would place her on the bed with great ceremony. Instead, he dumped her, causing an outraged squeal.

"I can't have you believing I forgive you completely."

He grinned, brushed the items to the side of the bed, and jumped on the mattress next to her. They spent the rest of the day like the two friends they were. Stephen talked mostly about himself and his past. He told her about Elizabeth, and what had transpired between him and her father, of the tragedy surrounding the Phillips family, and his helplessness in aiding her. Samantha expressed shock to find out he had a half-brother and a sister. They talked long into the day and on into the night, ordering room service for every meal.

Once in a while, Stephen would steal a kiss. He never carried it further than the simple gesture. She would need to love him before they shared a bed again. He was positive he'd never let her go if he touched her again. If she decided after today to push him back into the friend zone, he'd be a broken man.

CHAPTER 33

*W*ith nothing left to do but bask in his own misery, Joe went home. Samantha's book taunted him from where it rested on the kitchen table. It begged him to crack the spine and discover what mysteries it held.

The inscription read: *"A heart will always recognize its other half. May you find your one true soulmate. Sammy."* She hadn't prefaced it with a name.

As the story unfolded, so did his life. Memories rushed back, crowding his brain. Without a doubt, he was Michael Anselin.

Although she'd stated her novel was fiction, it was really their story. His recollection was so clear. Meeting her for the first time on the beach. Their first kiss at her parents' house. The first time they'd made love. The last time. He remembered the bet. She'd told the story correctly; she'd scratched on the eight ball. Then, as now, she believed he'd never won. She'd beat herself.

Oh, God, Sammy! What have I done?

With the memories came the devastation. She'd been pregnant when he left. He'd never known. Michael broke down and sobbed for all he'd lost. And he had lost it all.

How was he supposed to tell Sammy who he was after this morning? Her having sex—and he refused to consider it making love—with Stephen, spoke volumes. His Sammy would never sleep with another man. Not if she believed there was the remotest possibility he could still be alive. The joke was on them both because he looked so similar to who he had been, but still different enough to cause doubts for her.

More than ever, Michael wanted their life back. But it was too late for him. Only last night, she'd severed the tie to the past. Could he do that to her? Could he destroy what she'd started to rebuild?

As he pondered that question, he poured himself a shot and tossed it back. Michael welcomed the burn of the alcohol to distract himself from the crushing blow to his heart. He rubbed his chest. The literal ache was almost more than he could bear. Another shot of whiskey followed the first. Dulling the pain was all he could hope for.

He marveled at the capricious nature of fate. Would he have ever recovered his memory if Sammy hadn't approached him in the restaurant? *Probably not.*

Her demon had been right, Michael was never going home. But he wanted to. Dear God, how he wanted to! Wanted to drink beer and watch football with James. Wanted to play ball on the beach with Sassy. But most importantly, he wanted to spend long hours talking and making love with Sammy. He wanted to hold her and remember what it was like to feel complete.

Her love humbled him. She'd spent two years with unwavering devotion. Could he have been so strong? So sure he was right? Doubtful. And a mental hospital... *Good God!* But she'd come out fighting. He'd been impressed with her as Joe, but he was damned proud of her now that he knew the truth.

Stephen had to have recognized him by the tattoo on his shoulder. His look of guilt as Michael had turned around last night was unmistakable. If that asshole had ever read her book—and Michael had no doubt he had—he would've made the connection to the main character's tat. Sammy had written how the couple had worked for hours to perfect the design for his parents to be commemorated in ink.

She also would've known who he was last night if they'd carried through with making love. He was a stomach sleeper, so even had she initially missed the tattoo, she'd have seen it at some point during the night. He was confident had they made it to bed, he wouldn't have left anytime soon.

Fury replaced his grief. It pounded through his veins and knocked against his skull. Needing a release for the pent-up rage, he pummeled the closest wall, creating a huge hole in the drywall. When his assault on the wall did nothing to alleviate his anger, he went on a rampage, smashing anything not nailed down. Michael was consumed with a need to destroy.

Finally, chest heaving from sobs, he collapsed on the floor, his back resting against the overturned sofa.

"Fuck!" he screamed. *"Fuuuckkkk!"*

The desire to do something stupid like hunt Stephen down and beat him to a bloody pulp overwhelmed Michael. Violence had never been his way, but his wrath could not be contained. He had only one true friend left, if he hadn't completely destroyed their relationship. And so he dialed her number.

"Beth?"

"Joe. Somehow I didn't expect to hear from you anytime soon."

"Beth, I need to talk to you. Can you come over?"

"I don't think it's a good idea."

"I remembered who I am," he rasped out.

"I'm on my way."

Eighteen minutes later, Elizabeth rang the bell. As she ventured into the apartment, she recoiled from the destruction. With gingerly steps, she moved farther into the room, careful not to grind the smashed glass into the carpet.

"Holy shit! Joe, what the hell happened here?"

She struggled to straighten an overturned chair. Huffing from exertion, she flopped into it.

"Joe, you've been crying." Elizabeth shifted to get a clearer view of his face.

His need for comfort was powerful. Michael stumbled the four feet to where she sat. Reaching down, he hauled her up and into his arms. Seconds morphed into minutes, and still he was reluctant to release her. He drew strength from her. Sweet, selfless Beth. She'd taken care of him from day one.

After he had his emotions mostly in check, he released her to right the sofa. Side by side, hand in hand, they sat. "Beth, I'm Michael Anselin."

"But—"

"No, don't interrupt. I'll tell you all I remember. I'm not very clear on the accident itself, but I know now why I was chasing that guy through traffic." He inhaled and exhaled before he continued. "Samantha Holt was my girlfriend, soon to be my fiancée. I had an engagement ring I intended to give her that Christmas." Michael rose to pace. Each memory fought to be the utmost in his mind. "I was here on business, and I was getting ready to leave the hotel. I wanted to call Sammy one last time to let her know I was on my way home and to ease her fears. She'd been having bone-chilling nightmares, and she was worried I wouldn't return home. She kept telling me something terrible was going to happen. *Ohmygod!*" Michael jerked to a stop, stricken.

"Jo… uh, Michael, what is it?"

"The plane, Beth. The one that crashed the same day as the accident, I was supposed to be on that plane. If I hadn't stopped to call Sammy, I would have been killed," Michael said, feeling pole-axed. Grief and guilt stole his breath. "My friend was on that flight. Roger must've died in the crash."

Trying to divert his attention, Elizabeth questioned him about the guy he'd been chasing across the highway.

"I knew him, too. Or sort of. He delivered pizza to my room the night before. The resemblance between us was unreal. I almost asked about his family."

"Now that you mention it, he did look like you. I didn't recall that before this moment. I wonder who he really was."

Someday soon, Michael intended to find out. The guy had been a douchebag, but if he had family he'd left behind, they deserved to know the truth. "As I came out of my hotel room, he grabbed my duffle bag. It held my wallet, phone, and e-ticket." He scrubbed his face with his hands and dragged in a deep breath. "That must be how they identified him. Some lazy bastard dropped the ball. *I knew it!* It was all such a clusterfuck. To think, if that person had done their job properly, Sammy wouldn't have gone through all of this."

"Would you have wanted her to see you in a coma? Or trying to be brave through your recovery and all the painful therapy sessions?"

That particular point had not occurred to him. No, he wouldn't have wanted her to be there for the coma, surgeries, or any of the rest of it. What if she'd been there when he woke up and was forced to deal with his memory loss? She'd have been distressed and forced to cater to him while she was pregnant. It wouldn't have been fair to her. But was it any better to spend eight months in a psych ward?

"Beth, Stephen knew who I was last night. He didn't say anything to Sammy. He could have ended her search!" He became incensed again. Stephen had betrayed Sammy's trust. "That son of a bitch," he swore, jumping up to pace.

"Don't judge him too harshly, Jo... er... Michael. God, I'm never going to get used to calling you that."

"He had our future in the palm of his hand, Beth. He's a fucking coward. He was afraid she would leave with me. I know it." He was seething. Christ, he should've given in to the instinct to beat the hell out of the fuckhead.

"Please calm down." She stood and placed a hand on his chest. "Stephen's a doctor, Michael. He would've done what he thought was best for her mental stability. You don't know what she must've suffered. Or how emotionally stable she came out of it, for that matter."

"Bullshit. He saw the tattoo on my shoulder. If he read her book, he knew. It has to be the reason the anger left him so abruptly. Why he sat there, not saying a damned thing. He did what was best for *him*, Beth. *Not* her. Not Sammy. That rotten sonofabitch!"

"I'm telling you to give him the benefit of the doubt. I know Stephen, and he would never purposely hurt her. If he didn't tell her, then maybe he wasn't sure who you were."

"How exactly do you know him? Why are you so sure he's such a fucking saint?"

"It's a long story. He was a friend of my father's. Granted, I haven't seen him in close to a decade, but the general character of a person doesn't drastically change. If I learned anything from my dad, I learned that."

"A decade is a long time. You can't be sure what he is or isn't capable of," he argued.

ELIZABETH DIDN'T HAVE A RESPONSE. MICHAEL WAS RIGHT. STEPHEN could have his own hidden agenda. What did she really know about him other than he'd been her father's colleague? She certainly hadn't known he was engaged. Perhaps she never knew him the way she believed.

Michael stopped pacing to look at her. "I need to talk to him and find out what exactly he knows."

"I don't think that's a good idea."

"I need this cleared up."

She looked into his eyes. They burned with an inner fire. Michael was furious with Stephen. It would be in everyone's best interest if she acted as mediator. *If only to save Stephen's worthless hide.* He had an unhealthy habit of inciting the men in her life to violence. She crossed to where she'd dropped her purse and picked it up.

"You're leaving?"

She glanced up to see defeat on Michael's face. In the time she had known him and throughout his entire recovery, she'd never seen such a distraught look. Her choice was clear; she had to help him restore his old life, if at all possible.

"Michael, I think you should know, Stephen really was trying to find out the truth about you. He came to me yesterday and asked about the accident. I told him everything I could recall. I also told him about your memory loss. I think it may be why he never said anything last night. I can't begin to understand what went on between you three, or how he saw the tattoo on your shoulder, but I can certainly guess." She swallowed past the lump in her throat. "He loves her. Maybe he didn't have enough time to process what he discovered. Maybe he didn't know how you'd react." She sighed and walked back to where he stood. "I'm not saying he is innocent of any wrongdoing, but give him a chance to make it right, okay?"

Elizabeth picked up her cell and dialed Stephen. If he agreed to meet, she'd suggest neutral ground. She cast a glance around Michael's wrecked apartment. Definitely not here.

CHAPTER 34

Sammy heard Stephen's cell phone ring while he was in the shower. Since it was awfully late for a social call, she surmised it might be important. "Hello?"

"I'm looking for Stephen Montgomery. Is he available?"

"Who should I say is calling?"

"An old friend," came the terse reply.

"Hang on a sec."

Poking her head around the bathroom door, she covered the receiver and called to him. "You have a phone call from a woman who says she's an old friend. Stephen, it sounds like the woman from the restaurant."

Through the steamed glass, she saw his expression alter as the import of her words registered. Cutting the water off, he wrapped a towel around his hips and snatched the phone from her hand.

"Bethy? What is it? What's wrong?"

Stephen glanced to where Sammy stood in the doorway joining the two rooms. He checked his watch.

"Yes. Where?"

He listened for a few seconds, then nodded as if the woman on the phone could see him. "Okay, see you then."

After Stephen disconnected, he stared at the phone in his hand for a long moment.

"Is everything all right?"

"I need to go meet Beth." He grabbed a shirt and jeans from the closet.

"Now?" she asked incredulously. "Stephen, it's nine o'clock."

"I know. I'm sorry, Samantha. She said she needs to talk to me."

"I didn't mean to make it sound like an objection. I'm just surprised. I hate to see our day come to an end. Do you want me to wait up for you?"

"No. I really don't know what the problem is. There is little point to wait up." He finished dressing and picked out a pair of socks. "Besides, you have another book signing tomorrow morning you need to be awake for. Don't tell me you forgot again?"

She grinned. His question didn't require an answer, because she *had* forgotten, and he knew it. She was terrible with her schedule. When she returned home, she intended to hire Margie as her assistant.

She stepped over to where he was putting on his shoes. As she stood in front of him, she felt compelled to stare at his handsome face. Did anyone else have eyes that dark or a smile as bright?

Her Stephen. Today, she had come to view him as more than a best friend. He was hers now. Did she love him? *Yes.* Not the all-consuming love she held for Michael. Stephen wasn't her one true love, but he was the kind of man who appeared into your life without much fanfare and wormed his way into your heart. Without warning, you were left dealing with a love that crept up and surprised you. The kind of love that made for a beautiful partnership.

Samantha's stare unnerved Stephen. He couldn't put his finger on it. Could she see what he was hiding? He certainly hoped not. She'd never forgive his one lapse in judgment. Nor would she understand why he hadn't told her Michael was alive. It was the one secret he intended to take to his grave and pray she never discovered.

He stood up and placed a kiss on her forehead. "See you tomorrow at breakfast."

"Be careful driving."

"Always."

Stephen got to Elizabeth's place in just under thirty minutes. All the windows were ablaze. Apprehension assailed him. Something was about to go very wrong with his life. Was Samantha rubbing off on him? Could he get premonitions by osmosis? Shaking off his unease, he made his way to Elizabeth's apartment.

At his knock, Michael opened the door. The reason for his trepidation was staring him straight in the face. "You remembered who you were." It was a statement, not a question. He knew.

"Yes." Michael bristled.

Stephen stepped in and around Michael, then tossed his keys on the table and went to where Elizabeth sat on the sofa. He gazed down into her serious face. Her disappointment was clear to see. No words would come to excuse his actions.

"Stephen, Michael suspects you knew it was him last night. Did you?" The accusation was in her tone. She embodied an avenging angel, ready to do battle.

Stephen sank across from her into an armchair. Agitated, he ran his fingers through his hair and took a deep breath. He watched Michael perch on the edge of the sofa next to Elizabeth, and he wanted to knock the bastard sideways to distance the two of them.

"Yes," he said softly.

Michael exploded into action, pacing back and forth. He held his head in his hands as if in great pain.

"Why?" burst from Elizabeth.

"Why didn't I say something then?" At her nod, Stephen continued, "Even though I suspected who he might be, I couldn't be sure. I thought I recognized his tattoo, but a lot of men have tattoos. Also, I'd been drinking all afternoon after I left you, Beth. I wasn't myself last night. When Samantha showed up at the door with Joe—"

"*Michael!* My goddamn name is *Michael!*"

"With Michael," Stephen allowed. "I lost it. My jealousy took hold.

Like I said, I had my suspicions but no proof. Then Samantha asked him to leave. It was only when he shifted to put on his shirt, I saw the tattoo." He ran his hand through his hair and shook his head. "I was frozen with indecision. You told me he didn't remember who he was. And, in all honesty, I couldn't bear the thought of losing her. I love her." He was amazed at the calm in his own voice. Inside, he was a bundle of nerves and regret.

"You don't lie to people you love," Michael snarled.

He reminded Stephen of a wounded tiger. Stalking around, growling, taking swipes at anyone who came too close. The accusation and hatred radiating from him was well deserved. Stephen had gambled the other man wouldn't remember. He'd lost the roll of the dice.

Stephen rose and strode to where Michael was pacing.

"If you want to take a swing at me, go ahead. I deserve it and worse. It will probably be the hardest thing I've ever had to do, but I'll tell her who you are tomorrow. Not until after her signing though because it will upset her. She'll want to honor her commitment, but she'd want to see you more. Fair enough?"

MICHAEL SEARCHED THE OTHER MAN'S FACE FOR SIGNS OF DECEIT. Finding none, he stormed away. He thought about Sammy. About all they'd shared together. About her new career, and of how she'd bounced back from this godawful disaster. The love they'd had could be hailed as all-consuming. Was it emotionally healthy? What was best for her? Him? Would they be able to move past the tragedy and all the recent mistakes?

"Tell me about today, after I left. I saw you by the elevator as I was leaving. Did you and Sammy patch things up?" he asked with quiet dread.

"Would you believe me if I said we did?" Stephen inquired. At Michael's nod, he said, "Yes."

Michael closed his eyes and inhaled a deep, ragged breath. A difficult decision had to be made. No matter what he chose to do, someone would get his or her heart ripped apart. Maybe it would be better if that someone was him.

"I don't want you to tell Sammy who I am," he said roughly.

The shock on Stephen's and Beth's faces almost triggered his laughter. Had the circumstances not been so dire, perhaps he'd have given into the desire.

"Do you realize what you're giving up? It means saying goodbye forever: to your family, a life with Samantha, all your old friends and relationships," Stephen argued. "You can't possibly know what you're saying."

"My family died almost nine years ago. Sammy has moved on, and any friends I once had think I'm dead. There's nothing left to give up. My life as Michael effectively ended with the accident."

"Michael, you are being ridiculous! That woman never gave up hope you were alive for almost two years," stressed Beth.

He didn't know why she fought so hard to make him see reason. Maybe because, in spite of how crappy he'd treated her, she still wanted to believe in happy endings? Michael tugged a lock of her shiny hair and mustered a half-smile. Without looking at Stephen, he said, "Stephen, tell me truthfully. Did Sammy put aside her search for me? Has she come to terms with my supposed death?"

"She said she has." Stephen grimaced and shook his head. "Truthfully, I don't believe she's moved on at all. As flattering as it would be if my lovemaking had changed her mind, I'm not naive enough to believe it."

To Michael, hearing Stephen talk so casually about sex with Sammy was like a knife to the chest. He'd hidden it from her yesterday, but he hated that she'd slept with the guy. Yesterday, he didn't have a right to be pissed. Today he did.

"If you value your life, never talk about touching Sammy in my presence," Michael growled menacingly.

"You're a fucking idiot! You know that?" Stephen raged.

Beth stepped in when their fury was about to come to blows. "Michael, Stephen is right. You can't do this. You *are* being a fucking idiot."

He snorted. "Quite probably. But it's settled. Sammy must never know that I didn't die in that accident." Michael was firm.

"I cannot live with that decision," Stephen said, anger in every line of his body.

"You were ready to before you walked through that door tonight, weren't you?"

The question hit a nerve. Michael saw it in the way Stephen flinched. The righteous routine was all for show.

"That was before I knew you remembered your past. I refuse to live with a guilty conscience for the rest of my life. To see Samantha's misery on every anniversary of your supposed death? Don't ask it of me, Michael. I can't do it. Not to her."

"How upright and noble you've suddenly become," Michael sneered. He shrugged off Beth's hand and leaned closer to Stephen. "I've made my choice. Now go back to her," Michael's tone held the strength of unbending steel.

"You're making a rash decision. Today, we changed our tickets for a flight out tomorrow night. I want you to come to the airport to see us off." He held up his hand when Michael would have interrupted. "If, by that time, you still feel the way you do and you can actually look in her eyes to say goodbye, I will adhere to your decision. But, if you don't show up, I'll tell her who you are and where to find you."

Stephen snatched his keys from the table and made his way to the door. He extended a goodbye to Beth. His eyes bore into Michael's as he said, "Michael, I'll see you tomorrow night at six o'clock. Dallas/Ft. Worth. Delta Air Lines check-in. Don't be late."

As the door closed behind him, Beth glanced at Michael. She asked him what he thought of Stephen's ultimatum.

"I intend to be there at six o'clock to say goodbye."

CHAPTER 35

"Stephen, what happened last night?" Sammy finally asked. Holding an upbeat, one-sided conversation throughout breakfast was exhausting. It was obvious to anyone who cared to notice, Stephen was mulling over a problem.

"Nothing."

His abruptness surprised her. Apparently, Stephen became surly when troubled. As more human traits emerged from her once stuffy doctor, Sammy delighted in the change. Still, he wasn't telling her what she wanted to know. Never one to back down, she tried another tactic. "Would you say you've ever lied to me before?"

"Why?" Stephen asked with ill-temper.

"I might as well have been talking to that wall all morning. There's something bothering you, and I want to know what it is."

"I told you it was nothing."

His voice held an edge she'd never heard before.

"And you're a liar," she said with a calmness she didn't feel. "Did you sleep with Elizabeth last night?"

"What the hell kind of question is that?"

"You were gone awfully late. I just wondered."

"And would it bother you if I had?"

"Yes," she replied honestly, looking to diffuse the situation.

His expression softened marginally, and he lost his belligerence. "Well, I didn't. But I don't want to talk about last night. You don't need to worry about anything right before your signing."

"Worry about what?"

"Samantha, please let it go. I promise to tell you later today," he sighed and smiled, although it didn't reach his eyes.

"Are we still leaving today?"

"Yes. We need to check our bags at about six o'clock. Our flight is at seven-fifteen. Is that still what you want?"

Joe's face came to mind. It was better to leave. To start anew. So why did the knowledge she'd never see him again make her feel so close to shattering?

"Yes. I need to get a few things from my room before I go to the bookstore. I'll meet you back here in a few minutes." She ended their conversation as quickly as she could. She didn't want him to discern the lie on her face.

On her way back to her room, she stopped by the front desk to check for messages. There weren't any. She shouldn't have felt so depressed by Joe's silence, but she did. She racked her brain, trying to remember if she had ever heard his last name. The urge to call him and apologize was strong. It would be better to end everything on a less bitter note. The problem was, he had never told her his full name or bothered to give her his cell number.

She could always call his friend's restaurant where they had gone the other day, but it was still early in the day. It was doubtful anyone would be there yet. Joe had given her the impression he worked there. Maybe she should stop by on her lunch break? She rejected the idea as soon as it hit. She'd told Stephen it was over with Joe, and she didn't want to earn Stephen's mistrust should he stumble upon them again.

No, it would be better to cut and run. Letting go of the past was imperative. Anything else was insanity. Although, after eight months in as a guest of Brookhaven, she was entitled to a bit of crazy now and again.

So why did she feel so terrible? Stephen's mood must be rubbing off on her. Perhaps she had more of Annie's empathic ability than she realized. She shrugged off the wave of negativity and gathered her things for the bookstore event.

The day breezed by. Book sales were decent for a newbie, and her newfound fans all told her they eagerly anticipated her next novel. For the first time in her life, she felt as if she'd chosen the right path.

Early next year, she'd dig into the settlement money and treat herself to a long vacation. *Ireland.* It was past time to stop viewing the funds as blood money and start using them to make her life easier. Two weeks by herself, exploring castle ruins, should help clear her head and allow her heart to start the healing process. If she intended to have a real relationship with Stephen, she had to patch that gaping hole left by Michael. Stephen would understand and most likely encourage her time alone to find herself.

She intended to park her ass on the Cliffs of Moher and plot her second story. Ghosts in the ruins to go along with the synopsis she'd pitched earlier this year? She needed to confer with James to learn the ins and outs of hauntings.

Sammy was putting the finishing touches on her packing when Stephen knocked and strolled through the connecting door. He still seemed to be in a somber mood.

"Are you ready to tell me about last night?" she asked.

"No. Are you ready to go?"

"What's with the cloak-and-dagger stuff, Stephen? I promise not to swoon at your feet."

Her choice of words finally cracked his shell and made him smile. He rushed to her and scooped her into his arms, crushing her to him.

"God, how I love you," he said roughly. "Only you would use the word 'swoon.'"

Nothing needed to be said in return. She sensed he was still not ready to confide in her, so she hugged him, offering comfort the best way she knew how.

THE AIRPORT WAS CROWDED, WHICH WASN'T UNUSUAL FOR THIS TIME OF day. Still, the sheer number of people made Sammy antsy. Stephen, not so subtly, searched the people coming and going, and Sammy was curious who he was looking for. He'd refused to go to the check-in desk, and so here they sat. Time dragged. It was making her nuts. She was impatient in the best of situations.

"What time is it?"

"Ten 'til six," Stephen replied with exaggerated patience to offset her impatience.

However, she recognized an underlying tension in his tone. Without a doubt, he was waiting for someone, but for the life of her, she couldn't fathom who.

"Who are we waiting for, Stephen?"

"Joe."

Her whole body jerked to attention at the sound of his name. "Joe?" she squeaked.

"Yes."

She hadn't seen that one coming. Some psychic she was. Before she could comment, relief flooded Stephen's features. He stood and waved. Sammy shifted and rose on the tips of her toes to get a better view. Joe spotted them the instant he cleared the main doors. The expression on his face bordered on tortured as he approached. The two men communicated silently before Joe turned to her.

"What are you doing here?" she asked in confusion.

"I saw Stephen last night at Elizabeth's. He said you were leaving today. I needed to come and see you off."

She ignored the stab of pain. They had no more ties to one another. If he wanted to spend his time with his ex-girlfriend, who was she to argue?

His intensity disturbed her. In his eyes, a fire burned. Love glowed, fierce and true. It spoke to her heart. Sammy tried to shut down that line of thinking. Fanciful. She was just being ridiculous. Her connection to Michael no longer existed. Sharing Joe's thoughts was impossible. Her mental denials didn't slow down her hammering heart though.

Emotions disabled her speech. She looked at Stephen. A thoughtful frown played on his face. Why had Stephen told Joe they were leaving today? Was it because he didn't want her to be upset they'd parted in anger?

The invisible hand holding her heart contracted. She turned back to Joe and impulsively threw her arms around his neck. Breathing in his scent. Feeling as if she had come home as he gathered her close. Their hug seemed to last forever but was over too soon.

"Goodbye, Sammy Darlin'," he whispered with a catch in his throat. He caressed the side of her face and hesitated a moment before smiling. The smile contrasted sharply with the sorrow in his eyes.

"Promise me you'll have a good life," his voice was gruffer than she'd ever heard it.

"I promise," she choked out. "You, too... Joe."

She needed to make a conscious decision to unclench her hands and release the material of his shirt. The world around her dimmed as he drifted away. It took all the willpower she owned and more not to break down sobbing like a small child as he shuffled through the busy airport on his way to the exit. Sammy continued to watch Michael leave her life, making no move to stop him.

"You know who he is, don't you?" Stephen asked, solemn.

"Yes. I've always known."

Sammy smiled without humor when he stared at her with a floored expression.

"How... wha... then *why?*" he stammered, clearly reeling from the impact.

It was almost humorous to see Stephen floundering and frustrated. She put him out of his misery. "I knew the first time I touched the casket in the church. Then again when I touched his arm on our first night here."

"You've known all this time? Why didn't you say anything?" he demanded angrily.

"I knew he was *Joe*. The Michael I once knew wasn't residing in his body."

"What the fuck does that even mean? It makes no damned sense."

"It does if you think about it. Michael was absent. He'd become Joe. The man I loved was gone. He had no memories of me or our life together. But he had new memories starting. With Elizabeth. It was all there," she explained, looking back the way Michael had gone. Her breath caught in her chest to see him walking away. "It's why I was so devastated and torn. I wanted Michael back. Except I literally couldn't see that happening. Each vision I had was the same. And honestly, I couldn't stop myself from spending time with him when he kept showing up. I kept praying his memories would return. But they never did."

Stephen's anger drained as quickly as it appeared. Understanding her reasoning had helped him realize she hadn't been toying with him these last few days. He pulled her close and kissed the top of her head before releasing her with a long-suffering breath.

"He's remembered everything."

She gave a humorless chuckle. "I know that, too. Yesterday would be my guess, based on the frantic phone call last night and all the secrecy."

"Then why, for God's sake, are you not chasing him down?"

"Because he doesn't love me enough to fight for me. He's made a decision that will affect our lives. It's the second time he's done that without consulting me."

"*Jesus, Samantha!* You don't understand. Don't let him walk away. He's doing it for *you!*"

"For me? Right. If it were for me, he'd stay," she argued bitterly.

"Don't be stupid. You're much smarter than that."

"Why are you pushing this, Stephen? I thought you loved me?" she cried. "I love you. I've told you that."

His sorrowful mocha eyes met her probing gaze. He placed a hand on either side of her face and kissed her with a tenderness she hadn't really experienced in over two years. He tried to ease her ache. However, she knew nothing would, except being with the one man she truly loved beyond all others.

"But you'll always love him more," he told her softly, effectively ending any argument. "You need to hurry."

Involuntarily, her body jerked forward like a puppet dangling on strings, but she forced her limbs to mind. She was done chasing him.

"Go after him, Samantha."

Because he had been watching her closely, he knew the moment she made the decision, and he smiled.

"I do love you, Stephen," she gushed, hugging him one last time before she turned to run after Michael.

"Michael," she hollered. "Michael, wait."

She knew he had heard her because he paused for the briefest of seconds on his way to the exit.

"Michael, *please!* Don't leave!" She yelled, running as fast as she could. Not caring that she appeared desperate to the onlookers gaping at her, she shouted his name for all she was worth while she knocked people out of her way.

Focused on Michael, she stumbled over a small carry-on in her path. The face-plant broke her will. Too wrung out to continue, she collapsed on the floor in a heap. Her one true heart was about to leave her behind. He didn't care enough to stay, and she couldn't go through that loss again.

"Please, Michael. I can't do this again. *I just can't!*" she sobbed quietly into her folded arms, over and over again. It was impossible for him to hear her now. But she didn't care. She couldn't stop the words from pouring out. "I love you. Don't leave me again. Please, don't leave me."

Michael heard Sammy calling his name. Every second he was in this fucking, crowded airport tortured him. Each step away from her became harder to take. He gave up the fight and spun around just as she fell. He stopped, too stunned to move. Once again, he had brought her to this type of emotional breakdown. He met Stephen's fierce glare, understanding what his rival silently relayed. Slowly, he started to walk back to her. Two steps, and then he ran.

"Sammy!" pounded through his brain and out of his mouth with every step.

When he reached her, she was incoherent. He didn't think twice about waving off the TSA guards who'd rushed toward them or before sitting down on the floor and gathering her into his lap.

"I'm here. I'm here, Sammy Darlin'. Please don't cry. *Please.*" Holding her head to his heart, he repeated it over and over again, trying to penetrate her hysteria. He wasn't sure how he accomplished it, but he eventually did.

"Don't leave me. P-please," she begged, sandwiching his face between her palms. "I t-thought you were l-lost to me. I thought I w-would never find y-you."

"I won't, darlin'. Never again. I promise," he whispered fiercely, tears trailing down his face.

Michael looked at Stephen, who slowly closed the distance between them. He appeared as wrecked as the two of them. Dropping her bag, Stephen turned as if to go. He cast Michael a half smile.

"Thank you," Michael mouthed.

Stephen nodded before flipping him off.

Michael had to grin. He wondered if, in another lifetime, they might've been friends. Or would they both have been at odds over the same woman again? He closed his eyes and hugged her tight. Sammy, this woman who was his other half. He felt whole again for the first time in two years.

EPILOGUE

ONE YEAR LATER...

"Stephen called," Michael told Sammy when she emerged from her writing cave. "He said he has some important news."

She dropped a light kiss on his lips and avoided his arms when he would've dragged her into his lap. She rubbed her heavily rounded belly. "Food first. Our peanut needs sustenance. Reference Stephen, I'll bet ten-to-one odds he's taking the job in North Carolina with his brother, Trace."

"Like I'd bet you. I swear, pregnancy has heightened your psychic skill." Michael grinned and gave her ass a light pat. "Sit. I'll take care of dinner."

"I want mac and cheese."

"Then mac and cheese you shall have, my love. And I won't even dirty the kitchen doing it."

"Pfft. I'll believe that one when I see it." Sammy smiled as he eased her into his favorite recliner. "So, back to Stephen. When do we get the scoop?"

Michael checked his watch. "Within the next ten minutes. He's bringing dinner. Mac and cheese if I'm not mistaken."

Laughter bubbled up. "There's no way either of you knew I would ask for that!"

"Oh, but I did." He knelt at her feet and nudged her legs apart to settle between her thighs. He rubbed his nose against hers. "It's Thursday, and your cravings are like clockwork, Sammy Darlin'."

"Mmhmm." She tangled her fingers in his thick lion's mane of hair. It was almost back to pre-accident length, and she loved it. "I have other cravings."

"Yes, but those are going to have to wait. I need more than five minutes to satisfy you properly."

His mouth covered hers as his hands trailed her outer thighs to cup her ass. She moaned and deepened their kiss.

The doorbell rang. Sassy rushed to the foyer and began to whine.

"He's early. Can't you tell him to drop the food and go?" she murmured against his lips.

"I'd bury his body in the backyard if you wanted me to," he responded with a short laugh and nip of her lower lip.

She had no doubt he would, too. Michael and Stephen had settled into a semi-friendly pact. But if Sammy gave him the go-ahead, Michael would gladly dump Stephen's body in the Intracoastal Waterway.

"When did you turn so bloodthirsty?" Her fingers trailed his scar from temple to cheek. "Is this influencing you?"

"Argh, lassie! It be at that!"

The doorbell sounded again, and Sassy became more frantic and audible in her excitement. Sammy placed her palm on his face and lightly shoved. "Your pirate is worse than your Englishman, you tool. Now get my booty before Sassy has a stroke."

"Don't toss around the offer of booty so lightly, darlin'." He winked and rose. "I may bar the door and take you up on it."

She bit her lip against the giggle. "After he leaves, we'll play Anne Bonny and Calico Jack. I'll let you shiver me timbers."

His laughter echoed in the living room and through the foyer as he left to answer the door. When he returned, his smile was wiped clean, and strain tightened the skin around his eyes. In his wake was

Stephen, who sported roughly the same expression. Only Sassy was thrilled to have two of her favorite men in one place.

Sammy heaved an internal sigh. Maybe Stephen had been right when he told her his relocation was for the best. As selfish as she was, she couldn't continue to keep him as her close friend any longer. It wasn't fair to either one. She blinked away the building moisture and pasted on a wide smile. If tonight was goodbye, she'd not weep her way through it.

"Michael told me you are catering to my cravings and brought me the good stuff."

"I am." Stephen held up two bags, shook them, then handed them off to Michael. "He assured me the mac and cheese from the CBW was by far your favorite."

She sent Michael a grateful look and a soft smile. Since they'd been home, he'd gone out of his way to provide everything she could possibly desire. He didn't raise much of a fuss when she met Stephen for the occasional lunch to catch up on Brookhaven gossip. Michael seemed to understand Stephen's importance in her life. But now, it was time to let him go. Adulthood only became more difficult the older she got.

Stephen held out a hand to haul her to her feet, and she waddled her way into the dining room to plop down again. She stared grumpily at her swollen feet and thickening calves. *Fuck, was she developing cankles?*

When both men laughed, she glanced up.

"I said that out loud, didn't I?" A flush started somewhere around her baby bump and spread quickly over her cheeks.

Michael kissed the crown of her head. "Our princess will be here soon enough, and your ankles will be back to normal in no time."

Although Stephen tried to hide it, Sammy didn't fail to notice the envy in his dark gaze. Holding out her hand to him, palm up, she channeled her energy. When he placed his palm in hers, the vision struck.

"You should leave for North Carolina before the end of the month,

Stephen," she said softly. "You've got quite the future ahead of you." One he so richly deserved.

His full lips twisted, and Sammy wasn't as unaffected as she'd like to pretend. He was going to make the woman she'd seen in her premonition a very happy lady indeed.

LATER THAT NIGHT, AS MICHAEL HELD SAMMY WITHIN THE CIRCLE OF his arms, he rubbed his cheek against the softness of her hair. "Any regrets?"

She drew back slightly to see his expression. "Regrets? For what?"

"Me. Stephen. The way things worked out." How he managed to ask when the jealousy was nearly crushing his vocal cords was anyone's guess.

A beatific smile blossomed on Sammy's face. "Not a one."

"I've never asked before, but why, if you knew who I was the whole time, didn't you tell me when we met again in Dallas?"

She frowned and stared at him, concern clouding her eyes. "Has that been bothering you all this time? Babe, it's been a year."

He shrugged his embarrassment and toyed with the hand clasped in his.

"Instinct," she finally said. "I told you once, Joe wasn't you. Not the you I'd known. Other than a smattering of missing memories, you'd become a great guy who seemed content with his life the way it was."

"Stephen told me tonight you were going to let me leave, even knowing who I was."

Sammy remained quiet for a long moment. Michael could see she needed the time to gather her thoughts on the subject, so he didn't speak.

"I felt like I was holding you back. That maybe the reason you were with me was out of habit. I thought my baggage weighed too heavily on you and it's why you wanted to go to Dallas to begin with. Maybe that's why I thought you were saying goodbye at the airport, too." She squeezed his hand between both of hers. "I didn't want to ruin things for you, and I couldn't see a future for us together. Not with your memories gone. I saw three different scenarios when I touched you for the first time in the restaurant. The one where I told you who you were ended the worst."

"*Jesus, Sammy.* I had no idea."

"I never mentioned it because I didn't want to burden you. And I don't know what forces shifted or aligned to help you regain your memories, but I'm grateful you did. I'm grateful you came back for me." She placed his warm palm flat against her belly where their daughter began her evening exercises. "So grateful."

His vision blurred as he stared down into her loving countenance. "Me, too, Sammy Darlin'. Me, too."

"It's why you tolerate Stephen, isn't it?"

"He forced the issue. I owe him."

"He doesn't think so. He just wants us to be happy."

"And we are, aren't we?" The huskiness in his voice betrayed his deep need to know.

"Exceedingly."

STAY TUNED FOR BOOK TWO IN THE HOLT FAMILY SERIES. GABE AND Margie are sure to delight!

FROM THE AUTHOR...

Thank you for taking the time to read *FINDING YOU!*

Be sure to join my mailing list for news on current releases, potential sales, new-to-you author introductions, and contests each month. But if it gets to be too much, you can unsubscribe at any time. Your information will always be kept private. No spam here!

Join my Facebook Reader Group. While the standard pages and profiles on Facebook are not always the most reliable, I have created a group for fans who like to interact. This group entitles readers to "fan page only" contests, as well as an exclusive first look at covers, excerpts and more. Cromer's Carousers is the most fun way to follow yet! I hope to see you there!

ALSO BY T.M. CROMER

ONE WISH